FLOTSAM

ALSO BY ERICH MARIA REMARQUE

ALL QUIET ON THE WESTERN FRONT
THE ROAD BACK
THREE COMRADES
FLOTSAM
ARCH OF TRIUMPH
SPARK OF LIFE
A TIME TO LOVE AND A TIME TO DIE
THE BLACK OBELISK
HEAVEN HAS NO FAVORITES
THE NIGHT IN LISBON
SHADOWS IN PARADISE

Erich Maria Remarque

FLOTSAM

Translated from the German by
DENVER LINDLEY

Fawcett Columbine
The Ballantine Publishing Group • New York

A Fawcett Columbine Book
Published by The Ballantine Publishing Group

http://www.randomhouse.com

Library of Congress Catalog Card Number: 97-90643

ISBN: 0-449-91247-7

Manufactured in the United States of America

Cover design by Ruth Ross

First Ballantine Books Edition: January 1998

10 9 8 7 6 5 4 3 2 1

PART I

To live without roots
takes a stout heart

Chapter One

KERN awoke with a start out of a seething blackness and listened hard. Like all hunted creatures he was completely conscious at once, alert and ready for flight. As he sat motionless on the bed, his thin body bent forward, he debated how he could get away if the stairs were already occupied.

The room was on the fourth floor. A window opened toward the courtyard, but it had no balcony or cornice from which the gutters could be reached. Flight in that direction was out of the question. There was only one other way: along the corridor to the attic and from there across the roof to the next house.

Kern glanced at the illuminated dial of his watch. It was a little after five. The room was still almost black. On the two other beds the sheets gleamed indistinctly gray in the darkness. The Pole, who slept next to the wall, was snoring.

Cautiously Kern slid out of bed and crept to the door. At the same instant the man in the middle bed moved. "Is something wrong?" he whispered.

Kern made no reply; he kept his ear pressed to the door.

The other sat up and fumbled among the things on the iron bedstead. A pocket flash went on, catching in its wavering circle of pale light a section of the brown door, from which paint was scaling, and the figure of Kern, with mussed hair, in rumpled underwear and socks, at the keyhole listening.

"Damn it, what's up?" hissed the man on the bed.

Kern straightened. "I don't know. Something woke me, something I heard."

"Something! What was it, you fool?"

"Downstairs, something downstairs. Voices, steps, something like that."

The man got up and came to the door. He was wearing a yellow shirt from under which a pair of hairy, muscular legs protruded in the glow of the flashlight. He listened for a while, then asked, "How long you been staying here?"

"Two months."

"Been a raid in that time?"

Kern shook his head.

"Aha! You've been hearing things. When you're asleep a fart sometimes sounds like thunder."

He threw the light in Kern's face. "Well, well, barely twenty, eh? Refugee?"

"Of course."

"*Jesus Christus tso sięm stało —*" the Pole in the corner gurgled suddenly.

The man in the shirt let the beam of light slide across the room. Out of the darkness emerged a wild, black beard, a great gaping mouth and two deep-set, staring eyes under bushy brows.

"Shut up about Jesus Christ, Polack," growled the man with the flashlight. "He's not alive any more. Died as a volunteer at the Somme."

"*Tso?*"

"There! There it is again!" Kern sprang toward his bed. "They're coming upstairs. We've got to get across the roof."

The other spun around like a top. There was a sound

of closing doors and lowered voices. "Damn it! Get going! Polski, run for it! Police!"

He snatched his things from the bed. "Know the way?" he asked Kern.

"Yes. Along the hall to the right, up the stairs behind the sink."

"Let's go!" The man in the shirt opened the door noiselessly.

"*Matka boska!*" gurgled the Pole.

"Shut up! Don't tell them anything!"

The man drew the door shut. He and Kern raced along the narrow, dirty hall. They ran so silently they could hear the leaky tap dripping in the sink.

"Turn here," Kern whispered, swung around the corner and collided with something. He staggered, saw a uniform and tried to turn back. At the same instant he received a blow on the arm. "Stand still! Raise your hands!" someone commanded out of the darkness.

Kern let his things tumble to the floor. His left arm was numb from the blow that had hit his elbow. The man in the shirt looked for a second as if he were going to throw himself on the voice in the darkness. But then he caught sight of the barrel of a revolver, which a second policeman was holding against his chest. Slowly he raised his arms.

"Turn around!" ordered the voice. "Stand by the window!"

The two obeyed.

"See what's in that stuff," said the policeman with the revolver.

The second policeman searched the clothes lying on the floor. "Thirty-five schillings — a flashlight — a pipe — a pocketknife — a louse comb — nothing else — "

"No papers?"

"Couple of letters."

"No passports?"

"No."

"Where are your passports?" asked the policeman with the revolver.

"I haven't one," Kern said.

"Of course not." The policeman poked his revolver into the ribs of the man in the shirt. "And you? Do I have to ask you separately, you son of a bitch?"

The man turned around slowly. "What do you mean, 'son of a bitch'?" he asked.

The policemen looked at each other. The one without a revolver began to laugh. The other licked his lips. "Just look," he said slowly, "a fine gentleman! His Excellency, the Bum! General Stinker!" He drew back his arm suddenly and struck the man on the chin. "Keep your hands up!" he roared as the other staggered.

The man looked at him. Kern thought he had never seen such a look. "I mean you, you bastard," said the policeman. "Will you talk now? Or do you want me to jog up your brains again?"

"I haven't a passport," the man said.

" 'I haven't a passport,' " the policeman mimicked. "Of course Herr Son of a Bitch hasn't a passport. That's what we thought. Go on, get your clothes on, quick!"

A group of policemen came running along the hall, pulling open doors. One of them with shoulder stripes approached. "Well, what have you caught?"

"A couple of birds that were trying to fly away over the roof."

The officer looked at them. He was young. His face was narrow and pale. He wore a carefully trimmed, small, black mustache and smelled of toilet water. Kern recognized it; it was Eau de Cologne 4711. His father had owned a perfume factory; that's how he knew about such things.

"We'll take special care of these two," the lieutenant said. "Handcuffs!"

"Are the Viennese police allowed to strike a man while making an arrest?" asked the man in the shirt.

The officer looked up. "What's your name?"

"Steiner. Josef Steiner."

"He hasn't a passport and he threatened us," explained the policeman with the revolver.

"There's a lot more allowed than you think," the officer said sharply. "Get them downstairs!"

The two put on their clothes, and the policemen got out handcuffs. "Come, my pets. There, now, you look better. Fit as if they were made to order."

Kern felt the cold steel on his wrists. It was the first time in his life he had been fettered. The steel rings didn't hinder him much in walking. But it seemed to him that they had shackled more than just his hands.

Outside was the light of early morning. Two police wagons stood in front of the house. Steiner made a wry face. "First-class funeral. Pretty fine, eh kid?"

Kern did not answer. He was hiding the handcuffs under his coat as well as he could. A few milkmen were standing in the street, watching eagerly. In the houses opposite windows had been raised. Faces gleamed like dough in the dark openings. A woman giggled.

About thirty people had been arrested and were now being loaded into the uncovered wagons. Most of them climbed in silently. The owner of the building was among them — a fat, bright-blond woman of fifty. She alone was raising an angry protest. Several months before she had converted, in the cheapest possible fashion, two empty floors of her dilapidated house into a kind of *pension*. Word soon got around that one could sleep there without being reported to the police. The woman had only four legitimate boarders who had passports and were registered — a peddler, a rat-killer, and two whores. The others crept in after dark. Almost all were emigrants and refugees from Germany, Poland, Russia, and Italy.

"Get in, get in!" the lieutenant was saying to the landlady. "You can explain all that at the police station. You'll have time enough for it there."

"I protest — " screamed the woman.

"Protest all you like. Right now you come along with us."

Two policemen seized the woman under the arms and lifted her into the wagon.

The lieutenant turned toward Kern and Steiner. "Now, these two. Keep a special eye on them."

"*Merci*," said Steiner and got in. Kern followed him.

The wagons drove off. "Have a good time!" shrieked a woman's voice from one of the windows.

"Slaughter those refugees!" a man roared after them. "It'll save you food. *Heil Hitler!*"

The streets were still almost empty and the police cars moved rather fast. Behind the houses the sky receded, became brighter and wider and of a transparent blue; but the prisoners stood in a dark group on the wagons like willows in the autumn rain. Two of the policemen were eating sandwiches. They washed them down with coffee out of flat-bottomed tin cans.

Near the Franz Josef Bridge a vegetable truck crossed the street. The police cars stopped with a jolt and then started on again. At that moment one of the prisoners climbed over the side of the second car and jumped off. He fell diagonally across the mudguard, became entangled in his coat, and struck the pavement with the sound of a cracking branch.

"Stop! Back up!" shouted the leader. "Shoot if he moves!"

The truck jolted to a stop. The policemen scrambled down. They ran to the place where the man had fallen. The driver looked around. When he saw that the man wasn't trying to get away, he slowly backed up the machine.

The man lay prostrate. He had struck the pavement with the back of his head. Lying there with arms and legs spread out in his open overcoat, he looked like a great bat that had crashed to earth.

"Bring him back!" shouted the lieutenant.

The policemen bent over. Then one straightened up. "He must have broken something. He can't stand."

"Of course he can stand. Put him on his feet."

"Give him a good kick. That'll fix him up," the policeman who had struck Steiner advised casually.

The man groaned. "He really can't stand," reported the other policeman. "His head's bleeding, too."

"Damnation!" The leader climbed down. "No one is to move!" he shouted up at the prisoners. "Damned riffraff. Nothing but trouble."

The wagon now stood close to the fallen man. Kern could see him clearly from above. He recognized him. He was an emaciated Russian Jew with a ragged, gray beard. Kern had slept a few times in the same room with him. He remembered clearly how the old man had stood at the window in the early morning, with the phylacteries over his shoulders, bending slowly back and forth in prayer. He was a peddler of yarns, shoelaces, and thread, and had been expelled from Austria three times.

"Come on, get up!" the officer ordered. "What did you want to jump out of the wagon for anyway? Had too much of a record to face, eh? Been stealing and God knows what besides."

The old man moved his lips. His staring eyes were turned toward the lieutenant.

"What's that?" the latter asked. "Did he say something?"

"He says he did it because he was afraid," said the policeman kneeling beside him.

"Afraid? Of course he was afraid. Because he's broken the law. What's he saying now?"

"He says he's done nothing wrong."

"Everyone says that. But what are we going to do with him? What's wrong with him anyway?"

"Someone ought to get a doctor," Steiner said from his place in the wagon.

"Shut up!" the lieutenant barked nervously. "Where are we going to find a doctor at this hour? We can't leave him lying here on the street indefinitely. Later they'd say we did this to him ourselves. The police get blamed for everything."

"He ought to be in a hospital," Steiner said. "Right now."

The officer was confused. He saw now that the man was seriously injured and that made him forget to silence Steiner. "Hospital! They won't take him in just like that.

You have to have a certificate. That's something I can't arrange alone. First I have to report the case."

"Take him to a Jewish hospital," Steiner said. "They'll take him in there without a certificate or a report. Even without money."

The lieutenant stared at him. "How do *you* happen to know so much?"

"We ought to take him to the dispensary," one of the policemen proposed. "There's always an intern or a doctor there. They can find out what's wrong. And at least we'll be rid of him."

The lieutenant had made up his mind. "All right, lift him in. We'll drive by the public dispensary. One man can stay there with him. What a damned nuisance!"

The policemen hoisted the man up. He groaned and turned very pale. They placed him on the floor of the wagon. He shuddered and opened his eyes, which shone with unnatural brilliance in his sunken face. The lieutenant bit his lips. "What a fool trick! Jumping out of a truck, an old man like him. Go on, but drive slow."

Under the wounded man's head a pool of blood slowly formed. His gnarled fingers scrabbled over the floorboards of the truck. His lips slowly retracted baring his teeth. It was as though someone else were laughing silently and scornfully behind a death-shadowed mask of pain.

"What's he saying?" the lieutenant asked.

The policeman knelt down again and steadied the old man's head against the jolting of the truck. "He says he wanted to get to his children," he reported. "Now they'll starve to death."

"Oh, nonsense. They won't starve. Where are they?"

The policeman bent down. "He won't say. Otherwise they'd be deported. None of them has a permit."

"That's a lot of nonsense. What's he saying now?"

"He says he wants you to forgive him."

"What?" the lieutenant asked in amazement.

"He says he wants you to forgive him for the trouble he has caused you."

"Forgive him? What does he mean by that?" Shaking his head, the officer stared at the man on the floor.

The car stopped at the dispensary. "Carry him in," the lieutenant ordered. "Take it easy. And you, Rohde, stay with him till I telephone." They lifted the injured man. Steiner bent over him. "We'll find your children. We'll look after them," he said. "Do you understand, friend?" The Jew closed his eyes and opened them again.

Then three policemen carried him into the building. His dangling arms dragged helplessly over the pavement as though he were already dead. After a short time two policemen came back and got in again. "Did he say anything else?" asked the lieutenant.

"No. He was green in the face. If it's his spine he won't last long."

"Fair enough, just one Jew the less," the policeman who had hit Steiner said.

" 'Forgive,' " muttered the lieutenant. "What a thing to say! Funny fellow — "

"Especially in these times," Steiner said.

The lieutenant threw back his shoulders. "Shut up, you Bolshevik," he roared. "We'll teach you to be fresh."

The prisoners were taken to the Elisabeth Street police station. The handcuffs were taken off Steiner and Kern, and they were put with the others in a large dim room.

Most of them were sitting in silence. They were used to waiting. Only the fat, blond landlady kept up a steady lamentation.

About nine o'clock they were summoned upstairs one after the other.

Kern was led into a room where there were two policemen, a clerk in plain clothes, the lieutenant, and a middle-aged police captain. The captain was sitting in a swivel chair smoking cigarettes. "Fill in the form," he said to the man at the table.

The clerk was a thin, acidulous individual who looked like a herring. "Name?" he asked in an astonishingly deep voice.

"Ludwig Kern."

"Date of birth?"

"November 30, 1916, in Dresden."

"So you're a German —"

"No. No nationality. Deprived of citizenship."

The captain looked up. "At twenty-one? For what reason?"

"None. My father was deprived of citizenship. Since I was a minor, I was too."

"What had your father done?"

Kern was silent for a moment. A year's experience as a refugee had taught him to be cautious of every word he spoke to the authorities. "He was falsely denounced as politically unreliable," he said finally.

"Are you a Jew?"

"My father is — Not my mother."

"Aha . . ."

The captain flicked the ashes from his cigarette onto the floor. "Why didn't you stay in Germany?"

"They took our passports away and told us to leave. We

would have been locked up if we had stayed; and if we were going to be locked up anyway we wanted it to be somewhere else — not in Germany."

The captain laughed dryly. "I can understand that. How did you get across the border without a passport?"

"All you needed then, for short trips across the Czech border, was an identification card. We had that. With it you were allowed to stay for three days in Czechoslovakia."

"And after that?"

"We got permission to stay for three months. Then we had to leave."

"How long have you been in Austria?"

"Three months."

"Why haven't you reported to the police?"

"Because then I'd have been ordered to leave immediately."

"Indeed!" The captain struck the arm of his chair with the palm of his hand. "How do you happen to know that?"

Kern did not mention the fact that he and his parents had reported to the police the first time they had crossed the Austrian border. They had been deported the same day. When they came back again, they did not report.

"Perhaps it isn't so?" he asked.

"It's not your place to ask questions here. You just answer," the clerk said sharply.

"Where are your parents now?" asked the captain.

"My mother is in Hungary. She was allowed to stay because she is Hungarian by birth. My father was arrested and deported while I was away from the hotel. I don't know where he is."

"What's your profession?"

"I was a student."

"How have you lived?"

"I have some money."

"How much?"

"I have twelve schillings with me. Friends are keeping the rest for me." Kern owned nothing besides the twelve schillings. He had earned them peddling soap, perfume, and toilet water. But if he had admitted that, he would have been liable to additional punishment for working without a permit.

The captain got up and yawned. "Are we through?"

"There's one more downstairs," said the clerk.

"It will be the same story. Lots of bleating and not much wool." The captain made a wry face at the lieutenant. "Nothing but illegal immigrants. Doesn't look much like a Communist plot, does it? Who lodged that complaint anyway?"

"Someone who runs the same sort of place, only he has bedbugs," said the clerk. "Professional jealousy probably."

The captain laughed. Then he noticed that Kern was still in the room. "Take him downstairs. You know the sentence. Two weeks' detention and then deportation." He yawned again. "Well, I'm going out for a goulash and beer."

Kern was taken into a smaller cell than before. Beside him there were five prisoners there, among them the Pole who had slept in the same room.

In a quarter of an hour they brought Steiner in. He sat down beside Kern. "First time in the coop, kid?"

Kern nodded.

"Feel like a murderer, don't you?"

Kern made a face. "Just about. Prison — You know, I can't get over my early feeling about that."

"This isn't prison," Steiner explained, "this is detention. Prison comes later."

"Have you been in prison?"

"Yes." Steiner smiled. "You'll get a taste of it too, kid. The first time it will hit you hard. But not again. Particularly not in winter. At least you have peace while you're in. A man without a passport is a corpse on parole. All he's really expected to do is commit suicide — there's nothing else."

"And with a passport? There's no place where you get a permit to work too?"

"Of course not. You only get the right to starve to death in peace — not on the run. That's a good deal."

Kern stared straight ahead.

Steiner slapped him on the shoulder. "Keep your chin up, Baby. In return for all this you have the good fortune to live in the twentieth century, the century of culture, progress, and humanity."

"Isn't there anything at all to eat here?" asked a little man with a bald head, sitting in a corner on one of the plank beds. "Not even any coffee?"

"All you have to do is ring for the head waiter," Steiner replied. "Tell him to bring the bill of fare. There are four menus to choose from. Caviar if you want it, of course."

"Food very bad here," said the Pole.

"Why, there's our Jesus Christ!" Steiner looked at him with interest. "Are you a regular guest?"

"Very bad," repeated the Pole. "And so little — "

"Oh God," said the man in the corner, "and I have a roast

chicken in my trunk. When are they going to let us out of here anyhow?"

"In two weeks," Steiner answered. "That's the usual punishment for refugees without papers, eh, Jesus Christ? I bet you know that."

"Two weeks," agreed the Pole. "Or longer. Very little food. And so bad. Thin soup."

"Damn it! By then my chicken will be spoiled," the bald-head groaned. "My first chicken in two years. I saved up for it, groschen by groschen. I was going to eat it today."

"Postpone your anguish till tonight," Steiner said, "then you can assume you would already have eaten it and that will make it easier."

"What nonsense is that you're talking?" The man stared indignantly at Steiner. "Are you trying to tell me that would be the same thing, you twaddler? When I haven't really eaten it? And besides, I'd have saved a drumstick for tomorrow."

"Then wait until tomorrow noon."

"That not bad for me," the Pole broke in, "I not eat chicken."

"It can't possibly be bad for *you* — you haven't a roast chicken lying in your trunk," growled the man in the corner.

"If I had chicken, still not bad. I not eat her. Not stand chickens. Vomit up afterwards." The Pole looked very satisfied and smoothed his beard. "For me that chicken no loss."

"No one's interested in that, you fool!" the bald-head shouted angrily.

"Even if chicken here — I not eat same," announced the Pole triumphantly.

"Good God! Did anyone ever hear such drivel?" The owner of the chicken in the trunk pressed his hands in desperation to his head.

"Apparently he can't lose on roast chicken," Steiner said. "As far as they are concerned, our Jesus Christ is immune. A Diogenes among roast chickens. How about stewed chicken?"

"Truly not," the Pole announced firmly.

"And chicken paprika?"

"Not at all chicken." The Pole beamed.

"I'm going crazy!" howled the tormented owner of the chicken.

Steiner turned around. "And eggs, Jesus Christ, chicken's eggs?"

His smile disappeared. "Little eggs, yes — love little eggs." An expression of yearning stirred his untidy beard. "Very much love."

"Thank God, at last a flaw in this perfection."

"Very much love little eggs," the Pole insisted; "four eggs, six eggs, twelve eggs — six boiled, other six fried. With little potatoes. Little fried potatoes and bacon."

"I can't listen to any more of this. Nail him to the cross, this gluttonous Jesus Christ!" stormed the Chicken in the Trunk.

"Gentlemen," said a pleasant bass voice with a Russian accent, "why all this excitement about an illusion? I smuggled a bottle of vodka through. May I offer you some? Vodka warms the heart and soothes the spirit." The Russian uncorked the bottle, took a drink, and handed it to Steiner. The latter drank and handed it to Kern. Kern shook his head.

"Drink, Baby," Steiner said. "It's part of this business. You've got to learn."

"Vodka very good," the Pole agreed.

Kern took a small swallow and handed the bottle to the Pole, who tilted it to his lips with an accomplished gesture.

"That egg-fiend is swigging it all up," growled the Man with the Chicken, tearing the bottle away from him. "There's not much left," he said regretfully to the Russian after he had drunk.

The latter waved it aside. "It doesn't matter, I'm getting out tonight at the latest."

"Are you sure of that?" Steiner asked.

The Russian made a little bow. "Yes. I might almost say, unfortunately. As a Russian I have a Nansen passport."

"Nansen passport!" repeated the Chicken admiringly. "That makes you one of the aristocracy of men without a country."

"I'm sorry you haven't the same advantage," the Russian said politely.

"You got the start of us there," Steiner replied. "You were the first. You got the lion's share of the world's sympathy. We only have the leftovers. People pity us, but we're a nuisance and unwanted."

The Russian shrugged his shoulders. Then he handed the bottle to the last man in the cell, who had hitherto sat in silence. "Please have a swallow too."

"No thanks," the man replied arrogantly. "I don't belong in your crowd."

They all looked at him.

"I have a passport, a country, a permit to stay here and a permit to work."

They were all silent. "Pardon the question," the Russian said presently in a hesitant tone, "but then why are you here?"

"Because of my profession," the man explained haughtily. "I'm no fly-by-night refugee without papers. I'm a substantial pickpocket and professional gambler, with full rights of citizenship."

At noon there was bean soup without beans. In the evening the same thing, only this time it was called "coffee" and a piece of bread came with it.

At seven o'clock there was a knock on the door. The Russian was released, as he had predicted. He said goodby as though to old friends. "In two weeks I'll look in at the Café Sperler," he said to Steiner. "Perhaps by then you'll be there and I may have something for you. Goodby."

By eight o'clock the substantial citizen and cardsharp was ready to capitulate. He brought out a package of cigarettes and handed them around. Everyone began to smoke. The twilight and the glowing cigarettes gave the cell an almost homelike air. The pickpocket explained that the police were just giving him a routine going-over to see if they could pin anything on him during the last six months. He didn't think they could. Then he proposed a game and conjured up a pack of cards out of his coat.

It had grown dark and the electric light had not been turned on. But the cardsharp was equal to the situation. He waved his hands again and produced a candle and matches. The candle was stuck in a ledge in the wall where it gave a dim flickering light.

The Chicken, the Pole, and Steiner drew up. "We're not playing for money, are we?" the Chicken asked.

"Of course not." The cardsharp smiled.

"Aren't you going to play too?" Steiner asked Kern.

"I can't play cards."

"That's something you'll have to learn. What else can you do in the evenings?"

"Not today — tomorrow."

Steiner turned around. The light dug deep furrows in his face. "Is there something the matter with you?"

Kern shook his head. "No. Just a little tired. I'll lie down for a while on the bunk."

The cardsharp was already shuffling. He had an elegant, brisk way of letting the cards snap together. "Who deals?" asked the Chicken. The substantial citizen offered the cards around. The Pole drew a nine, the Chicken a queen, Steiner and the cardsharp each an ace.

The cardsharp glanced up quickly. "A tie."

He drew another ace. He smiled and handed the deck to Steiner. The latter casually flipped up the lowest card in the deck — the ace of clubs.

"What a coincidence!" The Chicken laughed.

The cardsharp did not laugh. "Where did you learn that trick?" he asked Steiner in amazement. "You belong to the profession?"

"No, I'm an amateur. That's why recognition by an expert pleases me so."

"It's not that." The cardsharp looked at him. "The fact is I invented the trick."

"Really?" Steiner pressed out his cigarette. "I learned it in Budapest. In prison, before I was deported. From a man named Katscher."

"Katscher! Now I understand." The cardsharp sighed with relief. "So that's where it came from! Katscher is a pupil of mine; you learned it well."

The cardsharp handed him the deck and looked inquiringly at the candle. "The light is bad — but of course we're

only playing for fun, gentlemen, aren't we? Strictly above-
board."

Kern lay down on his bunk and closed his eyes. He was
full of an unformulated gray sadness. Since the hearing that
morning he had been thinking steadily of his parents — for
the first time in a long while. He saw his father as he had
appeared when he had returned from the police station.
A business competitor had denounced him for talking
against the State — in order to bankrupt his small laboratory
for the manufacture of medicinal soap, perfumes, and toilet
water, and then to buy it up for a song. The plan had succeeded, as a thousand others had at that time. After six
weeks' detention, Kern's father had come back a completely
broken man. He never spoke of his experiences; but he sold
his factory to his competitor at a ridiculous price. Soon
afterward came the order to leave, and with it the beginning
of an endless flight. From Dresden to Prague; from Prague
to Brünn; from there by night over the border into Austria; the next day past the police back into Czecho, two
days later slipping secretly across the border to Vienna —
making improvised splints from branches for his mother's
arm, broken during the night; from Vienna to Hungary; a
couple of weeks with his mother's relatives; then the police
once more; the farewell to his mother, who was allowed to
remain because she was of Hungarian descent; the border
once more; Vienna once more; the heartbreaking business
of peddling soap, toilet water, suspenders, and shoestrings;
the constant dread of being denounced and caught; the
night when his father did not return; the months alone,
stealing from one hiding place to another . . .
Kern turned over, bumping someone as he did so. On the

bunk beside him lay something that looked like a bundle of rags in the darkness. It was the final occupant of the cell, a man of about fifty who had hardly moved all day.

"I beg your pardon," Kern said. "I didn't see you — "

The man made no reply. Kern noticed that his eyes were open. He knew this condition; he had often encountered it on the road. The best thing to do was to leave the man alone.

"Damnation!" the Chicken suddenly shouted from the corner where the card players were. "What a fool I am! What a terrible fool!"

"How's that?" Steiner asked calmly. "The queen of hearts was exactly the right card."

"That's not what I mean. But that Russian could have sent me my chicken. God in Heaven, what a contemptible fool I am! A simple, weak-minded idiot!"

He looked around him as though the world had come to an end.

Kern suddenly discovered that he was laughing. He didn't want to laugh, but now he found he could not stop. He laughed until his whole body shook, and he didn't know why. Something inside him was laughing and throwing everything into confusion — sadness, the past, and all his memories.

"What's up, Baby?" Steiner asked, glancing up from his cards.

"I don't know. I'm laughing."

"Laughter's always a good thing." Steiner threw down the king of spades, stealing a dead-certain trick from the speechless Pole.

Kern reached for a cigarette. All at once everything seemed simple. He decided to learn how to play cards tomorrow. And he had the strange feeling that this resolve had changed his whole life.

Chapter Two

FIVE days later the cardsharp was released. They had not been able to prove anything against him. He and Steiner parted friends. The cardsharp had improved his time by completing Steiner's education in the methods of his pupil Katscher. As a parting gift he gave him the deck of cards and Steiner began to instruct Kern. He taught him skat, jass, tarots, and poker — skat for emigrants; jass to be played in Switzerland; tarots for Austria; and poker for all other occasions.

Two weeks later Kern was summoned upstairs. A police sergeant led him into a room where a middle-aged man was sitting. The place seemed gigantic and so brilliantly lighted that Kern had to squint. He had grown accustomed to the cell.

"You are Ludwig Kern, a student, of no nationality, born November 30, 1916, in Dresden?" the man asked indifferently, glancing at a document.

Kern nodded. His throat was suddenly so dry he could not speak. The man looked up.

"Yes," Kern said huskily.

"You have resided in Austria without reporting to the police . . ."

The man hastily read through the record. "You have been sentenced to fourteen days' detention and have now served your time. You will be expelled from Austria. You are forbidden to return under penalty of imprisonment.

Here is the official order of deportation. You are to sign here in evidence of the fact that you have taken cognizance of this order and understand that to return will make you liable to punishment. Here at the right."

The man lit a cigarette. Kern looked in fascination at the pudgy, thick-veined hand holding the match. In two hours this man would shut up his desk and go to dinner. Afterwards, perhaps, he would play a game of tarots and drink a few glasses of vintage wine. About eleven he would yawn, pay his check and announce: "I'm tired. I'm going home to bed." Home. To bed. At that time the woods along the border would be wrapt in darkness, strangeness, fear; and lost in them — alone, stumbling and tired, with a yearning for men and a dread of men — would be the tiny, flickering spark of life called Ludwig Kern. And the reason for this difference was that a piece of paper called a passport divided him from the bored official behind the desk. Their blood had the same temperature, their eyes the same structure, their nerves reacted to the same stimuli, their thoughts ran in the same channels — and yet an abyss separated them, nothing was the same for both; satisfaction for one was agony for the other, they were possessor and dispossessed, and the abyss that separated them was only a scrap of paper on which there was nothing but a name and a few meaningless dates. . . .

"Here at the right," said the official, "first and last name."

Kern got possession of himself and signed.

"To which border do you wish to be taken?" asked the official.

"The Czech border."

"All right. You will leave in an hour. You will be escorted there."

"I have a few things at the place I was staying. Can I get them?"

"What are they?"

"A bag with shirts and that kind of thing."

"All right. Tell the officer who is to take you to the border. You can stop on the way."

The sergeant led Kern downstairs again and took Steiner back with him.

"What happened?" asked the Chicken, eagerly.

"We're going to get out in an hour."

"Jesus Christ!" said the Pole. "Then that crap start again."

"Would you rather stay here?" asked the Chicken.

"If eating better — and me with little guard job — I very glad staying."

Kern took out his handkerchief and cleaned up his suit as best he could. His shirt was very dirty after two weeks' wear. He reversed the cuffs which he had been carefully protecting. The Pole looked at him. "In one, two years all that — all the same," he predicted.

"Where are you going?" asked the Chicken.

"Czecho. And you? To Hungary?"

"Switzerland. I've thought it over. Come along. From there we'll get them to push us into France."

Kern shook his head. "No, I'm going to try to get to Prague."

A few minutes later Steiner was brought in. "Do you know the name of the policeman who hit me in the face when we were arrested?" he asked Kern. "Leopold Schaefer. He lives at Number 27, Trautenau Alley. They read it to me as part of the record. Of course it didn't say that he hit me. Just that I had threatened him." He looked at Kern. "Do you think I am going to forget that name and address?"

"No," Kern said. "Certainly not."

"Neither do I."

A plain-clothes man from the Criminal Bureau took Steiner and Kern away. Kern was excited. Once out of the building, he stopped involuntarily. The scene that met his eyes was as soothing as a soft breeze from the south. The sky was blue with a first hint of dusk over the houses, the gables caught the last red light of the sun, the Danube shimmered, and shiny busses pushed their way through the streams of people hurrying home or strolling about the streets. A group of girls in bright dresses hurried by laughing. Kern thought he had never seen anything so beautiful.

"Let's go," said the official.

Kern winced. He noticed that a passer-by was staring hard at him and he looked down at himself in shame.

They walked along the streets with the official between them. Tables and chairs had been set out in front of the cafés, and everywhere people were sitting and talking cheerfully. Kern lowered his head and began to walk faster. Steiner looked at him in good-natured derision: "Well, kid, that's not for us, eh? That sort of thing?"

"No," Kern answered and pressed his lips together.

At the boardinghouse the landlady received them with a mixture of annoyance and sympathy. She gave them their things at once; nothing had been stolen. While he was still in the cell Kern had made up his mind to put on a clean shirt, but now after walking through the streets he decided not to. He took the shabby valise under his arm and thanked the landlady.

"I'm sorry you've had so much trouble," he said.

The landlady dismissed the matter. "Take care of yourself," she said, "and you too, Herr Steiner. Where are you off to?"

Steiner made an aimless gesture. "The usual way of the border-bugs, from bush to bush."

The landlady stood hesitating a moment, then walked briskly to a walnut cupboard carved in the form of a medieval castle. "Here's a drink to start you on your way —"

She brought out three glasses and a bottle.

"Plum brandy?" Steiner asked. She nodded and offered the official a glass too. The latter smoothed his mustache. "After all, we fellows are only doing our duty," he explained.

"Of course." The landlady refilled his glass. "Why aren't you drinking?" she asked Kern.

"I can't," Kern said. "Not on an empty stomach."

"So that's it." The landlady looked him over carefully. She had a cold, pudgy face which now unexpectedly softened. "Heavens, he's still growing," she murmured. "Franzi," she shouted, "a sandwich."

"Thanks, that's not necessary." Kern blushed. "I'm really not hungry."

The waitress brought in a thick ham sandwich. "Don't put on airs," said the landlady, "go to it."

"Don't you want half?" Kern asked Steiner. "It's too much for me."

"Don't talk — eat," Steiner said.

Kern ate the sandwich and drank a glass of the brandy, then they took their leave. They rode out of the city by trolley. Kern suddenly felt very tired. The rattling of the car lulled him. As though in a dream he saw the houses glide past, factories, streets, inns with tall walnut trees, meadows, fields in the soft blue dusk of the evening. He was full of food and that affected him like drunkenness. His thoughts became vague and shrouded in dreams — dreams of a white house among blooming chestnut trees; of a deputation of solemn men in morning coats, come to hand him a scroll of honorary citizenship, and of a dictator in uniform who got down on his knees and weepingly implored his forgiveness.

It was almost dark when they reached the customs house. The official from the Criminal Bureau turned them over to the customs men and then plodded back through the lilac-colored dusk.

"It's still too early," said an officer who was stopping and searching cars. "About nine-thirty is the best time."

Kern and Steiner sat down on a bench in front of the door and watched the cars coming up. After a while a second customs man came out. He led them to the right from the customs house along a path. They went through fields that smelled strongly of dew-wet earth, past a few houses with lighted windows, and a patch of woods. Presently the official stopped. "You go on from here. Keep to the left so that you'll be hidden by the bushes, until you come to the Morava. It's not deep now. You can easily wade across."

The two started. It was very quiet. After a while Kern looked around. The figure of the customs man was a black silhouette against the sky. He was watching them. They went on.

On the bank of the Morava, they undressed and made bundles of their clothes and belongings. The river was marshy and had a brown-and-silver look. There were stars in the sky and some clouds through which the moon occasionally broke.

"I'll go first," Steiner said. "I'm taller than you."

They waded through the river. Kern felt the cool water rising stealthily about his body as though it would never release him. In front of him, Steiner was slowly and cautiously feeling his way forward. He held his knapsack and clothes above his head. The moon glistened on his broad shoulders. In the middle of the river he stopped and looked around. Kern was close behind him. He smiled and nodded to him.

They climbed out on the opposite bank and dried themselves hastily with their handkerchiefs. Then they dressed and went on. After a while Steiner stopped. "Now we're across the border," he said. His eyes were bright, almost glassy, in the light that filtered through the trees. He looked at Kern. "Is there anything different about the trees here? Or the smell of the wind? Aren't these the same stars? Do men die differently here?"

"No," Kern said. "All that's the same. But I feel different."

They found a place under an old beech tree where they were hidden from sight. In front of them lay a gently sloping meadow. In the distance gleamed the lights of a Slovakian village. Steiner opened his knapsack and looked for cigarettes. He glanced at Kern's valise. "I've found a knapsack more practical than a bag. It isn't so conspicuous. People take you for a harmless hiker."

"They check up on hikers too," Kern said. "Everyone who looks poor gets checked up on. A car would be the best thing."

They lit cigarettes. "I'm going back in an hour," Steiner said. "And you?"

"I'll try to make Prague. The police aren't so bad there. It's easy to get a permit to stay for a few days. After that we'll see. Perhaps I'll find my father and he can help me. I've heard that he's there."

"Do you know where he's living?"

"No."

"How much money have you?"

"Twelve schillings."

Steiner searched his pockets. "Here's some more. It ought to get you to Prague."

Kern looked up quickly. "Go ahead, take it," Steiner said. "I still have enough for myself."

He showed a couple of bills. In the shadow of the trees Kern couldn't see what they were. He hesitated for an instant, then he took the money.

"Thanks," he said.

Steiner did not reply. He was smoking and the recurrent glow of his cigarette etched his face in light and shadow. "Why are you on the road, anyway?" Kern asked hesitantly. "You're not a Jew."

Steiner was silent for a while. "No, I'm not a Jew," he said finally.

There was a rustling in the woods behind them. Kern leaped to his feet. "A rabbit or a squirrel," Steiner said. Then he turned to Kern. "Here's something you can think about, kid, when you're feeling low: You are out of the country, your father is out, your mother is out. I'm out too —but my wife is in Germany. I don't know what's happening to her."

The rustling behind them came again. Steiner pressed out his cigarette and leaned back against the bole of the beech tree. A breeze was blowing. The moon hung above

Flotsam

the horizon, chalk-white and pitiless, as it had been on that
last night . . .

* * *

After his escape from the concentration camp, Steiner
had hidden for a week at a friend's house. He had sat in a
locked attic room, ready to flee over the roof at the first
suspicious sound. When it got dark, his friend brought him
bread, preserves, and a couple of bottles of water. On the
second night he brought a few books. Steiner read them
feverishly, all day long, over and over, trying not to think.
He dared not strike a light or smoke. He had to satisfy
the needs of nature in a pot hidden in a cardboard box. His
friend took it away after dark and brought it back again.
They had to be so careful that they barely whispered to
each other. The maids who slept near by might have heard
and given them away.

"Does Marie know I'm out?" Steiner had asked, on the
first night.

"No. The house is being watched."

"Has anything happened to her?"

His friend shook his head and went away.

Steiner always asked the same question. Every night. On
the fourth night his friend finally brought him the news
that he had seen her. Now she knew where he was. He had
had a chance to whisper the news to her. Tomorrow he
would see her again — in the market-day crowd. Steiner
spent the whole following day writing a letter, which the
friend was to give her secretly. In the evening he tore it up.
Perhaps she was being watched. For the same reason, he
asked his friend not to meet her again. He spent three more
nights in the room. Finally his friend came with money, a

ticket, and some clothes. Steiner cut his hair and bleached it with peroxide. Then he shaved off his mustache. In the morning he left the house, wearing a laborer's jacket and carrying a box of tools. He had intended to leave the city immediately, but he weakened. It was two years since he had seen his wife. He walked to the market place. An hour later his wife came. He began to shake. She walked past him, however, without seeing him. He followed her and, when he was close behind her, he said: "Don't look around. It's me. Go on! Go on!"

Her shoulders quivered and she threw back her head. Then she went on. She seemed to be listening with every fiber of her body.

"Have they done anything to you?" asked the voice behind her.

She shook her head.

"Are you being watched?"

She nodded.

"Now?"

She hesitated, then shook her head.

"I'm going to leave immediately. I'll try to get across the border. I won't be able to write you. It's too dangerous for you."

She nodded.

"You must get a divorce from me."

The woman paused in her stride for an instant. Then she went on.

"You must get a divorce from me. You must go tomorrow and say that you want to divorce me because of my political views. You must say that you hadn't realized before what they were. Do you understand?"

His wife did not move her head. She walked straight on, holding herself rigidly erect.

"You must understand me," Steiner whispered. "It's only to make you safe. I would lose my mind if they did anything to you. You must divorce me, then they'll leave you alone."

His wife made no reply.

"I love you, Marie," Steiner said softly through his teeth, and his eyes swam with emotion. "I love you and I won't go unless you promise. I'll go back unless you promise. Do you understand me?"

After an eternity, it seemed to him that his wife nodded.

"You promise?"

His wife nodded slowly. Her shoulders sagged.

"I'm going to turn now and come back along the walk to the right. You turn left and come around to meet me. Don't say anything, don't make a sign — I just want to see you — once. Then I'll go. If you hear nothing, it will mean I got across."

His wife nodded and walked faster.

Steiner turned and went along the alley to the right. It was lined with butchers' stalls. Women with market baskets were bargaining in front of the booths. The meat glistened bloody-white in the sun. The smell was intolerable. The butchers were shouting. But suddenly all that was gone. The hacking of the cleavers on the wooden blocks became the distant whetting of scythes. The step and face of his beloved brought with them familiar scenes — a meadow, a cornfield, birch trees, freedom, and the wind. Their eyes sought each other's and would not part, and in them were pain and happiness and love and separation — the essence of life itself, full and sweet and wild — and renunciation like a barrier of a thousand flashing knives.

They moved and stopped in unison and they went on without being aware of it. Then suddenly Steiner's eyes were empty of sight and it was a while before he could even distinguish the kaleidoscopic colors that unrolled meaninglessly before him without penetrating to his mind.

He blundered on, began to walk faster, as fast as he could without attracting attention. He knocked a side of slaughtered pig off a butcher's table and heard the curses of the butcher like the rumbling of a drum. He ran around the corner of an alley and stopped.

He saw her walking away from the market place. She moved very slowly. At the corner of the street she halted and turned around. For a long time she stood with face upraised and eyes very wide. The wind tugged at her clothes and pressed them against her body. Steiner did not know whether she saw him. He dared not signal to her, for he felt she might run back to him. After a long time she lifted her hands and pressed them against her breasts. She held herself toward him — she held herself toward him in an agonized, empty and blind embrace, with open mouth and eyes tight closed. Then she turned slowly away, and the shadowy ravine of the street swallowed her up.

Three days later Steiner crossed the border. The night was bright and windy and a chalk-white moon hung in the sky. Steiner was hard, but once he had the border behind him, he turned, still dripping with cold sweat, and, like a man possessed, whispered back the name of his wife.

* * *

He took out another cigarette. Kern lit it for him.

"How old are you?" Steiner asked.

"Twenty-one. Almost twenty-two."

"Well, well, almost twenty-two. No laughing matter is it, Baby?"

Kern shook his head.

For a time Steiner was silent. Then he said: "At twenty-one I was in the war. In Flanders. That was no joke either. This sort of thing is a hundred times better. Can you understand that?"

"Yes." Kern turned toward him. "It's better than being dead, too. I know all that."

"Then you know a lot. Before the war very few people knew that."

"Before the war! That was a hundred years ago."

"A thousand." Steiner laughed. "When I was twenty-two I was in a field hospital. I learned something there. Do you want to know what?"

"Yes."

"All right." Steiner drew on his cigarette. "There was nothing much wrong with me. A flesh wound, not very painful. But beside me lay my friend. Not just any friend — my friend. A piece of shrapnel had torn open his belly. He lay there and screamed. No morphine, see? There wasn't even enough for the officers. On the second day he was so hoarse he could only groan. He begged me to finish him off. I'd have done it, too, if I had known how. On the third day we had pea soup at noon. Thick soup with bacon, the kind we had before the war. Up to then all they had given us was a sort of dishwater. We ate it. We were frightfully hungry. And while I lapped up mine with delight, like a starving ox, I saw, over the rim of the dish, my friend's face with its split, gaping lips and I saw that he was dying in agony; two hours later he was dead. And I had devoured a meal, and it had tasted better than anything in my life."

He paused.

"You were dreadfully hungry," Kern said.

"No, that's not the point. It's this: a man can gasp out his life beside you — and you feel none of it. Pity, sympathy, sure — but you don't feel the pain. Your belly is whole and that's what counts. A half-yard away someone's world is snuffed out in roaring agony — and you feel nothing. That's the misery of the world. Make a note of it, Baby. That's why progress is so slow, and things slip back so fast. Do you believe it?"

"No," Kern said.

Steiner laughed. "All right. But think about it sometimes. Maybe it will be a help."

He stood up. "I'm off. Back. The customs man isn't expecting me now. He kept watch for the first half-hour. Early tomorrow he'll be on the lookout again. It won't occur to him that I might crawl back in the meantime. That's the psychology of a customs man. Thank God the prey usually gets to be smarter than the hunter. Do you know why?"

"No."

"Because he has more at stake." He slapped Kern on the shoulder. "That's why the Jews have become the slyest people in the world. It's the first law of life: Danger sharpens the wits."

He gave Kern his hand. It was big and dry and warm. "Good luck. Perhaps we'll run into each other again. I'm often at the Café Sperler in the evenings. You can ask for me there."

Kern nodded.

"Well, take care of yourself. And don't forget the deck of cards. It's a distraction and it doesn't make you think. That's important for people without a place to live. You're not bad at jass and tarots. At poker you must take more chances. Bluff more."

"All right," Kern said. "I'll learn to bluff. And thank you. For everything."

"You'll have to get over being thankful. No, don't do that. Perhaps it will be a help. I don't mean with others, that's neither here nor there. I mean what it does for you yourself. Warms your heart when you can feel it. And remember this: Anything's better than war."

"And better than being dead."

"I don't know about being dead. But better than dying, anyhow. So long, Baby."

"So long, Steiner."

Kern sat where he was for a time. The sky had become clear and the landscape was peaceful; there were no people in it. Kern sat quietly in the shadow of the beech tree. The bright translucent green of the foliage above him was like a great sail attached to the earth and driving it before a gentle breeze through infinite blue space — past the beacon lights of the stars and the light-buoy of the moon.

Kern decided to try to get to Pressburg that night, and from there to Prague. It was always safest in a city. He opened his bag and took out a clean shirt and a pair of socks. He knew it was important to look neat, in case he met anyone on the road. Then, too, a change would help him shake off the prison atmosphere.

He felt strange standing naked in the moonlight. As though he were a lost child. Quickly he picked up the fresh shirt from the grass and pulled it over his head. It was a blue shirt — chosen because it showed the dirt less. In the moonlight it looked pale gray and violet. He resolved not to lose courage.

Chapter Three

KERN arrived in Prague in the afternoon. He left his bag at the station and went at once to the police. He had not made up his mind to report; he simply wanted peace to consider what he should do next. The police station was the best place for that purpose. There were no policemen there wandering around asking for papers.

He sat down on a bench in the hall. Opposite him was the office in which aliens were interviewed.

"Is the official with the pointed beard still here?" he asked a man sitting beside him.

"I don't know. The one I've seen has no beard."

"Well, maybe he has been transferred. How are things here now?"

"Not bad," the man said. "You can get a permit for a few days all right. But after that it gets tough. There are too many here."

Kern thought it over. If he secured a permit to stay for a few days he could get, as he had learned from previous experience, cards entitling him to food and a place to sleep for about a week, from the Committee for Refugees. But if they wouldn't give it to him he ran the risk of being locked up and put back across the border.

"Your turn next," said the man beside him.

Kern glanced up. "Don't you want to go first? I'm in no hurry."

"Fine."

The man got up and went inside. Kern decided to see what luck the other would have before making up his mind whether to go in. He strolled restlessly up and down the corridor. Finally the man came out. Kern rushed up to him. "How did it go?" he asked.

"Ten days!" the man beamed. "What luck! And without even asking for it. He must be in a good humor. Or perhaps it was because there aren't so many here today. Last time I only got five days."

Kern pulled himself together. "Then I'll try it too."

The official did not have a pointed beard. Nevertheless Kern thought he had seen him before. Perhaps he had had the beard shaved off in the interval. He was toying with a handsome mother-of-pearl pocketknife. "Immigrant?" he asked, glancing at Kern with weary fishlike eyes.

"Yes."

"From Germany?"

"Yes. I got here today."

"Any papers?"

"No."

The official nodded. He snapped shut the blade of his knife and opened the corkscrew. Kern noticed that in the mother-of-pearl handle there was also a nailfile. The official began carefully smoothing his thumb nail with it. Kern waited. It seemed to him that the nail of this weary man before him was the most important thing in the world. He hardly dared breathe for fear of disturbing him and making him angry. He just locked his hands unobserved behind his back.

Finally the nail was finished. The official inspected it with satisfaction and looked up. "Ten days," he said. "You may stay here ten days. Then you must get out."

Kern felt the tension snap. He thought he was falling but he was just taking a deep breath. Then he quickly got control of himself. He had learned to exploit his opportunities. "I'd be grateful to you," he said, "if I could have two weeks."

"Can't be done. Why?"

"I'm waiting for my papers to be sent to me and I need a permanent address. Then I want to go to Austria."

Kern was afraid he had ruined everything at the last instant; but once started he could not stop himself. He lied fluently and fast. He would just as gladly have told the truth, but he knew he had to lie. The official, on the other hand, knew he had to believe those lies, for there was no possibility of checking up on them. So it came about that both were almost convinced that they were talking about the truth.

The official shut the corkscrew of his knife with a snap. "All right," he said. "As an exception, two weeks. But after that there will be no extension."

He took out a form and began to fill it in. Kern looked at him as though it were an archangel writing. He could hardly conceive that everything had worked out this way. Up to the last instant he expected the official to look in the card index and find out that he had already been in Prague twice. And so to avoid this he gave a different first name and a false birth date. Then he could always maintain that it had been his brother.

But the official was much too weary to look up anything. He pushed the form toward Kern. "Here! Are there more outside?"

"No, I don't think so. At least when I came in there was no one else there."

"Fine."

The man took out his handkerchief and began lovingly to polish the mother-of-pearl handle of his knife. He hardly noticed when Kern said thanks and then rushed out as if his permit might even now be taken away from him.

Not until Kern was outside in front of the gate of the building did he pause and look around him. Sweet heaven, he thought, overcome with emotion. Sweet blue heaven! I'm back again. I have not been locked up; I don't have to be afraid for fourteen days — fourteen whole days and fourteen nights, an eternity! God bless the man with the mother-of-pearl knife. I hope before long he finds one with a disappearing watch and a pair of gold scissors in it.

Beside him at the entrance stood a policeman. Kern touched the permit in his pocket, then with sudden decision approached the policeman. "What time is it, officer?" he asked.

He had a watch of his own but it was a rare experience for him to be able to approach a policeman without being afraid.

"Seven," growled the policeman.

"Thanks." Kern walked slowly down the steps. He would have liked to run. Now for the first time he believed all this was true.

The big waiting room of the Committee for the Aid of Refugees was overcrowded with people. But strangely enough it gave the impression of being empty. The people stood and sat in the half-darkness like shadows. Almost no one spoke. Each of them had told and repeated a hundred times all the facts that concerned him. Now there was only one thing left to do — wait. This was the last barrier against despair.

More than half of those present were Jews. Beside Kern sat a pale man with a pear-shaped head holding a violin case on his knees. On the other side crouched an old man with a scar running across his bulging forehead. He was restlessly opening and closing his hands. Beside him, pressed close together, sat a blond young man and a dark girl. They were holding hands tightly as though they feared that if their attention wandered for so much as an instant they might even here be torn away from each other. They were not looking at each other; they were looking somewhere in space or into their past, and their eyes were empty of emotion. Behind them sat a fat woman who was silently weeping. The tears ran out of her eyes over her cheeks and chin and onto her dress; she paid no attention to them and made no attempt to stop them. Her hands lay limp in her lap.

In this atmosphere of silent resignation and sorrow a child was unheedingly at play. It was a girl of about six with black hair and sparkling eyes. Impatiently and quickly she skipped around the room.

Finally she stopped in front of the man with the pear-shaped head. She looked at him for a while and then pointed to the case he was holding on his knee. "Is there a violin in there?" she asked boldly in a piping voice.

The man looked at the child a moment as though he did not understand, then he nodded.

"Show it to me," the girl said.

"Why?"

"I want to see it."

The violinist hesitated an instant, then opened his case

and took out an instrument wrapped in a violet silk cloth. With loving hands he unwrapped it.

The child stared at the violin for a long time, then she cautiously raised one hand and touched the strings.

"Why don't you play?" she asked.

The violinist made no reply.

"Go ahead, play something," the girl repeated.

"Miriam!" A woman with an infant at her breast was calling from the other side of the room in a low, vehement voice. "Come here to me, Miriam."

The girl paid no attention to her. She was looking at the violinist. "Don't you know how to play?"

"Yes, I know how."

"Then why don't you play?"

The violinist looked around in embarrassment. His big, finely sculptured hand lay around the throat of the violin. The attention of some of those near by had been attracted and they were staring at him. He did not know which way to look.

"After all, I can't play here," he said finally.

"But why can't you?" the girl asked. "Do play, it's so tiresome here."

"Miriam!" the mother called.

"The child is right," said the old man with the scar on his forehead sitting beside the violinist. "Go ahead and play. It will entertain us all and I don't think there is any rule against it."

The violinist still hesitated. Then he took the bow out of the case, tightened it, and raised the violin to his shoulder. Through the room floated the first clear notes.

It seemed to Kern as though he felt a caress, as though a hand were smoothing away something inside him. He tried to resist but could not. A shiver ran through him, then suddenly he was filled with a comforting sense of warmth.

The door of the office opened and the head of the secretary appeared. He came in, leaving the door open behind him. There was a light in the office and the short crooked figure of the secretary was sharply silhouetted in the doorway. He looked as if he were about to say some-thing — but then he tipped his head to one side and listened. Slowly and silently, as if pushed by an invisible hand, the door behind him swung shut.

Only the violin was there. It filled the heavy, dead air of the room and seemed to transform everything, to melt to-gether the voiceless loneliness of the many little beings cowering in the shadow of the walls and to unite them in one great, yearning lamentation.

Kern put his arms around his knees. He let his head sink and allowed the flood to stream over him. He felt as if it were sweeping him away somewhere — to himself and to something very alien. The little black-haired girl crouched on the floor beside the violinist. She sat silent and motion-less and looked at him.

The violin was silent.

Kern, who could play the piano a little, knew enough about music to tell that the playing had been magnificent.

"Schumann?" asked the old man beside the violinist.

The latter nodded.

"Go on playing," said the girl. "Play something that will make us want to laugh."

"Miriam," called her mother.

"All right," said the violinist.

He raised his bow again.

Kern looked around and saw bowed heads and the shim-mer of raised white faces, he saw sorrow and despair and the soft transfiguration wrought for a few instants by the melody of the violin. He saw this; and he thought of the many similar rooms he had seen, filled with exiles whose one crime was to have been born and to be alive. This existed and at the same time this music existed too. It was incomprehensible. It was at once an undying comfort and a hideous irony. Kern saw that the violinist's head rested against his instrument as though on the shoulder of a loved one. I won't give up, he thought, as the twilight deepened through the big room; I will not give up, life is wild and sweet and I do not know it yet; it is a melody, a shout, a cry from distant forests, from undiscovered horizons, in unknown nights — I will not give up. . . . It was some time before he noticed the music had stopped.

"What's that called?" the girl asked.

"German Dances, by Franz Schubert," the violinist said huskily.

The old man beside him laughed. "German Dances!" He rubbed the scar on his forehead. "German Dances!" he repeated.

The secretary turned the light-switch by the door. "Next," he said.

Kern was given an order entitling him to a sleeping place in the Hotel Bristol, and ten tickets for meals at the dining hall on Wenceslaus Square. When he had the tickets in his hand he suddenly realized that he was tremendously hungry, and rushed through the streets for fear he would get there too late.

He was not too late to get in, but all the seats were

taken and he had to wait. Among those who were eating, he saw one of his former professors at the University. He wanted to go up and shake hands with him; but when he had reflected a moment, he decided not to. He knew that many emigrees did not care to be reminded of their former lives.

Presently he saw the violinist come in and stand looking about in bewilderment. He motioned to him; the violinist appeared surprised but came over slowly.

Kern was embarrassed. On first seeing the man again, he had believed he was an old acquaintance; now he suddenly realized that they had not yet spoken to each other.

"I beg your pardon," he said flushing, "but I heard you playing a while ago and it occurred to me you might not know your way around here."

"As a matter of fact, I don't. Do you?"

"Yes, I have been here twice before. Have you been out of the country for long?"

"Two weeks. I arrived here today."

Kern noticed that the professor and someone beside him were getting up. "There are two free places," he said quickly. "Come on."

They pushed their way between the tables. The professor came toward them through the narrow space. He looked at Kern uncertainly and stopped. "Don't I know you?"

"I was one of your students," Kern said.

"Ah, yes, to be sure." The professor nodded. "Tell me, do you happen to know anyone who could use a vacuum cleaner? With ten per cent discount and easy payments? Or a record player and radio combined?"

For an instant Kern was amazed. The professor had been an authority on cancer research. "No, unfortunately I don't," he said sympathetically. He knew what it meant to sell vacuum cleaners and phonographs.

"I rather thought you wouldn't." The professor looked at him absent-mindedly. "I beg your pardon," he said, as if he were speaking to someone entirely different, and went on.

There was barley soup with boiled beef. Kern emptied his plate ravenously. When he looked up, the violinist was sitting beside him with his hands on the table, his plate untouched.

"Aren't you going to eat?" Kern asked in amazement.

"I can't."

"Are you ill?" The pear-shaped head of the violinist looked a sick yellow under the chalky light of the un-shaded bulbs on the ceiling.

"No."

"You ought to eat," Kern said.

The violinist made no reply. He lighted a cigarette and smoked rapidly. Then he pushed his plate to one side. "It's impossible to live this way!" he exclaimed finally.

Kern looked at him. "Haven't you a passport?" he asked.

"Yes, but — " The violinist nervously crushed out his cigarette. "Even so it's impossible to live this way! De-prived of everything! With no ground under one's feet!"

"My God!" Kern said. "You have a passport and you have your violin — "

The violinist glanced up. "But that hasn't anything to do with it," he exclaimed irritably. "Can't you understand that?"

"No, I can't."

Kern was tremendously disillusioned. He had thought that anyone who could play like that must be a superior person. Someone from whom you could learn . . . And now he saw, sitting there, an embittered man who, though he was fifteen years Kern's senior, seemed to him like a spoiled child. The first phase of emigration, he thought. He will soon quiet down.

"Aren't you really going to eat your soup?" he asked.

"No."

"Then give it to me. I'm still hungry."

The violinist pushed the plate toward him. Kern ate the soup slowly. Every spoonful contained strength to withstand misery and he didn't want to lose any of it. Then he stood up. "Thank you for the soup. I'd have liked it better if you had eaten it yourself."

The violinist looked at him. Furrows disfigured his face. "That's something you're not old enough to understand," he said apologetically.

"It's easier to understand than you think," Kern replied. "You're unhappy, that's all."

"What do you mean, that's all?"

"It's not much. You begin by thinking there is something extraordinary about it. But you'll find out, when you've been out in the world a while longer, unhappiness is the commonest thing there is."

He went outside. To his surprise he saw the professor strolling up and down on the opposite side of the street. His attitude — hands clasped behind his back, body bent slightly forward — was the same one he had assumed when he walked up and down on the lecture platform elucidating some new and complicated discovery in the domain of cancer research. Only now he was probably thinking about vacuum cleaners and phonographs.

Kern hesitated a moment. He had never accosted a professor. But now, after his experience with the violinist, he walked over to him.

"I beg your pardon, Professor," he said, "for speaking to you. I would never have believed that I would be in a position to give you advice. But now I should like to try."

The professor paused. "Please do," he replied distractedly. "Please do. I shall be grateful for any advice. What was your name?"

"Kern. Ludwig Kern."

"I shall be grateful for any advice, Herr Kern. Quite unusually grateful. Really!"

"It is hardly advice. Only the lesson of experience. You are trying to sell vacuum cleaners and phonographs. Give it up. It is a waste of time. Hundreds of emigrees here are trying that. It is as hopeless as trying to sell life insurance."

"That was the next thing I was going to try," the professor interrupted excitedly. "Someone told me it was easy to do and you could earn good money at it."

"He offered you a commission for every policy you sold, didn't he?"

"Yes, of course. A good commission."

"But nothing else? No expenses and no salary?"

"No, nothing of that sort."

"I could make you that offer. It doesn't mean a thing. Professor, have you sold a single vacuum cleaner? Or a phonograph?"

The professor looked at him helplessly. "No," he said, strangely embarrassed, "but I hope very soon — "

"Give it up," Kern replied; "that's my advice. Buy a handful of shoelaces or a few boxes of shoe polish or some packages of safety pins. Little things that anyone can use. Peddle them. You won't earn much, but now and then you'll sell something. Of course, hundreds of emigrants are trading in them too. But people buy safety pins sooner than vacuum cleaners."

The professor looked at him thoughtfully. "I hadn't thought of that at all."

Kern smiled in embarrassment. "I can believe it. But think it over. It's better, as I know from experience. Earlier I, too, tried to sell vacuum cleaners."

"Perhaps you're right." The professor extended his hand. "Thank you. You are very kind." His voice was suddenly strangely soft and submissive as if he were a student who had come to class badly prepared.

Kern bit his lip. "I was at all of your lectures — " he said.

"Yes, yes — " The professor made a distracted gesture. "Thank you, Herr — Herr — "

"Kern. But it's of no importance."

"On the contrary, it is important, Herr Kern. I beg your pardon — my memory has not been very good recently. Thank you many times. I believe I shall try it, Herr Kern."

The Hotel Bristol was a dilapidated little frame building that had been rented by the Refugees' Aid. Kern was assigned a bed in a room in which two other refugees were staying. He felt very sleepy after the meal he had eaten and went to bed at once. The two others were not there and he did not hear them come in.

In the middle of the night he was wakened by screams. He sprang out of bed immediately and, without pausing for thought, seized his bag and his clothes, dashed through the door and down the hall. Outside everything was quiet.

At the head of the stairs he stopped, put down his valise and listened — then he rubbed his eyes with his fist. Where was he? What was up? Where were the police?

Slowly memory came back to him. He looked down at himself and smiled with relief. He was in Prague, in the Hotel Bristol, and had a permit that was good for fourteen days. Silly to get in such a fright. Probably he had had a nightmare. He turned around. This mustn't happen again, he thought, if I get jumpy that will be the last straw. Then everything's up. He opened the door and groped in the dark for his bed. It was to the right, beside the wall. He quietly put down his valise and hung his clothes over the foot of the bed. Then he felt for the blanket. Suddenly, just as he was about to lie down, his hand encountered something soft and warm and breathing. He shot bolt upright.

"Who's that?" a girl's voice inquired sleepily.

Kern held his breath. He had got into the wrong room.

"Is someone there?" the voice asked again.

Kern stood rigid. He felt sweat break out all over him. After a while he heard a sigh and the sound of the girl turning over. He waited a few minutes. But everything remained silent and there was only the sound of a deeper breathing in the darkness. He reached quietly for his things and slipped cautiously out of the room.

A man in a shirt was standing in the corridor now in front of Kern's room and was staring at him through his eyeglasses. He watched Kern come out of the neighboring room carrying his things. Kern was too confused to give any explanation. He went silently through the open door, past the man, who did not move out of the way for him, put his things away and got into bed. Before doing so he carefully ran his hand over the cover. There was no one lying under it.

The man stood for a while in the doorway, with the faint light from the hall glittering on his eyeglasses. Then he came in and closed the door with a sharp snap.

At that instant the screaming began again. Kern understood it now. "Don't hit me! Don't hit me! For Christ's sake don't hit me! Please, please! Oh . . ."

The screaming changed to a hair-raising gurgle and died away. Kern sat up. "What's the matter anyway?" he inquired in the darkness.

A switch clicked and the light came on. The man with the eyeglasses got up and went to the third bed, where lay a gasping, sweat-drenched man with wild eyes. The other man brought a glass of water and held it to his mouth. "Drink this. You've just been dreaming. You're safe."

The man drank thirstily, his Adam's apple bobbing up and down in his thin throat. Then he fell back exhausted, shut his eyes and gave a deep sigh.

"What's it all about?" Kern asked again.

The man with the eyeglasses came over to his bed. "What's it all about? Someone who has dreams. Who dreams aloud. Released from a concentration camp a couple of weeks ago. Nerves, see?"

"Yes," Kern said.

"Are you staying here?" asked the man with the eyeglasses.

Kern nodded. "I seem to have a touch of nerves myself. When he began to scream a while ago I dashed out. I thought the police were raiding the place. After that I got into the wrong room."

"So that was it."

"Please excuse me," said the third man. "I'll stay awake now. Excuse me."

"Oh nonsense," said the man with the eyeglasses, going back to his bed. "Your nightmares don't bother us a bit. Do they, young man?"

"Not a bit," Kern repeated.

There was a click and the room became dark. Kern lay down, but for a long time he could not go to sleep. That had been strange, that experience in the next room. The soft breast under the thin sheet. He could still feel it, and it seemed to him as if his hand were no longer the same.

Later he heard the man who had cried out get up and seat himself beside the window. His bowed head was revealed against the brightening gray of the dawn like the somber statue of a slave. Kern watched him for a time and then fell asleep.

*   *   *

Josef Steiner had no trouble getting back across the border. He knew the ground well and his experience of wartime patrol duty stood him in good stead. He had been a company guide and in 1915 had received the Iron Cross for a dangerous reconnaissance on which he had captured a prisoner.

In an hour's time he was out of the danger zone. He took the trolley for Vienna. There were not many people in the car. The conductor recognized him. "Back already?"

"A ticket to Vienna, second class," Steiner said.

"Quick work," said the conductor.

Steiner glanced at him. "I know all about it," the conductor went on. "People are sent out under guard every day — you soon get to know the officers. It's a nasty business. You rode out in this car, but you wouldn't remember that."

"I have no idea what you're talking about."

The conductor laughed. "You'll remember. Look, stand on the back platform. If an inspector comes along jump off — but that's not likely at this hour. You'll save the price of a ticket."

"Thanks."

Steiner got up and went to the back of the car. He felt the wind on his face and saw the lights of the little vineyard villages rush by. He filled his lungs, enjoying the headiest of all intoxications, the intoxication of freedom. His blood tingled and he felt the strong glow of his muscles. He was alive. He had not been caught; he was alive and had escaped.

"Have a cigarette, brother," he said to the conductor who had joined him at the rear of the car.

"All right. But I can't smoke it now. Thanks."

"I can smoke mine, though."

"Yes." The conductor laughed good-naturedly. "That's where you have it over me."

"Yes," Steiner said, drawing the fragrant smoke deep into his lungs, "that's where I have it over you."

He went to the rooming house where the police had picked him up. The landlady was still sitting in her office. She was startled at sight of Steiner.

"You can't stay here," she said quickly.

"Oh, yes I can," Steiner said, putting down his knapsack.

"It's out of the question, Herr Steiner. The police may come back any time. Then they'll shut up my house."

"Dear Luise," Steiner said equably, "the safest place during the war was a fresh shell-hole. Another hardly ever landed immediately in the same place. So, for the time being, your flea-bag is one of the safest in Vienna."

The landlady ran her hands distractedly through her hair. "You're the ruination of me," she announced pathetically.

"How nice! That's what I've always wanted to be! Someone's ruination! You're a romantic creature, Luise." Steiner looked around. "Is there still a little coffee and a drop to drink?"

"Coffee? And a drink?"

"Yes, dear Luise! I knew you would understand me. Such a pretty woman! Is that still the bottle of plum brandy in the cupboard?"

The landlady looked at him helplessly. "Yes, of course," she said at last.

"Just the thing!" Steiner fetched the bottle and two glasses. "Won't you have one too?"

"I?"

"Yes, you. Who else?"

"No."

"Oh, come, Luise! Have one as a favor to me. There's something unfriendly about drinking alone. Here — " He filled a glass and offered it to her.

The landlady hesitated, then took the glass. "Oh, very well. But you won't try to stay here, will you?"

"Only for a few days," Steiner said pacifyingly, "not more than a few days. You bring me luck. And I have plans afoot." He smiled. "And now the coffee, dear Luise."

"Coffee? I have no coffee here."

"Yes you have, my child. It's standing right over there. And I bet it's good."

The landlady laughed in exasperation. "Aren't you the one! Besides, my name is not Luise; my name is Therese."

"Therese, you are a dream."

The landlady brought him the coffee. "Old Seligmann's things are still here," she said, pointing to a bag. "What in the world shall I do with them?"

"Was that the Jew with the gray beard?"

The landlady nodded. "He's dead. I heard that much and no more — "

"Well, that's enough for one man. Don't you know where his children are?"

"How should I know? I can't bother my head about things like that."

"That's true." Steiner pulled the bag toward him and opened it. A number of rolls of yarn of various colors fell out. Under them, carefully packed, lay a box of shoelaces. Then came a suit, a pair of shoes, a Hebrew book, some shirts, a couple of cards of horn buttons, a small chamois bag containing one-schilling pieces, two phylacteries and a white prayer robe wrapped in tissue paper. "Not much for a whole life, eh, Therese?"

"Many have less."

"That's right too." Steiner examined the Hebrew book and found a slip of paper stuck under the paper inside the cover. Carefully he drew it out. There was an address written in ink on it. "Aha! I'll make inquiries here." He stood up. "Thanks for the coffee and the brandy, Therese. I'll be late tonight. You'd better put me in a room on the ground floor opening on the court. Then I can get out quick."

The landlady was about to say something, but Steiner raised his hand. "No, no, Therese! If the door is locked on my return, I'll come back with the whole Vienna police force. But I'm sure it won't be locked. To give lodging to the homeless is a commandment of God. You'll get a thousand years of bliss in Heaven for doing it. I'll just leave my knapsack here."

He left. He knew it was pointless to continue the conversation and he understood the extraordinarily persuasive effect that personal belongings exert upon people who lead regular lives. His knapsack would be more effective in finding quarters for him than any amount of pleading. By its voiceless presence alone it would overcome the landlady's last objections.

Steiner went to the Café Sperler. He wanted to find the Russian, Tschernikoff. During detention they had agreed to wait there after midnight for each other on the first and second day after Steiner's release. The Russians had had fifteen years more experience in being men without a country than the Germans. Tschernikoff had promised Steiner to look about and see whether forged passports could be bought in Vienna.

Steiner sat down at a table in the corner. He intended to order something to drink, but the waiters paid no attention to him. You did not have to order anything here; most of the people had no money.

The place was a typical emigrees' exchange. It was full of people. Many of them were sleeping sitting up on benches and chairs; others lay on the floor with their backs against the wall. They were filling in the time until the café was closed by sleeping for nothing. From five in the morning until noon they would stroll about and wait for the café to open again. Most of them were intellectuals. They had the hardest time adjusting themselves.

A man in a checked suit with a face like a full moon seated himself beside Steiner and regarded him for a while with lively black eyes. "Something to sell?" he asked finally. "Jewelry? Even old jewelry? I pay cash."

Steiner shook his head.

"Suits? Shirts? Shoes?" The man looked at him searchingly. "A wedding ring perhaps?"

"Go away, you vulture," Steiner snarled. He hated these peddlers who tried to cheat bewildered emigrees out of their last few belongings for a couple of groschen.

He called to a passing waiter. "You there! A cognac."

The waiter glanced at him in bewilderment and came over. "Did you ask for a lawyer? There are two here. Over there in the corner is Lawyer Silber of the Court of Appeals in Berlin: one schilling per consultation. At the round table beside the door is Judge Epstein of the Munich Circuit Court: fifty groschen per consultation. Just between us, Silber is better."

"I don't want a lawyer, I want a cognac," Steiner said.

The waiter put his hand to his ear. "Did I understand you correctly? A cognac?"

"Yes. A drink that tastes better if the glasses aren't too small."

"Very well. I beg your pardon, but I'm a little hard of hearing. And then I'm not used to the word any more. Coffee is almost the only thing that's ordered here."

"All right. Then bring me the cognac in a coffee cup."

The waiter brought the cognac and remained standing by the table. "What's the matter?" Steiner asked. "Do you want to watch me drink it?"

"You have to pay in advance. That's the rule here. Otherwise we'd go bankrupt."

"If that's the rule, here you are." Steiner paid.

"That's too much," the waiter said.

"The change is your tip."

"Tip?" The waiter rolled the word on his tongue. "My God," he said with emotion, "that's the first one in years! Thank you, sir. That makes a fellow feel like a man again!"

A few minutes later the Russian came in. He saw Steiner immediately and sat down with him.

"I was beginning to think you'd left Vienna, Tschernikoff."

The Russian laughed. "With us the probable is always the improbable. I found out everything you wanted to know."

Steiner emptied his glass. "Can you get papers?"

"Yes. Even very good ones. The best forgery I have seen in years."

"I've got to get out of the country," Steiner said. "I've got to have papers. I'd rather run the risk of a penitentiary with a false passport than stand this constant anxiety and these trips to the lock-up. What have you seen?"

"I was in the Hellebarde Café. That's where the people do business now. They are the same ones as seven years ago. Reliable enough in their way. To be sure the cheapest papers cost four hundred schillings."

"What can you get for that?"

"The passport of a dead Austrian. Good for one year more."

"One year. And then?"

Tschernikoff looked at Steiner. "Abroad it might be extended. Or a skillful hand could alter the date."

Steiner nodded.

"Besides, there are two passports that belong to dead

German refugees. But they cost eight hundred schillings apiece. Completely forged ones are not to be had under fifteen hundred. I wouldn't recommend them to you anyway."

Tschernikoff tapped the ash off his cigarette. "For the time being there's nothing to be expected from the League of Nations in your case. For those who have come into the country illegally without a passport, nothing at all. Nansen is dead; he was the one who got our passports for us."

"Four hundred schillings?" Steiner said. "I have twenty-five."

"You'll be able to beat them down a little. To three hundred and fifty, I'd say."

"Compared to twenty-five it's all the same. But that doesn't make any difference; I'll see to it that I get the money. Where is the Hellebarde?"

The Russian drew a slip of paper out of his pocket. "Here is the address. Also the name of the waiter who acts as go-between. He calls the people up when you tell him to. He gets five schillings for doing it."

"Fine. I'll see how I make out." Steiner put the slip away carefully. "A thousand thanks for taking so much trouble, Tschernikoff."

"Not at all," the Russian waved away the thanks. "One does what one can when there's a chance. You never know when you'll be in the same fix yourself."

"Yes." Steiner stood up. "I'll look you up again here and tell you how it comes out."

"Fine. I'm often here about this time. I play chess with the South German master. The man over there with the ear-locks. Never thought in normal times that I'd have the good fortune to play with an expert like that." Tschernikoff smiled. "Chess is a passion of mine."

Steiner nodded to him. Then stepping over a few young people who were lying asleep with open mouths along the wall, he went to the door. At Circuit Judge Epstein's table sat a pudgy Jewess. Epstein was lecturing unctuously and she sat with folded hands staring at him as though at an unreliable god. In front of her on the table lay fifty groschen. Epstein's hairy left hand lay close beside them like a great spider in wait.

Outside Steiner took a deep breath. The soft night air seemed like wine after the stale smoke and gray misery of the café. I must get away, he thought, I must get away at any price. He looked at his watch. Although it was late he decided to try to find the cardsharp.

The little bar, which the cardsharp had told him was his hangout, was almost empty. Only two showily dressed girls were perched like parrots on high chairs with their feet on the nickel railing of the bar.

"Has Fred been here?" Steiner asked the barkeep.

"Fred?" The barkeep looked at him sharply. "What do you want with Fred?"

"I want to repeat the Lord's Prayer with him, brother. What did you think?"

The barkeep reflected for a while. "He left an hour ago," he said finally.

"Will he be back?"

"Couldn't tell you."

"All right, then I'll wait. Give me a vodka."

Steiner waited for about an hour. He thought over all the things he could turn into cash. But it didn't amount to more than about seventy schillings. The girls had paid him only cursory attention. They sat around for a while longer, then strutted out. The barkeep began to shake and throw dice by himself.

"Shall we throw a round?" Steiner asked.

"Go ahead."

They threw and Steiner won. They went on playing. Steiner threw four aces twice in succession. "I seem to have luck with aces," he said.

"You have luck anyway," the barkeep replied. "What sign were you born under?"

"I don't know."

"You seem to be a Lion. At least you have the sun in the constellation of Leo. I know a little about astrology. Last round, eh? Fred won't be back. He never comes as late as this. Needs sleep and steady hands."

They shook and Steiner won again. "See?" said the barkeep in a satisfied tone, pushing over five schillings. "You are most certainly a Lion, with Neptune in the ascendant, I should say. What month were you born in?"

"August."

"Then you're a perfect Lion. You'll have magnificent luck this year."

"To make up for that I'm taking on a whole forest full of lions." Steiner emptied his glass. "Tell Fred I was here, will you? Say that Steiner asked for him. I'll stop in tomorrow about eight."

"Right."

Steiner went back to the rooming house. The way was long and the streets empty. Above him hung the star-studded sky, and over the walls drifted from time to time the heavy scent of lilacs in bloom. My God, Marie, he thought, this can't go on forever.

Chapter Four

KERN was standing in a drugstore near Wenceslaus Square. He had spied in the window a couple of bottles of toilet water bearing the label of his father's laboratory.

"Farr's Toilet Water!" Kern fondled the bottle the druggist had brought out of the case. "Where did you get this?"

The druggist shrugged his shoulders. "I don't remember now. It comes from Germany. We've had it for a long time. Do you want to buy that bottle?"

"Not just this one. Six —"

"Six?"

"Yes, six to begin with. More later on. I sell it. Of course I must have a discount."

The druggist looked at Kern. "Are you an emigree?" he asked.

Kern put the bottle down on the counter. "Do you know," he said angrily, "that question is gradually beginning to bore me — when it's asked by someone who is not a member of the police. Especially when I have a permit in my pocket. All you have to do is tell me what discount you'll give."

"Ten per cent."

"That's ridiculous. How can I make any money that way?"

"You can have the bottle at twenty-five per cent discount," said the owner of the store coming in from the back room. "Thirty per cent if you take ten. We'd be glad to get rid of that old stuff."

"Old stuff?" Kern gave the man an offended look. "That's very fine toilet water, don't you know that?"

The owner of the store indifferently dug into his ear with his little finger. "Maybe so. In that case, of course, you'll be satisfied with twenty per cent."

"Thirty is the very least. That hasn't anything to do with the quality. You can give me thirty per cent and it can be good toilet water just the same, can't it?"

The druggist made a face. "All toilet waters are the same. The only thing that makes some better than others is advertising. That's the whole secret."

Kern looked at him. "It's perfectly certain that there's not going to be any more advertising for this. And so according to you it's very bad. In that case, thirty-five per cent would be the right discount."

"Thirty," the owner rejoined. "Now and then someone asks for it."

"Herr Bureck," the druggist said. "I think we can let him have it at thirty-five per cent if he takes a dozen. The man who inquires for it now and then is always the same one. And he doesn't buy any of it; he just wants to sell us the formula."

"The formula? Dear God, as if we didn't have enough trouble!" Bureck lifted his hands in despair.

"The formula?" Kern pricked up his ears. "Who is it that wants to sell you the formula?"

The druggist laughed. "Someone or other. He says he formerly owned the laboratory himself. All lies of course! The things these emigrees think up!"

Kern was breathless for an instant. "Do you know where the man lives?" he asked.

The druggist shrugged his shoulders. "I think we have the address lying around somewhere. He has given it to us a couple of times."

"I think it's my father."

The two stared at Kern. "Really?" said the druggist.

"Yes, I think that's who it is. I've been looking for him for a long time."

"Bertha!" the owner shouted excitedly to a woman who was working at a desk in the back of the store. "Have we still got the address of the man who wanted to sell us a formula for toilet water?"

"Do you mean Herr Strna? Or that old windbag who's been in here loafing around a couple of times?" the woman shouted back.

"Hell!" The proprietor looked at Kern in embarrassment. "I'm sorry." He went quickly to the back of the store.

"That comes from sleeping with the help," the druggist remarked sneeringly behind his back.

The owner came back snorting after a while with a slip of paper in his hand. "Here's the address. It is a Herr Kern, Siegmund Kern."

"That's my father."

"Really?" The man gave the paper to Kern. "This is the address. The last time he was here was about three weeks ago. You understand, of course — "

"Oh, that doesn't make any difference. But I'd like to go there right away. I'll come back later about the bottles."

"Of course. There's time enough for that."

The house to which Kern had been directed was situated in Tuzarova Street, near the covered markets. It was dark and musty and smelled of damp walls and boiled cabbage. Kern climbed slowly up the stairs. It was strange, but he was a little afraid to see his father again after so long a time — experience had taught him that things never got any better.

On the third floor he rang. After a while there was a sound of shuffling footsteps behind the door and a piece of cardboard was pushed away from a round peephole. Kern could see one black eye peering at him.

"Who's there?" a woman's voice inquired sullenly.

"I want to see someone who lives here," Kern said.

"No one lives here."

"That's not true, you live here, don't you?" Kern looked at the name on the door. "Frau Melanie Ekowski? But I don't want to talk to you."

"Well then?"

"I want to talk to a man who lives here."

"There's no man living here."

Kern stared at the round black eye. Perhaps it was true that his father had left long since. He felt suddenly empty and discouraged.

"What's his name supposed to be?" asked the woman behind the door.

Kern lifted his head with reawakened hope. "I'd rather not shout that through the whole house. If you'll open the door I'll tell you."

The eye disappeared from the peephole. A chain rattled. This is a regular fortress, Kern thought. He was pretty sure now that his father still lived here; otherwise the woman wouldn't have questioned him.

The door opened. A powerful Czech woman, with a broad face and red cheeks, stood there examining Kern from head to toe.

"I want to speak to Herr Kern."

"Kern? Don't know him. He doesn't live here."

"Herr Siegmund Kern. I am Ludwig Kern."

"Ah?" The woman eyed him suspiciously. "Anyone could say that."

Kern took his permit out of his pocket. "Here — please look at this paper. The first name has been purposely changed; but you can see the other one."

The woman read the whole document through slowly. It took a long while. Then she gave it back. "Relative?"

"Yes." Something kept him from saying more. He was now practically certain that this was where his father lived.

The woman had made up her mind. "Doesn't live here," she declared curtly.

"All right," Kern said; "then I shall tell you where I live. In the Hotel Bristol. I shall only be here for a couple of days; I should like to see Herr Siegmund Kern before I go. I am not going to be a burden to him. I have something to give him," he added, glancing at the woman.

"Really?"

"Yes. The Hotel Bristol. Ludwig Kern. Good day."

He went down the stairs. Good heavens, he thought, a pretty Cerberus he has guarding him! However — it's better to be guarded than betrayed.

He went back to the drugstore. The owner rushed up to him. "Did you find your father?" His face was full of the curiosity of a man whose life is completely lacking in excitement.

"Not yet," Kern said, suddenly displeased. "But he lives there. He wasn't at home."

"Think of that! That's a real piece of luck, isn't it?"

The man folded his arms on the counter and launched into a discourse on strange coincidents in life.

"That's not the way it is with us," Kern said. "With us

it's a strange coincidence when anything goes normally. And how about the toilet water? I can only take six bottles right now. I haven't money for any more. What discount will you give me?"

The owner reflected for a moment. Then he announced magnanimously, "Thirty-five per cent. Something like this doesn't happen every day."

"All right."

Kern paid and the druggist wrapped up the bottles. The woman named Bertha had meanwhile come out from the back of the shop in order to look at the young man who had found his father. She was excitedly munching something.

"Look here," said the owner. "There's something I wanted to say — the toilet water is very good. Really very good."

"Thanks!" Kern took the package. "In that case I'll hope to be back soon to get the rest."

Kern returned to the hotel. He planned to fetch some cakes of soap and bottles of perfume and try peddling them in town. The man from the concentration camp who lived in the same room had loaned him money with which to lay in a stock.

As he stepped into the hall he saw someone come out of the room next to his. It was a girl of medium height, wearing a bright dress and carrying a couple of books under her arm. At first Kern paid no attention to her. He was busy figuring out the prices for his toilet water. But suddenly he realized that the girl had come out of the room into which he had blundered the night before, and he stopped short. He had a feeling that she might even now recognize him.

The girl went quickly down the stairs without looking around. Kern still waited for a while, then he went quickly down the corridor after her. He had suddenly become very curious to know what she looked like.

He went down the stairs and looked about, but the girl was nowhere to be seen. He went to the door and looked up and down the street. It lay empty in the afternoon sunlight. There were only a couple of police dogs romping on the sidewalk. Kern went back into the hotel.

"Didn't someone just go out?" he asked the doorman, who was also the waiter and handyman.

"Only you!" The doorman stared at him. He expected Kern to burst into laughter at his joke.

Kern did not laugh. "I mean a girl," he said. "A young lady."

"No ladies live here," the doorman replied sullenly. He was offended because his wit had been wasted. "Only women."

"So no one went out?"

"What do you mean by all these questions? Are you from the police?" The doorman was now openly hostile.

Kern looked at him in amazement. He could not understand what had got into the man. He had completely missed the joke. He got a package of cigarettes out of his pocket and offered one to the doorman. "Thanks," the latter said frostily. "I smoke a better brand."

"I can believe that."

Kern put the cigarettes away. He stayed there for a moment reflecting. The girl must still be in the hotel; perhaps she was in the sitting room. He went back.

The sitting room was long and it opened on a cement terrace which, in turn, led to a walled garden in which grew a couple of lilac bushes.

Kern glanced through the glass door. He saw the girl sitting at a table. She was leaning on her elbows reading. There was no one else in the room. Irresistibly drawn, Kern opened the door and stepped in.

The girl glanced up as she heard the door. Kern was embarrassed. "Good afternoon," he said tentatively. The girl looked at him. Then she nodded and went on reading.

Kern took a seat in one corner of the room. After a while he stood up and got a couple of newspapers. Suddenly he seemed ridiculous in his own eyes and wished that he were outside again. But it seemed almost impossible to get up again so soon and walk out.

He unfolded the newspapers and began to read. After a while he saw the girl reach for her handbag and open it. She took out a silver cigarette case and snapped it open. Then she closed it without taking out a cigarette and put it back in the bag.

Kern quickly laid the paper aside and got up. "I see you've forgotten your cigarettes," he said. "May I help you out?"

He drew out his package. He would have given a great deal to have a cigarette case. The package was crushed and torn at the corners. He offered it to the girl. "Of course I don't know whether you like this kind. The doorman just refused them. They weren't good enough for him."

The girl looked at the label. "They're the same kind I smoke," she said.

Kern laughed. "They're the cheapest you can buy. That's almost like telling the story of your life."

The girl looked at him. "I guess this hotel tells it anyway."

"That's true."

Kern struck a match and lit the girl's cigarette. The pale reddish light illuminated her narrow, tawny face with its well-defined dark eyebrows. Her eyes were clear and large and her mouth full and soft. Kern could not have said whether the girl was pretty or whether he liked her; but he had the strange feeling of a quiet and remote connection with her — his hand had rested on her breast before he knew her. He saw her breast rise and suddenly, although he knew it was silly, he hid his hand in his pocket.

"Have you been abroad long?" he asked.

"Two months."

"That's not long."

"It's an eternity."

Kern glanced up in surprise. "You're right," he said, "two years is not long. But two months is an eternity. There's this advantage, though: the longer it lasts, the shorter the months become."

"Do you think it will last long?" the girl asked.

"I don't know. I don't think about it any more."

"I do all the time."

"So did I when I had been away for two months."

The girl was silent. Her head was bowed in thought and she was smoking slowly with deep inhalations. Kern looked at the heavy, wavy black hair that framed her face. He would have liked to say something striking and brilliant but nothing occurred to him. He tried to remember how the worldly heroes of the many books he had read had behaved in similar situations, but his memory had dried up and probably, too, the heroes had never found themselves in a refugee's hotel in Prague.

"Isn't it too dark to read?" he asked finally.

The girl started as though her thoughts had been far away. Then she slammed shut the book that was lying in front of her. "No. But I'm not going to read any more anyway. There's no point in it."

"Sometimes it's a distraction," Kern said. "When I can get hold of a detective story I read it through at one sitting."

The girl smiled wearily. "This is no detective story, it's a textbook on inorganic chemistry."

"Really? Then you were in college?"

"Yes. In Würzburg."

"I was at Leipzig. At first I took my textbooks with me too. I didn't want to forget anything. But then later on I sold them. They were too heavy to carry around. And I bought toilet water and soap with the money so I would have something to peddle. That's the way I make my living now."

The girl looked at him. "I don't find you very encouraging."

"I certainly don't want to discourage you," Kern said quickly. "My case was entirely different. I had no papers at all. You probably have a passport."

The girl nodded. "I have a passport but it expires in six weeks."

"That's nothing. You can surely get it extended."

"I don't believe so."

The girl got up.

"Won't you have another cigarette?" Kern asked.

"No thanks. I smoke a great deal too much."

"Someone said to me once that a cigarette at the right moment is better than all the ideals in the world."

"That's right." The girl smiled, and all at once she

seemed very beautiful to Kern. He would have given a great deal to go on talking with her but he didn't know what to do to make her stay.

"If I can be helpful in any way," he said hastily, "I should be glad. I know my way around here in Prague. I've been here twice before. My name is Ludwig Kern and I live in the room to the right beside yours."

The girl glanced at him quickly. Kern thought he had given himself away. But she casually extended her hand. He felt a firm pressure. "I shall gladly call on you if there's anything I don't know about," she said. "Many thanks."

She took her books from the table and went up the stairs. Kern stayed for a while in the sitting room. Suddenly he knew all the things he should have said.

* * *

"Try it again, Steiner," the cardsharp said. "Heaven knows I'm more nervous about your debut at that clip joint over there than if I were going to play at the Jockey Club."

They were sitting in the bar and Fred was giving Steiner a final rehearsal before turning him loose for the first time against a couple of minor cardsharps in a neighboring dive. This was the only way Steiner could see to get some money — aside, of course, from burglary and highway robbery.

They practised the ace trick for about half an hour. Then the pickpocket was satisfied and got up. He was wearing a dinner coat. "I must be off now. To the opera. A big first-night crowd. Lotte Lehmann is singing. Really important art always makes good business for us. People get absent-minded, see?" He shook hands with Steiner.

"One thing more that's just occurred to me. How much money have you?"

"Thirty-two schillings."

"That's not enough. The boys will have to see more than that before they'll bite." He reached in his pocket and drew out a hundred-schilling note. "Here, pay for your coffee with this; then one of them will come up to you. Give the money back to the proprietor for me; he knows me. And now: play fast and look out when you get the four queens. They're out for blood then!"

Steiner took the bill. "If I lose this money I can't pay you back."

The pickpocket shrugged his shoulders. "Then it's gone and that's all there is to it. Just artist's luck. But you won't lose it. I know those fellows. Just good enough to cheat hayseeds. No class to them. Are you nervous?"

"I don't think so."

"Even if you are you have a chance. The fellows over there don't know that you understand their game. Before they find out they'll be caught, and there's not much they can do about it. Well, so long."

"So long."

Steiner went over to the dive. On the way he reflected that it was strange that there was no other human being who would have loaned him one quarter of the sum the cardsharp had unhesitatingly handed over. The comradeship of those who have lost their way, he thought. Always the same, thank God.

In the front room of the dive a couple of games of tarots were in progress. Steiner seated himself by the window and ordered a brandy. He ostentatiously drew out his wallet, in which he had stuffed a sheaf of paper to make it look fat, and paid with the hundred-schilling note.

A minute later an emaciated-looking man came up and invited him to join a small poker game. Steiner refused in bored tones. The man persisted.

"I haven't enough time," Steiner explained. "Not more than half an hour, and that's not enough for a game."

"Oh nonsense, nonsense," the thin man said, showing a set of badly decayed teeth. "Many a man has won his fortune in a half-hour, neighbor."

Steiner saw the two others at a neighboring table. One had a fat face and a bald spot. The other was dark and hairy and his nose was too big. Both were watching him with studied casualness. "If it really is just for half an hour," Steiner said in apparent hesitation, "I might try my luck."

"Of course, of course," the thin man answered heartily.

"And I can stop when I feel like it?"

"Naturally, neighbor, when you feel like it."

"Even if I'm winning?"

The fat man at the table twisted his lips and glanced over at the dark man: they seemed to have caught a real hayseed. "But that's just the time to stop, the very time to stop," the thin man bleated happily.

"All right then."

Steiner seated himself at the table. The fat man shuffled and dealt. Steiner won a few schillings. When the deal came to him he felt along the edges of the cards, then he shuffled again, broke the pack where he had felt something, ordered a drink and took that opportunity to look at the marked card. He saw it was the kings that had been nicked. Then he shuffled again and dealt. At the end of a quarter of an hour he had won about thirty schillings. "Why, that's fine!" bleated the thin man. "Shall we shove the bets up a bit?"

Steiner nodded. He won the next hands, too, in which the stakes were higher. Then the fat man dealt. His fat, pink hands were really too small to manipulate the cards. Steiner saw, however, that he was very adroit. Steiner lifted his hand. He had three queens.

"How many?" asked the fat man, chewing on his cigar.

"Four," Steiner said. He noticed that the fat man was startled: Steiner should have drawn only two cards. The fat man pushed four toward him. Steiner saw that the first was the missing fourth queen. Naturally he had no hand now and threw his cards down exclaiming: "Damnation, a bust!" The three looked at each other and passed too.

Steiner knew that he would have no chance to pull anything except when he himself dealt. And so his chances were one to three. The pickpocket had been right. He would have to act fast before the others caught on. He tried the ace trick in its simple form. The pig played against him and lost. Steiner looked at his watch. "I must be off; last round."

"Now, now, neighbor," bleated the thin man. The two others said nothing.

On the next deal Steiner had four queens in his original hand. He drew one card. A nine. The hairy dark man drew two cards. Steiner saw that the thin man dealt them to him from the bottom of the deck with a flick of the fingers. He knew what was up, but he went on raising to twenty schillings and then dropped out. The dark man shot him a glance and raked in the pot. "What kind of cards did you have?" barked the thin man, turning up Steiner's hand. "Four queens! And you passed, you simpleton? Why, there was all the money in the world in that hand! . . . What did you have?" he asked the dark man.

"Three kings," the latter replied with a wry face.

"There. You see, you see. You'd have won, neighbor!
. . . How high would you have gone with three kings?"

"With three kings I'd bid up to the moon," the dark
man replied sullenly.

"I made a mistake," Steiner said. "Thought I had only
three queens. I mistook one of them for a jack."

"What a way to play!"

The dark man dealt. Steiner got three kings and drew
the fourth. He bet fifteen schillings and then passed. The
pig drew his breath in audibly. Steiner had won about
ninety schillings and there were only about two more hands
to play.

"What did you have that time, neighbor?" The thin
man made a quick attempt to turn up Steiner's cards. Steiner
struck his hand away. "Is that the custom here?" he asked.

"Oh, excuse me. But you get curious, you know."

On the next deal Steiner lost eight schillings. He would
not bet any more. Then he took the cards and shuffled
them. He had been paying close attention and placed the
three kings under the deck so that he could deal them to
the fat man. It worked. The dark man stayed in for ap-
pearances. The fat man drew one card. Steiner gave him
the last king. The fat man gulped and exchanged a glance
with the others. Steiner made use of this moment for the
ace trick. He discarded three of his cards and dealt himself
the two last aces that lay on the top of the deck.

The fat man began to bet. Steiner laid down his cards
and went with him, hesitantly. The dark man doubled. At
a hundred schillings he dropped out. The fat man raised
the bet to a hundred and fifty. Steiner called him. He was
not entirely sure of his position. That the fat man had four
kings he knew, but he didn't know what the fifth card
might be. If it was the joker, Steiner was lost. The thin

man jiggled on his seat. "May I look?" he asked, reaching for Steiner's cards.

"No." Steiner put his hand on the cards. He was amazed at this transparent impudence. The thin man would immediately have telegraphed Steiner's hand to the fat man, with his foot.

The fat man became unsure of himself. Steiner had been so cautious hitherto that he must have a strong hand. Steiner noticed the hesitation and increased his bets. At a hundred and eighty the fat man stopped. He laid four kings on the table. Steiner sighed with relief and turned up his four aces.

The thin man whistled through his teeth. Then it became very quiet as Steiner pocketed the money.

"We'll play another round," the dark man said suddenly in a harsh voice.

"Sorry," Steiner said.

"We'll play another round," repeated the dark man, sticking out his chin.

Steiner got up. "Next time."

He went to the counter and paid. Then he pushed a folded hundred-schilling note toward the proprietor. "Please give that to Fred."

The proprietor raised his eyebrows in surprise. "Fred?" "Yes."

"All right." The proprietor grinned. "The boys fell for it! Went fishing for a mackerel and met a shark."

The three men were standing at the door. "We'll play another round," the dark man said, blocking the passage. Steiner looked at him.

"You can't get away with that, neighbor," bleated the thin man. "Impossible, sir."

"Let's not kid ourselves," Steiner said, "war is war. Everyone has to lose sometime."

"Not us," said the dark man. "We'll play another round."

"Or you fork over what you've won," the fat man added.

Steiner shook his head. "It was an honest game," he said with an ironic smile. "You knew what you wanted and I knew what I wanted. Good night."

He tried to push his way between the dark man and the thin man and in doing so felt the strength of the dark man's muscles. At this moment the proprietor came up. "No rough stuff in my place, gentlemen!"

"That's what I'm trying to avoid," Steiner said. "I want to leave."

"We'll go with you," the dark man said.

The thin man and the dark man went ahead. Then came Steiner, and behind him the fat man. Steiner knew that only the dark man was dangerous. He had made a mistake in going in front. At the moment when he was passing through the door Steiner kicked out behind and caught the fat man in the stomach. At the same time he drove his fist like a hammer into the base of the dark man's skull so that he went reeling down the steps and hit the thin man. With a leap Steiner got out and away and raced down the street before the others had recovered themselves. He knew it was his one chance, for on the street he would have had no show against three men. He heard shouting and looked around as he ran — but no one was following him. They had been too much surprised.

He went slower and came gradually into more populated streets. He paused in front of a mirror in the window of a dress shop and looked at himself. Cardsharp and cheat, he thought. But — half a passport! He nodded to his reflection and walked on.

Chapter Five

KERN was sitting on the wall of the old Jewish cemetery, counting his money in the shine of a street light. He had been peddling all day in the neighborhood of Holy Cross Mountain. It was a poor district, but Kern knew that poverty inclines people toward charity and not toward calling the police. He had earned thirty-eight crowns. It had been a good day.

He put the money in his pocket and tried to decipher the names on the weather-beaten headstones beside him, leaning haphazardly against the wall. "Rabbi Israel Loew," he said aloud, "dead long years ago, certainly a man of great learning in your time and now a handful of dust and bones down there, what do you think I should do now? Go home and be satisfied or go on working and try to raise my profits to fifty crowns?"

He drew out a five-crown piece. "So it doesn't matter much to you, old man? Well then, let's put the question to the emigrees' goddess — Chance. Heads we'll be satisfied, tails we'll go on peddling."

He spun the coin in the air and tried to catch it. It rolled out of his hand and fell on the grave. Kern climbed over the wall and carefully picked it up. "Tails! And on your grave! You're giving me your personal advice, Rabbi! Off we go!"

He approached the nearest house as though about to storm a fortress.

On the ground floor no one answered. Kern waited a while and then went up the stairs. On the second floor a pretty maid came to the door. She caught sight of the brief case, made a wry face, and closed the door without saying a word.

Kern went on up to the third floor. After he had rung twice a man came to the door wearing an unbuttoned vest. Kern had hardly begun to speak when the man indignantly interrupted him. "Toilet water? Perfume? What a nerve! Man, can't you read? Trying to sell me, the district agent for Leo's Toilet Preparations, me of all people, your rubbish! Get out!"

He slammed the door. Kern struck a match and looked at the brass plate on the door. It was true; Josef Schimek was himself a wholesale dealer in perfume, toilet water, and soap.

Kern shook his head. "Rabbi Israel Loew," he murmured, "what's the meaning of this? Is it possible we didn't understand each other?"

On the fourth floor he rang again. A friendly fat woman opened the door. "Come right in," she said pleasantly when she saw him. "You're a German, aren't you? A refugee? Just come right in!"

Kern followed her into the kitchen. "Sit down," said the woman. "I'm sure you must be tired."

"Not very."

It was the first time since he had been in Prague that anyone had offered Kern a chair. He seized the rare opportunity and sat down. Excuse me, Rabbi, he thought, I was premature. Excuse me, Rabbi Israel, I am young. Then he unpacked his wares.

The fat woman stood comfortably in front of him with

her arms crossed over her stomach watching him. "Is that perfume?" she asked, pointing to a little bottle.

"Yes." Kern had really expected her to be interested in the soap. He lifted the bottle as though it were a precious jewel. "This is the famous Farr perfume. A product of the Kern Company. Something quite out of the ordinary! Not like that lye made by the Leo Company that Herr Schimek represents."

"Well, well — "

Kern opened the bottle and gave it to the woman to smell. Then he took a little glass rod and rubbed some of it on her fat hand. "Try it yourself."

The woman sniffed at the back of her hand and nodded. "It smells good. But haven't you anything but those little bottles?"

"Here's a larger one. And then I have one that is very big. This one. But it costs forty crowns."

"That makes no difference. It's the big one I want; I'll take it."

Kern could hardly believe his ears. That meant eighteen crowns profit. "If you take the big one I'll give you a cake of almond soap free," he announced happily.

"Fine. One can always use soap."

The woman took the bottle and the soap and went into the next room. Kern meanwhile put away his things. Through the half-open door came the smell of cooked meat. He determined to treat himself to a first-class dinner. The soup at the eating place on Wenceslaus Square wasn't really filling.

The woman came back. "Well, thank you very much, and good-by," she said cordially. "Here's a sandwich to take with you."

"Thanks." Kern stood there waiting.

"Was there something else?" the woman asked.

"Well, yes." Kern laughed. "You haven't given me the money yet."

"Money? What money?"

"The forty crowns," Kern said in amazement.

"Oh, so that's it! Anton!" the woman shouted into the next room. "Come here a minute, will you? There's someone here asking for money."

A man in suspenders and a sweat-stained shirt came out of the next room. He was wiping his mustache and chewing. Kern saw that there was a strip of braid down his trousers, and a nasty suspicion suddenly rose in his mind. "Money?" the man asked hoarsely, digging a finger into his ear.

"Forty crowns," Kern replied. "But you can just give me the bottle back if that's too much. And you can keep the soap."

"Well, well!" The man came closer. He smelled of stale sweat and fresh, boiled loin of pork. "Come with me, my boy." He went to the door of the next room and opened it wide. "Do you know what that is?" he asked, pointing to the coat of a uniform hanging on a chair. "Do you want me to put that on and go with you to the police station?"

Kern recoiled a step. He already saw himself in jail serving a two weeks' sentence for illegal peddling. "I have a residential permit," he said as casually as he could. "I can show it to you."

"You'd better show me your permit to work," the man replied, staring at Kern.

"That's at the hotel."

"Then we can go straight to the hotel. Or would you prefer to call the bottle a present, eh?"

"Oh, all right." Kern turned toward the door.

"Here, don't forget your sandwich," the woman said, grinning broadly.

"Thanks, I don't want it." Kern opened the door.

"Just listen to that. He's ungrateful too!"

Kern shut the door behind him and went quickly down the stairs. He didn't hear the thundering laughter that followed his flight. "Magnificent, Anton!" the woman said proudly. "Did you see the way he skipped? As if he had bees in his pants. Even quicker than the old Jew this afternoon. I'll bet he took you for a police captain and saw himself already in the coop!"

Anton grinned. "They're all afraid of any kind of a uniform! Even if it belongs to a postman. That's gravy for us. We're not doing so badly with the emigrees, are we?" He put his arm around his wife's breasts.

"That's a good perfume." She pressed herself against him. "Better than the hair tonic we got from the old Jew this afternoon."

Anton hitched up his trousers. "Slather yourself with it tonight and I'll have a countess in bed with me. Is there still some pork in the pot?"

When he was on the street Kern stopped. "Rabbi Israel Loew," he said miserably, looking in the direction of the cemetery, "that was a fine trick you played on me! Forty crowns. Forty-three really, counting the cake of soap. That's a net loss of twenty-four."

He went back to the hotel. "Has anyone been here to see me?" he asked the doorman.

The latter shook his head. "Not a soul."

"Are you sure?"

"Absolutely. Not even the President of Czechoslovakia."

"He wasn't the one I was expecting," Kern said.

He went upstairs. It was strange he had not heard from his father. Perhaps he really wasn't there; or he might have been picked up by the police in the meantime. He decided to wait a few days more and then go again to Frau Ekowski's.

In his room he found the man named Rabe who screamed at night. He was just starting to undress.

"Going to bed so early?" Kern asked. "Before nine o'clock?"

Rabe nodded. "It's the best thing for me to do. Then I shall sleep until midnight. That's the time I always get my attacks. It was at midnight that they usually came for us when we were in the bunker. After that I shall sit up for a couple of hours at the window. Then I can take a sleeping powder and get through the night all right."

He placed a glass of water beside his bed. "Do you know what calms me most when I sit by the window at night? Saying poems to myself. Old poems from my school days."

"Poems?" Kern asked in amazement.

"Yes, very simple ones. For example, the one they sing to children in the evening: —

> "Gentle Jesus, meek and mild,
> Look on me, a little child;
> Pity my simplicity,
> Suffer me to come to Thee."

He stood in his white underwear like a tired, friendly ghost in the half-darkened room, and slowly repeated the verses of the lullaby in a monotonous voice, staring with lifeless eyes through the window out into the night.

"It calms me," he repeated, and smiled. "I don't know why, but it comforts me."

"Really?" Kern said.

"It sounds crazy, but it does calm me. Afterwards I feel quiet and somehow as if I were at home."

Kern was uncomfortable. His skin felt prickly. "I don't know any poems by heart," he said. "I have forgotten them all. It seems an eternity since I was in school."

"I had forgotten them too. But now suddenly I remember them all again."

Kern nodded and stood up. He wanted to get out of the room. Then Rabe could sleep and he wouldn't have to think about him.

"If one only knew what to do with the evenings!" Kern said. "Evenings are the worst time of all. I haven't had anything to read for a long while. And to sit down there and discuss for the hundredth time how fine things used to be in Germany, and when they're going to be better again, that's something I just can't stand."

Rabe sat down on his bed. "Go to the movies. That's the best way to kill an evening. Afterwards you don't know what you've seen; but at least you haven't been thinking about anything."

He took off his socks. Kern watched him thoughtfully. "The movies . . ." he said. It occurred to him that perhaps he could invite the girl from next door to go with him. "Do you know the people here in the hotel?" he asked.

Rabe laid his socks on a chair and wiggled his bare toes. "A few. Why?" He stared at his toes as though he had never seen them before.

"The ones in the next room?"

Rabe reflected. "Old Schimanowska lives there. She was a famous actress before the war."

"I don't mean her."

"He means Ruth Holland, a pretty young girl," said the man with the eyeglasses who was the third occupant of the room. He had been standing listening in the doorway for some time. His name was Marill, and he had formerly been a delegate to the Reichstag. "That's right, isn't it, Kern, you old Don Juan?"

Kern blushed.

"It's strange," Marill went on. "People blush at the most natural things. But never at mean ones. How was business today, Kern?"

"A complete catastrophe. I lost money."

"Then spend some more. That's the best way to keep from getting complexes."

"I was going to," Kern said. "I'm planning to go to the movies."

"Bravo. With Ruth Holland, I assume, judging from your cautious inquiries."

"I don't know. I haven't met her."

"You haven't met most people. You have to get started sometime. Get going, Kern. Courage is the fairest adornment of youth."

"Do you think she'd go with me?"

"Of course. That's one of the advantages of this filthy life of ours. What with fear and boredom, everyone's thankful to be distracted. So no false modesty! Fire away and forget your cold feet!"

"Go to the Rialto," Rabe said from the bed. " 'Morocco' is playing there. I've found that foreign countries are best for distraction."

" 'Morocco' is always good," Marill remarked, "even for young girls."

Rabe sighed and drew the covers around him. "Sometimes I wish I could sleep for ten years."

"Then you'd like to be ten years older?" Marill asked.

Rabe looked at him. "No," he said, "then my children would be grown up."

Kern knocked at the door of the next room. A voice from inside answered indistinctly. He opened the door and stopped short. He had come eye to eye with Schimanowska.

She had a face like a barn owl. The heavy rolls of fat were covered with thick white powder and gave the appearance of a snow-covered mountain landscape. Her black eyes were like deep-set holes and she stared at Kern as though she might fly at him any moment with her claws. In her hands she held a brilliant red shawl with some knitting needles sticking in it. Suddenly her face was contorted and Kern thought that she was going to leap upon him. But then a kind of smile came over her features. "What do you want, my young friend?" she asked in a resonant, moving, dramatic voice.

"I'd like to speak to Fräulein Holland."

The smile disappeared as though it had been wiped off. "Oh really?"

Schimanowska looked at Kern contemptuously and then set up a great clatter with her knitting needles.

Ruth Holland was crouched on her bed. She had been reading. Kern saw it was the same bed by which he had stood the night before. He felt his color mounting. "There's something I want to ask you," he said.

The girl got up and went out into the hall with him.

Schimanowska's snort, like that of a wounded horse, followed them.

"I wanted to ask if you'd go to the movies with me," Kern said when they were outside. "I have two tickets," he added untruthfully.

Ruth Holland looked at him.

"Or perhaps you have some other engagement?"

She shook her head. "No, I have no engagement."

"Then come along. Why should you sit all evening in that room?"

"Oh, I'm used to it."

"So much the worse. After two minutes I was glad to get out again. I thought I was going to be eaten alive."

The girl laughed. Suddenly she seemed very childlike.

"Schimanowska just looks that way. She has a kind heart."

"Maybe so. But you can't see it by looking at her. The picture starts in fifteen minutes. Shall we go?"

"All right," Ruth Holland said, and it was as if she were making a resolve.

At the ticket window Kern hurried ahead. "Just a minute, I'm going to pick up the tickets. They're being held for me."

He bought two tickets and hoped she hadn't noticed. But in a moment that didn't matter; the important thing was that she was sitting beside him.

The room grew dark. On the screen appeared the native quarter of Marrakesh. The wastes of the desert blazed, sun-drenched and exotic, and through the hot African night came the monotonous and exciting beat of the tambourines and flutes. . . .

Ruth Holland leaned back in her seat. The music swept

over her like a warm rain — a warm, monotonous rain from which memory arose tormentingly. . . .

She was standing beside the moat in Nuremberg. It was April. In front of her in the darkness stood the student Herbert Binding with a crumpled newspaper clenched in his hand.

"You understand what I mean, Ruth?"

"Yes, I understand, Herbert! It's easy to understand."

Binding nervously twisted the copy of the *Stürmer*. "My name in the paper for keeping company with a Jewess! For being a profaner of the race! That means ruin, do you understand?"

"Yes, Herbert. My name is in the newspaper too."

"That's something entirely different! How can it affect you? You can't go to the University even as it is."

"You're right, Herbert."

"So this is the end, isn't it? We've separated, and we'll have nothing more to do with each other."

"Nothing more. And now good-by."

She turned around and walked away.

"Wait — Ruth — listen a minute!"

She stopped and he came up to her. His face was so close to hers in the darkness that she could feel his breath. "Listen," he said, "where are you going now?"

"Home."

"You don't have to right away — " His breathing became heavier. "We understand each other, don't we? And that's not going to change! But after all you could — we could — it just happens that tonight there is no one at my house, you understand, and we wouldn't be seen." He reached for her arm. "We don't have to part like this, so formally I mean; we could just once more —"

"Go!" she said. "At once!"

"But be reasonable, Ruth." He put his arm around her shoulders.

She looked again at the handsome face, at the blue eyes, at the waves of blond hair — the face she had loved and had implicitly trusted. Then she struck it. "Go!" she screamed, tears streaming from her eyes. "Go!"

Binding recoiled. "What, strike me? Why, you dirty Jewish slut! Would you strike me?"

He seemed about to spring at her.

"Go!" she screamed shrilly.

He looked around. "Shut your mouth!" he hissed. "Do you want to bring down the whole neighborhood on my neck? Maybe that would suit your plans! I'm going, yes, indeed, I'm going! Thank God I'm rid of you!"

"*Quand l'amour meurt . . .*" sang the woman on the screen, her dark voice drifting through the noise and smoke of the Moroccan Café. Ruth ran her hand across her forehead.

Compared to that, all the rest had been unimportant — the anxiety of the relatives with whom she was living; her uncle's urgent advice to take a trip so that he would not become involved; the anonymous letter informing her that if she did not disappear within three days her hair would be cut off and she would be pulled through the streets in a cart, with placards on her breast and back labeling her as a defiler of the race; the visit to her mother's grave; the wet morning when she had stood in front of the War Memorial from which the name of her father, who had fallen in Flanders in 1916, had been scratched out because he was a Jew; and then the hasty, lonesome trip across the border to Prague, taking with her her mother's few pieces of jewelry . . .

Once more the music of flutes and tambourines came from the screen. Above it rolled the march of the Foreign Legion — a quick, stirring clarion-call above the company of those proceeding into the wilderness, fighters without home or country.

Kern bent toward Ruth Holland. "Do you like it?"

"Yes."

He reached in his pocket and handed her a small bottle. "Eau de Cologne," he whispered. "It's hot in here. Perhaps you will find this refreshing."

"Thanks." She sprinkled a few drops on her hand. Kern did not see that suddenly there were tears in her eyes.

"Thanks," she said again.

* * *

Steiner was sitting in the Hellebarde Café for the second time. He handed the waiter a five-schilling note and ordered coffee.

"Want me to telephone?" the waiter asked.

Steiner nodded. He had played cards a few times and with varying luck in other bars and now possessed about five hundred schillings.

The waiter brought him a stack of newspapers and went away. Steiner picked up one of the papers and began to read, but he soon laid it aside; he wasn't much interested in what was happening in the world. For someone swimming under water only one thing matters: to get to the surface again; the color of the fishes isn't important.

The waiter put a cup of coffee and a glass of water in front of him. "The gentlemen will be here in an hour."

He remained standing beside the table. "Fine weather today, isn't it?" he asked after a while.

Steiner nodded and stared at the wall on which hung an exhortation to prolong your life by drinking malt beer.

The waiter shuffled back behind the counter. But presently he returned, bringing a second glass on a tray.

"I don't want that," Steiner said. "Bring me a Kirsch."

"Yes, sir, at once."

"Have one yourself."

The waiter bowed. "Thank you, sir. You have some feeling for people like us. That's rare nowadays."

"Nonsense," Steiner said. "I'm bored, that's all."

"I've known people to hit on worse ideas when they were bored," the waiter said.

He tossed off his drink and began to scratch his throat. "I know why you're here, sir," he confided. "And if you'll let me give you some advice, I'd like to recommend the dead Austrian. There are dead Rumanians, too, and they're cheaper — but who knows how to speak Rumanian?"

Steiner looked at him narrowly.

The waiter stopped scratching his throat and began massaging the back of his neck. Simultaneously he scratched the ground with one foot like a dog. "Of course the best of all would be an American or an Englishman," he said thoughtfully. "But when do you find an American dying in Austria? And if that should happen, in an automobile accident for instance, how are you going to get hold of his passport?"

"I think a German passport is better than an Austrian," Steiner said. "Harder to check on."

"That's true. But all you can get with it is a permit for residence, not for work. But if you take the dead Austrian you can work anywhere in the country."

"Till you're caught."

"Yes, of course, but who's ever caught in Austria? Only the wrong people — "

Steiner had to laugh. "You know, I might be the wrong person. Just the same it's dangerous."

"As for that, sir," the waiter said, "they say that it's even dangerous to pick your nose."

"Yes; but you don't get put in the penitentiary for that."

The waiter began cautiously rubbing his nose — but he didn't pick it. "I mean it all for the best, sir," he said. "And I've had a lot of experience here. A dead Austrian is much the best buy."

It was about ten o'clock when the two dealers in passports arrived. The conversation was carried on by one of them, a lively birdlike fellow. The other sat there, large and bloated, saying nothing.

The spokesman brought out a German passport. "We have talked this over with our associates. You can have your own name put on it. The personal description will be washed out and your own substituted. Except, of course, the place of birth. You will have to accept Augsburg for that because that's where the seal is from. All this will come to two hundred schillings more, naturally enough. It's precision work, you understand."

"I haven't that much money," Steiner said. "And I don't attach any importance to my name."

"Then take it the way it is. We'll just change the photograph and we'll make you a present of the raised lettering that runs along the edge of the picture."

"No good. I want to work, and with this passport I won't be able to get a permit."

The spokesman shrugged his shoulders. "In that case there's only the Austrian. With that you can work."

"And suppose someone makes inquiries at the office where it was issued?"

"Who's going to? Unless you get into trouble."

"Three hundred schillings," Steiner said.

The spokesman started. "We have fixed prices," he said in an injured tone. "Five hundred, not a groschen less."

Steiner was silent.

"Now if it had been the German passport, we might have made a deal. They're common enough. But an Austrian passport is very rare. When does an Austrian need a passport? Not when he's at home, and when does he ever go abroad? Especially now, with the embargo on currency! It's a gift at five hundred."

"Three hundred and fifty."

The spokesman became excited. "Three hundred and fifty is what I myself paid the bereaved family. You have no idea how much work this sort of thing requires. Commissions and expenses, too. Conscience comes very high, my friend. To snatch something like this, fresh from the grave, you have to lay down cold cash and lots of it. Money's the only thing that dries tears and assuages grief. You can have it for four hundred and fifty. We're losing money, but we like you."

They agreed at four hundred. Steiner brought out a

photograph which he had had made for a schilling at an automat. The two took it away and came back in an hour with the passport in order. Steiner paid them and put it in his pocket.

"Good luck," said the spokesman. "And now let me give you a tip. When it runs out there is one way of extending it. Wash out the date and change it. The only trouble is with the visas. The longer you can get along without them, the better — you can extend the date correspondingly."

"Why, we could have done that now," Steiner said.

The spokesman shook his head. "It's better for you as it is. You have a genuine passport which you might have found. Changing a photograph isn't as serious as forgery. And you have a year's time. A lot can happen in a year."

"Let's hope so."

"You'll be discreet about all this, won't you? It's to everyone's advantage. Of course if you have a customer who means business — you know how to reach us. Till then, good night."

"Good night."

"*Strszecz miecze,*" said the silent man.

"He doesn't speak German," said the spokesman, grinning at Steiner's expression. "But he has a wonderful touch with seals. Only strictly serious customers, remember."

Steiner went to the station. He had left his knapsack in the checkroom there. On the previous evening he had left the rooming house and had spent the night on a bench in the park. In the morning he shaved off his mustache in the station washroom, and after that he had his picture taken.

He was filled with exuberant satisfaction. Now he was the workman Johann Huber from Graz.

On the way he stopped suddenly. There was still one score to be settled from the time when his name had been Steiner. He went to a telephone and looked for a number. "Leopold Schaefer," he murmured to himself. "Number 27, Trautenau Alley." The name was branded in his memory.

He found the number and called up. A woman answered.

"Is Officer Schaefer at home?" he asked.

"Yes. I'll call him right away."

"That's not necessary," Steiner replied quickly. "This is the police station at Elisabeth Promenade. There will be a riot at twelve o'clock. Policeman Schaefer is to report here at a quarter of twelve. Have you got that?"

"Yes. At quarter of twelve."

"Good." Steiner hung up.

Trautenau Alley was a narrow, silent street of bleak, cheap houses. Steiner examined Number 27 carefully. There was nothing to distinguish it from the others; but it seemed to him especially repulsive. Then he went on a way and waited.

Officer Schaefer came blustering importantly out of the house. Steiner approached him so that they would meet at a dark spot. Then he lurched against him with his shoulder.

Schaefer reeled. "Are you drunk, fellow?" he roared. "Can't you see that you have before you an officer on duty?"

"No," Steiner replied. "I only see a God-damn' son of a bitch! A son of a bitch, understand?"

Schaefer was speechless for a moment. "Man," he said then in a low voice, "you must be crazy. I'll make you pay for this. Come on, off to the station-house!"

He tried to draw his revolver. Steiner kicked him in the arm, moved in suddenly and did the most insulting thing one man can do to another; he struck Schaefer with his open hand on both sides of the face.

The policeman emitted a gurgle and leaped at him. Steiner ducked to the side and landed a left hook on Schaefer's nose which immediately began to bleed. "Son of a bitch!" he growled. "Miserable turd! Cowardly carcass!"

He chopped his lips with a sharp right and felt the teeth break under his knuckles. Schaefer reeled. "Help!" he shouted in a high thick voice.

"Shut your trap," Steiner snarled, and placed a sharp right to the chin followed by a short left straight to the solar plexus. Schaefer gave a gulp like a bullfrog and pitched to the ground like a pillar.

Lights went on in a few windows. "What's the matter this time?" a voice cried.

"Nothing," Steiner replied from the darkness, "only a drunk."

"Devil take these rumpots!" the voice shouted angrily. "Cart him off to the police!"

"That's just where he's going!"

"Smack him a couple of times on his drunken snout."

The window was slammed shut. Steiner grinned and disappeared around the nearest corner. He was sure that Schaefer had not recognized him with his altered face. He crossed a few more streets until he came to a populated district. Then he walked more slowly.

Magnificent and yet enough to make you puke, he thought. Such a laughable little bit of revenge! But it makes up for years of flight and submission. You have to take your opportunities as they come. He stopped under a street light and took out his passport. Johann Huber! Workman! You are dead and moldering somewhere in the soil of Graz, but your passport is still alive and valid in the eyes of the authorities. I, Josef Steiner, am alive; but without a passport I am dead in the eyes of the authorities. He laughed aloud. Let's exchange, Johann Huber! Give me your paper life and take my paperless death. If the living won't help us, it's up to the dead!

Chapter Six

SUNDAY evening Kern returned to the hotel. In his room he found Marill in a state of great excitement. "Someone at last!" he shouted. "Damn this roost! Not a living soul in it, today of all days! Everyone gone out! Everyone away! Even the damned proprietor!"

"What's the matter?" Kern asked.

"Do you know where to find a midwife? Or any kind of woman's doctor?"

"No."

"No, of course you don't!" Marill stared at him. "You're a sensible fellow. Come along with me. Someone has to stay with the woman. Then I can go out and look for a midwife. Can you do that?"

"Do what?"

"See that she doesn't thrash around. Reason with her. Do anything."

He dragged Kern, who had no idea what was happening, along the hall to the floor below and opened the door of a small room in which there was not much but a bed. On the bed a woman lay groaning.

"The seventh month. Miscarriage or something of the sort. Calm her if you can. I'll get a doctor."

He was out of the room before Kern could reply.

The woman on the bed groaned. Kern approached on tiptoe.

"Can I get you anything?" he whispered.

The woman continued to groan. Her faded, blond hair was soaked with sweat and dark patches of freckles stood out on her gray face. Her eyes were rolled up under half-closed lids; only the whites could be seen. Her thin lips were drawn back and her teeth tightly clenched. They gleamed a clear white in the half-darkness.

"Can I get you anything?" Kern repeated.

He looked around. A thin, cheap coat lay tossed over a chair. By the bed stood a pair of worn shoes. The woman lay there, completely dressed, as though she had dropped suddenly on the bed. There was a water bottle on the table and beside the washstand stood a suitcase.

The woman groaned. Kern did not know what to do. The woman began to toss. He remembered what Marill had told him and the little he had learned during his year at the University, and tried to hold down the woman's shoulders. But it was as if he were trying to hold a snake.

While he was still struggling and she was slipping away from him and pushing him off, she suddenly raised her arms and in an instant had driven her fingers with all her strength, clawlike, into his arm.

He stood as though riveted to the spot. He would never have guessed she had such strength. She twisted her head slowly as though it were on a pivot and groaned so hideously that it seemed her breath must be coming out of the earth.

Her body jerked and suddenly from beneath the blanket, which she had pushed aside, Kern saw a dark red stain creep, spread out on the sheet and grow larger and larger. He tried to pull himself free, but the woman held him in a grip of iron. As though bewitched he stared at the stain, which became a broad ribbon, reached the edge of the sheet and began, drop by drop, to form a dark pool on the floor.

"Let me go! Let me go!" Kern dared not pull his arm away for fear of jarring her. "Let me go," he groaned. "Let me go."

Suddenly the woman's body grew slack. She released her grip and fell back among the pillows. Kern seized the blanket and lifted it. A wave of blood welled out and splashed on the floor. He leaped up, horrified, and ran instinctively to the room where Ruth Holland lived.

She was there, sitting alone among her open books. "Come!" Kern gasped. "A woman is bleeding to death downstairs."

They ran down together. The room had become darker. In the window sunset flamed, throwing a dismal light over the floor and table. A reflection, caught in the water bottle, sparkled like a ruby. The woman lay quite still. She seemed to have stopped breathing.

Ruth Holland threw back the blanket. The woman was swimming in blood. "Turn on the light," the girl called.

Kern rushed to the switch. The light of the weak bulb blended with the red of sunset in a somber glow. Bathed in this reddish-yellow haze lay the woman on the bed. She appeared to be nothing but a formless belly with disheveled, bloody clothes, from which protruded spraddled, white legs, smeared with blood. Her black stockings had worked down and her legs themselves had a strangely twisted and lifeless look.

"Give me the towel! We must stop the bleeding! Perhaps you can find something."

Kern saw that Ruth had rolled up her sleeves and was loosening the woman's clothes. He gave her the towel from the washstand. "The doctor must be here soon. Marill has gone for him."

Searching for bandage material, he hastily emptied out the contents of the suitcase.

"Give me anything you can find!" Ruth called.

On the floor lay a heap of baby clothes — little shirts, belly bands, diapers, and among them a few knitted sweaters of pink and light-blue wool, trimmed with silk bows. One of them was unfinished; a pair of knitting needles was still sticking in it. A ball of soft blue yarn fell and rolled noiselessly across the floor.

"Get me something!" Ruth threw away the blood-soaked towel. Kern gave Ruth the belly bands and diapers. Then he heard steps on the stair and immediately after the door flew open to admit Marill and the doctor.

"Damn it, what's this?" The doctor took one long stride, pushed Ruth Holland aside and bent over the woman. After a while he turned to Marill. "Call number 2167. Braun is to come at once with everything necessary for anesthesia, Braxton-Hicks operation. Have you got it? In addition, everything for severe hemorrhage."

"Right."

The doctor looked around. "You can go," he said to Kern. "The young lady will remain. Get hot water. Give me my bag."

Ten minutes later the second doctor came. With the help of Kern and a few people who had arrived in the meantime, the room next to the one where the woman lay was transformed into an operating room. The beds were pushed aside, tables placed close together, and the instruments laid out. The proprietor brought the strongest bulbs he had and screwed them into the lamps.

"Hurry, hurry!" The first doctor was raging with impatience. He pulled on his white gown and had Ruth Holland button it. "Put one on too." He threw her a gown. "Perhaps we'll need you here. Can you stand the sight of blood? Will it make you sick?"

"No," Ruth said.

"Good girl, fine."

"Perhaps I can help too," Kern said. "I've had two semesters of medicine."

"Not just now." The doctor glanced over his instruments. "Can we begin?"

The light glistened on his bald spot. The door to the room was taken off its hinges. Four men carried the bed with the softly moaning woman through the corridor and into the room. Her eyes were wide open; her white lips quivered.

"Come on, steady it there!" barked the doctor. "Lift it higher! Careful now, damn it, careful!"

The woman was heavy. Drops of perspiration stood on Kern's forehead. His eyes met Ruth's. She was pale but calm and so changed that he hardly recognized her. She belonged now to the bleeding woman.

"There! Everyone out who isn't needed!" snapped the doctor with the bald spot. He took the woman's hand. "It won't hurt. It's very easy." His voice had suddenly become like a mother's.

"My child must live," whispered the woman.

"Both of you will — both," the doctor answered softly.

"My child — "

"We'll just turn it around a little to avoid the shoulder presentation. Then it will come like lightning. Just be calm, quite calm. Anesthesia!"

Kern was standing with Marill and a few others in the room the woman had left. They were waiting for a chance to be useful. From next door came the subdued murmurs of the doctors. Scattered on the floor lay the pink and blue sweaters.

"A birth," Marill said to Kern. "That's how it is when someone comes into the world. Blood, blood and screams! Do you understand, Kern?"

"Yes."

"No," Marill said. "You don't and I don't. A woman, only a woman, can understand. Don't you feel like a swine?"

"No," Kern replied.

"You don't? Well, I do." Marill polished his eyeglasses and looked at Kern. "Ever slept with a woman? No! Otherwise you'd feel like a swine too. Is there any chance of getting a drink here?"

The waiter appeared from the back of the room. "Bring me a half-bottle of cognac," Marill said. "Yes, yes, I have money to pay for it. Just go ahead and bring it."

The waiter disappeared and with him went the proprietor and two other people. Kern and Marill remained alone. "Let's sit here by the window," said the latter. He pointed toward the sunset. "Pretty, isn't it?"

Kern nodded.

"Yes," Marill said. "All sorts of things side by side. Those are lilacs down there in the garden, aren't they?"

"Yes."

"Lilacs and ether. Blood and cognac. Well, *prost!*"

"I brought four glasses, Herr Marill," said the waiter, placing a tray on the table. "I thought perhaps — " he motioned with his head toward the next room.

"Good."

Marill filled two glasses. "Do you drink, Kern?"

"Not often."

"That's a Jewish sin — abstinence. On the other hand you know more about women. But that's the last thing women want. *Prost!*"

"*Prost!*"

Kern emptied his glass. It made him feel better. "Is that only a miscarriage," he asked, "or something else?"

"Yes. Four weeks too soon. Overexertion, that's the cause. Traveling, changing trains, excitement, hurrying around, and all that sort of thing, see? Just what a woman in her condition ought not to do."

"And why — "

Marill refilled the glasses. "Why — " he said. "Because she wanted her child to be a Czech. Because she did not want him to be spit at in school and called a stinking Jew."

"I understand," Kern said. "Didn't her husband come with her?"

"Her husband was locked up a couple of weeks ago. Why? Because he was in business and was more enterprising and industrious than his competitor on the next corner. So what do you do if you're the competitor? You go and denounce the industrious fellow; you accuse him of treasonable speeches, of having cursed the government or of holding communistic theories. Anything at all. Then he gets locked up and you take over his customers. See?"

"I've watched it happen," Kern said.

Marill emptied his glass. "A crude age. Peace is stabilized with cannon and bombers, humanity with concentration camps and pogroms. We're living in a time when all standards are turned upside-down, Kern. Today the aggressor is the shepherd of peace, and the beaten and hunted are the troublemakers of the world. What's more, there are whole races who believe it!"

A half-hour later they heard a thin, squalling cry from the next room.

"Damn it," Marill said, "they've done the trick! One more Czech in the world! We'll have a drink to that! Come on, Kern! To the greatest mystery in the world, birth. You know why it's a mystery? Because later on one dies. *Prost!*"

The door opened and the second doctor came in. He was spattered with blood and he was sweating. In his hands he held a squalling object as red as a lobster. He was slapping it on the back. "It's alive," he growled. "Is there anything here — " He reached for a pile of diapers. "These will have to do — young lady!"

He handed the child and the diapers to Ruth. "Bathe and wrap up — not too tight. The old woman in there, the proprietress, knows how — but keep it away from the ether, leave it in the bathroom — "

Ruth took the child. Her eyes seemed to Kern twice as large as usual. The doctor sat down at the table. "Is that cognac?"

Marill poured him a glass. "How does a doctor feel," he asked, "when he sees new bombing planes and guns built every day but no new hospitals? After all, the only purpose of the former is to fill the latter."

The doctor glanced up. "Up shit creek," he said. "That's how! A nice job; you sew them up with the best modern technique so they can be torn to pieces again with the most primitive savagery. Why not kill the children at once? It's much simpler."

"My dear fellow," answered former deputy Marill, "killing children is murder. Killing grown-ups is a prerogative of national honor."

"In the next war there'll be plenty of women and children killed too," the doctor muttered. "We stamp out cholera — and it's a harmless little ailment compared to a dose of war."

"Braun!" called the doctor from the next room. "Quick!"

"Coming!"

"Damnation! Things don't seem to be going right," Marill said.

After a while Braun came back. He looked worn out. "Tear in the wall of the uterus," he said. "Nothing to be done. The woman's bleeding to death."

"Nothing to be done?"

"Nothing. We've tried everything. The hemorrhage won't stop."

"Couldn't you try a transfusion?" asked Ruth, who was standing in the doorway. "You could use my blood."

The doctor shook his head. "It wouldn't help, my child. If it doesn't stop — "

He went back, leaving the door open. The rectangle of bright light had a ghostly look. The three sat in silence. Presently the waiter tiptoed in. "Shall I clear off?"

"No."

"Will you have something to drink?" Marill asked Ruth. She shook her head.

"Do. Take some. It will do you good." He poured her half a glass.

It had become dark. Across the roofs the last wan greenish-orange light still lingered on the horizon. In it swam the pale moon, pitted with holes like an old brass coin. Voices floated up from the street, loud, self-satisfied and unaware. Suddenly Kern thought of Steiner and of what he had said. . . . When someone dies beside you, you don't feel it. That is the misfortune of the world. . . . Sympathy is not pain, sympathy is dissimulated joy — a sigh of relief that it is not oneself or someone one loves.

He looked over at Ruth. He could no longer see her face.

"What's that?" Marill asked, listening.

The long, full note of a violin swept through the gathering night. It died away, rose again, swelling higher and higher, triumphant and defiant — then came a series of bubbling runs, more and more tender, and a melody emerged, simple and sad as the waning light.

"It's here in the hotel," Marill said, peering through the window, "above us on the fourth floor."

"I think I know him," Kern replied. "He's a violinist I've heard once before, but I didn't know he was living here."

"That's no ordinary violinist. He's much more than that."

"Shall I go up and ask him to stop?"

"Why?"

Kern motioned toward the next room. Marill's eyeglasses flashed. "No. Why do that? One can always be sad. And death is everywhere. It all belongs together."

They sat and listened. After a long time Braun came out of the next room. "All over," he said. "Exit. She didn't suffer much. And she knows her child is alive. We were able to tell her that." The three stood up. "We can bring her back in here," Braun said. "The other room is being used."

The woman, white and now thin, lay amid the confusion of blood-soaked cloths, basins, pitchers and the piles of bloody wadding. She wore a detached, austere expression and nothing mattered to her any more. The doctor with the bald spot was working over her. There was something shocking and improper in the contrast — full, lusty, vigorous, relentless life beside the peace of fulfillment.

"Leave her covered," the doctor said. "It's just as well

for you not to see any more. It was rather much, even so, wasn't it, little lady?"

Ruth shook her head.

"You behaved like a soldier. No shirking. Do you know what I, Braun, would like to do now? Go and hang myself. Simply go to the next window and hang myself."

"You saved the child; that was a fine achievement."

"Hang myself! You see, I know that we did all we could; you're helpless in that situation. Nevertheless I could hang myself."

His fleshy face grew red with rage above the collar of the bloodstained gown. "For twenty years I've been doing this. And every time a patient slips through my fingers I'd like to hang myself. Silly, isn't it?" He turned to Kern. "Get the cigarettes out of the left-hand pocket of my coat and put one in my mouth. Yes, little lady, I know what you're thinking. All this, and then I smoke. I'm going to wash up." He stared at his rubber gloves as though they were to blame for everything and moved heavily into the bathroom.

They carried the bed with the dead woman out into the hall and back to her own room. There were a few people outside, those who lived in the big room. "Couldn't they have taken her to a hospital?" asked a scrawny woman with a throat like a turkey gobbler.

"No," Marill said. "Otherwise they'd have done it."

"And is she going to stay here all night? Who will be able to sleep with a corpse in the next room?"

"Then stay awake, grandmother," Marill replied.

"I'm no grandmother," snorted the woman.

"That's obvious."

The woman gave him a withering look. "And who's to clean up the room? We shall never be rid of the smell. They could just as well have used Number 10, over on the other side!"

"You see," Marill said to Ruth, "this woman is dead. Her child had need of her and very likely her husband too. But that sterile ironing board out there is still alive. Probably she'll live to a great old age to be a plague to her fellowmen. That's a puzzle no one can solve."

"Evil is stronger; it can withstand more," Ruth replied grimly.

Marill looked at her. "Where did you find that out?"

"Nowadays it's hard to miss."

Marill made no reply but watched her thoughtfully. The two doctors came in. "The proprietress has the child," said the one with the bald spot. "Someone will come to get it. I'm going to telephone about that right away. And about the woman. Did you know her well?"

Marill shook his head. "She came a few days ago. I have only talked to her once."

"Perhaps she has some papers. The authorities will want them."

"I'll look."

The doctors left. Marill searched the dead woman's suitcase. There was nothing in it except baby clothes, a blue dress, some underwear and a bright-colored rattle. He put the things back again. "Strange how all this suddenly seems dead too."

In her handbag he found a passport and a certificate from the Frankfurt police. He held it up to the light. "Katharina Hirschfeld, *née* Brinkmann, from Munster, born March 17, 1901."

He stood up and looked at the dead woman, at the blond hair and the narrow, hard, Westphalian face. "Katharina Brinkmann who married Hirschfeld."

He looked at the passport again. "Still good for three years," he murmured. "Three years, three years for someone else. The certificate from the police is enough for a grave."

He put the papers in his pocket. "I'll look after this," he said to Kern. "And I'll get a candle. I don't know why, but I have a feeling someone ought to sit with her for a while. It doesn't do any good, of course — but I have a funny feeling that someone ought to sit with her for a while."

"I'll stay," Ruth said.

"So will I," Kern said.

"Fine. I'll come back later and relieve you."

The moon had grown brighter. Night had engulfed the sky, deep blue and spacious. Its breath, scented with earth and flowers, drifted into the room.

Kern stood with Ruth at the window. It seemed to him that he had been a long way off and had come back again. Darkly within him lingered his terror at the screams of the woman in childbirth and at her convulsed and bleeding body. He heard the soft breathing of the girl beside him and he looked at her tender young mouth. He knew suddenly that she, too, belonged to this dark mystery that encircled love with a ring of horror, he sensed that the night too was a part of it, and the flowers and the heavy scent of earth and the sweet notes of the violin over the roofs; he knew that if he turned around the pale mask of death

would stare at him in the flickering light of the candle, and
for this very reason he felt all the more strongly the warmth
beneath his skin which made him shiver and led him to seek
for warmth, only for warmth, and for nothing but
warmth —

A strange hand took his and placed it around the smooth
young shoulders beside him.

Chapter Seven

MARILL was sitting on the cement terrace of the hotel fanning himself with a newspaper. Some books lay in front of him. "Come here, Kern," he called. "Evening is approaching, the time when beasts seek solitude and man looks for company. How are you making out with your permit?"

"It's still good for a week." Kern sat down beside him.

"A week in prison is a long time; a week of freedom is short." Marill tapped the books in front of him. "Exile is educational! At my advanced age I'm learning French and English."

"There are times when I can't stand the word 'exile,'" Kern said morosely.

Marill laughed. "Nonsense! You're in the best of company. Dante was an exile. Schiller had to leave his country. Heine. Victor Hugo. Those are just a few. Look up there at pale Brother Moon — an exile from the earth. And Mother Earth herself — an old emigree from the sun." He squinted. "Of course it might have been better if that particular migration had never taken place and we were still roaring around as fiery gases. Or as sun spots. Don't you agree?"

"No," Kern said.

"Right." Marill went on fanning himself with the newspaper. "Do you know what I've just been reading?"

"That the Jews are to blame because it hasn't rained."

"No."

"That a shell fragment in the belly is the only true happiness for a he-man."

"Not that either."

"That the Jews are bolshevists because they are so busy accumulating possessions."

"That's not bad! Go on."

"That Christ was an Aryan. The illegitimate son of a German legionnaire —"

Marill laughed. "No, you'll never guess. Matrimonial notices. Just listen to this. 'Where is the dear, sympathetic man who will make me happy? A maiden lady of deeply sensitive nature, distinguished and noble character, with a love for everything good and beautiful and a first-class knowledge of the hotel business, seeks a soul of similar tastes, between thirty-five and forty years of age, in a good business — '" He glanced up. "Between thirty-five and forty! Forty-one lets you out — that's confidence, isn't it? Or this: 'Where shall I find my complement? A lady and housekeeper of happy and profoundly inquiring nature, with her zest for life, her temperament and spirit unimpaired by the daily routine, possessed of inner beauty and a talent for friendship, is seeking a gentleman with adequate income, a love of art and sport, who at the same time must be a good fellow' — Magnificent, isn't it? Or let's take this: 'A spiritually lonesome man of fifty, of sensitive nature, younger in appearance than his years, orphaned — '" Marill paused. "Orphaned," he reflected, "at fifty! What a pathetic creature, this defenseless fifty-year-old!

"Here, my boy." He held out the newspaper to Kern. "Two pages! Each week two full pages in this one newspaper. Just look at the headings — absolutely crawling with souls, kindness, comradeship, love and friendship! Paradise, that's what it is! The Garden of Eden in the wasteland of politics. It's encouraging. It's refreshing. It makes you see that in these miserable times fine people still exist. Always sets you up, something like that — "

He threw down the paper. "Why shouldn't there be a notice like this: 'Commandant of a concentration camp, kind disposition, sensitive soul — ' "

"That's just what he'd consider himself," Kern said.

"Absolutely! The more primitive a man is the better he believes himself to be. You can see that from these notices. Blind conviction," Marill grinned, "that's what gives one impetus! Doubt and tolerance are the characteristics of civilized man. Again and again they destroy him. It's the old story of Sisyphus — one of the profoundest symbols of humanity."

Suddenly the hotel clerk appeared, and announced excitedly: "Mr. Kern, there is someone here to see you. He doesn't look like a policeman."

Kern got up quickly. "All right, I'll come."

At first glance Kern failed to recognize the indigent elderly man. It was as though he were looking at a hazy, unfocused image on the ground glass of a camera, which only gradually became sharper and revealed familiar features.

"Father!" he exclaimed, deeply shocked.

"Yes, Ludwig." The elder Kern wiped the perspiration from his forehead. "It's hot," he said in a tired voice.

"Yes, very hot. Come into this room where the piano is. It's cool in here."

They sat down. But almost immediately Kern got up to

fetch a lemonade for his father. He was much disturbed. "We haven't seen each other for a long time, Father," he said cautiously as he came back.

The elder Kern nodded. "Will you be able to stay here, Ludwig?"

"I don't believe so. You know how it is. They're very decent about it. Two weeks' permit and then perhaps two or three days more — but after that, it's the end."

"Do you intend to stay on illegally?"

"No, Father. There are too many emigrees here; that's something I didn't know. I'll try to get back to Vienna. It's easier to earn a living there. Now tell me how you're doing?"

"I have been sick, Ludwig. Grippe. I got up for the first time a few days ago."

"So that was it." Kern breathed more easily. "You were sick. Are you all right now?"

"Yes, you can see for yourself — "

"And what are you doing, Father?"

"I have found a place for myself."

"You're certainly well guarded," Kern said smiling.

The old man looked at him with such a tormented and embarrassed expression that he paused in surprise. "Aren't things going well with you, Father?" he asked.

" 'Well,' Ludwig? What does well mean for people like us? A little peace is a great deal. I have an occupation; I keep books. It isn't much but it's something to do. At a coal dealer's."

"But that's splendid! How much do you earn?"

"I don't earn anything — just pocket money. But I get my board and lodging."

"That's a good deal. I'll come and see you tomorrow, Father."

"Yes — yes — Or I could come here."

"But why should you exert yourself? I'll come to see you."

"Ludwig — " the elder Kern gulped. "I'd rather come here."

Kern looked at him in amazement and suddenly he understood everything. That formidable woman at the door . . .

For an instant his heart beat like a trip hammer against his ribs. He wanted to leap up, seize his father and carry him away; in a daze he thought of his mother, of Dresden, of their quiet Sunday mornings together — then he looked at the doomed man in front of him, who was watching him with dreadful humility, and he thought: he's done for, finished. The tension snapped and he felt nothing but infinite pity.

"They deported me twice, Ludwig. If I had been there just one more day they would have found me. They weren't unkind. But they cannot keep us all here, you know. I became sick; it rained all the time. Pneumonia with a relapse. And then — she nursed me. Otherwise I should have died, Ludwig. And she doesn't mean any harm — "

"I'm sure she doesn't, Father," Kern said calmly.

"I do some work, too. I earn my keep. It doesn't — you know — it isn't that way. But I just can't go on sleeping on benches and being frightened all the time, Ludwig — "

"I can understand that, Father."

The old man stared straight ahead. "Sometimes I think your mother ought to divorce me. Then she could go back to Germany."

"Is that what you want?"

"No, not for myself. For her. After all, I am to blame

for everything. If she wasn't married to me she could go back. I am to blame. For you, too. It's on my account you no longer have a country."

Kern was finding it a hideous experience. This man was no longer his brisk and cheerful father of the Dresden days; this was a pathetic, helpless old man who was related to him and who could no longer cope with life. In bewilderment he got up and did something he had never done before. He put his arms around his father's narrow, bowed shoulders and kissed him.

"You do understand, Ludwig?" murmured Siegmund Kern.

"Yes, Father. It doesn't matter. It doesn't matter at all." With the palm of his hand he gently patted his father's bony back and stared over his shoulder at a picture hanging above the piano, a picture of a snow slide in the Tyrol.

"Well, I'll go now — "

"Yes."

"I'll just pay for the lemonade. I brought along a package of cigarettes for you too. You've grown big, Ludwig, big and strong."

Yes, and you've grown old and shaky, Kern thought. If I only had one of those fellows from across the border, one of the men who brought you to this — if I only had him here, so that I could smash his stupid, fat, complacent face! "You're looking well too, Father," he said. "The lemonade has been paid for. I'm earning a little money now. And do you know how? With our old stock. With your almond cream and your Farr toilet water. A druggist here still has a supply, and I buy from him."

Siegmund Kern's eyes brightened a little. Then he smiled sadly. "And now you have to go around peddling it. You must forgive me, Ludwig."

"Oh, nonsense!" A lump rose in Kern's throat and he

had to swallow suddenly. "It's the best school in the world, Father. You learn about life from the bottom up. And about people too. After that, there's not much chance of being disillusioned."

"Just don't get sick."

"No, I'm pretty well toughened."

They went out. "You have so much hope, Ludwig."

My God, Kern thought, he calls this hope. Hope! "Everything will get straightened out again," he said. "It can't go on this way."

"Yes — " the old man stared in front of him. "Ludwig," he said softly, "when we're all together again — and your mother is there too — " He gestured as though brushing something away. "We'll forget all about this — we'll not even think about it any more, eh?"

He spoke softly with a kind of childish trustfulness, in a voice that was like the twittering of a tired bird. "If it weren't for me you would be going on with your studies now, Ludwig," he said plaintively and a little mechanically, like someone who has brooded over a consciousness of guilt for so long that the phrases have become automatic.

"If it weren't for you I wouldn't be alive," Kern replied.

"Keep healthy, Ludwig. Won't you take the cigarettes? After all I'm your father. I'd like to do something for you."

"All right, Father, I'll keep them."

"Don't forget me altogether," the old man said and his lips suddenly began to quiver. "I meant well, Ludwig." He kept repeating the name again and again as though unwilling to relinquish it. "Even if I didn't succeed, Ludwig. I meant to take care of all of you, Ludwig."

"You did take care of us, as long as you could."

"Well, I'll be going now. The best of luck to you, my child."

Child, Kern thought — which of us two is the child?

He watched his father walk slowly down the street. He had promised to write, and to see him again. But he knew that actually he was seeing him for the last time. He looked after him, wide-eyed, till he was out of sight. And he had a feeling of emptiness.

He went back. Marill was still sitting on the terrace reading his paper with an expression of loathing and contempt. Strange, Kern thought, how fast something can fall to pieces — in the time someone else spends quietly reading the newspaper. *Orphan, fifty years old* — His face twitched in bitter amusement. An orphan — as if one couldn't be that without one's father and mother being dead.

Three days later Ruth Holland left for Vienna. She had received a telegram from a friend with whom she could stay, and she planned to try to get work and to attend lectures at the University.

On the evening of her departure she went with Kern to the Black Pig Restaurant. Hitherto they had both eaten every day at the soup kitchen; but for their last evening Kern had proposed a special celebration.

The Black Pig was a smoky little place where the food was cheap but very good. Marill had told Kern about it. He had also told him the exact prices and had particularly recommended the specialty of the house, veal goulash. Kern had counted his money and decided it would be enough to include cheese cake for dessert afterward. Ruth had once told him she loved it.

But an unpleasant surprise awaited them on their arrival. There was no more goulash; they had come too late.

Kern studied the bill of fare apprehensively. Most of the other dishes were more expensive. The waiter, standing beside him, ran through the list in a singsong voice: "Smoked meat with sauerkraut, pork chops and green salad, chicken paprika, fresh pâté de foie gras — "

Pâté de foie gras, thought Kern — the fool seems to think we're multimillionaires. He handed the menu to Ruth. "What would you like instead of goulash?" he asked. He had calculated that if he ordered chops, the cheese cake would be out of the question.

Ruth merely glanced at the menu. "Frankfurters and potato salad," she said. It was the cheapest item.

"Nonsense," Kern protested, "that's not the thing for a farewell dinner."

"I'm very fond of it. After the fare at the soup kitchen it's a feast."

"And how would you like to make your feast of pork chops?"

"Much too expensive."

"Waiter," Kern ordered, "two pork chops, and see that they're big ones."

"They're all the same size," the waiter replied indifferently. "What do you wish first? Soup, hors d'oeuvres, relishes?"

"Nothing," Ruth said before Kern could consult her.

They ordered a carafe of cheap wine and the waiter moved off scornfully — as though he knew by intuition that Kern had already spent a half-crown of the money that was to have been his tip.

The place was almost empty. A single guest sat at a table in the corner. He had a broad, red face marked by dueling scars, and he was wearing a monocle. He sat with a glass of beer in front of him, watching Kern and Ruth.

"Too bad that fellow's sitting there," Kern said.

Ruth nodded. "If it were only someone else. But he — he reminds you — "

"Yes, you can be sure he's no exile," Kern said. "More likely the opposite."

"We'll just not look in that direction."

But Kern couldn't help it. He noticed that the man went on staring at them steadily.

"I can't make out what he wants," he said angrily. "He keeps right on looking at us."

"Perhaps he's an agent of the Gestapo. I've heard this town is crawling with spies."

"Shall I go over and ask him what he wants?"

"No!" Ruth laid her hand on Kern's arm in terror.

The chops were served. They were crisp and tender, and fresh green salad came with them. But Ruth and Kern did not enjoy them as much as they had anticipated; they were too nervous.

"He can't be here on our account," Kern said. "No one knew that we were coming here."

"That couldn't have been it," Ruth agreed. "Perhaps he is here by accident. There's no doubt, though, that he's watching us."

The waiter carried out the dishes. Kern looked after him disconsolately. He had planned this meal as a treat for Ruth, and now the fellow with the monocle had spoiled it. Angrily he got up; he had made up his mind. "Just a moment, Ruth — "

"What are you going to do?" she asked anxiously. "Stay here!"

"No, no, this has nothing to do with the man over there. I'm just going to speak to the proprietor."

As a precaution he had put two small bottles of perfume

in his pocket before he left the hotel. Now he meant to see if he could arrange with the proprietor to trade one of them for two pieces of cheese cake. They were worth a good deal more, but that didn't matter. After the failure of the chops, Ruth should at least have the dessert she liked best. Perhaps he could arrange for coffee as well.

He went out and made his proposal to the proprietor. The latter immediately got red in the face. "Aha, trying to run out without paying your check! Think you can eat here and not pay for it, do you? Well, my friend, there's just one thing for you — the police!"

"I can pay for what I've eaten!" Kern angrily tossed the money on the table.

"Count it carefully," the proprietor said to the waiter. "Pack up your trash," he snapped at Kern. "What are you trying to get away with anyway? Are you a guest or a peddler?"

"For the time being I'm a guest," Kern declared furiously, "and you are — "

"One moment!" said a voice behind him.

Kern spun around. The stranger with the monocle was standing directly behind him. "May I ask you a question?"

The man moved a few steps away from the counter. Kern followed him. His heart was beating wildly. "You're German exiles, aren't you?" the man asked.

Kern stared at him. "What's that to you?"

"Nothing," the man replied calmly. "Only I happened to hear what you were just talking about. Will you sell me the perfume?"

Kern thought he knew now what the man wanted. If he sold him the perfume then he would be guilty of peddling without a license and could be arrested immediately and deported.

"No," he said.

"Why not?"

"I have nothing to sell. I'm not a peddler."

"Then let's trade. I shall give you what the proprietor refused to give — pastry and coffee."

"I don't understand at all what you want," Kern said.

The man smiled. "I know you're suspicious. But let me explain. I live in Berlin and in an hour I'm going back there. You can't go back."

"No," Kern said.

The man looked at him. "That's the reason I'm standing here and it's the reason I should be glad to do you this small favor. I was a company commander during the war. One of my best men was a Jew. Now will you give me the little bottle?"

Kern handed it to him. "I beg your pardon," he said. "I thought something quite different about you."

"I can well imagine." The man laughed. "And now you must not leave the young lady alone any longer. Very likely she is already frightened. I wish you both the best of luck." He shook hands with Kern.

"Thanks. Thanks very much."

Kern went back bewildered. "Ruth," he said, "either this is Christmas or I'm crazy."

The waiter appeared immediately. He was carrying a tray with coffee and a three-tiered silver stand piled with pastries.

"Why, what's this?" Ruth asked in amazement.

"These are the wonders of Kern's Farr Perfume."

Kern beamed and poured out the coffee. "Now we each

have the right to our choice of pastries. What would you like, Ruth?"

"A piece of cheese cake."

"Here's your cheese cake. I'll take a chocolate cream puff."

"Shall I pack up the rest for you?" asked the waiter.

"The rest? What do you mean?"

The waiter indicated the three tiers with a sweep of his hand. "This has all been ordered for you."

Kern looked at him in complete amazement. "All this for us? Where is the — isn't the gentleman coming — "

"He left some time ago. Everything has been taken care of. So now — "

"Wait," Kern said hastily, "for heaven's sake wait. Ruth, have an éclair? Or one of these flaky ones? Or a seed cake?"

He filled her plate and took a few more for himself. "There," he said, sighing with contentment, "please put up the rest in two packages. You're to take one with you, Ruth. My, it's nice to be able to do something for you for once."

"The champagne is already on ice," said the waiter, picking up the silver stand.

"Champagne! That's a good joke!" Kern laughed.

"No joke." The waiter pointed toward the door where the proprietor himself had appeared, carrying an ice-filled cooler from which protruded the neck of a champagne bottle.

"You won't hold it against me." The latter smiled ingratiatingly. "Of course I was only joking before — "

Kern leaned back in his chair, wide-eyed. The waiter nodded. "Everything's paid for."

"I'm dreaming," Kern said, rubbing his eyes. "Have you ever had champagne, Ruth?"

"No. Up to now I've only seen it in the movies."

Kern with difficulty regained his composure. "My man
—" He addressed the proprietor in a dignified tone. "You
see what a bargain I offered you: a bottle of the world-
famous Kern perfume in exchange for two ridiculous
pieces of cheese cake. Now you see what a connoisseur is
willing to pay for it."

"No one can know everything," the proprietor apolo-
gized. "Drinks are more in my line."

"Ruth," Kern said, "from today on I believe in miracles.
If a white dove were to fly in through the window this
minute, carrying in its beak two passports for us, good for
five years, or an unrestricted work permit — it wouldn't
astonish me a bit!"

They emptied the bottle. It would have seemed a sin to
leave even a drop. They didn't especially like the taste, but
they went on drinking and became merrier and merrier,
and at the end they were both a little drunk.

When they were ready to leave Kern picked up the
packages of pastries and prepared to give the waiter a tip.
But the waiter waved him aside. "It's all been attended
to — "

"Ruth," Kern stammered, "life is overwhelming us. Another day like this and I'd become a romantic."

The proprietor stopped them. "Have you any more of
that perfume? I thought perhaps for my wife — "

Kern was alert at once. "It just happens that I have one
more bottle with me, the last." He pulled the second bottle
out of his pocket. "But not on the same terms as before,
my friend. You missed your chance. The price is twenty
crowns —" he held his breath — "seeing it's you!"

The proprietor made a lightning calculation. He had overcharged the captain thirty crowns for the champagne and pastry, so he would still be ten crowns to the good. "Fifteen," he offered.

"Twenty." Kern made a move to put the bottle away.

"All right then." The proprietor brought a ragged bill out of his pocket. He decided to tell his beloved, the buxom Barbara, that the bottle had cost fifty. In that way he could avoid buying her the hat she had been begging for all week, which was priced at forty-eight crowns. Two birds with one stone . . .

Kern and Ruth went to the hotel. They picked up Ruth's bag and then went to the station. Ruth had become very quiet. "Don't be sad," Kern said. "I'll be following you soon. In a week at the latest I'll have to leave here, I'm sure of that. Then I'll come to Vienna. Do you want me to come to Vienna?"

"Yes, come! But only if it's best for you."

"Why don't you just say: Yes, come?"

She looked at him a little guiltily. "Doesn't what I said mean more?"

"I don't know. It sounded cautious."

"Yes." She suddenly looked sad. "That's what it was — cautious."

"Don't be sad," Kern said. "A while ago you were so gay."

She looked at him helplessly. "Don't pay any attention to me," she murmured. "Sometimes I don't make sense. Perhaps it's because of the wine. Pretend it's the wine anyway. Come along, we still have a few minutes."

They sat down on a bench in the park and Kern put his arm around her shoulders. "Be happy, Ruth. The other does no good. I know that sounds foolish, but it isn't foolish for us. We bitterly need what little gaiety we can get. We especially."

She looked straight ahead. "I'd like to be gay, Ludwig. I guess I'm serious by nature. I'd like so much to take things lightly and to make people happy. But what I say always turns out to be awkward and heavy." She spoke the word angrily. And Kern suddenly noticed that tears were streaming down her cheeks. She wept without a sound, angry and helpless. "I don't know why I'm crying," she said, "I have no reason to, especially now. But perhaps that's why I'm crying. Don't look at me — don't look at me."

"Darling, don't," Kern said.

She leaned forward and put her hands on his shoulders. He drew her to him and kissed her. Her eyes were closed and her mouth was shut savagely and stubbornly as though to refuse him.

"Ah —" She became calmer. "Do you know —" Her head dropped against his shoulder, her eyes remained closed — "Do you know . . ." Her mouth opened and her lips became as soft as a fruit.

They walked on. At the station Kern disappeared and bought a bunch of roses, silently blessing the man with the monocle and the proprietor of the Black Pig.

Ruth was filled with confusion when he presented her with the flowers. She blushed, and all the sadness left her face. "Flowers," she said. "Roses! Why, I'm having a send-off like a movie star."

"You're having a send-off like the wife of an extremely successful businessman," Kern declared proudly.

"Businessmen don't give flowers, Ludwig."

"Yes, they do. The youngest generation has revived the custom."

He put her bag and the package of pastries in the luggage net. She got out with him. On the station platform she took his head in her hands and looked at him earnestly. "It was good that you were here." She kissed him. "Now go, go on while I'm getting into the train. I don't want you to see me cry again. Otherwise you'll think that's all I can do. Go —"

He didn't go. "I'm not afraid of good-bys," he said. "There have been so many in my life. This is not good-by." The train began to move. Ruth waved. Kern stood where he was until the train was out of sight. Then he went back. He had a feeling that the whole city had died.

At the entrance to the hotel he met Rabe. "Good evening," Kern said, drawing out his package of cigarettes and offering them to him. Rabe recoiled and lifted his arm as though to ward off a blow. Kern looked at him in astonishment. "I beg your pardon," Rabe said, greatly embarrassed. "That's just a kind of — a sort of involuntary reaction —"

He took a cigarette.

For two weeks Steiner had been a waiter at the Green Tree Inn. It was now late at night. The proprietor had gone to bed two hours before.

Steiner lowered the shutters. "Closing time!" he said.

"Let's have one more, Johann," said one of the guests, a master carpenter, with a face like a cucumber.

"All right," Steiner replied. "Barack?"

"No. No more of that Hungarian stuff. Let's go to work on a good plum brandy."

Steiner brought the bottle and glasses. "Have one yourself," the master carpenter invited.

"Not tonight. Either I stop drinking right now or I'll have to get drunk."

"Get drunk then." The master carpenter rubbed his knobbly face. "I'll get drunk too. Just imagine: a third daughter. In comes the midwife this morning and says, 'My congratulations, Herr Blau, on your third fine daughter.' And I'd thought that surely this time it would be a boy. Three girls and no heir! Isn't that enough to drive a man crazy? Isn't that enough to drive a man crazy, Johann? After all, you're a human being, you must understand how I feel!"

"And how!" Steiner said. "Shall we use bigger glasses?"

The master carpenter struck the table with his fist. "You're God-damned right, that's the thing! Bigger glasses, that's what we want! And to think it never occurred to me!"

They took bigger glasses and drank for an hour. By that time the master carpenter was badly mixed up and was lamenting the fact that his wife had borne him three sons. Clumsily he counted out the money and staggered away with his drinking companions.

Steiner cleaned up.

He poured himself another tumbler of brandy and tossed it off. His head was roaring. He sat down at the table and brooded. Then he got up and went into his room. He rummaged among his things, got out his wife's photograph and looked at it for a long time. He had never heard from her. Nor had he written to her. Because he assumed her mail would be opened. He believed she had divorced him.

"Damn it!" He got up. "Maybe she's been living with someone else for months and has forgotten all about me." With a jerk he tore the photograph in two and tossed the pieces to the floor. "I've got to get out! If I don't, this thing will drive me nuts. I am a man who lives by himself. I am Johann Huber. I'm not Steiner any more. All that's over!"

He emptied another glass, then shut the place up and went out on the street. In the neighborhood of the Ring a girl accosted him. "Will you come with me, dearie?"

"Yes."

As they walked along together the girl eyed him curiously. "You haven't looked at me once."

"Yes I have," Steiner replied without lifting his eyes.

"I don't think you have. Do you like me?"

"Yes. I like you."

"You know what you want, don't you?"

"Yes," he said, "I know what I want."

She pushed her arm through his. "What are you going to give me, my pet?"

"I don't know. How much do you want?"

"Are you going to stay all night?"

"No."

"How would twenty schillings be?"

"Ten. I'm a waiter. I don't earn much."

"You don't look like a waiter."

"There are people who don't look like presidents of countries, still that's what they are."

The girl laughed. "You're funny. I like funny people.

All right, we'll call it ten. I have a beautiful room. Just you wait. I'll make you happy."

"Will you?" Steiner said.

The room was a red plush-lined box, with plaster statues, and little crocheted covers over the tables and chairs. On the sofa sat a row of carnival dolls, Teddy bears and stuffed monkeys. Above them hung an enlarged photograph of a pop-eyed sergeant-major in dress uniform and waxed mustache.

"Is that your husband?" Steiner asked.

"No, the landlady's dear departed."

"She must have been glad to get rid of him, eh?"

"You have no idea!" The girl was slipping out of her blouse. "She still howls for him, he was such an amazing fellow. Capable, if you know what I mean."

"Then why has she hung him in your room?"

"She has another picture in her own room. Bigger and brighter. Of course only the uniform is brighter, you understand. Come and unhook me behind, will you?"

Steiner felt her firm shoulders under his hands. He was surprised. He knew from his time in the army what the flesh of whores was like — always somewhat too soft and gray.

The girl threw her blouse on the sofa. Her breasts were full and firm. They suited her strong shoulders and neck. "Sit down, my pet, and make yourself comfortable," she said. "Waiters and our kind always have tired legs."

She pulled her dress over her head.

"Damn it," Steiner said. "But you're beautiful."

"Lots of people have told me that" — the girl carefully folded her dress. "If this won't disturb you — "

"On the contrary, it does disturb me. It disturbs me a lot."

She turned half around. "You're always making jokes. You're a funny fellow."

Steiner looked at her.

"What makes you stare at me like that?" the girl said. "You're enough to frighten a person. Jesus, just like a stabber. Haven't had a woman for a long time, have you?"

"What's your name?" Steiner asked.

"You'll laugh — Elvira. It was one of my mother's ideas. She was always trying to be refined. Come on to bed."

"No. Let's have something to drink," Steiner said.

"Have you money?" the girl asked quickly.

Steiner nodded. Elvira went to the door, naked and unembarrassed. "Frau Poschnigg!" she shouted. "Something to drink."

The landlady appeared as quickly as if she had been listening behind the door. She was a roly-poly person, tightly laced in black velvet. Her cheeks were red and her eyes glistened like marbles. "We could give you champagne," she said eagerly. "Like sugar!"

"Brandy," Steiner said. "Plum brandy, pear brandy, Enzian, whatever you have."

The women exchanged a glance. "Pear brandy," Elvira said. "Some of the kind from the top shelf. It costs ten schillings, my pet."

Steiner gave her the money. "Where did you get a skin like that?" he asked.

"Not one pimple, is there?" Elvira pirouetted in front of him. "Only redheads have skins like that."

"Oh yes," Steiner said. "That's something I hadn't noticed before — you have red hair."

"I had my hat on, darling."

Elvira took the bottle from the landlady. "Have one with us, Frau Poschnigg?"

"If I may?" The landlady seated herself. "You're lucky, Fräulein Elvira!" she sighed. "Now look at me, a poor widow — always alone — " The poor widow gulped down the drink and immediately poured another. "Here's your health, kind sir!"

She got up and glanced coquettishly at Steiner. "Well then, my very best thanks! And have a good time."

"I think you might get somewhere with her, my pet," Elvira remarked.

"Give me that tumbler," Steiner said. He filled it and drank it down.

"Jesus." Elvira looked at him anxiously. "You're not going to start breaking things up, darling? This is expensive furniture, you know. It cost a lot of money, my pet."

"Sit down here," Steiner said. "Beside me."

"Perhaps we better go out somewhere. To the Prater or into the woods."

Steiner raised his head. He felt the brandy pounding behind his forehead, pounding against his eyeballs with soft hammer-blows. "Into the woods?" he asked.

"Yes, into the woods. Or into a cornfield. Now that it's summer."

"A cornfield — in summer? How'd you hit on a cornfield?"

"The way anyone would," Elvira chattered hastily and anxiously. "Because now it's summer, my pet! That is when you go into a cornfield sometimes, you know."

"Don't hide that bottle, I'm not going to wreck your room. You said a cornfield in summer?"

"Yes, of course, in summer, my pet; in winter, it's too cold."

Steiner filled his glass. "Damn it! How you smell — "

"Redheads all smell alike, my pet."

The hammers beat faster. The room reeled. "A cornfield — " Steiner said slowly and heavily, "and the night wind — "

"Come to bed now, darling. Get undressed — "

"Open the window — "

"Why the window's open, my pet. Come, I'll make you happy."

Steiner drank. "Were you ever happy?" he asked, staring at the table.

"Of course, often."

"Oh, shut your mouth. Turn out the light."

"Get undressed first."

"Turn out the light."

Elvira obeyed. The room became dark. "Come to bed, my pet."

"No. Not to bed. Bed is something else. Damn it, not to bed!"

With unsteady hand Steiner poured brandy into his glass. His head was roaring. The girl crossed the room. She came to the window and paused a moment, looking out. The pale glow from the street lights outside fell over her dark shoulders. Behind her head was the night sky. She raised her hand to her hair — "Come here," Steiner said hoarsely.

She turned and came toward him softly and silently. She was like a ripe cornfield, dark and unknowable, with the scent and the skin of a thousand women, and of one. "Marie," Steiner murmured.

The girl laughed low and tenderly. "Just see how drunk you are, my pet — my name is Elvira. . . ."

Chapter Eight

KERN succeeded in getting his permit extended for five days; then he was ordered to leave. He was given a railroad pass as far as the border and he rode to the customs house.

"No papers?" asked the Czech official.

"None."

"Go inside. There are some others there now. About two hours from now is the best time."

Kern went into the customs building. Three people were there — a very pale man, accompanied by a woman, and an old Jew.

"Good evening," Kern said.

The others muttered an indistinct reply.

Kern put down his valise and seated himself. Wearily he closed his eyes. The trip later on would be long he knew, and he wanted to get some sleep.

"We'll get across," he heard the pale man say. "You'll see, Anna; and then everything will be better."

The woman said nothing.

"We're sure to get across," the man began again. "Absolutely sure. Why shouldn't they let us across?"

"Because they don't want us," the woman answered.

"But after all we're human beings — "

You poor fool, Kern thought. He heard indistinctly the man's continued murmuring; then he fell asleep.

He awoke when the customs man came to get them.

They went across fields and came to a leafy woods which lay in front of them like a solid black block in the darkness.

The official stopped. "Follow this path and keep to the right. When you get to the road, turn left. Good luck."

He disappeared into the night.

The four stood hesitating. "What shall we do now?" the woman asked. "Does anyone know the way?"

"I'll go ahead," Kern said. "I was here once before, a year ago."

They groped their way through the dark. The moon had not yet risen. The grass was wet, and they could feel its strange, invisible touch against their ankles. Then came the woods and swallowed them up in its breathing darkness.

They walked for a long time. Kern heard the others behind him. Suddenly flashlights blazed in front of them and a harsh voice shouted: "Halt! Stand where you are!"

With a sidewise leap Kern got away. He plunged into the darkness, striking against trees and groping his way; he plowed through a blackberry thicket and threw his valise into it. There was the sound of running feet behind him. He turned. It was the woman. "Hide yourself!" he whispered. "I'm going to climb this tree!"

"My husband — Oh this — "

Kern hurriedly climbed the tree. Crouching in a fork, he could feel the soft, rustling foliage beneath him. The woman stood motionless below; he could not see her, he just felt her standing there. In the distance he heard the old Jew talking.

"Bosh!" the harsh voice answered. "Without a passport you don't get across. That's all there is to it!"

Kern strained his ears. After a while he could hear the low voice of the other man answering the guard. So they had caught them both. At that instant there was a rustling under him. The woman was going back, muttering to herself.

For a time everything was quiet. Then the beams of the flashlights began to sweep beneath the trees. Footsteps approached. Kern pressed himself against the tree-trunk. He was well hidden by the thick leaves under him. Suddenly he heard the piercing, hysterical voice of the woman. "This is where he must be. He climbed a tree, here — "

The beam was directed upward. "Come down!" the harsh voice shouted. "Otherwise we'll shoot."

Kern considered the situation; there was nothing to be done. He climbed down. The blinding flashlights were thrust into his face. "Passport?"

"If I'd had a passport I wouldn't have climbed that tree."

Kern looked at the woman who had given him away. She was disheveled and almost out of her mind. "You'd have liked that, wouldn't you?" she hissed at him. "To get away and leave us here! All of us are going to stay," she screamed, "all of us."

"Shut your mouth!" roared the guard. "Stand close together!" He turned his light on the group. "We really ought to throw you into prison, you know that well enough! Unauthorized entry! But what's the use of feeding you? About-face! Back to Czechoslovakia! But make a note of this: next time we'll shoot at sight!"

Kern got his valise out of the thicket. Then the four went back silently in single file, followed by the guards with the flashlights. They could see nothing of their opponents but the white circles of the flashlights; it gave them an eerie feeling as if voices and light had captured them and were now driving them back.

Presently the lights stopped moving. "March straight

ahead," commanded the coarse voice. "Anyone who returns will be shot."

The four went on until they could no longer see the lights behind the trees.

Kern heard behind him the gentle voice of the man whose wife had betrayed him. "You must excuse her — she was beside herself — forgive her — I am certain she feels sorry now —"

"That makes no difference to me," Kern said over his shoulder.

"But you must understand," the man whispered; "the shock, the fear —"

"Sure, I understand." Kern turned around. "Forgiving is too much trouble. I'd rather forget."

He stopped. They were in a little clearing. The others stopped too. Kern lay down on the grass and put his valise under his head. The others whispered together. Then the woman approached. "Anna," her husband said.

The woman placed herself in front of Kern.

"Aren't you going to show us the way back?" she asked sharply.

"No," Kern replied.

"It's your fault they caught us. You louse!"

"Anna!" her husband said.

"Leave her alone," Kern said. "It always helps to get it out of your system."

"Get up!" screamed the woman.

"I'm staying here. You can do what you like. Straight ahead and turn to the right beyond the woods; that'll take you to the Czech customs house."

"You Jewish bum!" the woman screamed.

Kern laughed. "I thought that was coming."

He watched the pale man whispering to his hysterical

wife and urging her to leave. "He's planning to go back," she sobbed. "I know he's planning to go back. And he'll get across. He must take us — it's his duty — "

The man led her slowly away toward the woods. Kern was fumbling for a cigarette when something dark bobbed up a couple of yards in front of him like a gnome popping out of the earth. It was the old Jew who had also been lying down. He straightened up and shook his head. "These Christians!"

Kern made no reply. He lit his cigarette.

"Do we stay here all night?" the old man asked softly.

"Till three. That's the best time. They are on the lookout now. If no one comes back they'll get tired."

"Waiting is something I can do too," the old Jew said contentedly.

"It's a long way and we'll have to crawl part of it," Kern replied.

"It don't matter. I'll turn into a Yiddish Indian in my old age."

They sat in silence. Gradually the stars appeared from among the clouds. Kern recognized the Great Bear and the North Star.

"I've got to get to Vienna," the old man said presently.

"There's really no place I have to get to," Kern replied.

"That's how it is sometimes." The old man began to chew a blade of grass. "Later on there'll be some place or other you have to get to. That's the way it goes. You just have to wait."

"Yes," Kern said. "That's what you have to do. But what is one waiting for?"

"For nothing really," the old man replied calmly. "When it comes it's nothing. Then you start waiting again for something else."

"Maybe so." Kern stretched out again. He felt the bag under his head. It was nice to feel it there.

"I am Moritz Rosenthal from Godesberg-on-the-Rhine," the old man said after a while. He got a thin gray ulster out of his knapsack and threw it around his shoulders. It made him look even more like a gnome. "Sometimes it's ridiculous to have a name, isn't it? Especially at night — "

Kern looked up at the dark sky. "And when one has no passport. Names have to be written down, otherwise they don't belong to you."

The wind caught in the tops of the trees and made a murmuring sound as though beyond the forest lay an ocean. "Do you think the fellows over there will shoot?" Moritz Rosenthal asked.

"I don't know. Probably not."

The old man rocked his head. "There's one advantage in being sixty-five: There's not so much of your life left to risk — "

Steiner had finally found out where old Seligmann's children were hidden. The address that had been stuck in the Hebrew prayer-book had been right; but meanwhile the children had been taken somewhere else. It took Steiner a long time to find out where: everyone took him for a police spy and distrusted him.

He got the bag from the rooming house and started off. The house was situated on the east side of Vienna. It took him more than an hour to get there. He climbed up the stairs. On each floor there were the doors to three flats. He struck matches and read the names. Finally on the fifth floor he found an oval brass plate with the inscription: SAMUEL BERNSTEIN, CLOCKMAKER. He knocked.

Beyond the door he heard a sound of scurrying and of moving furniture. Then a cautious voice asked: "Who's there?"

"I have something to deliver," Steiner said: "a bag."

Suddenly he felt he was being watched and turned around quickly.

The door to the apartment behind him had opened noiselessly. An emaciated man in shirt sleeves stood at the entrance. Steiner put down the bag.

"Whom do you want?" the man in the doorway asked.

Steiner looked at him. "Bernstein isn't in," the man added.

"I have old Seligmann's things here," Steiner said. "This is where his children are supposed to be. I was present when he met his end."

The man examined him for a moment longer. Then he shouted: "It's all right to let him in, Moritz."

There was the rattling of a chain, a key grated in the lock and the door of the Bernstein flat opened. Steiner strained his eyes in the dim light. "Why —" he said. "Why, it can't be! But of course it is, it's Father Moritz!"

Moritz Rosenthal stood in the doorway. In one hand he held a wooden spoon. An ulster was draped around his shoulders. "It's me," he replied. "But who — Steiner?" he said suddenly, in pleased surprise. "I might have guessed! My eyes certainly are getting bad! I knew you were in Vienna. When was the last time we saw each other?"

"That was about a year ago, Father Moritz."

"In Prague?"

"In Zürich."

"Right, in the prison in Zürich. Nice people there. I've

been getting a little confused recently. Six months ago I was in Switzerland again. Basle. Excellent food there; unfortunately no cigarettes like in the state prison in Locarno. There they even had a camellia bush in the cell. I was sorry to have to leave. Milan was nothing by comparison." He broke off. "Come in, Steiner. We're standing here, like old criminals, exchanging reminiscences in the corridor."

Steiner went in. The flat consisted of a kitchen and one room. There were a couple of chairs, a table and two mattresses with blankets. A number of tools were spread out on the table. Amid them stood some cheap clocks and a painted case with baroque angels who supported an antique clock the second hand of which was a little figure of Death with a scythe that swung back and forth. On a curved bracket above the hearth hung the kitchen lamp with a chipped, greenish-white burner. A large soup kettle was steaming on the iron ring of a gas-cooker.

"I was just stewing something for the children," Moritz Rosenthal said. "Found them here like mice in a trap. Bernstein is in the hospital."

The three children of the late Seligmann were crouching beside the hearth. They were not looking at Steiner. They were staring at the soup kettle. The eldest was a boy of about fourteen; the youngest was seven or eight.

Steiner put down the bag. "Here's your father's bag," he said.

The three children looked at him simultaneously, almost without moving. They barely turned their heads.

"I saw him," Steiner said. "He spoke of you — "

The children looked at him and made no reply. Their eyes glittered like polished, round, black stones. The flames of the gas burner hissed. Steiner was uncomfortable. He had a feeling that he ought to say something friendly and human, but everything that occurred to him seemed trite and false in the face of the destitution emanating from these three silent children.

"What's in the bag?" the eldest asked presently. He had a colorless voice and spoke slowly, stiffly and cautiously.

"I don't remember exactly. Various things of your father's. And some money."

"Does it belong to us now?"

"Of course. That's why I brought it."

"Can I take it?"

"Why, naturally!" Steiner said in surprise.

The boy got up. He was thin, dark and tall. Slowly he approached the bag, his eyes fastened on Steiner. With a quick animal movement he seized it and then sprang back as though he were afraid Steiner would tear his prize away from him. He immediately dragged the bag into the next room. The two other children followed close behind him, pushing each other like two big, black cats.

Steiner looked at Father Moritz. "Well, yes," he said, relieved. "Of course they've known about it for some time — "

Moritz Rosenthal stirred the soup. "It doesn't mean very much to them now. They saw their mother and two brothers die. This doesn't hurt them so much now. What happens often no longer hurts so much."

"Or it hurts even more," Steiner said.

Moritz Rosenthal peered at him from wrinkle-circled eyes. "Not when you're very young. Not when you're very old either. The period in between is the bad time."

"Yes," Steiner said. "Those lousy fifty years in between, they're the ones."

Moritz Rosenthal nodded placidly. "That's all over for

me." He put the cover on the pot. "We've found places for them already," he said. "Mayer is taking one with him to Rumania. The second is going to an orphanage in Locarno. I know someone there who will pay for him. For the time being the oldest is going to stay here with Bernstein — "

"Do they know they're going to be separated?"

"Yes. But even that doesn't bother them much. They're rather pleased at the prospect." Rosenthal turned around. "Steiner," he said, "I knew him for twenty years. How did he die? Did he jump down?"

"Yes."

"They didn't throw him off?"

"No. I was there."

"I heard about it in Prague. They said there that he had been pushed off. So I came here. To look after the children. Promised him once that I would. He was still young. Barely sixty. Never thought it would happen that way. He was always a little crazy, though, after Rachel died." Moritz Rosenthal looked at Steiner. "He had a lot of children. That's often the case with Jews. They love their families. But actually they oughtn't to have any." He drew his ulster around his shoulders as though he were chilly and suddenly he looked very old and tired.

Steiner got out a package of cigarettes. "How long have you been here, Father Moritz?" he asked.

"For three days. Got caught once at the border. Came across with a young man you know. He talked to me about you. Kern, his name was."

"Kern? Yes, I know him. Where is he?"

"Somewhere here in Vienna. I don't know exactly."

Steiner got up. "I'll just see if I can find him. *Auf*

Wiedersehen, Father Moritz, old wanderer. Heaven knows where we'll see each other again."

He went into the bedroom to say good-by to the children. They were sitting on one of the mattresses with the contents of the bag spread out in front of them. The balls of yarn were carefully arranged in a little pile; beside them the shoelaces, the little bag of schillings and a few boxes of sewing silk. The shirts, shoes, suit and other belongings of old Seligmann were still in the bag. The eldest child looked up as Steiner came in with Moritz Rosenthal. Instinctively he spread his hands over the things on the mattress. Steiner paused.

The boy looked up at Moritz Rosenthal. His cheeks were fiery and his eyes shone. "If we sell those," he said excitedly, pointing to the things in the bag, "we'll have about thirty schillings more. Then we can take all the money and lay in a stock of materials too — corduroy, buckskin and even stockings — you can earn more with that. I'll begin tomorrow. I'll begin at seven o'clock tomorrow morning." He looked at the old man very earnestly and eagerly.

"Fine!" Moritz Rosenthal patted the youngster's narrow head. "Tomorrow at seven you begin."

"Then Walter won't have to go to Rumania," the boy said, "he can help me. We'll get along all right. Then only Max will have to go away."

The three children looked at Moritz Rosenthal. Max, the youngest, nodded. It seemed fair to him.

"We'll see. We'll talk it over later."

Moritz Rosenthal accompanied Steiner to the door. "No time for grief," he said. "Too much want, Steiner."

Steiner nodded. "I hope the boy doesn't get caught right away — "

Moritz Rosenthal shook his head. "He'll be on the look-out. He knows a good deal. We learn young."

Steiner went to the Café Sperler. He had not been there in some time. Since he had had his false passport he had been avoiding those places where he had been known before.

Kern was sitting on a chair by the wall. He had put his feet on his bag, leaned his head back and gone to sleep. Steiner cautiously took a seat beside him. He didn't want to wake him up. Somewhat older, he thought. Older and more mature . . .

He looked around the place. Beside the door squatted Circuit Judge Epstein with a couple of books and a glass of water on the table in front of him. He sat there alone and discontented; there was no anxious client in front of him with fifty groschen in his hand. Steiner looked around; apparently his rival, Lawyer Silber, had stolen his clientèle. But Silber was not there.

The waiter came up without being called. His face was radiant. "You here again?" he asked familiarly.

"So you remember me?"

"You bet! I was worried about you. The police are getting sharper. Cognac again, sir?"

"Yes. What's become of Lawyer Silber?"

"He's among the missing, sir. Arrested and deported."

"Aha! Has Herr Tschernikoff been here lately?"

"Not this week."

The waiter brought the cognac and put the tray on the table. At that moment Kern opened his eyes. He squinted; then jumped to his feet. "Steiner!"

"Here you are," the latter said casually. "Just drink this cognac; there's nothing so refreshing as brandy after you've been asleep sitting up."

Kern drank the cognac. "I've been here twice before looking for you," he said.

Steiner smiled. "With your feet on your bag. So you've no place to stay, eh?"

"That's right."

"You can stay with me."

"Really? That would be fine. Up to now I've had a room with a Jewish family but I had to leave today. They're afraid to keep anyone for more than two days."

"You won't need to worry at my place. I'm living way out of town. We can start right away. You look as if you needed sleep."

"Yes," Kern said. "I'm tired. I don't know why."

Steiner motioned to the waiter. He came galloping up like an old and experienced war-horse at the signal for battle. "Thanks," he said expectantly, even before Steiner had paid. "A thousand thanks, sir!"

He looked at the tip. " 'Kiss your hand," he stammered overcome. "My humblest thanks, Count!"

"We've got to go to the Prater," Steiner said when they were outside.

"I'm ready to go anywhere," Kern replied. "I feel fine now."

"We'll take the trolley. Better on account of your bag. Still toilet water and soap?"

Kern nodded.

"I've changed my name since I saw you, but you can

go on calling me Steiner. I keep it as my stage name any-way. Then I can always say it's a pseudonym. Or the other way about. Depending."

"What are you now anyway?"

Steiner laughed. "For a while I was a substitute waiter. When the regular man got out of the hospital I had to leave. Now I'm an assistant in the Potzloch Entertainment Enterprises. Shooting gallery manager and mind reader. What are your plans?"

"I haven't any."

"Perhaps I can get you a job with us. People are always needed from time to time to help out. I'll tackle old Potzloch about it tomorrow. The advantage is that the police don't bother people in the Prater. You don't even have to report."

"My God," Kern said, "that's wonderful. I've been wanting to stay for a while in Vienna."

"Really?" Steiner glanced at him sidewise. "Have you?"

"Yes."

They got out and walked through the darkened Prater. Steiner stopped in front of a gipsy wagon a little apart from the city of tents. He unlocked the door and lighted a lamp. "Here we are, Baby. The next thing is to conjure up a bed for you."

Out of a corner he pulled a couple of blankets and an old mattress and spread them on the floor beside his own bed. "I'll bet you're hungry, eh?"

"I hardly know."

"There's bread, butter and salami in the little box. Fix a sandwich for me too."

There was a gentle knocking on the door. Kern put down his knife and listened, his eyes darting to the window. Steiner laughed. "The old dread, eh kid? It's a cinch we'll never get over it. Come in, Lilo," he called.

A slender woman entered and paused in the doorway. "I have company," Steiner said. "Ludwig Kern, young but already an experienced exile. He's going to stay here. Can you make us some coffee, Lilo?"

"Yes."

The woman got out an alcohol stove, lighted it, put on a small pot of water and began to grind coffee. She did all this almost noiselessly, with slow, graceful movements.

"I thought you were asleep long ago, Lilo," Steiner said.

"I can't sleep."

The woman had a deep, husky voice. Her face was narrow and regular and her dark hair was parted in the middle. She looked like an Italian, but she spoke German with a harsh Slavic accent.

Kern was sitting in a broken wicker chair. He was weary, not in mind alone — a sleepy relaxation, such as he had not known in a long time, had come over him. He felt protected.

"A pillow," Steiner said. "The one thing we need is a pillow."

"That doesn't matter," Kern replied. "I can fold up my coat or get some underwear out of my bag."

"I have a pillow," the woman said.

She let the coffee come to a boil, then got up and went out in her shadowy, noiseless way.

"Come and eat," Steiner said, pouring coffee into two handleless blue cups.

They ate the bread and sausage. The woman came back, bringing a pillow. She laid it on Kern's bed and sat down at the table.

"Don't you want coffee, Lilo?" Steiner asked.

She shook her head. Silently she watched the two men eat and drink. Then Steiner got up. "Time to sleep. You're tired, kid, aren't you?"

"Yes. I'm getting sleepy again."

Steiner ran his hand over the woman's hair. "You go to sleep too, Lilo — "

"Yes." She got up obediently. "Good night."

Kern and Steiner went to bed. Steiner blew out the lamp.

"Do you know," he said presently out of the warm darkness, "a man ought to live as though he were never going back."

"Yes," Kern replied. "As far as I'm concerned that's not hard to do."

Steiner lit a cigarette. He smoked slowly. The reddish point of light gleamed brighter each time he inhaled the smoke. "Would you like one too?" he asked. "They taste entirely different in the dark."

"Yes." Kern felt Steiner's hand as he gave him the package and the matches.

"How was it in Prague?" Steiner asked.

"All right." Kern was silent for a while, smoking. Presently he said, "I met someone there."

"Was that what brought you back to Vienna?"

"Not just that. But she is in Vienna too."

Steiner smiled in the darkness. "Remember, Baby, you're a wanderer. Wanderers should have no adventures that will tear out pieces of their hearts when they have to move on."

Kern was silent.

"I'm saying nothing against adventures," Steiner added.
"And nothing against the heart. Least of all against those
who provide us with a bit of warmth on the way. Only
against us perhaps. Because we take — and aren't able to
give much in return."

"I don't think I can give anything at all in return." Kern
suddenly felt very discouraged. What abilities had he? And
what could he give Ruth? Only his feeling for her and
that seemed to him like nothing at all. He was young and
ignorant and nothing more.

"Nothing at all is better than a little, Baby," Steiner said
reassuringly. "It's almost all there is."

"It depends on whom — "

Steiner smiled. "Don't be worried, Baby. Whatever your
heart says, is right. Throw yourself into it. But don't get
caught halfway." He crushed out his cigarette. "Sleep well.
Tomorrow we'll go to see Potzloch — "

"Thanks. I'm certain to sleep well here."

Kern put out his cigarette and burrowed his head into
the strange woman's pillow. He was still discouraged; but
also almost happy.

Chapter Nine

DIRECTOR Potzloch was a lively little man with a ragged mustache, a tremendous nose, and eyeglasses that were always slipping off. He was constantly in a great rush, particularly when there was nothing to do.

"Quick! What's up?" he asked when Steiner came to him with Kern.

"We need another assistant," Steiner said. "To clean up during the day and help with the telepathic experiments in the evening. Here he is." He pointed to Kern.

"Is he any good?"

"He's just what we need."

Potzloch squinted. "One of your friends? How much does he want?"

"Board, lodging and thirty schillings. For the time being."

"A fortune!" screamed Director Potzloch. "The salary of a movie star! Do you want to ruin me, Steiner? Why, you'd pay almost that much to a day laborer who was registered with the police," he added more calmly.

"I'll stay even without pay," Kern answered quickly.

"Bravo, young man! That's the way to become a millionaire. Only the unassuming get ahead in life!" Potzloch snorted, grinning, and made a quick grab for his slipping glasses. "But you little know Leopold Potzloch, the last of the philanthropists. You will receive wages, fifteen schillings cash a month. Wages, I say, dear friend. Wages, not salary. From today on you are an artist. Fifteen schillings wages is more than a thousand in salary. Has he any special talent?"

"I can play the piano a little," Kern said.

Potzloch jammed the glasses violently onto his nose. "Can you play softly — background music?"

"My soft music is better than my loud."

"Good!" Potzloch transformed himself into a field marshal. "Have him practise something Egyptian. In the scene where the mummy is sawed in pieces and the one with the lady without legs we can use a little music."

He disappeared. Steiner looked at Kern and shook his head. "You confirm my theories," he said. "I have always considered the Jews the dumbest and most blindly trustful people in the world. We could easily have got thirty schillings out of him."

Kern smiled. "There's one thing you don't take into account — the feeling of panic that a couple of thousand years of pogroms and ghettos have bred into us. If you make allowance for that, the Jews are really insanely rash. And what's more I'm really only a miserable mongrel."

Steiner grinned. "All right. All right. Come along now and eat matzoth. We're going to celebrate the Feast of the Tabernacles. Lilo's a marvelous cook."

Potzloch's show consisted of three parts: a carrousel, a shooting gallery and the Panorama of the Wonders of the World. Steiner instructed Kern that same morning in the first of his duties. He was to sweep out the carrousel and polish the brass trappings of its more imposing horses. Kern set to work. He polished not only the horses but also the stags which careered to the music, and the swans and elephants. He was so absorbed in his job that he did not hear Steiner approach. "Come along, kid, lunch."

"What, food again?"

Steiner nodded. "Yes, again. You've got out of the habit, haven't you? Now you're among artists; they have the most bourgeois customs in the world. There's even time off in the afternoon for coffee and cakes."

"This is Utopia!" Kern crawled out of a gondola to which a whale was harnessed. "My God, Steiner," he said. "Everything's been so wonderful lately that it worries me. First in Prague — and now here. Yesterday I had no idea where I was going to sleep; and today I have a job, a place to live and someone comes to call me for lunch! I still don't believe it!"

"You must believe it," Steiner replied. "Don't think about it; take it as it comes. That's the classic motto for travelers."

"I hope it lasts a while longer!"

"It's a lifetime job," Steiner said. "At least for three months. Until it gets too cold."

Lilo had set up a rickety table in the grass in front of the gipsy wagon. She brought out a big dish of vegetable soup with meat in it, and joined Steiner and Kern at the table. It was clear weather with a hint of autumn in the air. Some pieces of laundry were hanging in the field and between them played a pair of greenish-yellow brimstone butterflies.

Steiner stretched out his arms. "A healthy life! And now off to the shooting gallery."

He showed Kern the guns and how to load them. "There

are two kinds of marksmen," he explained. "The ambitious and the greedy."

"Just as in life," bleated Director Potzloch, who happened to be passing.

"Those with ambition try the trick shots," Steiner continued his explanation. "They're not dangerous. The greedy ones want to win something." He pointed to a number of shelves at the back of the gallery which were filled with Teddy bears, dolls, ash trays, bottles of wine, bronze figurines, household goods, and similar objects.

"And they are supposed to win something. Something from the lower shelves, to be exact. But if anyone gets fifty or above then he has a chance at the upper shelves where the prizes are worth as much as ten schillings. In that case you put one of Director Potzloch's original magic cartridges in his gun. They look exactly like the others. We keep them right here at the side. The man will be astounded when he suddenly makes a score of two or three. A little less powder, see?"

"Right."

"Above all never change the gun, young man," warned Director Potzloch, who suddenly appeared again behind them. "The boys are distrustful about guns. But not about cartridges. And you must keep a sense of proportion. People are to win, but we must make a profit — you must balance one consideration against the other. If you can do that successfully you're an artist in living. A word to the wise is sufficient. Anyone who shoots often enough naturally has a right to the third shelf."

"Anyone who shoots up five schillings' worth of powder is allowed to win a bronze goddess," Steiner said. "Worth one schilling."

"Young man," Potzloch said suddenly, in earnest warning, "I call your attention to one thing in particular — the chief prize. That is never to be won, understand? It is a private possession from my house. A showpiece!"

He pointed to a hammered-silver fruit basket with twelve silver dishes and cutlery. "You must die before you let anyone get a sixty. Promise me that."

Kern promised. Potzloch wiped the perspiration from his forehead and made a grab for his glasses. "The very thought makes me shudder," he gasped. "My wife would murder me. It's an heirloom, young man!" he shouted. "An heirloom, in this traditionless age! Do you know what an heirloom is? Never mind, you wouldn't know — "

He scurried away. Kern looked after him. "It's not so bad," Steiner said. "Anyhow our rifles date from the time of the siege of Troy. And besides, Lilo will help you out if things get ticklish."

They went over to the exhibit of the Wonders of the World. It was a booth covered with colored posters and raised three steps above ground level. In front of it was a little ticket office, built in the shape of a Chinese pagoda — one of Leopold Potzloch's inspirations. Steiner pointed to a poster that represented a man with lightning shooting out of his eyes. "Alvaro, the Telepathic Wonder — that's me, Baby. And you'll be my assistant." They went into the booth which was half-dark and musty-smelling. There were a few rows of disordered chairs standing like ghosts. Steiner got up on the platform. "Now pay attention! Someone in the audience will hide something on another member of the audience; usually it's a cigarette case, match-box, compact or occasionally a pin. Heaven knows how people are always able to produce a pin. I have to find it. I invite an interested member of the audience up to the platform, take him by the hand and go to work. If you're the person you lead me straight to the place and the harder you squeeze my hand the closer I am to the hidden object. A light tapping with the middle finger means that I have the right one. It's easy. I go on searching until you tap; you show me whether to go higher or lower by moving your hand up or down."

Director Potzloch bustled in with a great commotion. "Is he getting the hang of it?"

"We're just going to rehearse it," Steiner replied. "Sit down, Director, and hide something on yourself. Do you happen to have a pin?"

"Of course!" Potzloch seized the lapel of his coat.

"Of course he has a pin!" Steiner turned his back. "Hide it. And then you come here, Kern, and lead me."

Leopold Potzloch took the pin with a guileful expression and stuck it between the soles of his shoe.

"Go ahead, Kern!" he said.

Kern went to the platform and took Steiner's hand. He led him to Potzloch and Steiner began to search.

"I'm ticklish, Steiner," Potzloch snorted and began to giggle.

After a few minutes Steiner found the pin. They repeated the experiment with a matchbox. Kern learned the signals, and the time it took Steiner to find Potzloch's box of matches became shorter and shorter.

"Very good," Potzloch said. "Practise that some more this afternoon. But here's the principal thing: When you take the part of a spectator, you must hesitate, see? Otherwise the audience will smell a rat. That's why you've got to hesitate. Go ahead, Steiner. I'll show him."

He sat down on a chair beside Kern. Steiner went up to the stage. "And now, ladies and gentlemen, I invite one of you to come up here on the stage," he thundered in a barker's voice into the empty room. "The thought transference will take place through nothing more than the touch of my hand. Not a word will be spoken, but the hidden object will be brought to light."

Director Potzloch bent forward as though he were about to get up and say something. Then he began to hesitate. He squirmed about in his chair, straightened his eyeglasses and looked around in embarrassment. Then he smiled apologetically, got up halfway, giggled, quickly sat down again, finally pushed himself up, and strode, at once solemn, self-conscious, curious and hesitant, toward Steiner, who was convulsed with laughter.

When he got to the stage he turned around. "Now just copy that, young man," he said encouragingly to Kern, smiling with self-satisfaction.

"That can't be copied," Steiner shouted.

Potzloch beamed at the flattery. "Self-consciousness is hard to portray. As an old ham actor I know that. Genuine self-consciousness, I mean."

"This fellow was born self-conscious," Steiner explained. "He won't have any trouble."

"That's fine! Now I've got to go over to the carrousel." Potzloch dashed off.

"A volcanic temperament," Steiner remarked admiringly. "Over sixty years old! Now I'll show you what you have to do when you don't have a chance to hesitate — when someone else does the hesitating. There are ten rows of chairs here. The first time you run your hand over your hair you show me the number of the row where the object is. Simply that many fingers. The second time how many seats from the left it is. Then you unobtrusively touch the spot on yourself where the thing is hidden. Then I'll be able to find it — "

"Is that all you need?"

"That's all. People are amazingly lacking in imagination in such matters."

"It seems too simple to me."

"Trickery has to be simple. Complicated schemes almost always misfire. We'll try out the act again this afternoon. Lilo helps too. Now I'll show you the music box. It's a museum piece. One of the first pianos ever built."

"I don't think I can play well enough."

"Nonsense. Just pick out a couple of pretty tunes. In the scene with the sawed-up mummy play it with the sustaining pedal; for the lady without legs make it gay and staccato. No one hears it anyway."

"All right. I'll practise a little and then play it for you."

Kern climbed into the cubbyhole behind the stage, from which the piano leered at him with yellow teeth. After some reflection he chose the Death March from "Aïda" for the mummy, and for the missing legs an informal piece called "The Junebug's Wedding Dream." He pounded away on the piano and thought about Ruth, Steiner, the peaceful weeks ahead, and about supper, and was sure he had never been so well off in his life.

A week later Ruth appeared in the Prater. She came just at the moment when the evening performance of the Wonders of the World was beginning. Kern found a place for her in the front row. Then he disappeared excitedly to do his stint at the piano. In celebration of the occasion he changed his program. In the scene with the mummy he played the "Japanese Torchlight Serenade," and for the lady without legs, "Shine, Little Glowworm." They were very effective. Later, for Mongo, the Australian Wild Man, he added of his own accord the Prologue from "Bajazzo," his best accomplishment, which gave him a good opportunity for runs and chords.

Outside Leopold Potzloch stopped him. "Splendid," he said admiringly. "Much more fire than usual! Been drinking?"

"No," Kern replied. "Just a matter of mood —"

"Young man!" Potzloch made a grab for his glasses. "It's clear that up to now you have been deceiving me! I really ought to ask you to hand back your wages. From today on it's your duty always to be in the right mood. An artist can do that, understand?"

"Yes."

"And to make up to me, from now on you will play an accompaniment for the trained seals too. Something classical, see?"

"All right," Kern said. "I know a part of the Ninth Symphony. That will be appropriate."

He went into the hall and sat down in the back row. Way up in front, between a hat with a feather and a man with a bald spot, he saw Ruth's head through the haze of cigarette smoke. Suddenly it seemed to him the tiniest and most beautiful head in the world. Once in a while it disappeared as the spectators swayed with laughter; then amazingly it was there again like a vague and distant vision, and it was hard for Kern to believe that it belonged to someone with whom he would presently be talking and beside whom he would walk.

Steiner appeared on the stage. He wore a black jacket on

which astrological symbols were painted. A fat woman hid her lipstick in a young man's handkerchief pocket and Steiner invited someone to come up to the stage.

Kern began to hesitate. He hesitated in really masterly fashion; even when he was halfway to the stage he made as though to go back to his seat. Potzloch threw him an approving glance — mistakenly, for this was no piece of finished artistry, it was only that Kern suddenly felt that he could not walk past Ruth.

But after that everything went smoothly and easily.

After the performance Potzloch motioned Kern over to him. "Young man," he said. "What's happened to you today? You did a first-class job of hesitating. There was even nervous sweat on your forehead. Sweat is hard to represent, as I know myself. How did you manage it? Hold your breath?"

"I think it was stage fright."

"Stage fright?" Potzloch beamed. "At last! The genuine excitement of a true artist before his entrance. Let me tell you something: you play an accompaniment for the seals from now on and for the Wild Man from the outskirts of Cologne as well, and I'll give you a five-schilling raise. Agreed?"

"Agreed!" Kern said. "And ten schillings advance."

Potzloch stared at him. "So you've learned the word 'advance' already." He drew a ten-schilling note from his pocket. "Now there can be no more doubt: You're actually an artist!"

"Well, children," Steiner said, "run along! But be back here to eat at nine o'clock. There'll be hot piroshki, the national dish of Holy Russia. Won't there, Lilo?"

Lilo nodded.

Kern and Ruth walked across the field behind the shooting gallery toward the uproar of the merry-go-rounds. The lights and music of the amusement park rolled to meet them like a bright sparkling wave and broke over them in a foam of carefree gaiety.

"Ruth!" Kern took her arm. "You're going to have a big evening tonight. I'm going to spend at least fifty schillings on you."

"You'll do nothing of the sort!" Ruth stopped.

"Yes I will! I'll spend fifty schillings on you. But I'll do it the way the German Reich does. Without having them. You'll see. Come along!"

They went to the Ghost Ride. It was a giant maze with tracks that rose high in the air over which tiny cars shot to the accompaniment of laughter and screams. People were crowding up to the entrance. Kern pushed his way through, drawing Ruth with him. The man at the ticket window caught sight of him. "Hello, George," he said. "Here again? Go right in!"

Kern opened the door of one of the low cars. "Step in!"

Ruth looked at him in amazement.

Kern laughed. "This is how it goes! Pure magic! We don't have to pay."

They whizzed off. The car went up a steep incline and then pitched downward into a dark tunnel. A monster in chains rose screeching before them and made a grab at Ruth. She screamed and pressed close to Kern. Next moment a grave opened and a number of skeletons rattled out a grisly death march with their bones. Then the car shot out of the tunnel, whirled around a curve and pitched into a new shaft. Another car was rushing toward them with two people in it pressed close together and staring at them in terror; a collision seemed inevitable — then the

car careened around a curve, the mirrored reflection disappeared and they flew into a steaming hell in which
clammy hands swept across their faces.

"Cheers you up, doesn't it?" Kern shouted.

"Not me," Ruth shouted back and closed her eyes.

They ran over a wailing old man, then emerged again
into the light and the car stopped. They got out. Ruth
rubbed her eyes. "How fine all this suddenly seems," she
said smiling, "the light, the air, the breeze, the fact that
you can move and breathe."

"Have you ever been to a flea circus?" Kern asked.

"No."

"Then come along!"

"Good evening, Charlie," said the woman at the door.
"This your day off? Go right in. Alexander II is on now."

Kern looked complacently at Ruth. "Again, nothing to
pay," he explained. "Come on."

Alexander II was a strong, reddish flea who was making
his first solo appearance before the public. His trainer was
a trifle nervous; hitherto Alexander II had only acted as
the left lead horse in a tandem and he possessed a wild and
incalculable temperament. The audience, which, including
Ruth and Kern, consisted of five people, observed him
intently.

But Alexander II gave a flawless performance. He
trotted, he climbed and swung on a trapeze, and got
through the climax of his act, with a balancing pole, without so much as a sidewise glance.

"Bravo, Alfons," Kern said, shaking the proud trainer's
much-bitten hand.

"Thanks. How did you like it, Madame?"

"It was marvelous!" Ruth shook hands with him too.
"I don't understand at all how you do it."

"It's perfectly simple. All training. And patience. Someone told me once that you could train stones if you had enough patience." The trainer grinned slyly. "Do you know, Charlie, I played a little trick on Alexander II. I had the beggar dragging a cannon around for a half-hour before the performance. The heavy mortar. That tired him out. And tiredness makes for obedience."

"Cannon," Ruth said. "Have fleas got cannon now too?"

"Even heavy field artillery." The trainer let Alexander II take a good bite on his lower arm as reward. "It's our most popular number, Madame. And popularity brings in the cash!"

"But they don't shoot at one another," Kern said. "They don't exterminate themselves — that's where they're less smart than we."

They went to the auto scooters. "Greetings, Peperl!" the man at the entrance howled through the metallic uproar. "Take number seven, she bumps good and hard!"

"Don't you get the feeling that I'm Mayor of Vienna?" Kern asked Ruth.

"Better than that; I think you own the Prater."

They roared away, collided with other cars and were soon caught in the whirlpool. Kern laughed and took his hands off the wheel; Ruth tried hard to steer, frowning earnestly. Finally she gave it up, turned to Kern as though to apologize and then smiled — that rare smile which lighted up her face and made it tender and childlike. It was the full red mouth one noticed now and not the solemn eyebrows.

They made the rounds of a half-dozen booths and sideshows — from the calculating sea lions to the Indian fortuneteller; nowhere did they have to pay. "See," Kern said proudly, "they get my name wrong everywhere, but we get in free. That's the highest form of common courtesy."

"Will they let us ride on the big ferris wheel free too?" Ruth asked.

"Certainly! As artists in the employ of Director Potz-loch. They'll treat us as honored guests. Come along, we'll go there now."

"Hello, Schani," said the man at the ticket window. "Brought your fiancée, I see."

Kern nodded and blushed, avoiding Ruth's eye.

The man took two colored postcards from a pile beside him and handed them to Ruth. They were pictures of the ferris wheel with a panorama of Vienna. "Souvenirs for you, Fräulein."

"Thank you very much."

They got into one of the cars and sat down by the window. "I just let that reference to fiancée pass," Kern said. "It would have taken too long to explain."

Ruth laughed. "As a result we have this special honor — the postcards. The only trouble is probably neither of us knows anyone to send them to."

"No," Kern said. "I don't know anyone. Those I can think of have no address."

The car drifted slowly upward and beneath it the panorama of Vienna unfolded gradually like a great fan. First the Prater with its bright strings of lighted avenues like double-stranded pearl necklaces around the dark neck of the forest — then like a giant ornament of emeralds and rubies the garish blaze of the amusement park — and finally the myriad lights of the city itself, more almost than the eye could take in, and beyond them the thin dark haze of the mountain ranges.

They were alone in the car which rose higher and higher in a gentle curve and then glided parallel to the earth so that it seemed to them suddenly as if it were no

longer a car — but as though they were sitting in a noiseless airplane while the earth turned slowly beneath them —
as though they were no longer a part of it, as though they
were in a phantom airship that had no landing field anywhere and under them a thousand homes glided by, a
thousand lighted houses and rooms, lamps, welcoming
lights of evening, stretching away to the horizon, dwelling
places with sheltering roofs, which called and enticed, and
no one of them was theirs. They hung suspended in the
darkness of exile and the only light they had was the cheerless candle of yearning. . . .

The windows of the gipsy wagon were open. It was
sultry and very still. Lilo had spread a bright cover over
the bed and thrown an old velvet curtain from the shooting gallery over Kern's mattress. Two Chinese lanterns
hung in the windows.

"A Venetian night for modern vagabonds," Steiner said.
"Were you in the little concentration camp?"

"What do you mean?"

"The Ghost Ride."

"Yes."

Steiner laughed. "Bunkers, dungeons, chains, blood and
tears — the Ghost Ride has suddenly become modern, eh,
little Ruth?" He got up. "Let's have some vodka!"

He picked up the bottle from the table. "Have some,
Ruth?"

"Yes, a big one."

"And you, Kern?"

"A double one."

"Children, you're learning."

"I'm drinking out of pure high spirits," Kern explained.

"Give me a glass too," said Lilo, who had come in with a platter of brown piroshki. Steiner poured. Then he grinned and raised his glass. "Long live Melancholy, the dark mother of life's joy!"

Lilo put down the platter and brought an earthenware jar of pickles and a plate with black Russian bread. Then she took her glass and slowly emptied it. The light of the lanterns glittered in the clear liquid so that she seemed to be drinking out of a rose-colored diamond.

"Will you give me another glass?" she asked Steiner.

"As much as you want, melancholy little child of the steppes. Ruth, how about you?"

"I'll have another too."

"And another for me," Kern said. "I got a raise today."

They sat and ate the warm patties filled with meat and cabbage. Afterward Steiner seated himself cross-legged on his bed and smoked. Kern and Ruth sat down on Kern's mattress on the floor. Lilo moved back and forth cleaning up. Her huge shadow wavered across the walls of the wagon. "Sing something, Lilo," Steiner said presently.

She nodded and got her guitar which was hanging on the wall in a corner. In speaking her voice was husky but when she sang it was deep and clear. She sat in half-darkness. Her usually impassive face became animated, and her eyes took on a wild and melancholy brilliance. She sang Russian folk songs and the old lullabies of the gipsies. After a while she stopped and looked at Steiner. The light sparkled in her eyes.

"Go on singing, Lilo," Steiner said.

She nodded and plucked a few chords on the guitar. Then she began to hum, little melodies in a single key out of which now and then words rose like birds out of the darkness of the broad steppes, wanderers' songs, songs of brief peace beneath the tents, and in the restless light of the lanterns it seemed that the wagon, too, had become a tent, hastily pitched in the night, and that tomorrow all of them would have to press on.

Ruth was sitting in front of Kern leaning against him; her shoulders touched his knees and he felt the smoothness and warmth of her back. She rested her head against his hands. The warmth streamed through them into his blood and made him a helpless prisoner of unfamiliar desires. There was a dark something stirring within him and pressing upon him from without. It was in Lilo's deep and passionate voice and in the breath of the night, in the confused tumult of his thoughts and in the flashing tide that suddenly lifted him and bore him away. He laid his hands like a shawl around the slender neck in front of him and it nestled eagerly against them.

It was quiet outside when Kern and Ruth left. The booths were already covered with their gray tarpaulins, the noise had ceased, and after the uproar and the shouting, after the cracking of rifles and the shrill cries of the barkers, the forest had silently taken possession again, burying beneath it the gray and gaudy rash of tents.

"You don't want to go home just yet, do you?" Kern asked.

"I don't know. No, I don't."

"Let's stay here. We'll walk around. I wish tomorrow would never come."

"I wish so too. Tomorrow always means fear and uncertainty. How lovely it is here!"

They walked through the darkness. Above them the trees were motionless; wrapped in silence as though in an invisible soft wadding. There was not the slightest rustle of a leaf.

"Perhaps we're the only people still awake — "

"I doubt it. The police are always awake longer."

"There are no police here. Not one. This is the forest. How pleasant it is to walk here! Even our footsteps are silent."

"No, you can't hear a thing."

"I can: I hear you. Or perhaps it's me. Somehow I can't even imagine what it was like without you."

They walked on. It was so quiet that the silence seemed to be whispering — as though it were breathlessly awaiting a strange monster from far away.

"Give me your hand," Kern said. "I'm afraid you might suddenly no longer be here."

Ruth leaned close to him. He felt her hair against his face. "Ruth," he said, "I know this is nothing more than a brief feeling of belonging together amid all this flight and loneliness — but for us it means more than much that goes by a grander name — "

She nodded her head against his shoulder. They stood thus for a while. "Ludwig," Ruth said. "Sometimes I don't want to go on anywhere. I'd simply like to let myself drop into the earth and cease to exist."

"Are you tired?"

"No, not tired. I'm not tired. I could go on walking like this forever. It's so soft. Like walking on air."

A wind rose. The leaves above them began to rustle. Kern felt a warm drop on his hand. Another brushed his face. He looked up. "It's beginning to rain, Ruth."

"Yes."

The drops began to fall steadily and faster. "Take my coat," Kern said. "I don't need it. I'm used to this."

He put his coat around Ruth's shoulders. She could feel the warmth that lingered in it and suddenly she had a strange sense of being protected.

The breeze ceased. For an instant the forest seemed to hold its breath. Then lightning, wide and noiseless, blazed through the darkness; thunder followed at once and immediately the rain poured down as though the lightning had ripped open the sky.

"Come quick!" Kern shouted. They ran toward the carrousel, which stood dimly before them in the night under its gray canvas like the squat tower of a robber baron. Kern lifted an edge of the cover and they crawled inside and stood panting, as though suddenly protected inside a gigantic dark drum on which the rain beat down.

Kern took Ruth by the hand and drew her with him. Their eyes quickly grew used to the darkness. The shapes of horses reared like ghosts; the stags were turned to stone in eternal shadowy flight; the swans spread wings filled with mysterious shadows; and the peaceful and massive backs of the elephants stood blacker than the darkness itself.

"Come!" Kern drew Ruth to a gondola. He gathered up silk cushions out of the coaches and carriages and lined the bottom of the gondola. Then he pulled off the gold-embroidered cover from an elephant. "Come. There now, you have a coverlet fit for a princess!"

From without came the long-drawn roll of the thunder. The lightning threw faint, colorless light into the warm darkness of the tent — and with each flash, like the soft and distant vision of an enchanted Paradise, the animals emerged with their painted antlers and trappings, peacefully parading together in a never-ending circle. Kern saw Ruth's pale face with its dark eyes and, as he covered her, he felt her breast under his hand; unknown and strange again and exciting as it had been on that first night in the Hotel Bristol in Prague.

The storm came swiftly nearer. The roll of the thunder drowned out the drumming on the tight-stretched canvas roof, from which rain gushed in streams; the floor vibrated at the violent thunder claps, and in the reverberating silence that followed a last particularly heavy shock, the carrousel freed itself and began slowly turning. More slowly than by day, almost reluctantly, as though under the influence of a secret spell — the music too was slower than by day and oddly interspersed with pauses. It made only a half turn, as though awakened for an instant from its sleep — then it stopped and the organ too was silent, as though it had wearily broken down in the middle of a note, and there was only the murmuring of the rain, rain, the oldest lullaby in the world.

PART II

Chapter Ten

THE SQUARE in front of the University lay empty in the afternoon sunlight. The sky was clear and blue and above the roofs circled a flock of restless swallows. Kern was standing at the edge of the square waiting for Ruth.

The first students began to come through the big doors and down the steps. Kern craned his neck, searching for Ruth's brown beret. She was usually one of the first to come. But he did not see her. And then suddenly no more students were coming out. Instead a number of those who were outside were turning back. Something seemed to be wrong.

Suddenly, as though propelled by an explosion, a wildly confused and struggling mass of students poured out of the doorway. It was a free-for-all. Now Kern could distinguish the shouts: "Out with the Jews!" "Beat up the sons of Moses!" "Knock out their crooked teeth!" "Off with them to Palestine!"

He walked quickly across the square and stood by the right wing of the building. He had to avoid getting mixed up in the fight; at the same time he wanted to be as close as possible, so he could take Ruth away.

A small group of some thirty students were trying to escape. Packed close together, they were pushing their way down the stairs. They were surrounded by about a hundred others who were striking at them from all sides.

"Shove them apart!" shouted a big black-haired student who looked more Jewish than most of those under attack. "Get them one at a time!"

He put himself at the head of a group which, with wild shouts, drove a wedge into the crowd of Jews and then he began to seize individuals one at a time and throw them to the others who at once went to work belaboring them with fists, book satchels and canes.

Kern looked anxiously around for Ruth. He could not see her anywhere and he hoped she had stayed inside the University. At the top of the steps stood two professors. One of them had a rosy face and a gray Franz-Josef beard, parted in the middle; he was smiling and rubbing his hands. The other, a lean severe individual, was looking down impassively at the turmoil.

Some policemen came up hurriedly from the far side of the square. The one in front stopped near Kern. "Halt!" he said to the two others. "Don't interfere with this!"

The two stopped. "Jews, eh?" one of them asked.

The first nodded. Then he noticed Kern and looked at him sharply. Kern pretended he had heard nothing. Deliberately he lighted a cigarette and moved on a few steps with apparent aimlessness. The policemen folded their arms and watched the fight with relish.

A little Jewish student escaped from the tumult. He stood still for an instant as though dazed. Then he saw the policemen and ran up to them. "Come!" he shouted. "Quick! Help! They're being killed."

The policemen looked at him as though at some strange insect. They made no reply. The little fellow stared at them a moment in bewilderment. Then he turned without another word and went back toward the fight. He hadn't gone ten steps when two students separated themselves

from the seething mass and plunged toward him. "Izzy!"
one of them shouted. "Izzy's yammering for justice! You'll
get it!"

He knocked him down with a resounding blow in the
face. The youngster tried to get up. The other flattened
him with a kick in the stomach. Then the two seized him
by the legs and began to drag him over the pavement as
though he were a wheelbarrow. The little fellow was claw-
ing vainly for a fingerhold on the stones. His white face
staring back at the policemen was a mask of horror. His
mouth was a gaping black hole from which blood ran out
over his chin. He did not scream.

Kern's gums felt dry. It seemed to him that he had to
throw himself on the attackers. But he saw the policemen
were watching him and, stiff and convulsed with rage,
he walked across to the other corner of the square.

The two students passed close to him with their victim.
Their teeth flashed as they laughed and their faces showed
no trace of cruelty. They were simply beaming with can-
did, innocent pleasure — as though they were playing some
game and not dragging a bleeding human being.

Suddenly help came. A big, fair-haired student, who had
hitherto been standing idle, frowned with disgust as the
little fellow was dragged past him. He pushed up the sleeves
of his coat, took a couple of leisurely strides and with two
short, powerful blows knocked the little fellow's tor-
mentors to the ground.

He picked up the dirt-covered youngster by the collar
of his coat and put him on his feet. "There you are," he
growled. "Now get out of here quick!"

Thereupon, in the same slow and deliberate fashion, he
approached the seething pile. He picked out the black-
haired leader and gave him such a frightful crack on the

nose, followed immediately by a quick blow to the jaw, that he fell groaning to the pavement.

At that instant Kern caught sight of Ruth. She had lost her beret and was standing at the edge of the crowd. He ran to her. "Quick! Come quick, Ruth! We've got to get away from here!"

She didn't recognize him at first. "The police," she stammered, pale with emotion. "The police ought to help!"

"The police aren't going to help. They mustn't catch us here. We've got to get away, Ruth!"

"Yes." She looked at him as though she were waking up. Her expression changed. It was as if she were going to cry. "Yes, Ludwig," she said in a strange, broken voice. "Come along."

"Yes, hurry!" Kern took her arm and pulled her with him.

There was a shout behind him. The group of Jewish students had succeeded in breaking through. Some of them were running across the square. The fight changed ground, and suddenly Kern and Ruth were in the middle of it.

"Ah, Rebecca! Sarah!" One of the attackers tried to get his hands on Ruth.

Kern felt something like the snapping of a spring. He was much surprised to see the student slowly collapse to one side. He was not conscious of having hit him.

"Pretty punch!" someone beside him said admiringly.

It was the big fair-haired student, who had seized two others and was engaged in knocking their heads together. "No harm done," he said, dropping them like wet sacks and making a grab for two more.

Kern felt a cane strike his arm. He leaped forward, striking about him in a red fog. He smashed a pair of eyeglasses and jumped aside to avoid someone. Then there was a dreadful roaring in his head and the red fog turned black.

He came to at the police station. His collar was torn, his cheek was bleeding and his head kept on roaring. He sat up.

"Hello," said a voice beside him. It was the big blond student.

"Damn it!" Kern said. "Where are we?"

The other laughed. "In detention, my friend. A day or two and then they'll let us out."

"They won't let me out." Kern looked around. There were eight of them there. All Jews, except for the blond student. Ruth was not among them.

The student laughed again. "Why are you peering around like that? You think they pinched the wrong ones? You're mistaken, my friend. The guilty ones are not the attackers but those they attack. They are the cause of the disturbance. It's the latest psychology."

"Did you see what happened to the girl who was with me?" Kern asked.

"The girl?" The blond student reflected. "Nothing will have happened to her. What would happen? After all, girls don't get mixed up in a fist fight."

"Are you sure of that?"

"Yes. Fairly. And besides, the police got there just then."

Kern stared in front of him. The police. That was just it. But Ruth's passport was still valid. They couldn't do much to her. But even that was too much.

"Was anyone besides us arrested?" he asked.

The student shook his head. "I don't think so. I was the last one. And they hesitated about running me in."

"Are you sure you were the last?"

"Yes. Otherwise the rest would be here. We're still at the police station, you know."

Kern sighed with relief. Perhaps nothing had happened to Ruth.

The blond student looked at him ironically. "Feel sunk, don't you? That's the way it always is when you're innocent. It's easier when you've done something to deserve punishment. You know, I'm the only one who belongs here according to the good old-fashioned ideas of right and wrong. I got into it of my own free will. And I'm glad I did."

"It was decent of you," Kern said.

"The hell with decency!" The blond student made a sweeping gesture. "I'm an anti-Semite from away back. But you can't just stand and watch a slaughter like that. Incidentally, that was a pretty straight right of yours. Sharp and quick. Ever studied boxing?"

"No."

"Then you ought to learn. You have natural ability. Only you're too much of a hothead. If I were the Jewish Pope I'd ordain an hour's boxing lesson every day for my people. You'd see how quick the boys would get respect for you."

Kern cautiously felt his head. "At the moment I'm not in the mood for boxing."

"Rubber blackjack," the student commented matter-of-factly. "Our brave police force. Always on the winning side. Tonight your head will be better. Then we'll begin to practise. We've got to have something to do." He drew his long legs up on the bench and looked around. "We've

been here two hours already! Damned boring spot. If
we only had a deck of cards. Surely someone here would
know how to play blackjack or one of those games." He
measured the Jewish students with a contemptuous look.

"I have a deck with me." Kern reached in his pocket.
Steiner had made him a present of the pack that had belonged to the pickpocket. Since that time he had carried
it with him constantly as a sort of talisman.

The student looked at him admiringly. "Good for you!
Now don't tell me that the only thing you can play is
bridge. Every Jew can play bridge and nothing else."

"I'm a half-Jew. I play skat, faro, jass and poker," Kern
replied with pride.

"First-rate! You're ahead of me there. I can't play jass."

"It's a Swiss game. I'll teach you if you like."

"Good. In return I'll give you boxing lessons. An exchange of spiritual values."

They played until evening. The Jewish students meanwhile discussed politics and justice. They reached no con-
clusion. Kern and the student played jass at first, and later
poker. At poker Kern won seven schillings. He had learned
Steiner's lessons well. Gradually his head became clearer.
He avoided thinking about Ruth. There was nothing he
could do for her; brooding about her would make him dull.
And he wanted to have his wits about him when he was
brought before the judge.

The student threw down the cards and paid Kern. "Now
we come to the second part," he said. "Come on! We're
going to make a second Dempsey out of you."

Kern got up. He was still very weak. "I don't think I

can do it," he said. "My head won't stand another blow."

"Your head was clear enough to win seven schillings from me," the student replied grinning. "Come on, down with the inner cur! Give the Aryan ruffian inside you a chance to speak. Muzzle your humane Jewish half."

"I've been doing that for a year."

"Splendid! For the time being, then, we'll spare your head. Let's begin with the legs. The chief thing about boxing is to be light on your feet. You must dance. Dancing you knock out your opponents' teeth. Applied Nietzsche!"

The student assumed position, bent his knees, and took a number of steps alternately forward and back. "Imitate that."

Kern imitated it.

The Jewish students had stopped disputing. One of them, with eyeglasses, got up. "Would you teach me too?" he asked.

"Of course! Off with your glasses and at it!" The blond student slapped him on the shoulder. "Rise and foam, blood of Maccabees!"

Two more pupils applied. The rest remained seated on the bench, disdainful but curious.

"Two on the right. Two on the left." The blond student directed. "Now for a lightning course. We are going to make up for thousands of years of neglect in your education in barbarism. You don't hit with your arm, you hit with your whole body — "

He took off his coat. The others followed suit. Then he gave a short explanation of body movement and drilled them in it. The four hopped about zealously in the half-darkened cell.

The blond student cast a fatherly glance over his sweating pupils. "There," he announced after a while, "you've got that now. Practise it while you serve your week for inciting noble Aryans to race hatred. Now stop for a couple of minutes. Take a deep breath! And now I'll show you the short punch, the tricky middle ground of boxing."

He showed them how it was done. Then he rolled his coat into a ball and, holding it at the height of a man's head, made the others practise hitting it.

Just as they were getting well warmed up the door opened. A jailer came in with two steaming basins. "Why, this is — " Quickly he set down the basins and shouted back into the corridor: "Guard! Hurry! This crowd is going on fighting right here in the police station!"

Two guards rushed in. The blond student quietly laid down his coat. The four boxing pupils had quickly effaced themselves in the corners. "Rhinoceros!" the blond student said with great authority to the jailer. "Blockhead! Miserable prison oaf!" He turned to the guard. "What you see here," he said, "is an instruction period in modern humanism. Your appearance, with your eager hands on your blackjacks, is unnecessary. Understand?"

"No," said one of the guards.

The blond student looked at him pityingly. "Physical culture. Gymnastics. Bodily exercise. Now do you understand? Is that supposed to be our supper?"

"Sure," said the jailer.

The blond student bent over one of the bowls and screwed up his face in disgust. "Take it out!" he roared suddenly. "How dare you bring in this slop? Dishwater for the son of the President of the Senate? Do you want to be demoted?" He stared at the guards. "I'm going to make a complaint. I wish to speak to the police captain immediately! Take me to the Commissioner of Police at once. Tomorrow my father's going to make things hot for the Minister of Justice on your account."

The two guards stared up at him. They did not know whether they dared be rude or had better be careful. The blond student stared back fixedly.

"Sir," the older of the two said presently in a cautious tone, "this is the regular prison food."

"Am I in prison?" The student was a picture of injured dignity. "I am in detention. Don't you know the difference?"

"I do, yes —" The guard was now visibly shaken. "You can, of course, buy your own food, sir. That is your right. If you're willing to pay for it, the jailer can bring you a goulash —"

"At last someone is talking sense." The blond student's manner softened.

"And perhaps a beer too —"

The blond student looked at the guard. "I like you. I'm going to use my influence in your behalf. What's your name?"

"Rudolf Egger, your grace."

"Quite so. Carry on." The student got some money out of his pocket and gave it to the jailer. "Two orders of beef goulash with potatoes. A bottle of plum brandy —"

The guard Rudolf Egger opened his mouth. "Spirits —"

"Are allowed," the student finished the sentence. "Two pitchers of beer — one for the guard and one for us."

"Many thanks. Your servant, sir," said Rudolf Egger.

"If the beer isn't fresh and cold," the son of the President of the Senate explained to the jailer, "I'll saw your foot off. If it's good, you shall keep the change."

The jailer smiled happily. "It shall be as you say, Count." He beamed. "I can recognize genuine, golden Viennese humor."

The food came and the student invited Kern to join him. At first Kern refused. He saw the Jews eating their slop with earnest faces. "Be a traitor! It's the style nowadays," the student encouraged him. "Besides this is a meal between fellow card-players."

Kern sat down. The goulash was good and after all he had no passport and moreover was only half Jew.

"Does your father know you're here?" Kern asked.

"Good God!" The student laughed. "My father! He has a dry-goods business in Linz."

Kern looked at him in astonishment. "My friend," the student said calmly, "you seem not to know that we are living in the age of bluff. Democracy has given place to demagogy. A natural sequence. *Prost!*"

He uncorked the plum brandy and offered a glass to the student with spectacles. "Thanks, but I don't drink," the latter said in embarrassment.

"Of course not! I might have guessed it." The fair-haired student tossed off the glass himself. "For that very reason others will persecute you forever. How about us, Kern? Shall we kill the bottle between us?"

"Yes."

They emptied the bottle. Then they lay down on their plank beds. Kern thought he would be able to sleep. But he kept waking up. Damn it, he thought, what have they done with Ruth? And how long are they going to keep me locked up?

He was given two months in prison. Assault and battery, disorderly conduct, resisting the police, repeated illegal residence — he was surprised he hadn't been given ten years.

He said good-by to the blond student, who was released at that time. Then he was taken downstairs. He had to turn over his possessions and was given prison clothing. While he stood under the shower it occurred to him that he had felt depressed once because he was handcuffed. That seemed a tremendously long time ago. Now his only feeling about prison clothes was that they were a help; he wouldn't be wearing out his own things.

His fellow prisoners were a thief, a petty swindler, and a Russian professor from Kazan who had been picked up as a vagrant. All four were put to work in the prison tailor shop.

The first evening was bad. Kern remembered what Steiner had once told him — that he would get used to it. But nevertheless he sat on his bunk staring at the wall.

"Do you speak French?" the professor asked him suddenly from his bed.

Kern started. "No."

"Do you want to learn how?"

"Yes. We can start right now."

The professor got up. "You have to occupy yourself, you know. Otherwise your thoughts will start gnawing at you."

"Yes." Kern nodded. "Besides it will be useful. I'll probably have to go to France when I get out of here."

They sat down beside each other on a corner of the lower bunk. Above them the swindler was making a noise. He had a stump of a lead pencil and was covering the walls with obscene drawings. The professor was very thin. His prison clothes were much too big for him. He had a wild red beard and a childlike face with blue eyes. "Let's begin with the most beautiful and futile word in the world," he said with a charming smile that had no irony in it, "with the word 'freedom' — *la liberté*."

Kern learned a great deal during this time. At the end of three days he could talk without moving his lips to the prisoners in front of him and behind him during the exercise period in the courtyard. In the tailor shop he memorized French verbs in the same way with the professor. In the evening when he was tired of French, the thief taught him how to pick a lock with a wire and how to quiet watchdogs. He also taught him the times when all the various fruits ripened in the fields, and the technique of crawling unobserved into a haymow. The swindler had smuggled in with him a few copies of the *World of Fashion*. It was the only thing, aside from the Bible, that they had to read, and they learned from it how to dress at diplomatic receptions and on what occasions a red or white carnation was proper with a dinner coat. Unfortunately the thief was incorrigible on one point; he maintained that a black cravat was the right thing with tails — he had often enough seen waiters in restaurants dressed that way.

As they were being taken out of their cell on the morning of the fifth day, the jailer gave Kern a violent shove so that he lurched against the wall. "Look out, you ass!" he roared.

Kern pretended he couldn't stand up. He hoped in this way to get a chance to kick the jailer in the shins without being punished. It would have looked like an accident. But before he was able to do it the jailer plucked him by the sleeve and whispered: "Ask to leave the room in an hour. Say you have stomach cramps." Then he shouted, "Get going! Do you think we're all going to wait for you?"

During the walk Kern speculated as to whether the jailer was trying to get him in trouble. They hated each other. Later in the tailor shop he discussed the subject in a noise-less whisper with the thief, who was an expert on prisons.

"You can always leave the room," the latter explained. "That's a human necessity. No one can get you for that. Some people have to go often, and some not so often. That's nature. But after that look out!"

"All right. I'll just see what he wants. Anyhow it's a change."

Kern pretended to have stomach cramps and the jailer led him out of the room. He took him to the washroom and looked around. "Cigarette?" he asked.

They were forbidden to smoke. Kern laughed. "So that's it! No, my friend, you'll not get me that way."

"Oh, shut up! You think I'm trying to get you in trouble, do you? Do you know Steiner?"

Kern stared at the jailer. "No," he said presently. He guessed that this was a trick to catch Steiner.

"You don't know Steiner?"

"No."

"All right then, listen. Steiner has sent word to you that Ruth is safe. You need have no anxiety. When you get out you're to have yourself deported to Czecho and then come back. Now do you know him?"

Kern suddenly realized he was shaking. "Cigarette now?" the jailer asked. Kern nodded. The jailer took a package of Memphis and matches out of his pocket. "Here, take them! From Steiner. If you're caught, I don't know any-thing about it. And now sit down in there and smoke one of them. Blow the smoke down the can. I'll watch out-side."

Kern sat down on the toilet. He took out a cigarette, broke it in two and lit one of the halves. He smoked slowly with deep inhalations. Ruth was safe. Steiner was on the lookout. He stared at the dirty wall with its obscene drawings and thought this was the finest room in the world.

"Look," said the jailer as he came out. "Why didn't you tell me you knew Steiner?"

"Have a cigarette," Kern said.

The jailer shook his head. "I wouldn't think of it."

"Where did you know him?" Kern asked.

"He got me out of a mess once. A damned bad mess. Now come along."

They went back to the tailor shop. The professor and the thief looked at Kern. He nodded and sat down. "Everything all right?" the professor asked noiselessly.

Kern nodded again.

"Well, let's get on," the professor whispered into his red beard. "*Aller.* Irregular verb. *Je vais, tu vas, il . . .* ?"

"No," Kern said. "Today we'll take up something else. What's the word 'to love'?"

" 'To love'? *Aimer.* But that's a regular verb — "

"That's the very reason," Kern said.

The professor was released at the end of four weeks; the thief at the end of six; the swindler a few days later. Toward the end he tried to convert Kern to homosexuality; Kern was strong enough to keep him away. Finally he knocked him out with the short punch the blond student had taught him; after that he had peace.

He was alone for a few days; then he got two new cell mates. He spotted them immediately as refugees. One was middle-aged and very quiet; the younger was about thirty. They wore shabby clothes and you could see the care they had taken to keep them clean. The older one immediately lay down on his bunk.

"Where have you come from?" Kern asked the younger man.

"From Italy."

"How is it there?"

"It was good. I was there two years. Now it has changed. They are checking up on everything."

"Two years!" Kern said. "That really is something!"

"Yes, but it only took them a week to catch me here. Is it always that way?"

"It's been getting worse in the last six months."

The newcomer propped his head in his hands. "It's getting worse everywhere. What's going to happen now? How is it in Czechoslovakia?"

"Worse there too. Too many there. Have you been in Switzerland?"

"Switzerland is too small. They spot you right away." The man stared straight ahead. "What I should have done was to go to France."

"Do you know French?"

"Yes, sure." The man ran his hands through his hair.

Kern looked at him. "Shall we speak French? I've just been learning it and I don't want to forget."

The man rolled up his eyes in astonishment. "Speak French?" He gave a dry laugh. "No, I couldn't do that! Get thrown into jail and then carry on a French conversation — that's too ridiculous. You certainly have funny ideas."

"Not at all. It's just that I lead a funny life."

Kern waited a while to see whether the man would

change his mind. Then he climbed up on his bunk and
repeated irregular verbs until he fell asleep.

He awoke to find someone shaking him. It was the man
who had refused to talk French. "Help!" he gasped. "Quick!
He's hanged himself."

Kern sat up, still half asleep. In the pale gray of early
morning a black body hung in front of the window, its head
drooping. He leaped from his bunk. "A knife! Quick!"

"I haven't a knife. Have you?"

"Damn it, no. They took it away. I'll lift him. You try
to work the belt over his head."

Kern got onto the bunk and tried to lift the hanging
body. It was as heavy as the world, much heavier than it
looked. The clothes were cold and dead as he. Kern ex-
erted all his strength. He could scarcely lift him. "Hurry,"
he panted. "Loosen the belt. I can't hold him here forever."

"Yes." The other man climbed and went to work on the
hanged man's neck. Suddenly he stopped, reeled and vomited.

"You damn fool!" Kern roared. "Can't you go on? Get
him loose! Quick!"

"I can't look at him," groaned the other. "His tongue,
his eyes —"

"Then get down here. You lift him and I'll get him
loose."

He put the heavy body in the other man's arms and
sprang up on the bunk. The sight was hideous. The pale
and swollen face, the eyes protruding as though about to
burst, the thick black tongue — Kern felt for the thin leather

strap which had cut deep into the folds of the bloated neck. "Higher," he shouted, "lift him higher!"

He heard a gurgle below. The man was vomiting again. At the same instant he let the hanged man fall and the jerk drove his eyes and tongue out as though he were sneering hideously at the helplessness of the living. "Damnation!" In desperation Kern sought for something that would bring the man below him to his senses. Suddenly, like a flash of lightning, the scene between the blond student and the jailer went through his mind. "Why, you damned washerwoman!" he roared. "If you don't take hold immediately, I'll kick your guts out! Get going, you yellow-bellied coward." As he spoke he kicked and felt his foot strike home. He kicked again with all his strength. "I'll break your skull!" he screamed. "Go on and lift!"

The man kept quiet and lifted. "Higher!" Kern raged. "Higher, you filthy washrag." The man lifted higher and Kern succeeded in loosening the noose and slipping it over the hanged man's head. "All right. Now lower him."

Between them they laid the limp body on the bunk. Kern tore open his vest and trouser band. "Get the slit in the door open," he directed. "Call the guard. I'll begin artificial respiration."

He kneeled behind the grizzled head, took the cold dead hands in his warm, living ones and began to move the man's arms. He heard a wheezing rattle as the thorax rose and fell and sometimes he paused to listen; but there was no breathing. The man who wouldn't speak French was rattling at the slit in the door and shouting: "Guard! Guard!" It made a dull echo in the cell.

Kern went on working. He knew you were supposed to keep it up for hours — but after a while he stopped.

"Is he breathing?" the other asked.

"No." All at once Kern was desperately tired. "There's no sense in this. The man wanted to die. Why shouldn't we let him?"

"But, for God's sake — "

"Be quiet, man," Kern said very softly and viciously. He could not have stood another word. He knew exactly what the man was going to say. But he knew, too, that the other man would hang himself again if he survived. "You try it," he said more calmly after a moment. "This man probably knew why he had had enough."

A moment later the guard came. "What's the row? Are you all crazy?"

"Someone has hanged himself."

"Good God, what a nuisance! Is he still alive?"

The guard opened the door. He smelled strongly of bologna sausage and wine. He snapped on his pocket flashlight. "Is he dead?"

"Probably."

"Well, then, tomorrow morning's time enough. Sternikosch can bother his head with it. I don't know a thing about it."

He was going to leave. "Stop!" Kern said. "You'll get orderlies at once. From the emergency squad."

The guard stared at him.

"If you're not back here in five minutes, there'll be a scandal that will cost you your job."

"There's a chance he can still be saved! With oxygen!" shouted the other prisoner like a ghost from the background where he was raising and lowering the hanged man's arms.

"A nice beginning for the day," the guard growled as he left.

A few minutes later the orderlies came and took the hanged man away. Shortly afterward the guard came back. "You are to turn over your suspenders, belts and shoe-strings."

"I won't hang myself," Kern said.

"No matter. You're to hand them over."

They handed over their things and crouched on the bunk. There was a sour smell of vomit. "In an hour it will be light, then they can clean it up," Kern said.

His throat was dry and he was very thirsty. Everything inside him was dry and dusty. He felt as though he had swallowed coal dust and cotton. As though he would never be clean again.

"Horrible, wasn't it?" the other said presently.

"No," Kern replied.

That evening they were put in a larger cell in which there were already four men. Kern decided they were all refugees; but he paid no attention to them. He was very tired and climbed into his bunk. However, he couldn't sleep. He lay with open eyes staring at the little rectangle formed by the barred window. Later, around midnight, two more men were brought in. Kern could not see them, but he heard their voices.

"How long do you think it will be before we get out?" the voice of one of the newcomers inquired anxiously out of the dark.

There was a pause before an answer came. Then a bass voice growled, "Depends on what you've done. For murder with intent to rob, a life sentence; for political murder, a week."

"All I've done is to be picked up for the second time without a passport."

"That's more serious," grunted the bass voice. "You can be dead certain of four weeks."

"My God! And I have a chicken in my trunk. A roast chicken! It will be spoiled by the time I get out."

"That's a safe bet," agreed the bass voice.

Kern pricked up his ears. "Didn't you have a chicken in your trunk once before?" he asked.

"Yes, that's right," the newcomer replied in astonished tones. "How do you know that, sir?"

"Weren't you locked up that time too?"

"Yes, I was! Who's asking these questions? Who are you? How do you happen to know that, sir?" the voice from the darkness asked excitedly.

Kern laughed. He was suddenly laughing as if he were going to choke. It was like a spasm, a painful cramp, it released all the emotions that had been dammed up inside him — his rage at being imprisoned, his loneliness, his anxiety about Ruth, his struggle to keep his self-control, his horror at the hanged man; he laughed and laughed in violent outbursts. "The Chicken," he groaned. "As I live and breathe, the Chicken. And in the same fix. What a coincidence!"

"You call that a coincidence?" snarled the enraged Chicken. "A damned fatality, that's what it is."

"You seem to have bad luck with roast chickens," said the bass voice.

"Quiet!" snapped another. "A plague on your roast chickens! Is it decent to start an exile's stomach rumbling in the middle of the night?"

"Perhaps there is some profound relationship between him and chickens," the bass suggested oracularly.

"He might try roast rocking-horses," snorted the man without a country.

"Or stomach ulcers," whinnied a high falsetto.

"Perhaps in a previous existence he was a fox," the bass voice theorized, "and now the chickens are getting back at him."

The Chicken's protest penetrated the conversation: "What a God-damned low trick, to make fun of a man even when he's down on his luck!"

"What better time?" asked the bass voice soothingly.

"Quiet!" roared the guard from outside. "This is a respectable prison, not a night club."

Chapter Eleven

KERN signed his second order of deportation from Austria. It was for life. This time he felt no emotion whatever. It simply occurred to him as he signed that he would probably be back in the Prater by the following morning.

"Have you any other possessions in Vienna you want to take with you?" the official asked.

"No. Not a thing."

"You know that you will be liable to at least three months' imprisonment if you return to Austria?"

"Yes."

The official watched Kern for a while. Then he quickly reached in his pocket and pushed a five-schilling note toward him. "Here, buy a drink with this. I can't change the laws, you know. Ask for Gumpoltskirchener. It's especially good this year. And now off with you!"

"Thanks!" Kern said in amazement. It was the first time he had ever been given anything by the police. "Many thanks! I can certainly use this money."

"All right, all right! On your way now. Your escort is waiting in the vestibule."

Kern put the money in his pocket. Not only could he buy two glasses of Gumpoltskirchener with it, but he could also ride back to Vienna in the streetcar. That was less dangerous, and he would still have two schillings left over for unforeseen emergencies.

They went out the same way they had gone the first time with Steiner. Kern had a feeling that it had been ten years since then.

From the station at the end of the line they had to go on a way on foot. Presently they came to an inn that advertised new wine. There were a few tables and chairs in the front yard. Kern remembered the official's advice. "Shall we drink a glass of wine?" he asked his escort.

"What?"

"Gumpoltskirchener. It's especially good this year."

"We might as well. It's still too light for the customs."

They sat down in the front yard and drank the clear, dry Gumpoltskirchener. It was very quiet and peaceful there. The sky was clear and high and apple green. An airplane, like a distant falcon, soared off toward Germany. The proprietor brought out a hurricane lamp and put it on the table. It was Kern's first evening out of doors. For two months he had not seen the open sky. He sat still, enjoying the short period of peace that was still his. In an hour or two fear and flight would begin again.

"It's enough to make you puke," the official snarled suddenly.

Kern glanced up. "I think so too!"

"That's not what I mean."

"I suppose not."

"I mean with you refugees," the official explained dourly. "You detract from the dignity of our profession. Nothing but refugees to escort, day after day! From Vienna to the border, again and again. What sort of a life is that? A fellow never gets a decent job in handcuffs any more."

"Perhaps in a year or two you'll be taking us to the border in handcuffs," Kern replied dryly.

"That wouldn't make up at all!" The official looked at him contemptuously. "You're nothing at all in a political sense. I had the quadruple murderer Müller Second to escort, with orders to shoot at the first move. And then two years ago Bergmann, the woman killer, and later Brust, the ripper — not to mention Teddy Blümel, the corpse defiler. Those were the days! But you — you're enough to make a guy pass out with boredom!" He sighed and emptied his glass. "Well, anyhow — you do understand something about wine. Shall we drink another glass? This time I'll pay."

"All right." They drank the second round companionably. Then they left the inn. Meanwhile it had grown dark. Bats and moths swooped across their path. The customs house was brightly lighted. The old officials were still there. Kern's escort delivered him to them. "Sit down for a while inside," one of the customs men said. "It's still too early."

"I know," Kern replied.

"So you know that, do you?"

"Of course. The borders are our home."

In the first gray of dawn Kern was back in the Prater. He didn't dare go to Steiner's wagon to wake him up since he did not know what might have happened in his absence. He wandered around. Autumn had come while he had been in jail and the trees, clothed in brilliant foliage, shone through the mist. He paused for a while in front of the gray-draped carrousel. Then he lifted the canvas and crawled inside. He sat down in a gondola. He was safe there from strolling policemen.

He woke to hear someone laughing. It was broad daylight and the canvas cover had been thrown back. He shot to his feet. Steiner stood in front of him dressed in blue overalls.

Kern leaped out of the gondola. Suddenly he felt at home. "Steiner!" he shouted beaming. "I'm here again, thank God!"

"So I see. The prodigal son returned home from the police dungeons! Come here, let's have a look at you. A little pale and thin from prison grub. Why didn't you come in?"

"I didn't know whether you were still there."

"Yes, for the time being. But the first thing to do is to get some breakfast. After that the world looks different. Lilo!" Steiner shouted across to the wagon. "Our little one is back again. He needs a good big breakfast." He turned back to Kern. "You've grown and you look more of a man. Learned anything, Baby, while you were away?"

"Yes. That you've got to be tough if you don't want to be rubbed out. And that they are not going to get me down! Besides how to sew bags and speak French. And that giving orders often gets you farther than begging."

"Excellent!" Steiner grinned. "Excellent!"

"Where's Ruth?" Kern asked.

"In Zürich. She was ordered out of the country. Aside from that nothing happened to her. Lilo has letters for you. She is our post office. She's the only one who has proper papers, you know. Ruth sent her letters for you to her."

"In Zürich — " Kern said.

"Yes, Baby, is that bad?"

Kern looked at him. "No."

"She's living there with friends. You'll be in Zürich before long yourself, that's all. It's slowly getting hot here anyhow."

"Yes."

Lilo came up. She greeted Kern as though he had been out for a walk. For almost twenty years she had been living outside Russia; two months, so far as she was concerned, were nothing that had to be accounted for. She had seen men reappear from Siberia and China from whom no word had come in ten or fifteen years. In her deliberate fashion she put down on the table a tray with cups and a pot of coffee on it.

"Give him his letters, Lilo," Steiner said. "He'll not eat breakfast until he's seen them."

Lilo pointed to the tray. The letters were there, leaning against one of the cups. Kern tore them open. He began to read and suddenly he forgot everything. These were the first letters he had received from Ruth. They were the first love letters of his life. As though by magic a load fell from his shoulders — disappointment that she was not there, nervousness, anxiety, loneliness. He read, and the black ink marks began to light up as though they were phosphorescent. Here suddenly was a human being who cared for him, who was distracted about what had happened to him, and who told him that she loved him. Your Ruth. My God, he thought, your Ruth! Yours! It seemed almost impossible. Your Ruth. What had belonged to him so far? What had been his? A few bottles, a little soap, and the clothes he was wearing. And now a human being? The thick black hair, the eyes! It was almost impossible.

He looked up. Lilo had gone into the wagon. Steiner was smoking a cigarette. "Everything all right, Baby?" he asked.

"Yes. She says I'm not to come. She says I'm not to take any more risks on her account."

Steiner laughed. "The way girls write!" He poured a cup of coffee for Kern. "Now drink that and eat some breakfast."

He leaned against the wagon and watched Kern as he ate and drank. The sun came through the thin, white mist. Kern felt it on his face; he felt it as if he were inhaling wine. On the day before he had eaten his breakfast of lukewarm slops out of a discarded tin basin in a stinking room while a hobo named Leo gave a concert of farts — a specialty of his after waking. Now a soft fresh morning breeze caressed his hands, he was eating white bread and drinking good coffee, there were letters from Ruth in his pocket, and Steiner was beside him leaning against the wagon.

"There's one thing about having been in the hoose-gow," he said. "Afterwards everything's wonderful."

Steiner nodded. "What you really want to do is to start this evening, isn't it?" he asked.

Kern looked at him. "I want to leave and I want to stay here. I wish we could all go together."

Steiner gave him a cigarette. "Stay here for a day or two anyway," he said. "You look like hell. The prison grub has got you down. Feed yourself up a bit here. You'll need marrow in your bones for the trip. It's better to wait here a few days than to fold up on the road and get nabbed. Switzerland is no child's play. A strange country — you'll have to have all your wits about you."

"Is there anything for me to do here?"

"You can help in the shooting gallery. And in the evening with the mind reading. I had to get someone for that, to be sure; but two are always better anyhow."

"Good," Kern said. "You're probably right. I ought to pull myself together a bit before I start. Somehow I have a dreadful feeling of hunger. Not just in my stomach — in my eyes and my head, everywhere. I'd better wait till I'm straightened out a bit."

Steiner laughed. "Right! Here comes Lilo with hot piroshki. Make a good meal, Baby. I'm going now to wake up Potzloch."

Lilo put the platter in front of Kern. He began to eat again, feeling between times for his letters.

"Are you going to stay here?" Lilo asked in her slow, slightly harsh German.

Kern nodded.

"Don't be worried," Lilo said. "You mustn't be worried about Ruth. She will get along. I know faces."

Kern wanted to tell her that he wasn't worried for that reason; that he was only afraid she might be arrested in Zürich before he got there. But one look at the Russian woman's face, shadowed by an immense sadness, made him stop short. All his affairs seemed small and unimportant by contrast. However, she seemed to have read his thought. "It is not bad," she said. "So long as the other is alive, it is never bad."

It was two days later in the afternoon. A party of men wandered into the shooting gallery. Lilo was busy with a crowd of boys and the men approached Kern. "Come on! We want to shoot."

Kern gave one of them a rifle. First the men took a few shots at the clay figures, which they smashed, and at the little glass balls dancing in a jet of water. Then they began to study the list of prizes and called for targets in order to compete for them.

The first two men scored thirty-four and forty-four points. They won a plush bear and a silver cigarette case. The third, a thick-set man with bristling hair and a heavy brown shoebrush of a mustache, aimed long and carefully and made a forty-eight. His friends roared applause. Lilo glanced over quickly. "Five more shots!" the man ordered, pushing back his hat. "With the same gun."

Kern loaded. With the first three shots the man scored thirty-six points, a twelve each time. Kern saw that the silver fruit basket and cutlery, the heirlooms and family treasures, were in danger. He took one of Director Potzloch's magic bullets. The next shot was a six.

"Hold on!" The man laid down his gun. "There's something wrong here. I made a perfect shot that time."

"Perhaps you trembled a little," Kern said. "It's the same gun."

"I don't tremble," the man answered angrily. "An old police sergeant doesn't tremble. I know the way I shoot."

It was Kern's turn to tremble. A policeman even in plain clothes made him jumpy. The man stared at him. "There's something fishy here," he said menacingly.

Kern made no reply. He handed him the loaded rifle again. He had put a regular cartridge in it this time. The sergeant glanced at him again before he aimed. He scored another twelve and laid the rifle down. "Well?"

"It sometimes happens," Kern said.

"It sometimes happens? It does not happen! Four twelves

and a six! You don't even believe that yourself, do you?"

Kern said nothing. The man pushed his red face closer. "I've seen you somewhere before — "

His friends interrupted him. They were shouting for a free shot. The six was not to count. "You fellows did something to the cartridge!" they cried.

Lilo came up. "What's wrong?" she asked. "Can I be of service to you? This young man is new here." The others began to argue with her. The policeman took no part. He was looking at Kern and thinking hard. Kern met his glance steadily. He remembered all the lessons his stormy life had taught him. "I'll talk to the director," he said casually. "I have no authority to make decisions."

He was thinking of giving the policeman his free shot, but he already saw Potzloch writhing at the loss of his wife's family heirloom. He was caught between Scylla and Charybdis. Slowly he got out a cigarette and lighted it, forcing his hands not to tremble. Then he turned around and strolled over to Lilo.

Lilo was ready for him. She proposed a compromise. The policeman should take five more shots. In vain of course. The others were against it. Lilo had been watching Kern and had noticed that he was pale and that more was wrong than just a quarrel about Director Potzloch's magic bullets. Suddenly she smiled and seated herself on the counter facing the policeman. "Surely a fine fellow like you can shoot just as well a second time. Come on, try it. Five free shots for the King of the Sharpshooters!"

The policeman preened himself at this flattery. "A man with a hand like that would never be afraid," Lilo said, laying her own slender hand on the sergeant's powerful fist covered with reddish hair.

"Afraid! I don't know the word." The policeman thumped his chest and laughed woodenly. "This is even better than we asked for."

"That's what I thought!" Lilo looked at him admiringly and handed him the rifle.

The policeman took it, aimed carefully, and shot. A twelve. He looked proudly at Lilo. She smiled and loaded the gun again. The policeman scored fifty-eight.

Lilo beamed at him. "You're the best shot that's been here in years," she said. "Your wife need never be anxious."

"I have no wife."

She looked into his eyes. "I can tell that's only because you don't want one."

He grinned. His friends were raising an uproar. Lilo fetched the picnic basket he had won. He smoothed his mustache and then suddenly said to Kern, his eyes narrow and cold: "I'm not through with you yet. I'm coming back in uniform."

Then he took the basket, grinning, and went away with his friends.

"Did he recognize you?" Lilo asked quickly.

"I don't know. I don't think so. I've never seen him before. But he may have seen me somewhere."

"Go now. It's better not to let him see you again. Tell Steiner."

The policeman did not come back that day. But Kern decided to leave that evening anyway.

"I've got to get away," he said to Steiner. "I have a feeling that otherwise something is going to happen. I've been here for two days now and I think I'm in working order again. Don't you think so too?"

Steiner nodded. "Go ahead, Baby. I'll be on my way too in a couple of weeks. My passport is better anywhere than here. It's becoming dangerous in Austria. I've heard that everywhere in the last few days. Come along, we'll go to Potzloch."

Director Potzloch was in a rage about the picnic basket. "Worth thirty schillings, young man, at wholesale — " he trumpeted. "You're ruining me."

"He's leaving," Steiner said, and explained the situation. "The basket was a necessary sacrifice," he concluded. "Otherwise your family heirloom would have been lost."

This horrid thought made Potzloch pale. Then he brightened. "Well, well, that's different." He paid Kern his wages and led him over to the gallery. "Young man," he said, "you shall see what sort of man Potzloch is! Pick out some presents for yourself. As souvenirs. To be sold, of course. Only a fool keeps souvenirs; they embitter your life. You're going to try peddling, aren't you? Pick something out. Anything you like — "

He disappeared toward the Wonders of the World. "Go ahead and do it," Steiner said. "Trash always sells well. Take small, light things. And do it fast before Potzloch changes his mind."

But Potzloch didn't change his mind. In addition to the ash trays and dice that Kern had selected, he added of his own accord three little naked goddesses of genuine imitation bronze. "They'll be your biggest success in the smaller cities," he explained, leering and grabbing for his glasses. "Men in the small cities are full of suppressed desires. Small cities without brothels, that is. And now, God be with you, Kern! I've got to go to a meeting in protest against the amusement tax. A tax on amusement! That's typical of this century. Instead of giving a bounty for it!"

Kern packed his bag. He washed his socks and shirts and hung them up to dry. Then he had supper with Lilo and Steiner.

"Be sad, kid," Steiner said. "You have a right to be. The heroes of ancient Greece wept more often than our silly, sentimental modern women. They knew it did no good to hold it back. Our ideal is the impassive courage of a statue. Unnecessary. Be sad and then you'll soon be over it."

"Sadness is sometimes — the final happiness," Lilo said calmly, handing Kern a dish of borsch and cream.

Steiner smiled and ran his hand over her hair. "The final happiness in your case, young cosmopolite, is going to be a good meal. That's something a soldier understands. And you're a soldier, don't forget that — an advance guard; a patrol; a pioneer citizen of the world. In an airplane you can cross ten national boundaries in a day; each needs the others — and all are armed to the teeth with iron and powder against one another. That can't last. You are one of the first Europeans — never forget that. Be proud of it."

Kern smiled. "That's all well and good. And I am proud of it. But what am I going to do tonight when I'm alone?"

Kern took the evening train. He chose the cheapest class and the cheapest train and came by roundabout ways to Innsbruck. From there he went on by foot, hoping for a lift. He had no luck. In the evening he went to a small inn and ate an order of baked potatoes — food that was cheap and filling. That night he slept in a haystack. He made use of the technique that the thief had taught him in jail. It worked fine.

Next morning he got a ride as far as Landeck. The owner of the car bought one of Director Potzloch's goddesses for five schillings. Toward night it began to rain. He stopped at a little tavern and played tarots with a couple of loggers. He lost three schillings. This depressed him so much that he couldn't sleep until midnight. Then he realized that it was even worse to have paid two schillings for a night's sleep which he wasn't getting; at that thought he dozed off.

Next morning he went on. He stopped a car but the driver demanded five schillings fare. It was an Austro-Daimler worth fifteen thousand schillings. Kern passed it up. Later a peasant gave him a lift in his wagon and presented him with a thick sandwich. He slept that night in the hay. It was raining, and he spent a long time listening to the monotonous patter and smelling the sharp, musty, exciting odor of the wet, fermenting hay.

Next day he climbed the Arlberg Pass. He was nearly exhausted when a policeman on a bicycle overtook him near the top and arrested him. Nevertheless he had to walk the weary distance back to St. Anton beside the wheel. There they locked him up for the night. He didn't get a minute's sleep for fear they would find out that he had been in Vienna and would send him back there for trial. But they took his word that he wanted to get across the border and next morning they let him go.

This time he sent his valise by freight to Feldkirch; it was because of it that the policeman had spotted him. Next day he arrived in Feldkirch and recovered the valise. He waited until night, undressed and waded across the Rhine, holding his bags and clothes high above his head. Now he was in Switzerland. He spent two nights walking, hiding by day, until he had got past the danger zone. Then he expressed his valise and soon afterward found a car that took him to Zürich.

It was afternoon when he got to the station and left his bag at the checkroom. He knew Ruth's address but did not want to go there until after dark. For a while he stayed at the station; then he inquired in several Jewish stores about refugee aid societies. In a hosiery store he was given the address of a religious group and went there.

A young man received him. Kern explained that he had crossed the border the day before.

"Legally?" asked the young man.

"No."

"Have you papers?"

Kern looked at him in amazement. "If I had papers I wouldn't be here."

"Are you a Jew?"

"No. I am a half-Jew."

"Religion?"

"Protestant."

"Aha, Protestant. Then I'm afraid we can't do much for you. Our means are very limited, and as a religious organization our chief interest is naturally — you understand — in Jews of our faith."

"I understand," Kern said. "I fled from Germany because my father is a Jew. Here you can't help me because my mother is a Christian. Funny world!"

The young man shrugged his shoulders. "I'm sorry, but we have only private funds at our disposal."

"Could you at least tell me where I can stay for a couple of days without reporting to the police?" Kern asked.

"Unfortunately I can't. It's against the law. The regulations are very strict and we have to abide by them precisely. You must go to the police and see if you can get a permit."

"Well," Kern said, "I've had some experience with that sort of thing."

The young man looked at him. "Please wait a moment." He went into a back office and presently came out again. "This is an exception to our rule but we can help you out to the extent of twenty francs. Unfortunately there's nothing more we can do for you."

"Thank you very much. That's more than I had expected." Kern folded the note carefully and put it in his wallet. It was the only Swiss money he had.

He paused for a moment on the street, not knowing where to go.

"Well, Herr Kern," said a jeering voice behind him.

Kern whirled around. An elegant young man of about his own age stood smiling behind him. "Don't be alarmed. I just happened to be in there," he pointed to the door of the religious society. "This is your first time in Zürich, isn't it?"

Kern looked at him for a moment distrustfully. "Yes," he said finally. "As a matter of fact, it's my first time in Switzerland."

"That's what I thought. I guessed it from the way you told your story. Not very adroit, if you don't mind my saying so. There was no need for you to say you were a

Christian. But even so, you got some help from them. I'll
give you a couple of tips if you like. My name is Binder.
Shall we get some coffee?"

"Yes, fine. Is there an emigrees' café or something of the
sort around here?"

"Several. The best one for us is the Café Greif. It's not
far from here and the police haven't paid much attention
to it so far. At least there's been no raid up to now."

They went to the Café Greif. It resembled the Café
Sperler in Vienna as one egg resembles another.

"Where did you come from?" Binder asked.

"Vienna."

"Then there are some notions you'll have to change. Now
listen. You can, of course, apply to the police for a short-
term residential permit. Only for a couple of days, of
course; after that you'll have to get out. Without papers
your chances of getting it are, at the moment, less than
two per cent; your chances of being deported at once
about ninety-eight. You want to risk it?"

"Certainly not."

"Right. That's what I thought. For you would also be
running the risk of being refused the right to enter the
country again — for one year, three years, five years or
more, according. After that if you're caught, it means
prison."

"I know," Kern said. "It's the same everywhere."

"All right. You can postpone that by staying here illegally. Of course only until the first time you're picked
up. And that's a matter of luck and good management."

Kern nodded. "What are the chances of being allowed
to work?"

Binder laughed. "None at all. Switzerland is a small country and has enough unemployed of its own."

"Then it's the same old story; starve, legally or illegally, or get in trouble with the law."

"Precisely!" Binder replied with smooth assurance. "Now as to the question of districts. Zürich is hot. The police are very active. In plain clothes, too, which makes it ticklish. Only old-timers can get away with living here. Beginners haven't a ·chance. Just now French Switzerland is good, especially Geneva. Socialistic government. Tessin isn't bad, either, but the towns are too small. How do you work — straight or with trimmings?"

"What does that mean?"

"That means, do you simply try to get assistance, or do you do exactly the same thing under the pretense of peddling something?"

"I intend to peddle."

"Dangerous. Counts as work. Double penalty. Illegal residence and illegal work. Especially if someone enters a complaint against you."

"A complaint?" Kern asked.

"My dear friend," answered Binder, the expert, in a patiently instructive tone, "a year ago I was denounced by a Jew who has more millions than you have francs. He was outraged because I asked him for money to buy a ticket to Basle. And so if you're going to peddle, select small articles — pencils, shoelaces, buttons, gum erasers, toothbrushes, and so on. Never take a bag or box with you, or even a brief case. Brief cases have got lots of people into trouble. The best thing is to take everything in your pockets. That's easier now that it's fall because you can wear an overcoat. What do you deal in?"

"Soap, perfume, toilet water, combs, safety pins, and that sort of thing."

"Fine. The more worthless the merchandise, the greater

the profit. As a matter of principle, I don't sell anything at all. I simply ask people to help me out. In this way I avoid the statute against illegal work and am only guilty of begging and vagrancy. How about addresses? Have you any?"

"What kind of addresses?"

Binder leaned back and looked at Kern in amazement. "For heaven's sake," he said, "that's the most important thing of all! Addresses of people you can go to, of course. You can't just run around at random from door to door. You'd be laid by the heels in three days."

He offered Kern a cigarette. "I'll give you a number of reliable addresses," he went on. "Three series — pious Jews, mixed, and Christian. No charge. I myself had to pay twenty francs for my first list. Some of the people, of course, are dreadfully pestered; but at least they won't get you into trouble."

He examined Kern's suit. "Your clothes are all right. You have to be especially careful about that here in Switzerland. On account of the detectives. Your coat at least has to be good; on occasion it can cover a tattered suit, which might arouse suspicion. Of course there are a lot of people who will refuse to help you if your clothes are any good at all. Have you a likely story you can tell?"

He glanced up and noticed Kern's expression. "My friend," he said, "I know what you're thinking. I used to think the same thing. But take my word for it: to support yourself, even in misery, is a fine art. And charity is a cow that gives little milk and gives it grudgingly. I know people who have three different stories on tap — a sentimental story, a story of persecution, and a matter-of-fact story — according to what the man who's going to shell out a couple of francs wants to hear. They lie, of course, but only because they have to. The basic truth is always the same — want, flight and hunger."

"I know," Kern replied. "And I wasn't thinking of that at all. I was just amazed that you have so much precise information."

"It's the concentrated experience of three years' service in the fight for life. Yes, I've become tough. More than most. My brother couldn't take it. He shot himself a year ago."

For an instant Binder's face was twisted with pain. Then it became calm again. He stood up. "If you don't know where to sleep you can spend tonight with me. For a week I have a safe place, a room that belongs to a Zürich acquaintance of mine who is away on vacation. I'll be here from eleven o'clock on. Twelve o'clock is the police hour. Be careful after twelve. From then on the streets swarm with detectives."

"Switzerland seems damned hot," Kern said. "Thank God I met you. Otherwise I'd probably been nabbed the first day. Thanks from the bottom of my heart. You've helped me a lot."

Binder waved aside his thanks. "That's a matter of course with people who are at the very bottom. Comradeship of those outside the law — almost like that among criminals. Each one of us may be in the same fix tomorrow, and need help, himself. Well, then, till twelve!"

He paid for the coffee, gave Kern his hand and went out, self-assured and elegant.

Kern waited in the Café Greif until dark. He asked for a map of the city and traced out the way to Ruth's house.

Then he left the place and strode along the street, restless and impatient. It took him about a half-hour to find the house. It was in a quiet section, full of crooked streets; the house stood high and white in the moonlight. In front of the door he stopped. He looked at the big brass knocker and his impatience suddenly died. All at once he had ceased to believe that he only had to climb one flight of stairs to find Ruth. It was too easy after all those months. He was not used to easy things. He stared up at the windows. Perhaps she wasn't in that house at all. Perhaps she wasn't even in Zürich any more.

He walked past the house. A few blocks farther on he came to a tobacco store and went inside. A surly woman came out from behind the high counter.

"A package of Parisiennes," Kern said.

The woman gave him the cigarettes. Then she reached into a box under the counter, brought out some matches and laid them on the package. There were two books that had stuck together; the woman noticed it, pulled them apart, and threw one back into the box. "Fifty centimes," she said.

Kern paid. "May I use your telephone?" he asked.

The woman nodded. "The instrument's there in the corner to the left."

Kern looked up the number in the book. Neumann — there seemed to be hundreds of Neumanns in this city. Finally he found the right one. He picked up the receiver and gave the number. The woman stood at the counter watching him. Kern angrily turned his back on her. It was a long time before anyone answered.

"May I speak to Fräulein Ruth Holland?" he said into the black mouthpiece.

"Who is that?"

"Ludwig Kern."

The voice at the other end was silent for an instant. "Ludwig —" it came again as though breathless. "You, Ludwig?"

"Yes —" Kern suddenly felt his heart beating hard as though it were a hammer. "Yes — is that you, Ruth? I didn't recognize your voice. We've never talked to each other on the telephone."

"From where are you calling?"

"I am here. In Zürich. In a cigar store."

"Here?"

"Yes. In the same street as you."

"Then why don't you come here? Is there anything wrong?"

"No, not a thing. I got here today. I thought perhaps you weren't here any more. Where can we meet?"

"Here! Come here right away! The second floor. Do you know which house it is?"

"Yes, I know. But is it all right? I mean on account of the people you're staying with."

"There's no one here. I am alone. They've all gone away for the week end. Come!"

"Yes."

Kern put down the receiver. He looked around absently. It no longer seemed to be the same store. Then he went back to the counter. "How much was that call?" he asked.

"Ten centimes."

"Only ten centimes?"

"That's dear enough." The woman picked up the coin. "Don't forget your cigarettes."

"Oh, yes. Yes, to be sure."

Kern went out on the street. I'm not going to run now, he thought. Anyone who runs is likely to be suspected.

I'm going to keep hold of myself. Steiner wouldn't run in
my place either. I'm going to walk. No one will notice
anything unusual about me. But I can walk fast. I can walk
very fast. That's just as quick as if I ran.

Ruth was standing on the stairs. It was dark and Kern
could only see her indistinctly. "Look out," he said hurriedly in a hoarse voice, "I am dirty. My things are still
at the station. I haven't been able to wash or change my
clothes."

She made no reply. She stood on the landing leaning
forward waiting for him. He ran up the steps and suddenly she was beside him warm and real — life and more
than life.

She lay quiet in his arms. He heard her breathe and felt
her hair. He stood motionless and the vague darkness
around him seemed to tremble. Then he realized she was
crying. He started to move. She shook her head against
his shoulder without letting go of him. "Don't pay any
attention to me. This won't last long."

A door opened downstairs. Kern turned cautiously and
almost unnoticeably to one side in order to look down
the stairs. He heard steps. Then a switch snapped and the
lights went on. Ruth was startled. "Come, come in here
quick!" She pulled him through a doorway.

They were sitting in the Neumann family's living room.
It had been a long time since Kern had been in a home.
The room was middle-class and decorated without much

taste, with massive oak furniture, a modern Persian rug, a few chairs covered in rep and some lamps with bright-colored silk shades. But to Kern it appeared a vision of peace and an island of security.

"When did your passport expire?" he asked.

"Seven weeks ago, Ludwig." Ruth took two glasses and a bottle from the sideboard.

"Did you apply for an extension?"

"Yes. I went to the Consulate here in Zürich. They refused. I didn't expect anything else, of course."

"Nor did I really. Although I always keep hoping for a miracle. After all we're enemies of the State. Dangerous enemies of the State. That ought to make us feel important, oughtn't it?"

"It's all right with me," Ruth said, placing the glasses and the bottle on the table. "I have no advantage over you now and that's something."

Kern laughed. He put his arm around her shoulders and pointed to the table. "Now what's that, cognac?"

"Yes. The Neumann family's best cognac. I'm going to drink it with you because you are here again. It was awful without you. And it was awful to know you were in jail. They struck you, those criminals, and it was all my fault."

She looked at him. She smiled and Kern noticed that she was excited. Her voice was angry and her hands trembled as she filled the glasses. "It was hideous," she said once more, handing him his glass. "But now you're back again."

They drank. "It wasn't so bad," Kern said. "Really it wasn't."

Ruth put down her glass. She had emptied it in one gulp. She put her arms around Kern's neck and kissed him. "Now I'm not going to let you go away again," she murmured, "ever!"

Kern looked at her. He had never seen her this way before. She was entirely changed. Something alien that formerly had often stood between them like a shadow, something enigmatic, a sort of faraway sadness for which he had no name, had disappeared. Now she had unfolded and was wholly there, and for the first time he felt that she belonged to him. He had never been sure of it before.

"Ruth," he said, "I wish this ceiling would open to let in an airplane that we could fly away to an island with palms and coral where no one had ever heard of a passport or a residential permit."

She kissed him again. "I'm afraid they know all about them there, Ludwig. They're sure to have forts and cannon and men-of-war among the palms and coral and to be even more on guard than here in Zürich."

"Yes, of course. Let's have another drink." He took the bottle and poured. "But even Zürich is too dangerous. We can't hide here for long."

"Then let's leave."

Kern looked around the room, at the damask curtains, at the chairs, at the yellow silk lampshades. "Ruth," he said, motioning toward these things, "it will be wonderful to go away with you; it's the very best I've been able to imagine. But you've got to understand that we'll not have anything like this. There'll be country roads, haystacks and hiding places and dingy little boardinghouse rooms, with always the fear of the police, if we're lucky. And jail."

"I know all that and it doesn't matter. You don't need to worry about it. I have to leave here anyway. I can't stay any longer. My friends are afraid of the police because I have not registered. They'll be glad when I'm gone. I still have some money, Ludwig. And I'll help you peddle. I won't cost you much. I believe I'm quite sensible."

"So you even have money," Kern said, "and you're going to help me sell things! One more word from you and I'll begin howling like an old woman. Have you many things to take with you?"

"Not many. Anything I don't need I'll leave here."

"Good. What are we going to do with your books? Especially the thick ones about chemistry? Shall we leave them here for the time being?"

"I've sold my books. I followed the advice you gave me in Prague. You oughtn't to keep anything from your former life. Nothing at all. And you oughtn't to look back. That just makes you weary and useless. Books have brought me misfortune. I sold them. Besides they were much too heavy to carry around."

Kern smiled. "You're right, Ruth. You are sensible. I think we'll go first to Lucerne. George Binder, an expert on Switzerland, recommended it to me. There are a lot of foreigners there, so you're not so conspicuous and the police aren't so strict. When shall we leave?"

"Day after tomorrow early. We can stay here till then."

"Fine. I have a place where I can sleep. The only thing is I've got to be back at the Café Greif by twelve."

"You're not going back to the Café Greif at twelve! You're going to stay here, Ludwig. We'll not let you go out on the streets until day after tomorrow. Otherwise I'd die of fear."

Kern stared at her. "But can we do that? Isn't there a maid or someone who might give us away?"

"The maid has time off until noon Monday. She's coming back on the 11:40 train. The others get here at three in the afternoon. We have until then."

"God in heaven!" Kern said. "We have this whole apartment to ourselves until then?"

"Yes."

"And we can live here as though it belonged to us? With this living room and bedroom, a dining room of our own, and a lily-white tablecloth, and china, and probably silver knives and forks, and fruit knives for apples, and coffee in demitasses, and a radio?"

"All of it! And I'll cook dinner and put on one of Sylvia Neumann's evening dresses for you."

"And I'll put on Herr Neumann's dinner jacket this evening. No matter how big he is. While I was in prison I learned from the *World of Fashion* how one should dress."

"It will just about fit you."

"Magnificent! We must have a celebration." Kern leaped to his feet eagerly. "And I can even have a hot bath, can't I, with plenty of soap? That's something I haven't had in a long time. In prison there was only a kind of Lysol shower."

"Of course you can! A hot bath with the world-famous Kern-Farr perfume in it."

"I've just sold the last of that."

"But I still have a bottle. The one you gave me in the movie house in Prague. On our first evening. I've been saving it."

"That's the final touch," Kern said. "What a blessed spot Zürich is! Ruth, you overwhelm me. Things are starting to go right for us."

Chapter Twelve

THE VILLA that belonged to Arnold Oppenheim, Councilor of Commerce, lay close to Lucerne. It was a white house perched like a castle above the Lake of the Four Cantons. Kern laid siege to it for two days. In the list of addresses that the expert Binder had given him there was a note after Oppenheim's name: "German. Jew. Gives, but only under pressure. A nationalist. Say nothing about Zionism."

On the third day Kern was admitted. Oppenheim received him in a large garden full of asters, sunflowers and chrysanthemums. He was a good-humored–looking, powerful man, with stubby fingers and a small, thick mustache. "Have you just come from Germany?" he asked.

"No, I've been away for more than two years."

"And where are you from originally?"

"Dresden."

"Oh, Dresden." Oppenheim ran his hand over his gleaming bald head and sighed nostalgicly. "Dresden is a magnificent city. A jewel. Nothing can compare with the Brühl Terrace. Can it?"

"No," Kern said. He felt hot and he would have liked to have a glass of the wine that stood on the stone table in front of Oppenheim. But it did not occur to Oppenheim to offer it. He stared into the clear air, lost in thought. "And the Zwinger — the Castle — the galleries — I suppose you know all that well?"

"Not so very. I know it from the outside, of course."

"But my dear young friend!" Oppenheim looked at him reproachfully. "Not to know something like that! The noblest example of German Baroque! Haven't you ever heard of Daniel Pöppelmann?"

"Oh yes, of course!" Kern had never heard the name of the great architect of Baroque, but he wanted to please Oppenheim.

"Well, that's better," said Oppenheim, mollified, and leaned back in his chair. "Yes, our Germany! No one can copy it, eh?"

"Certainly not. And a good thing too."

"What's that — good? What do you mean by that?"

"Simply this — it's a good thing for the Jews. Otherwise they'd be done for."

"Oh, that! You're bringing politics into it. Now listen to me — 'done for, done for,' those are big words! Believe me things aren't so bad. There is a great deal of exaggeration. I have it on the best authority, conditions aren't nearly so bad as they're painted."

"Really?"

"Most certainly." Oppenheim bent forward and lowered his voice confidentially. "Let me tell you. Just between us, the Jews themselves are responsible for much of what is happening today. They have a huge responsibility. I tell you it's true and I know what I'm saying. Much of what they did wasn't necessary; it's a subject I know something about."

How much is he going to give me? Kern wondered. Perhaps enough to get us as far as Berne.

"Now just take the East Jews for example, the immigrants from Galicia and Poland," Oppenheim explained, taking a sip of cool wine. "Was there any good reason for letting all of them in? What business have such people in Germany anyway? I am just as much opposed to them as the government is. People keep saying Jews are Jews — but what is there in common between a dirty peddler, wearing a greasy caftan and those ridiculous earlocks, and an old aristocratic Jewish family that has been in the country for centuries?"

"The one migrated earlier than the other," Kern said thoughtlessly and stopped in alarm. The last thing he wanted to do was to irritate Oppenheim.

But the latter paid no attention; he was busy with his own problem. "The latter have been assimilated. They are valuable and important citizens, an asset to the nation — the others are just foreigners. That's it, my friend. And what have we to do with such people? Nothing, nothing at all! They should have been left in Poland!"

"But they're not wanted there either."

Oppenheim made a sweeping gesture and looked at him irritably. "That has nothing to do with Germany! That's something entirely different. We must be objective. I hate these wholesale condemnations. You can say what you like against Germany, the people there are active and accomplishing something! You'll have to admit that, won't you?"

"Of course." Twenty francs, Kern thought, will do for four days' lodging. Perhaps he'll give me even more.

"The fact that an individual sometimes has to suffer, or certain groups — " Oppenheim gave a quick snort. "Well, that's an unavoidable necessity of politics. There is no place for sentimentality in national politics. We simply have to accept that as a fact."

"Certainly."

"You can see for yourself," Oppenheim went on, "the

people are employed. National dignity has been enhanced. There have been extreme measures, of course, but that always happens at the beginning. It will be corrected. Just consider how our armed forces have been transformed. Why, it's unique in history! Suddenly we have become again a powerful nation. Without a large well-equipped army a country is nothing, absolutely nothing."

"I don't know anything about such matters," Kern replied.

Oppenheim gave him an irritated look. "But you should!" he declared getting up. "Especially abroad!" He made a quick grab for a gnat and methodically squashed it. "And now they're afraid of us again. Take my word for it, fear is the most important thing of all. It's only when the other fellow is afraid that you can accomplish anything."

"I know that," Kern said.

Oppenheim emptied his glass and took a few strides through the garden. Beneath them the Lake gleamed like a blue shield fallen from heaven. "And what about you?" he asked in an altered tone. "Where do you want to go?"

"To Paris."

"Why Paris?"

"I don't know. I want a goal of some sort, and they say it's easier to get on there."

"Why don't you stay in Switzerland?"

"Councilor Oppenheim," Kern said, suddenly breathless, "if I could only do that! If you would only help to make it possible for me to stay here. Perhaps you would give me a recommendation, or the chance to work. If you would use your name — "

"I can't do a thing," Oppenheim interrupted him quickly. "Nothing at all! Absolutely nothing! That's not what I meant, anyway. It was just a question. I have to remain politically neutral in every respect. I can't allow myself to become involved."

"But there's nothing political about this."

"Nowadays everything is political. Switzerland at present is my host. No, no, don't ask me anything like that." He was becoming more and more angry. "And what else did you want to see me about?"

"I wanted to ask whether you could use any of these trifles." Kern brought some of his wares out of his pockets.

"What have you here? Perfume? Toilet water? No use at all for them." Oppenheim pushed the bottle aside. "Soap? Soap is always useful. Here, show it to me. Fine. I'll take this piece. Wait a minute — " He reached in his pocket, hesitated for an instant, put a few coins back and laid two francs on the table. "There, I guess that's a good price, isn't it?"

"As a matter of fact, it's too much. The soap costs one franc."

"Well, let it go," Oppenheim said generously. "But don't tell anyone about this. As it is, I'm bothered to death."

"Councilor Oppenheim," Kern said with restraint, "for that very reason I will only accept the price of the soap."

Oppenheim looked at him in surprise. "Well, just as you like. It's a good principle, of course. Never accept gifts. That's always been my motto too."

That afternoon Kern succeeded in selling two cakes of soap, a comb and three cards of safety pins. The profit was three francs. Finally, more from indifference than hope, he went into a small linen store belonging to one Frau Sara Grünberg.

Frau Grünberg, a woman with untidy hair and a pince-nez, listened to him patiently.

"This isn't your regular business, is it?" she asked.

"No," Kern said, "and I'm not very good at it either."

"Would you like work? I happen just now to be taking inventory and I could use an extra man for two or three days. Seven francs a day and good food. You can come to-morrow at eight."

"Thank you," Kern said, "but — "

"I know — but no one's going to find out anything from me. And now give me a bar of soap. Here's three francs, is that enough?"

"It's too much."

"It is not too much. It's too little. Don't lose your nerve."

"Nerve alone won't get you far," Kern said, accepting the money. "But now and then you have a little luck as well. That's better."

"Then start right away and help me clean up. One franc an hour. Do you call that luck?"

"Certainly," Kern said. "Luck's something you've got to recognize when you see it. Then it comes oftener."

"Do you learn things like that on the road?" asked Frau Grünberg.

"Not on the road but in the intervals when I have a chance to think. I try to learn something then from what's been happening to me. Every day you learn something. Sometimes even from Councilors of Commerce."

"Do you know anything about linen?"

"Only the coarsest sort. A short time ago I spent two months in an institution learning how to sew. The simplest sort of articles, to be sure."

"Never does any harm," Frau Grünberg remarked. "For instance, I know how to pull teeth. Learned how twenty

years ago from a dentist. Who knows, perhaps I'll make
my fortune that way sometime."

Kern worked until ten o'clock in the evening and received a good supper and five francs in addition. That,
added to the rest, was enough for two days, and it raised
his spirits more than they would have been raised by a
hundred francs from Councilor Oppenheim.

Ruth was waiting for him in a little boardinghouse they
had selected from Binder's list of addresses. It was possible
to stay there for a few days without being reported to the
police. She was not alone. At the table beside her on the
little terrace sat a slim, middle-aged man.

"Thank heaven, you're here," Ruth said, getting up. "I
was worried about you."

"You mustn't worry. Whenever you feel inclined to
worry usually nothing happens. Accidents only occur when
you're not counting on them."

"That is a sophism but not a philosophy," said the man
who was sitting with Ruth.

Kern turned toward him and the man smiled. "Come and
have a glass of wine with me. Fräulein Holland will tell
you that I am harmless. My name is Vogt, and I used to be
a university instructor in Germany. Keep me company
with my last bottle of wine."

"Why your last?"

"Because tomorrow I'm going to become a lodger for
a while. I'm tired and I have to rest."

"A lodger?" Kern asked in perplexity.

"I call it so. You might add — in prison. Tomorrow I'm
going to report to the police and tell them I have been an

illegal resident in Switzerland for two months. As punishment I will be given a few weeks in jail because I have already been deported twice. The state boardinghouse. It is important to say you have been in the country for some time; otherwise breaking the order to stay out of the country counts as an act of self-preservation and you are simply put across the border again."

Kern looked at Ruth. "If you need money — I've earned quite a bit today."

Vogt waved aside the offer. "Thank you, no. I still have ten francs. That's all I need for the wine and the night. I am just tired; I want a little rest. And people like us can find that only in jail. I am fifty-five years old and not in very good health. I am really very tired of running around and hiding. Come and sit down with me. When one is so much alone company is a great pleasure." He filled the glasses. "It is Neuchâtel, sharp and clear as glacier water."

"But prison — " Kern said.

"The prison in Lucerne is good. I am acquainted with it — That's a luxury I grant myself, to choose where I want to go to jail. My only fear is that I won't be admitted. That I will appear before judges who are too humane and who will simply deport me. Then the whole thing will start over again. And for us so-called Aryans it's harder than for Jews. We have no religious organizations to help us — and no fellow believers. But let's not talk about these things — "

He lifted his glass. "We'll drink to the beauty of the world; that is imperishable."

They touched glasses with a clear tinkling sound. Kern drank the cool wine. The juice of the grape, he thought. Oppenheim. He sat down with Vogt and Ruth at the table.

"I thought that I was going to have to be alone again,"

Vogt said, "and now you're here. How beautiful the evening is with its clear autumn light!"

They sat for a long time in silence on the half-lighted terrace. A few late nocturnal butterflies were hurling their heavy bodies against the hot glass of the electric bulbs. Vogt leaned back in his chair with a rather absent-minded but very peaceful look on his thin face and in his clear eyes; and all at once it seemed to the other two that here was a man from some past century calmly and collectedly taking leave of his life and the world.

"Serenity," Vogt said thoughtfully after a pause, almost as though he were talking to himself, "serenity, calm daughter of tolerance, has been lost to our times. Too many things are required for it — knowledge, superiority to circumstance, tolerance and resignation in the face of the inevitable. All that has taken flight before the brutal military ideal which today is intolerantly trying to improve the world. Those who want to improve the world have always made it worse — and dictators are never serene."

"Nor are those to whom they dictate," Kern said.

Vogt nodded and slowly took a sip of the bright wine. Then he motioned toward the silver Lake sparkling in the light of the half-moon, and towards the mountains that surrounded it like the sides of a precious chalice. "No one can dictate to them," he said, "nor to the butterflies. Nor to the leaves of the trees. Nor, for that matter, to those — " He pointed to a few well-read books. "Hölderlin and Nietzsche. One wrote the purest hymns to life — the other conceived the divine dancer full of Dionysian ecstasy — and both went mad — as though nature had set a limit somewhere."

"Dictators don't go mad," Kern said.

"Of course not." Vogt got up smiling. "But they do not become sane either."

"Are you really going to the police tomorrow?" Kern asked.

"Yes, I am. Good-by, and thank you for wanting to help me. I am going down to spend an hour beside the lake."

He went slowly down the street. It was deserted and they could hear his steps for some time after he had disappeared.

Kern looked over at Ruth and she smiled at him. "Are you afraid?" he asked.

She shook her head.

"It's different with us," he said. "We're young, we'll get along."

Two days later Binder blew in from Zürich, cool, elegant and self-assured. "How are you?" he asked. "Everything all right?"

Kern told him about his experience with Councilor Oppenheim. Binder listened attentively. He laughed when Kern described how he had begged Oppenheim to use his influence in his behalf. "That was your mistake," he said. "That man is the most cowardly toad I know. But I'm going to launch a punitive expedition against him."

He went off and returned that evening with a twenty-franc note in his hand.

"Nice work," Kern said.

Binder shrugged in disgust. "It wasn't pretty; you can take my word for that. Herr Oppenheim, the nationalist, who understands everything because he's a millionaire. Money ruins the character, doesn't it?"

"And lack of it too."

"That's right. But not so often. I gave him a thorough scare with wild reports from Germany. Fear is the only thing that will make him give. Hoping to bribe fate. Doesn't it say that on the list?"

"No. It says: 'Gives, but only under pressure.'"

"That's the same thing. And perhaps sometime we'll run into Councilor Oppenheim as a fellow hobo on the road. That would make up to me for a lot."

Kern laughed. "He'll get around it somehow. But why are you in Lucerne?"

"It got a little too hot in Zürich. There was a detective after me. And besides — " his face darkened — "I come here from time to time to get letters from Germany."

"From your parents?"

"From my mother."

Kern was silent. He was thinking about his mother to whom he wrote occasionally. But he never received an answer because he was always changing his address.

"Do you like cake?" Binder asked after a while.

"Yes, of course. Have you some?"

"Yes, just wait a minute."

He came back with a package. It was a cardboard box in which there was a Madeira cake carefully wrapped in wax paper. "It came through the customs today," Binder said. "The people here got it for me."

"But you must eat it yourself," Kern said. "Your mother baked it with her own hands. I can see that."

"Yes, she baked it herself. That's the reason I won't eat it. I can't do it, not a bite."

"I can't understand that. Good Lord, if I had a cake from my mother I would be eating it for a month, a small slice every evening!"

"Don't misunderstand me," Binder said with suppressed

emotion. "She didn't send it to me. It was intended for my brother."

Kern stared at him. "But you said your brother was dead."

"He is, but she doesn't know it."

"She doesn't know it?"

"No, I can't tell her. I simply can't do it. She'll die when she finds out. He was her darling. She liked him better than me. He was better, too. That's why he couldn't stand it. I'll get through! Of course! You can see that." He threw Oppenheim's money on the floor.

Kern picked up the bill and put it back on the table. Binder sat down on a chair, lighted a cigarette, and drew a letter out of his pocket. "Here, just read this — this is her last letter. Came with the cake. When you read it you'll understand how this sort of thing makes you feel."

It was a letter written on pale blue paper in a delicate, slanting hand as though written by a young girl.

My dearest Leopold: —

Your letter reached me yesterday and I was so overjoyed to get it that I had to sit down and wait a while until I became calmer. Then I opened it and began to read. My heart is no longer so good after all this confusion, as you can well imagine. How happy I am that you have finally found work! Even if you don't earn much don't be worried; if you are industrious you will get ahead. Then later on you will have a chance to return to your studies. Dear Leopold, please look out for George. He is so rash and thoughtless. But as long as you are there, I am not worried. This morning I baked a Madeira cake for you, the kind you have always liked. I am sending it to you and hoping that it won't be too dry when it arrives, although of course it is all right for Madeira cake to be pretty dry. That's why I chose it instead of coffee ring, your favorite. That would be certain to dry out on the way. Dear Leopold, write me soon again if you have time. I am always so worried. Haven't you a picture of yourself? I hope we shall all soon be together again. Don't forget me.

Your loving MOTHER.

Greetings to George.

Kern put the letter back on the table. He did not place it in Binder's hand; he laid it near him on the table.

"A picture," Binder said. "Where can I get a picture?"

"Has she just received the last letter your brother wrote?"

Binder shook his head. "He shot himself a year ago. Since then I've been writing to her. Every week or two. In my brother's handwriting. I learned to copy it. She must not know. Absolutely not. Don't you agree that she must not know?"

He looked earnestly at Kern. "Tell me what you think."

"Yes. I believe it's better this way."

"She is sixty, and her heart is bad. Probably she won't live much longer. Very likely I'll be able to keep her from finding out. That he should have done it himself, you understand, that's something she would never be able to accept."

"Yes."

Binder got up. "I must write her again now. From him. Then it will be over. A picture — where can I get a picture?" He picked up the letter from the table. "Take the cake, I beg you. If you don't want it, give it to Ruth. You don't have to tell her the whole story about it."

Kern hesitated.

"It's a good cake. I'd like to take just a small slice — just so as to have — "

He took a knife out of his pocket, cut a narrow slice

Flotsam

from the edge of the cake and placed it in his mother's letter. "Do you know," he said then with a strange, disillusioned look, "my brother never really loved Mother very much. But I — I! Funny, isn't it?"

He went up to his room.

It was going on eleven in the evening. Ruth and Kern were sitting on the terrace. Binder came down the stairs. He was his cool and elegant self once more.

"Let's go somewhere," he said. "I can't go to sleep this early and I don't want to be alone tonight. Just for an hour. I know a place that's safe. Do it as a favor to me."

Kern looked at Ruth. "Are you tired?" he asked.

She shook her head.

"Do it as a favor to me," Binder repeated. "Just for an hour. Get a change of scene."

"All right."

He took them to a café where there was dancing. Ruth looked inside. "This is too elegant," she said. "This is not for us."

"For whom should it be if not for us cosmopolitans?" Binder replied sardonically. "Come on. It's not really so elegant when you get a good look at it. Just elegant enough to be safe from detectives. And a cognac here costs no more than anywhere else. On the other hand, the music is much better. And there are times when you need this sort of thing. Come on please. There's a table now."

They sat down and ordered drinks. "Here's to nothing!" Binder said, raising his glass. "Let's be gay. Life is short, and afterwards no one gives a damn whether we've had a good time or not."

"That's right." Kern raised his glass in turn. "We'll simply assume we're citizens of the country, won't we Ruth? People with a home in Zürich who are just making a trip to Lucerne."

Ruth nodded and smiled at him.

"Or tourists," Binder said, "rich tourists."

He emptied his glass and ordered another. "Have one too?" he asked Kern.

"Later."

"Have another. You'll get into the right mood faster. Please do."

"All right."

They sat at their table and watched the dancers. There were a number of young people there no older than themselves, but nevertheless the three felt like lost children, sitting there watching with wide-eyed interest but not belonging. It was not only their homelessness that lay like a gray ring around them; it was the joylessness of a youth that was without much hope or future. What's the matter with us, Kern thought. We were going to be gay. I have everything I could expect and almost more; what's wrong anyway?

"Do you like it?" he asked Ruth.

"Yes, very much," she replied.

The place became dark, colored spotlights swept across the floor and a beautiful slim dancer whirled into sight.

"Wonderful, isn't it?" Binder asked, applauding.

"Magnificent!" Kern clapped too.

"The music's excellent, don't you think?"

"First-rate."

They sat there, very eager to find things magnificent and to be happy and gay; but there were dust and ashes in everything and they could not understand why.

"Why don't you two dance?" Binder asked.

"Shall we?" Kern got up.

"I don't think I know how," Ruth said.

"I don't know how either. That makes us even."

Ruth hesitated an instant, then accompanied Kern to the dance floor. The colored lights flicked over the dancers. "Here comes the violet light," Kern said. "A good chance to dive in." They danced cautiously and rather shyly together. Gradually they became more confident, especially when they noticed that no one was paying any attention to them. "How nice it is to dance with you!" Kern said. "There are always fine new things to do with you. It's not just that you are there — everything around changes and becomes beautiful too!"

She moved her hand closer around his shoulder and pressed against him. Slowly they glided into the rhythm of the music. The spotlight swept over them like colored water and for an instant they forgot everything else — now they were just pliant young life drawn to one another and freed from the shadows of fear and distrust and flight.

The music stopped and they went back to their table. Kern looked at Ruth. Her eyes were shining and her face was animated. All at once it had a beaming, self-forgetful and almost bold expression. Damn it, he thought, if one could only live as one would like — and for an instant he felt an agonizing bitterness.

"Just look who's coming," Binder whispered.

Kern looked up. Arnold Oppenheim, Councilor of Commerce, was striding diagonally across the room on his way to the door. He paused beside their table and glowered down at them. "Very interesting," he snapped, "very instructive."

No one replied. "This is what I get for my generous assistance," Oppenheim went on indignantly. "My money is immediately squandered in bars."

"Man does not live by bread alone, Councilor," Binder replied calmly.

"That's pure rhetoric. Young people like you have no business in bars."

"And no business on the road either," Binder replied.

Kern turned to Ruth. "May I introduce this gentleman who is so upset about us. He is Councilor Oppenheim. He bought a cake of soap from me. I made a profit of forty centimes on the transaction."

Oppenheim was taken aback and looked at him angrily. Then he snorted something that sounded like "Impudence" and stamped away.

"What was that?" Ruth asked.

"The commonest thing in the world," Binder replied derisively. "Conscious charity. Harder than steel."

Ruth got up. "He's sure to get the police. We've got to leave."

"He's much too cowardly to do that. There would be unpleasant consequences."

"Let's go just the same."

"All right."

Binder paid the check and they started back for the boardinghouse. Near the railroad station they saw two men approaching from the opposite direction. "Careful," Binder whispered. "A detective. Act unconcerned."

Kern began to whistle quietly. He took Ruth's arm and strolled with deliberate slowness. He felt that Ruth wanted to walk faster. He pressed her arm, laughed, and wandered slowly ahead.

The two men went by them. One of them wore a bowler hat and was carelessly smoking a cigar. The other was

Vogt. He recognized them and on his face they saw an almost imperceptible expression of regret.

Kern looked around presently. The two men had disappeared.

"Bound for Basle. The twelve-fifteen train to the border," Binder announced with assurance.

Kern nodded. "Too humane a judge, as he feared."

They walked on. Ruth shivered. "All at once it seems scary here," she said.

"France," Binder replied. "Paris . . . A big city is best."

"Why don't you go there too?"

"I don't know a word of French. And besides I'm a specialist on Switzerland. And then too — " he stopped speaking.

They walked on in silence. A cool breeze was blowing from the direction of the Lake. Above them the sky was vast and iron-gray and alien. . . .

*　　*　　*

In front of Steiner sat the former lawyer, Dr. Goldbach II, once a member of the Court of Appeals in Berlin. He was the new telepathic assistant. Steiner had found him in the Café Sperler.

Goldbach was about fifty years old and had been ordered out of Germany because he was a Jew. He carried on a business in neckties and illegal legal advice. In this way he earned exactly enough to keep him from starving to death. His wife was thirty years old and very beautiful, and he was in love with her. At the moment she was paying her expenses by selling her jewelry; but he knew she would probably leave him before long. Steiner had listened to his story and got him the job of assistant for the evening performances. And so during the day he could carry on his other professions.

Very shortly it became apparent that Goldbach was not suited to the job. He kept getting confused and ruining the performances. And then in the evening he would come to Steiner in despair and beg not to be fired.

"Goldbach," Steiner said, "it was especially bad today. It really can't go on this way. Why, you're forcing me to be a genuine mind-reader."

Goldbach gazed at him like a dying sheep dog.

"It's all so simple," Steiner went on, "the number of steps you take to the first tent pole means the number of the row the person is sitting in. Closing your right eye means a woman — your left, a man. The number of fingers casually extended shows how many seats he is from the left. Extending your right foot means the object is hidden on the upper part of the body — the left foot, the lower part. The farther forward the foot, the farther up or down. We've already changed the system because you're so jittery."

The lawyer nervously ran his fingers around his collar. "Herr Steiner," he said, "I know it by heart. Heaven knows I practise it every day. It's as though I were possessed — "

"But, Goldbach," Steiner said patiently, "as a lawyer you must have had to keep much more complicated things in mind."

Goldbach· wrung his hands. "I know the Civil Code by heart. I know hundreds of citations and decisions. Believe me, Herr Steiner, my memory was the terror of the judges — but this thing is a jinx — "

Steiner shook his head. "But a child can remember it, Goldbach. Just eight different signs. And then four more for unusual cases."

"I know them all right. My God! I practise them every day. It's just the excitement that — "

Goldbach sat, a small huddled figure, on a stool and stared helplessly in front of him. Steiner laughed. "But you were never excited in the courtroom. You have conducted important cases in which you had to have complete and calm command of a complicated subject."

"Yes, yes, that was easy. But here! Before it begins I know every detail perfectly — the minute I step inside the tent I get everything confused in my excitement."

"For heaven's sake, what makes you so excited?"

Goldbach was silent for a moment. Then he said in a whisper, "I don't know. There's so much mixed up in it."

He got up. "Will you give me one more chance, Herr Steiner?"

"Of course. But tomorrow it has to work; otherwise we'll have Potzloch on our necks."

Goldbach fumbled in the pocket of his coat and brought out a tie wrapped in tissue paper. He offered it to Steiner. "I brought you a little present. You have so much trouble with me — "

Steiner waved it aside. "Put it away. We don't do that sort of thing."

"It doesn't cost me anything."

Steiner slapped him on the shoulder. "Attempted bribery by a lawyer. What additional punishment does that bring in a trial?"

Goldbach smiled feebly. "That's a question you must put to the prosecuting attorney. The only thing you ask a good defense counsel is, how much less does it bring? Besides, the amount of punishment is the same; only in such cases mitigating circumstances are ruled out. The last celebrated instance was the case of Hauer and Associates."

He became animated. "The defense had Freygang. An able man, but too fond of paradox. A paradox is admirable as byplay because it confuses the opposition; but it can't serve as the basis of a defense. That's where Freygang came to grief. He tried to plead extenuating circumstances for a country lawyer on the ground of — " he laughed appreciatively — "ignorance of the law."

"A brilliant inspiration," Steiner said.

"As a joke, yes; but not in a lawsuit."

Goldbach stood for a time with his head bent a little to one side, his eyes suddenly sharp between narrowed lids. He was no longer the pathetic exile and tie peddler, he was once more Dr. Goldbach II of the High Court of Appeals, the dreaded tiger of the legal jungles.

With quick step and erect bearing he walked along the main avenue of the Prater, as he had not walked in a long time. He did not notice the melancholy of the clear autumn night — he was standing in an overcrowded courtroom with his notes in front of him, taking the place of lawyer Freygang. He watched as the state's attorney finished the summing up for the prosecution and took his seat; he straightened his own robes, rested the knuckles of his hands lightly on the table, swayed a little as a fencer sways and then began in a metallic voice: "High Court of Appeals — Hauer, the accused — "

Sentence followed sentence, brief and pointed, inexorable in their logic. He took up the arguments of the State's attorney, one after the other. He appeared to agree with their conclusions, he appeared to prosecute and not to defend. The room became quiet, the judges lifted their heads. But suddenly, with an adroit twist, he changed ground, cited the statute on bribery and in four slashing questions revealed its ambiguity. Then with a snap like a whiplash he introduced the exonerating evidence, now carrying a wholly new weight.

He stopped in front of the house where he lived and slowly mounted the stairs — moving slower and slower and ever more hesitantly. "Has my wife come in?" he asked the sleepy maid who opened the door.

"She got in fifteen minutes ago."

"Thanks." Goldbach went along the hall to his room. It was narrow and had a single small window opening on the court. He brushed his hair and then knocked on the communicating door.

"Yes?"

His wife was sitting in front of a mirror intently studying her face. She did not turn around. "Well, what now?" she asked.

"How are things, Lena?"

"How do you expect them to be in a life like this? They're bad. What makes you ask such questions anyway?" The woman examined her eyelids.

"Were you out?"

"Yes."

"Where were you?"

"Oh, some place or other. I can't sit all day and stare at the walls, you know."

"I don't want you to do that. I'm happy if you have been entertained."

"Well, that makes everything fine, doesn't it?"

His wife began to rub cold cream into her skin, slowly and carefully. She spoke to Goldbach with no animation in her voice, with galling indifference as though she were addressing a stick of wood. He stood by the door and looked at her, hungry for a kind word. She had flawless, rosy skin that shone in the lamplight. Her body was soft and plump.

"Have you found anything yet?" she asked.

Goldbach seemed to shrink in size. "But, Lena, you know I have no permit to work. I went to my colleague Höpfner; but he can't do anything for me either. Everything takes so horribly long — "

"Yes, it's taken too long already."

"I'm doing all I can, Lena."

"Yes, I know. I'm tired."

"I'm going. Good night."

Goldbach closed the door. He was at a loss what to do. Should he burst in and beg her to understand him, plead with her to sleep with him for one night — or? He clenched his fists impotently. Beat her, he thought. Inflict on that rosy flesh all the humiliation and shame he had suffered, let himself go for once, release his rage, smash the room to bits and strike and strike again until that haughty and indifferent mouth screamed and whimpered and the soft body writhed on the floor.

He trembled as he listened. Karbatke — no, that wasn't right — Karbutke, that had been the man's name. He was a thick-set fellow with hair that grew low on his forehead and a face such as a layman pictures a murderer's to be. And because of that face it had been hard to plead for acquittal on the ground that the man had acted under the influence of passion. He had knocked his girl's teeth out, broken one arm and torn the corner of her mouth; even at the hearing her eyes were still swollen he had beaten her so; nevertheless she loved this ape with doglike devotion — perhaps because of it. The acquittal had been a

great success, a deeply penetrating psychological master-
piece of defense, as his colleague Cohn III had said at the
time in congratulating him.

Goldbach let his hands drop. He looked at the selection
of cheap imitation silk ties that lay on his table. Yes, at that
time among his colleagues in the lawyers' chambers, how
conclusively he had demonstrated that a woman's love demands a lord and master; at that time, when he was earning
sixty thousand marks a year and was giving Lena the
jewelry she was now selling for her own uses.

He strained his ears as she got into bed. It was something
he did every night and hated himself for doing, but he
could not help it. His cheeks became mottled as he heard
the springs creak. He clenched his teeth, went to the mirror
and looked at himself. Then he took a chair and placed it
in the middle of the room. "Let's assume that a woman in
the ninth row, three from the end, has hidden a key in her
shoe," he muttered. Carefully he took nine short steps to
the chair, winked his right eye quickly, ran three fingers
over his forehead and put his left foot forward — farther
forward — now he was completely absorbed; he saw
Steiner searching and pushed his foot even farther forward.

In the reddish light of the electric bulb, his shadow,
pathetic and grotesque, wavered across the wall.

*   *   *

At about this time Steiner was saying, "I wonder what
our kid's doing now, Lilo. Heaven knows, it's not just on
account of that miserable Goldbach — I really do miss him
often, that kid."

Chapter Thirteen

KERN and Ruth were in Berne. They were living in the Pension Evergreen, which was on Binder's list. You could stay there for two days without being reported to the police.

Very late on the second evening there was a knock at Kern's door. He had already undressed and was about to get into bed. For a moment he stood motionless. There was another knock. Noiselessly, on bare feet, he ran to the window. It was too high to jump down and there was no rainpipe by which he could climb to the ground. Slowly he went back and opened the door.

A man of about thirty stood outside. He was a head taller than Kern, had a round face with deep blue eyes, and crisp, light blond hair. In his hands he held a gray velour hat which he was twisting nervously.

"Excuse me," he said. "I am an emigree like you — "

Kern felt as if he had suddenly grown wings. Saved, he thought. It's not the police!

"I am very much embarrassed," the man went on. "Binding is my name — Richard Binding. I am on my way to Zürich and I haven't a single centime left to pay for a night's lodging. I am not going to ask you for money. I just want to enquire whether you will let me sleep here on the floor for the night."

Kern looked at him. "Here?" he said. "In this room? On the floor?"

"Yes. I'm used to it and I'll promise not to disturb you.

I've been on the road for three nights now. You know what it's like sleeping outdoors on benches in constant fear of the police. After that you're happy if you can find any place where you're safe for a couple of hours."

"I know. But just take a look at this room. There's not enough room anywhere for you to stretch out. How are you going to sleep here?"

"That doesn't matter," Binding declared eagerly. "It will work all right. Over there in the corner, for instance. I can sleep sitting up or leaning against the wardrobe. That'll work fine! When you just have a little peace, people like us can sleep anywhere, you know."

"No, that won't do." Kern thought for a moment. "A room here costs two francs. I can give you the money. That's the simplest thing to do. Then you can get a good night's rest."

Binding lifted his hands in protest. They were big and red and thick. "I won't take your money! I haven't come to that yet. Anyone who lives here needs his few groschen. And besides, I've already asked downstairs whether there wasn't some place I could sleep. There are no rooms free."

"Perhaps there'd be one if you had two francs in your hand."

"I don't believe so. The proprietor told me he would always give free lodging to anyone who had spent two years in a concentration camp. He actually didn't have an empty room."

"What?" Kern said. "You were in a concentration camp for two years?"

"Yes." Binding gripped his hat between his knees and produced a tattered document from his breast pocket. He unfolded it and handed it to Kern. "Here, take a look. This is my discharge from Oranienburg."

Kern took the sheet gingerly in order not to tear the fragile creases. He had never seen a discharge paper from a concentration camp. He read the contents, the printed matter and the typewritten name, Richard Binding — then he looked at the seal with the swastika and the neat, clear signature of the official; everything was in order. It was, in fact, orderly in a pedantic and bureaucratic fashion, and this made the whole thing almost uncanny — as though someone had come back from the Inferno with a residential permit and a visa.

He returned the document to Binding. "Listen," he said, "I know what we'll do. You take my bed and my room. I know someone here in the boardinghouse who has a larger room. I can sleep there perfectly well. So we'll both be taken care of."

Binding stared at him wide-eyed. "But that's altogether out of the question!"

"Not a bit of it. It's perfectly simple." Kern picked up his overcoat and pulled it on over his pajamas. Then he laid his suit over his arm and picked up his shoes. "You see, I'll take these along. Then I won't need to disturb you early in the morning. I can dress in the other room. I'm awfully glad to be able to do something for someone who has been through so much."

"But — " Binding suddenly seized Kern's hands. He looked as if he were about to kiss them. "My God, you're an angel!" he stammered. "A savior."

"Oh nonsense," Kern replied in embarrassment. "We help one another out, that's all. Otherwise what would become of us? Sleep well."

"I'll do that, heaven knows."

Kern wondered for a moment whether he should take his bag with him. He had hidden forty francs in a little side pocket in it. But the money was well hidden. The bag was snapped shut and he hesitated to show such open distrust of a man who had been in a concentration camp. Refugees don't steal from one another. "Good night. Sleep well," he said again and left.

Ruth's room was on the same corridor. Kern gave two short taps on the door. This was the signal they had agreed on. She opened the door at once. "Has something happened?" she asked in alarm when she saw the things in his hands. "Do we have to clear out?"

"No. I've just loaned my room to a poor devil who was in a concentration camp and who hadn't slept for a couple of nights. May I sleep here in your room on the chaise longue?"

Ruth smiled. "The chaise longue is old and rickety. But don't you think the bed is big enough for both of us?"

Kern stepped quickly into the room and kissed her. "Sometimes I really do ask the silliest questions," he said, "but it's just from embarrassment, you know. This is all so new to me."

Ruth's room was somewhat bigger than the other. Aside from the chaise longue the furniture was similar — but Kern noticed that it looked entirely different. Strange, he thought, it must be the few things of hers that are here — the little shoes, the blouse, the brown dress — what tender charm they have! When my things are in a room they only make it look untidy.

"Ruth," he said, "if we wanted to get married, do you know we couldn't possibly do it? Because we haven't any papers."

"I know. But that's the last thing for us to worry about. Why do we even have to have two rooms?"

Kern laughed. "Because of the high standard of Swiss

morality. It will wink at infringements of police regulations, but to live together without being married is out of the question."

He waited until ten o'clock next morning, then he went over to get his bag. He wanted to look up a few addresses without waking Binding. But the room was empty when he got there. Binding, presumably, was already on his way. Kern opened his bag. It was not snapped shut and this surprised him. He was certain he had closed it the night before. It seemed to him that the bottles were not lying in the same order as usual. The little envelope in the hidden side pocket was there. He opened it and saw immediately that the Swiss money was gone. Only two lonesome Austrian five-schilling notes fluttered out.

He made a thorough search everywhere. Even through his suit, although he was sure the money wasn't there. He never carried money with him because he might be arrested while away from home. In that event, Ruth would at least have the bag and the money. But the forty francs had disappeared. He sat down on the floor beside the bag. "That swindler," he said helplessly, "that damned swindler! How could anything like this happen?"

He remained sitting for a while, debating whether he should tell Ruth; but he decided not to do it until it was absolutely necessary. He didn't want to distress her until the last possible moment.

Finally he took out Binder's list and wrote down a number of Berne addresses. Then he filled his pockets with soap, shoelaces, safety pins and bottles of toilet water and went downstairs.

There he met the proprietor. "Do you know a man named Richard Binding?" he asked.

The proprietor pondered for a while, then he shook his head.

"I mean a man who was here yesterday evening. He asked for a room."

"No one asked for a room yesterday evening. I wasn't even here. I was bowling until twelve."

"Is that so? Did you have any free rooms?"

"Yes, three of them. They're still free for that matter. Were you expecting someone? You can have Number Seven on your corridor."

"No. I don't believe the man I was expecting will come back. He's probably already on his way to Zürich."

By noon Kern had earned three francs. He went into a cheap restaurant to get some bread and butter. Afterward he planned to go on peddling at once.

He stood at the counter and ate hungrily. Suddenly he almost dropped the bread. He had recognized Binding at one of the farthest tables.

He stuffed the rest of the bread into his mouth, swallowed it down and walked slowly to the table. Binding was sitting there alone, his elbows propped on the table. In front of him was a large dish of pork chops with red cabbage and potatoes which he was engrossed in eating.

He did not look up until Kern was right in front of him. "Look who's here!" he said casually. "How's tricks?"

"There are forty francs missing from my wallet," Kern said.

"That's a shame," Binding replied, swallowing a great mouthful of chop, "that certainly is a shame."

"Give me what you have left and we'll call the matter closed."

Binding took a swallow of beer and wiped his mouth. "The matter is closed as it is," he declared good-naturedly. "Or perhaps you thought there was something you could do about it?"

Kern stared at him. In his rage he had not yet realized that there was actually nothing he could do. If he went to the police, they would ask for his papers and then he himself would be locked up and subsequently deported.

He measured Binding through narrowed eyes. "Not a chance," the latter said. "I'm a very good boxer. Forty pounds heavier than you. Besides a row in a public place means the police and deportation."

At the moment Kern wouldn't have cared much what happened to him, but he had to think of Ruth. Binding was right: there was not the ghost of a chance for him to do anything. "Do you do this sort of thing often?" he asked.

"It's the way I live. And as you see I live well."

Kern almost choked with impotent bitterness. "At least give me back twenty francs," he said in a hoarse voice. "I need the money. Not for myself. For someone else to whom it belongs."

Binding shook his head. "I need the money myself. You got off cheap. For a measly forty francs you learned the greatest lesson of all — not to be trusting."

"Right." Kern stared at him. He wanted to leave but he simply couldn't. "All your papers — of course they are fakes too?"

"Just imagine," Binding replied, "they aren't at all. I was in a concentration camp." He laughed. "For theft, to be sure, from a district Party leader. A most unusual case!"

He reached for the last chop on the plate. The next

moment Kern had it in his hand. "Go ahead, make a fuss," he said.

Binding grinned. "I wouldn't think of it. I've had about all I want anyway. Have them bring you a plate and take some of the cabbage. I'm even ready to treat you to a glass of beer."

Kern made no reply. He was ready to kick himself for the thing that had happened. Quickly he turned around and walked away with the snatched chop still in his hand. At the counter he asked for a piece of paper to wrap it in. The girl behind the counter looked at him curiously. Then she fished two pickles out of a jar. "Here," she said, "take these too."

Kern accepted the pickles. "Thank you," he said, "thank you very much." Supper for Ruth, he thought. Hell and damnation, at a cost of forty francs!

At the door he turned around once more. Binding was watching him. Kern spat. Binding smilingly saluted with two fingers of his right hand.

*   *   *

Beyond Berne it began to rain. Ruth and Kern had not enough money left to take a train to the next large town. They had, to be sure, a small final reserve, but they did not want to touch this until they reached France. A car that was going their way gave them a lift for about fifty kilometers. After that they had to walk. Kern seldom took the risk of selling anything in the small towns. It made them too conspicuous. They would never spend more than one night in the same place. They would arrive late in the evening when the police stations were closed and would leave in the morning before they had opened again.

Thus they were always away from the place at the time when the report form should be handed in to the authorities. Binder's list failed them for this part of Switzerland; it mentioned only the larger towns.

Near Murten they slept in an empty barn. That night there was a cloudburst. The roof was in bad repair, and when they woke up they were drenched to the skin. They tried to dry their things, but they could not make a fire. Everything was wet and they had great difficulty in finding a spot where the rain had not come through. They went to sleep pressed close together to keep each other warm, but their coats which they used for covers were too wet — the cold woke them up again. So they waited for the first light of morning and then started on their way.

"Walking will warm us up," Kern said. "And in an hour we'll probably be able to get some coffee somewhere or other."

Ruth nodded. "Perhaps the sun will come out. Then we'll dry out fast."

But it remained cold and cloudy all day. Rain squalls drove across the fields. It was the first really cold day of the month; the clouds hung ragged and low, and during the afternoon there was a second heavy storm. Ruth and Kern took refuge in a small chapel. It was very dark, and after a while there was thunder, and flashes of lightning gleamed through the stained glass windows on which saints in blue and gold were holding scrolls in their hands describing the peace of heaven and of the soul.

Kern felt Ruth shivering. "Are you very cold?" he asked.

"No, not very."

"Come, it's better for us to walk around a little. I'm afraid you'll catch cold."

"I won't catch cold. Just let me sit this way for a little while."

"Are you tired?"

"No. I just want to sit here for a moment more."

"Wouldn't it be better for you to walk around? Just for a few minutes. It's not good for you to sit still in wet clothes for so long. This stone floor is too cold."

"All right."

They walked slowly around the chapel, their footsteps echoing in the empty space. They walked past the confessional boxes whose green curtains bellied out in the draught, around the altar into the sacristy and back.

"It's still nine kilometers to Murten," Kern said. "We'll have to try to find a place to stay nearer than that."

"We can manage nine kilometers all right."

Kern muttered something to himself.

"What are you saying?" Ruth asked.

"Nothing. I was just cursing a certain Binding."

She pushed her hand through his arm. "Forget about it. That's the simplest thing to do. What's more, I think it's going to stop raining."

They went outside. Drops were still falling, but above the mountains hung a gigantic rainbow. It spanned the entire valley like a many-colored bridge. Beyond the forest, between torn clouds, a burst of yellow-white light flooded the landscape. They could not see the sun; they only saw the light which streamed forth like a luminous mist.

"Come," Ruth said, "it's going to be better now."

That evening they came to a sheepfold. The shepherd, a taciturn middle-aged farmer, was sitting in front of the door. Two sheep dogs were lying beside him. They dashed out barking as the two approached. The farmer took his pipe out of his mouth and whistled them back.

Kern went up to him. "Could we sleep here for the night? We're wet and tired and can't go any farther."

The man looked at him for some time. "There's a hayloft up there," he said finally.

"That's all we need."

The man looked at him again for a time. "Give me your matches and your cigarettes," he said finally. "There's a lot of hay there."

Kern handed them over. "You'll have to climb up the ladder inside," the shepherd explained. "I'll lock the fold behind you. I live in the town. Tomorrow morning early I'll let you out."

"Thanks. Thanks very much."

They climbed up the ladder. It was dusky and warm up there. After a while the shepherd appeared, bringing them grapes and some cheese and black bread. "Now I'm going to lock up," he said. "Good night."

"Good night and many thanks."

They listened as he climbed down the ladder. Then they took off their wet things and lay down on the hay. They got their night clothes out of their bags and then began to eat. They were very hungry.

"How does it taste?" Kern asked.

"Wonderful." Ruth leaned against him.

"We're lucky, aren't we?"

She nodded.

Below them the shepherd was locking up. The hayloft had a round window. They crouched beside it and watched the shepherd walk away. The sky had cleared and was reflected in the lake. The shepherd walked slowly across the mowed fields with the thoughtful strides of a man who spends his days close to nature. There was no one else in sight. He walked in solitude across the fields and it seemed as though he were carrying the whole sky on his dark shoulders.

They sat at the window until that colorless hour before nightfall when the light makes all things gray. Behind them in the play of shadows the hay grew to a fantastic mountain range. Its smell mixed with the smell of peat and whisky that rose from the sheep. They could see them through the holes in the floor, a confused mass of woolly backs, and they could hear the thousand little sounds that gradually grew quieter and quieter.

Next morning the shepherd came and opened the sheep-fold. Kern went down. Ruth was still asleep. Her face was flushed and her breathing was rapid. Kern helped the shepherd unbar the fold and drive out the sheep.

"Would you let us stay here one more day?" he asked. "We'd be glad to help you in return if that's all right with you."

"There's not much you can do to help. But you're welcome to stay here if you like."

"Thanks."

Kern inquired about the addresses of Germans living in the town. The place was not included in Binder's list. The shepherd mentioned a few people and told him where they lived.

Kern started off in the afternoon when it was beginning to get dark. He found the first house without difficulty. It was a small white villa surrounded by a little garden. A tidy housemaid opened the door. She admitted him at once to a small reception room instead of making him stand out-side. A good sign, Kern thought. "May I speak to Herr Ammers or to Frau Ammers?" he asked.

"Just a minute."

The maid disappeared and presently returned. She led him into a living room, furnished in modern mahogany. The floor was so highly polished he almost lost his foot-ing. There were antimacassars on all the furniture. After a minute Herr Ammers appeared. He was a little man with a pointed white beard and a friendly manner. Kern de-cided to tell his true story.

Ammers listened sympathetically. "So you're an exile and have no passport or residential permit?" he said. "And you have soap and household things to sell?"

"Yes."

"I see." Herr Ammers got up. "My wife can take a look at your things."

He went out. After a little while his wife entered. She was a faded, sexless creature, with a face the color of over-cooked meat and pale, haddock eyes.

"What sort of things have you there?" she asked in a simpering voice.

Kern unpacked his wares, of which there were not very many left. The woman fussed over her selection, she looked at the sewing needles as though she had never seen anything of the sort before, she smelled the soap and tested the toothbrushes on her thumb, she asked about prices and finally decided to consult her sister.

The sister was an exact duplicate. Small though he was, the bearded Ammers must have ruled the house with an iron hand, for the sister, too, was completely subdued and had a quavering, frightened voice. At every other instant the two women glanced at the door. They dallied and hesitated until Kern finally began to lose patience and started to pack up his things. "Perhaps you'll think it over until morning," he said, for he saw that even now they could not make up their minds.

The wife looked at him in alarm. "Perhaps you'd like a cup of coffee?" she said.

Kern had not had any coffee in a long time. "If you have some made," he said.

"Yes, yes indeed. Just one minute."

She lumbered out, as awkward as a lopsided keg, but quickly nevertheless. The sister stayed in the room.

"A cup of coffee will taste fine," Kern said to make conversation.

The sister emitted a strangled laugh like a turkey gobbler and then was suddenly silent as though she had swallowed the wrong way. Kern looked at her in amazement. She bobbed her head and made a shrill piping sound through her nose.

The wife came in and put a steaming cup on the table in front of Kern. "Take your time drinking it," she said considerately. "There's no hurry and the coffee is very hot."

The sister gave a sudden brief laugh and then ducked her head nervously.

Kern never got to drink his coffee. The door opened and Ammers came in with short, springy steps, followed by a disgruntled-looking policeman.

With a pontifical gesture Ammers pointed at Kern. "Officer, do your duty. Here is an individual without a country and without a passport — banished from the German Reich!"

Kern stiffened. The officer looked at him. "Come with me," he growled.

For a moment Kern had the feeling that his brain had stopped working. He had anticipated everything but this. Slowly and mechanically, as though in a slow motion picture, he got his things together. Then he straightened up. "So that was the reason for your kindness and for the coffee," he said awkwardly and with difficulty, as though he must at all costs make himself clear, "just to keep me here." He clenched his fists and took a step towards Ammers, who recoiled. "Don't be afraid," Kern said softly, "I'm not going to touch you. I'll just curse you. I curse you and your children and your wife with the whole strength of my soul. May all the unhappiness in the world fall on you! May your children revolt against you and leave you alone in poverty, sickness and misery!"

Ammers turned pale. His beard trembled. "Protect me," he ordered the policeman.

"He hasn't injured you yet," the officer said phlegmatically. "Up to now he's only cursed you. If, for example, he had called you a dirty informer that might perhaps have been an injury — principally on account of the word dirty."

Ammers looked at him in a rage. "Do your duty!" he snapped.

"Herr Ammers," the officer announced calmly, "it's not your place to give me orders. Only my superiors can do that. You have denounced a man and I have come. You may leave the rest to me." He turned to Kern. "Follow me."

The two went out. Behind them the door was slammed shut. Kern walked silently beside the official. He still could not get his thoughts in order. Somewhere inside him an indistinct voice said *Ruth* — but he simply did not dare think further.

"My boy," said the policeman after a while, "sometimes

sheep go to call on hyenas. Don't you know who he is? He's the local spy of the German Nazi Party, and he has already denounced all sorts of people."

"My God!" Kern said.

"Yes," replied the officer, "that's what you call a prize boner."

Kern was silent. "I don't know — " he said dully after a moment. "All I know is there's a sick person waiting for me."

The policeman looked down the street and shrugged his shoulders. "That doesn't help a bit. And it has nothing to do with me. I've got to take you to the police station." He looked around. The street was empty. "I can't advise you to run for it," he went on. "There's no point. Of course I have a game leg and couldn't run after you, but I would shout at you and then if you didn't stop I'd draw my revolver." He looked Kern up and down for a couple of seconds. "Naturally that would take some time," he explained. "You might even get away from me, particularly at a place we're just coming to, where there are all sorts of alleys and corners and where shooting is out of the question. If you were to escape, I couldn't really do anything. Unless I had put you in handcuffs first."

Suddenly Kern was wide awake and filled with an unreasoning hope. He stared at the officer.

The officer walked on indifferently. "Do you know," he said thoughtfully after a pause, "sometimes people are too decent for their own good."

Kern felt his hands wet with excitement. "Listen," he said, "there's a person waiting for me who is helpless without me. Let me go. We are on our way to France. We want to get out of Switzerland. It won't make any difference one way or the other."

"I can't do that," the officer replied phlegmatically. "It's against the service regulations. I must take you to the police station. That's my duty. Of course if you were to escape from me there would naturally be nothing I could do about it." He stopped. "For example, if you were to run down that street, turn the corner and keep to the left — you'd be off before I could shoot." He glanced at Kern impatiently. "Well then, I'll just put you in handcuffs. Damnation, where did I put the things?"

He turned halfway round and began a thorough search of his pockets. "Thanks," Kern said and ran.

At the corner he took a quick look back. The officer was standing there, both hands on his hips, grinning after him.

* * *

Kern awoke and listened to Ruth's quick, shallow breathing. He felt her forehead; it was hot and damp. She was sleeping deeply but restlessly and he did not want to wake her. The smell of the hay was overpowering, although they had spread blankets and bed covers on top of it. After a while she awoke of her own accord and in a plaintive, childish voice asked for water. Kern brought her the pail and a cup and she drank thirstily.

"Are you hot?"

"Yes, very. But perhaps it's only the hay. My throat is parched."

"I hope you haven't a fever."

"I mustn't have a fever. I mustn't get sick. I'm not sick either. I won't be sick."

She turned over and pushed her head under his arm and went to sleep again.

Kern lay still. He wished he had a light to see how Ruth looked. He recognized from the damp heat of her face that she was feverish. But he had no flashlight. So he lay still, listening to her quick short breathing and watching the infinitely slow progress of the hand around the illuminated dial of his watch, which gleamed through the darkness like some pale and distant diabolical engine of time. Beneath them the sheep jostled each other, grunting from time to time, and it seemed to take years for the circle of the window to grow brighter, announcing the day.

Ruth awoke. "Give me some water, Ludwig."

Kern handed her the cup. "You have a fever, Ruth. Will you be all right alone for an hour?"

"Yes."

"I'm just going to run down to the village and get some medicine."

The shepherd came and opened the sheepfold. When Kern told him what had happened he made a wry face. "She must go to a hospital. She can't stay here."

"We'll see if she isn't better by noon."

Despite his fear of meeting the policeman or a member of the Ammers family, Kern ran to the drugstore and begged the druggist to lend him a thermometer. The assistant let him have one after he had put up money as a deposit. Kern bought a bottle of arcanol and ran back.

Ruth's temperature was 101.5. She took two tablets and Kern wrapped his jacket and her coat around her where she lay in the hay. By noon, despite the medicine, her temperature had risen to 102 degrees.

The shepherd scratched his head. "She needs nursing. If I were in your place I'd take her to the hospital."

"I won't go to the hospital," Ruth whispered hoarsely. "Tomorrow I'll be well again."

"It doesn't look like it to me," said the shepherd. "She ought to be in bed in a room and not here in a hayloft."

"No, it's warm and nice here. Please let me lie here."

The shepherd climbed down the ladder and Kern followed. "Why doesn't she want to leave?" the shepherd asked.

"Because then we'd be separated."

"That doesn't matter. You could wait for her."

"That's just what I couldn't do. If she's admitted to a hospital they will find out she hasn't a passport. Perhaps they might keep her there, although we haven't enough money; but afterwards the police would take her to the border and I wouldn't know where or when."

The shepherd shook his head. "And you haven't done anything? You haven't committed any crime?"

"We haven't passports and can't get them, that's all."

"That's not what I mean. You haven't stolen something somewhere, or swindled someone or anything like that?"

"No."

"And nevertheless they chase you as though they had a warrant for your arrest?"

"Yes."

The shepherd spat. "Perhaps someone can understand that. A simple fellow like me can't."

"I understand it," Kern said.

"You know, that might be a case of inflammation of the lungs, up there."

"Inflammation of the lungs?" Kern looked at him in terror. "Why that isn't possible! That might be fatal."

"Of course," said the shepherd. "That's why I'm arguing with you."

"I'm sure it's grippe."

"She has fever, high fever. And what it really is only a doctor can say."

"Then I'll get a doctor."

"Bring one here?"

"Perhaps I can get one to come. I'll see whether there's a Jewish doctor in the directory."

Kern went back to the village. In a tobacco store he bought two cigarettes and asked for the telephone book. He found the name of Dr. Rudolf Beer and went to him.

The consultation hour was over when he arrived and he had to wait for more than an hour. He occupied himself looking at papers and magazines; he stared at the pictures in them, unable to understand how there could still be tennis matches and receptions and half-naked women in Florida and happy people, while he sat there helpless and Ruth was sick.

Finally the doctor arrived. He was a young man and he listened to Kern in silence. Then he put some things in a bag and picked up his hat. "Come along. My car's downstairs. We'll drive out."

Kern gulped. "Couldn't we walk? It costs more in a car. And we have very little money."

"Let me worry about that," Beer replied.

They drove to the sheepfold and the doctor examined Ruth. She looked anxiously at Kern and silently shook her head. She did not want to leave.

Beer stood up. "She must go to the hospital. Congestion of the right lung. Grippe, and the danger of pneumonia. I will take her with me."

"No, I won't go to the hospital. We can't pay for it either."

"Don't concern yourself about the money. You have to leave here. You're seriously ill."

Ruth looked at Kern. "We'll talk it over," he said. "I'll come right away."

"I'll come to get you in half an hour," the doctor announced. "Have you warm clothes and blankets?"

"We have only this."

"I'll bring some things with me. See you in half an hour."

"Is it absolutely necessary?" Kern asked.

"Yes. She can't stay here lying on the hay. And there's no point either in putting her in a room. She belongs in a hospital — right away too."

"All right," Kern said. "Then I'll have to tell you what that means for us."

Beer listened to him. "You don't believe, then, that you'll be able to visit her?" he asked.

"No. In a couple of days word would get about and all the police would have to do would be to wait for me. But this way I have a chance of staying near her and of hearing from you how she is getting on and what is happening to her, and so of making my plans accordingly."

"I understand. You can come to me to inquire at any time."

"Thank you. Is her condition dangerous?"

"It might become dangerous. It's absolutely necessary for her to leave here."

The doctor drove off. Kern climbed slowly up the ladder to the loft. He had lost all power of feeling. The white face, with dark shadows where the eyes were, turned toward him out of the twilight of the low room. "I know what you're going to say," Ruth whispered.

Kern nodded. "There's nothing else to do. We must be thankful that we have found this doctor. I'm sure you are going to get into the hospital for nothing."

"Yes." She stared straight ahead. Then she suddenly sat bolt upright in panic. "My God, where will you stay when I'm in the hospital? And how shall we meet again? You can't come there, perhaps they'd arrest you."

He sat down beside her and took her hot hands comfortingly in his. "Ruth," he said. "This is a time for us to be very clear-headed and reasonable. I have thought it all over. I shall stay here in hiding. The shepherd has told me that I may. I shall simply wait for you. It's better for me not to go to the hospital to visit you. That would be talked about and they might grab me. But there's something else we can do. I'll come to the hospital every evening and look up at your window. The doctor will tell me where you are. That will be like a visit."

"At what time?"

"Nine o'clock."

"It's dark then and I won't be able to see you."

"I can only come when it's dark; otherwise it would be too dangerous. I mustn't let myself be seen during the day."

"You mustn't come at all. Just leave me; everything will be all right."

"I will come. I couldn't stand it otherwise. Now you must get dressed."

He moistened his handkerchief with water from the tin pail and washed and dried her face. Her lips were parched and hot. She laid her face on his hand. "Ruth," he said, "we must think things out. When you get well, if I'm not here any more, or if they deport you — make them send you to Geneva on the border. We'll agree to write each other care of General Delivery in Geneva. In that way we can be sure of meeting again. We'll write to each other care of General Delivery, Main Post Office, Geneva. And we'll give the doctor our addresses too, in case I'm arrested.

Then he can always see that each gets the other's. He has promised me to do it. I'll hear all about you through him and he'll give you the news about me. That way we can be quite sure of not losing each other."

"Yes," she whispered.

"Don't be worried, Ruth. I'm saying this only if worse comes to worst. This is only in case they catch me. Or in case they don't just let you go from the hospital. I really think they'll let you out without telling the police anything, and then we'll just start on together."

"And if they do find out?"

"All they can do is send you to the border. And I'll be waiting for you in Geneva at the Main Post Office."

He looked at her encouragingly. "Here is some money for you. Hide it, for you may need it for the trip."

He gave her what little money he had left. "Don't let them know at the hospital that you have it. You must keep it for the time afterward."

The doctor called to them from below. "Ruth," Kern said, and took her in his arms, "will you be brave, Ruth?"

She clung to him. "I will be brave. And I'll see you again."

"General Delivery in Geneva, if anything goes wrong. Otherwise I'll wait for you here. Every evening at nine o'clock I'll be standing outside and wishing you the best."

"I'll come to the window."

"You must stay in bed. Otherwise I won't come. Laugh just once now."

"Ready?" shouted the doctor.

She smiled through her tears. "Don't forget me."

"How could I? You're all I have."

He kissed her parched lips. The doctor's head appeared

through the opening in the floor. "All right," he said, "but now let's go."

They helped Ruth down and into the car and tucked her in. "Can I come to inquire this evening?" Kern asked.

"Of course. Are you going to stay here now? Yes, it's better. You can come to see me any time."

The car drove off. Kern remained where he was until he could no longer see it. He stood motionless, but he felt as though a great wind were pushing him backward.

At eight o'clock he went to Dr. Beer's. The physician was at home and reassured him; Ruth's temperature was high but at the moment there was no grave danger. It seemed to be an ordinary case of inflammation of the lungs.

"How long will it last?"

"If things go well, two weeks. And then a week of convalescence."

"How about money?" Kern asked. "We haven't any."

Beer laughed. "For the present she's in the hospital. Later on some charity will probably pay the expenses."

Kern looked at him. "And your fee?"

Beer laughed again. "Keep your couple of francs. I can live without them. You can come again tomorrow to inquire about her." He got up.

"Which room is she in?" Kern asked. "Which floor?"

Beer laid a bony index finger against his nose. "Wait a minute — Number 35, on the second floor."

"Which window is that?"

Beer blinked. "The second from the right I think; it won't do any good, though, she'll be asleep."

"That wasn't what I meant."

"Of course not," Beer replied.

Kern inquired the way to the hospital. He found it easily and looked at his watch. It was quarter of nine. The second window from the right was dark. He waited. He would never have believed that nine o'clock could come so slowly, but suddenly he saw a light go on in the window. He stood, tense in every muscle, watching the luminous rectangle. Once he had read somewhere about thought transference and now he tried to concentrate in order to send strength to Ruth. "Let her get well. Let her get well," he thought urgently and did not know to whom he was praying. He took a deep breath and exhaled it slowly, for he remembered that breathing played an important part in the book he had read. He clenched his fists and tensed his muscles, he rose on tiptoe as though about to spring from the ground, and he whispered again and again, up toward the square of light: "Get well! Get well! I love you!"

The light went out and he saw a shadow. She must stay in bed, he thought, suddenly filled with joy. She waved; he waved back wildly. Then he remembered that she could not see him. Desperately he looked around for a street light, for any light at all before which he could stand. There was none to be seen. Then an inspiration came. He pulled out of his pocket the package of matches he had got that morning with his two cigarettes, struck one of them and held it above his head.

The shadow waved. He waved back cautiously with the match. Then he tore out two more and held them so they lighted his face. Ruth waved eagerly. He signaled her to go back to bed. She shook her head. He held the light near his face and nodded emphatically. She did not understand him. He saw that he would have to go away to make her return to bed. He took a few steps to show her he was going. Then he threw all the burning matches high in the air. They fell flickering to the ground and went out. Kern went to the next corner and then turned around. The light continued to burn for an instant, then went out. And the window seemed darker than all the others.

* * *

"Congratulations, Goldbach," Steiner said. "For the first time today you were really good. Calm and confident and no mistakes. It was first-rate, the way you gave me the tip about the watch hidden in that woman's brassière. That was really hard."

Goldbach looked at him gratefully. "I don't know myself how it happened. It came suddenly like a revelation between yesterday and today. You just watch, I'm going to become a good assistant. I'll start tomorrow to think up new tricks."

Steiner laughed. "Come on, we'll have a drink to this happy occasion." He got out a bottle of apricot brandy and poured drinks. "*Prosit*, Goldbach!"

"*Prosit!*" Goldbach choked over his drink and put the glass down. "Excuse me," he said. "I'm not used to it any more. If you don't mind I'd like to go now."

"Sure. We're through for the day. But aren't you going to finish your drink?"

"Yes, thank you." Goldbach drank obediently.

Steiner shook hands with him. "And don't practise too many tricks. Otherwise I'll get lost among your subtleties."

"No, no."

Goldbach strode quickly down the boulevard to the city. He felt as light as though a heavy burden had fallen from his shoulders. But it was a lightness without joy — as though his bones were full of air and his will was a vapor which he could not control and which was at the mercy of every passing breeze.

"Is my wife in?" he asked the maid at the door.

"No," she replied and laughed.

"Why are you laughing?"

"Why shouldn't I laugh? Is there a law against laughing?"

Goldbach looked at her abstractedly. "I didn't mean that," he muttered. "Go ahead and laugh."

He walked along the narrow corridor to his room and listened through the partition. He heard nothing. Carefully he brushed his hair and his suit; then he knocked at the communicating door, despite the fact that the maid had said his wife was not there. Perhaps she's come in meanwhile, he thought. Perhaps the maid didn't see her. He knocked again. There was no reply. Cautiously he raised the latch and went in. The light on the dressing table was burning. He stared at it like a sailor watching a beacon. She'll be back right away, he told himself, otherwise the light wouldn't be on.

He already knew, somewhere in the emptiness of his bones, in the gray, scattered ashes in his veins, that she would not come back. He knew it below the level of his thought, but with the obstinacy of fear his mind held fast, as though to a projecting timber that would save him from the flood, to the meaningless words: She will certainly come back — otherwise the light would not be burning . . .

Then he discovered the emptiness of the room. The brushes and jars of cold cream were gone from in front of the mirror; the door of the closet was half-open, revealing that the rose and pastel-colored dresses were missing; the closet yawned black and abandoned. Only her scent was still in the room, a breath of life, but already fainter — memory and pain lying in wait. Then he found the letter and wondered dully why he had missed it for so long — it was lying in the middle of the table.

It was some time before he opened it. He knew everything anyway — why should he open it? Finally he slit the envelope with a forgotten hairpin that he found lying beside him on the chair. He read the letter but the words could not penetrate the sheath of ice around his brain; they remained dead, words out of a newspaper or book, accidental words that had no connection with him. The hairpin in his hand had more life.

He sat there quietly waiting for the pain and surprised that it did not come. There was only a dead feeling, an immense let-down, like the anxious moment before falling asleep when he had taken too much bromide.

He sat thus for a long time, staring at his hands which lay on his knees like dead white animals, like pale insentient sea-monsters with five flaccid tentacles. They were no longer his. No part of him was any longer his; he was a strange body with eyes turned inward, scrutinizing a paralysis that showed no sign of life but an occasional quiver.

Finally he got up and went back to his own room. He saw the ties lying on the table. Mechanically he got out a pair of scissors and began to cut the ties into pieces methodically, strip by strip. He did not let the fragments fall to the floor but pedantically gathered them up in the hollow of his hand and arranged them on the table in multicolored piles. In the midst of this automatic activity he suddenly realized what he was doing; he laid aside the scissors and stopped. But he forgot immediately what he had done. He walked stiffly across the room and sat down in a corner. He remained crouching there, continually rubbing his hands with a strangely weary, old man's gesture, as though he were cold and no longer possessed the vitality to warm himself.

Chapter Fourteen

JUST as Kern was throwing the last of his matches into the air a hand fell on his shoulder. "What's going on here?"

He jumped and, turning, saw a uniform. "Nothing," he stammered. "Excuse me. It's just a foolish game, nothing more."

The officer scrutinized him carefully. It was not the same one who had arrested him at Ammers' house. Kern looked anxiously up at the window. Ruth was no longer to be seen. Possibly she had not noticed anything; it was so dark. "I really beg your pardon," he said lightly, attempting a carefree smile. "It was just a sort of joke. You can see for yourself no harm could come from it. Just a few matches, that was all. I was trying to light a cigarette. It wouldn't burn properly, so I took a half-dozen matches at once and very nearly burned my fingers."

He laughed, waved his hand, and started to go on. But the officer kept hold of him. "Just a minute. You're not Swiss, are you?"

"Why do you think that?"

"I can tell by the way you talk. Why are you lying?"

"I'm not lying at all," Kern replied. "I was just interested in how you knew right away."

The officer looked at him suspiciously. "Perhaps we ought — " he murmured and turned on his flashlight. "Listen," he said suddenly, and his voice had a different ring, "do you know Herr Ammers?"

"Never heard of him," Kern replied as calmly as he could.

"Where do you live?"

"I only got here this morning. I was just going to look for an inn. Could you recommend one? One that's not too expensive."

"First of all come with me. There's a formal complaint by Herr Ammers that fits you exactly. We'll begin by looking into that."

Kern went along. He cursed himself for not having been more alert. The officer must have stolen up behind him on rubber soles. For a week everything had gone well and probably that was the trouble. He had got to feeling too safe. Surreptitiously he glanced about for a chance to run away, but the way was too short; a few minutes later they were at the police station.

The officer who had let him escape the first time was sitting at a table writing. Kern felt encouraged. "Is this the man?" asked the officer who had brought him in.

The first officer gave Kern a quick glance. "Might be. I can't say for sure. It was too dark."

"Then I'll call up Ammers. He'll know him."

He went out. "My boy," said the first officer, "I thought you were gone long ago. Now things are going to be tough. Ammers lodged a complaint."

"Can't I run away again?" Kern asked quickly. "You know that — "

"Out of the question. The only way is through the anteroom over there and that's where your friend's standing telephoning. No — you're up a creek now. And you tumbled into the hands of the sharpest man on our force, a fellow who's after promotion."

"Damnation!"

"Yes. Particularly since you ran away once. I had to make a report of that at the time because I knew Ammers would be snooping around."

"Jesus!" Kern said, taking a step backward.

"You might even say Jesus Christ," the officer remarked. "It won't help you this time. You'll get a couple of weeks."

A few minutes later Ammers came in. He had run so fast that he was panting. His pointed beard glistened. "Of course," he said, "that's the man! As big as life, the impudent scoundrel!"

Kern looked at him.

"This is one time he won't slip through your fingers, eh?" Ammers asked.

"No, this time he won't," the policeman agreed.

"The mills of the gods grind slow," Ammers declaimed unctuously, "but they grind exceeding fine. The jug that goes too often to the well will be broken."

"Do you know you have cancer of the liver?" Kern interrupted him. He hardly knew what he was saying or how he had hit upon the idea. He was suddenly raging mad, and without fully realizing his misfortune he concentrated all his thoughts automatically on a single point, to hurt Ammers in some way. He could not strike him, for that would increase his sentence.

"What?" In his amazement Ammers forgot to shut his mouth.

"Cancer of the liver; a typical case." Kern saw that his blow had struck home. Immediately he followed it up. "In a year the intolerable pain will set in. You will have a frightful death! Nothing to be done about it either! Nothing!"

"Why, that — "

"The mills of the gods . . ." Kern hissed. "What did you say? Slow, very slow!"

"Officer," Ammers chattered, "I demand that you protect me from this individual."

"Draw up your will," Kern snapped. "It's the one thing left for you to do. You'll be eaten out and rotted from the inside!"

"Officer!" Ammers looked around wildly seeking help. "It's your duty to defend me from these insults."

The first officer looked at him curiously. "So far he hasn't insulted you," he announced, "up to now he's just made a medical diagnosis."

"I demand that it be put on record," Ammers screamed.

"Just look." Kern pointed his finger at Ammers, who shrank back as though it were a snake. "The leaden-gray color of the skin during excitement, the yellowish eyeballs — unmistakable symptoms. A candidate for death! All you can do for him is to pray."

"Candidate for death," bawled Ammers, "put candidate for death in the record."

"Candidate for death is not an insult either," explained the first officer with visible enjoyment. "You won't be able to make a complaint stick on that ground. We're all candidates for death."

"The liver rots inside your living body!" Kern saw that Ammers had suddenly grown pale. He took a step forward. Ammers drew back as though fleeing Satan. "At first you don't notice anything," Kern explained in triumphant rage. "There is hardly enough to make a diagnosis. But when you notice it it's already too late. Cancer of the liver! The slowest and most dreadful death there is!"

Ammers could only stare at Kern. He made no reply.

Involuntarily he pressed his hand in the region of his liver.

"Now you be quiet!" snarled the second officer with sudden severity. "There's been enough of this! Take a seat over there and answer our questions. How long have you been in Switzerland?"

Kern was arraigned next morning before the District Court. The judge was a stout middle-aged man with a round red face. He was humane, but he could not help Kern. The law was clear.

"Why didn't you report to the police after illegally crossing the border?" he asked.

"Then I'd have been put straight out of the country again," Kern answered wearily.

"Yes, of course you would."

"And on the other side I'd have had to report to the nearest police station at once if I didn't want to break the law there. Then the next night they'd have brought me back to Switzerland. And from Switzerland back to the same place again. Then back to Switzerland. I'd have slowly starved to death between the customs houses, and if I hadn't, I'd have wandered forever from one police station to the other. What is there for us to do except break the laws?"

The judge shrugged. "I cannot help you. It is my duty to sentence you. The minimum punishment is fourteen days in prison. That is the law. We have it to protect our country from being flooded with refugees."

"I know."

The judge glanced at his notes. "All that I can do is to make a recommendation in your behalf to the Superior

Court that you be given detention and not a prison sentence."

"Many thanks," Kern said. "But it's all one to me. I have no pride left."

"It is not all one by any means," the judge explained with some vehemence. "On the contrary it is of great importance for full civil rights. If you are simply placed in detention then you will have no prison record. Perhaps that's something you hadn't thought about."

Kern looked for a while at the good-natured, unsuspecting man. "Full civil rights . . ." he said then. "What would I do with them? Why I haven't even the commonest civil rights. I am a shadow, a ghost, a dead man in the eyes of society. What have I to do with what you call full civil rights?"

The judge was silent for a while. "But you'll have to get papers of some sort," he said finally. "Perhaps an application could be made through a German consulate for identification papers."

"That was done a year ago by a Czechoslovakian court. The application was denied. We no longer exist so far as Germany is concerned. And for the rest of the world only as prey for the police."

The judge shook his head. "Hasn't the League of Nations done anything for you yet? After all there are many thousands of you; and you have to be allowed to exist somehow!"

"The League of Nations has spent a couple of years debating whether to give us identification papers," Kern replied patiently. "Each country represented there is trying to dump us on some other country. And so in all probability it will go on for a number of years."

"And meanwhile — "

"Meanwhile — you can see for yourself!"

"But, my God!" the judge said suddenly and helplessly in his soft, broad Swiss dialect. "Why, that's a terrific problem! What's to become of all of you?"

"I don't know. The more important thing is: What's to happen to me now?"

The judge ran his hand over his glistening face and looked at Kern. "I have a son," he said, "who is just about as old as you. If I were to picture him being hunted from place to place for no other reason than that he had been born — "

"I have a father," Kern replied. "If you were to see him . . ."

He glanced out the window. The autumn sun was shining peacefully on an apple tree in full fruit. Out there was freedom. Out there was Ruth.

"I should like to ask you a question," the judge said after a while. "It has no bearing on your case. But I should like to ask it nevertheless. Do you still believe in anything at all?"

"Oh, yes. I believe in holy egoism! In heartlessness! In lies! In hardness of heart!"

"That's what I feared. But what else could one expect?"

"That isn't all," Kern replied calmly. "I also believe in kindness and comradeship, in love and helpfulness. I have run into them more often perhaps than many people who have had an easy time."

The judge got up and moved heavily around his chair to face Kern. "It's good to hear that," he murmured. "If I only knew what I could do for you!"

"Nothing," Kern said. "By this time I know something about the laws, too, and I have a friend who's a specialist. Send me to jail."

"I will hold you for examination and send your case to the higher court."

"If it's going to lighten the sentence, fine. But if it's going to take longer, I'd rather go to jail."

"It won't take longer. I'll see to that."

The judge took a huge wallet out of his pocket. "There is only this simple form of help," he said uncertainly, taking out a folded bill. "It distresses me that I can do nothing more for you."

Kern took the money. "It's the only thing that really helps us," he replied, and thought: *Twenty francs! What luck! That will be enough to get Ruth to the border.*

Kern did not dare to write to her. It might have resulted in their finding out that she had been in the country for some time and then she might be arrested. As it was, she would probably just be asked to leave the country, or if luck was with her she might simply be released from the hospital.

The first evening he was unhappy and restless and could not sleep. He saw Ruth lying feverish on her bed and woke up because he dreamed she was being buried. He crouched on the plank bed and remained for a long time with his arms wrapped around his knees. He was determined not to let this panic get the upper hand, but at the same time he felt that it might be stronger than he was. It's the night, he thought, the night and the night fears. Daylight fears have a reasonable basis, but night fears are limitless.

He got up and walked back and forth in the little cell. He took long deep breaths, then he took off his coat and began to exercise. I mustn't lose control of my nerves, he thought, otherwise I'm licked. I must stay well. He began a series of bending and twisting exercises and gradually succeeded in concentrating his attention on his body. Then came the memory of the evening at the police station in Vienna and the student who had given him boxing lessons. He smiled wryly. If it hadn't been for him, he thought, I wouldn't have behaved toward Ammers as I did today. If it hadn't been for him and if it hadn't been for Steiner . . . If it hadn't been for this whole tough life. I want it to make me tough, too, but not to knock me out. I'll defend myself. He began to strike out with his fists, moving lightly on his feet; he threw a long right into the darkness with the whole weight of his body behind it, right, left, a couple of quick uppercuts, and suddenly the ghostly figure of the white-bearded, cancer-stricken Ammers gleamed in front of him, and the fight took on pith and moment. He hit him about the head and ears with short hooks and terrific straight punches, he smashed two devastating blows to the heart, followed by a pitiless punch to the solar plexus, and it seemed to him he heard Ammers fall groaning to the floor. But that wasn't enough. Panting with excitement, he made the shadow of his enemy get up again and again, and systematically beat him to bits, saving for the end, as a particular refinement, a couple of powerful hooks to the liver. When morning came he was so worn out and tired that he fell on the bed and went to sleep immediately, with the night fears safely behind him.

Two days later Dr. Beer came into his cell. Kern leaped to his feet. "How is she?"

"All right; everything normal."

Kern gave a sigh of relief. "How did you know I was here?"

"That was easy. You stopped coming to see me. So you had to be here."

"That's right. Does she know?"

"Yes. When you didn't make an appearance yesterday evening in your role of Prometheus she moved heaven and earth to get in touch with me. An hour later we knew definitely. By the way, that trick with the matches was a crazy idea."

"Yes, so it was. Sometimes you think you're very smart and then you make the silliest mistakes. For the moment I've been sentenced to fourteen days, but probably I'll be out in twelve days. Will she be well by then?"

"No. At least not well enough to travel. I think we should leave her in the hospital as long as possible."

"Of course." Kern thought a moment. "In that case I'll just have to wait for her in Geneva. Anyway I couldn't take her with me. I'll be deported of course."

Beer drew a letter from his pocket. "Here, I brought you something."

Kern eagerly snatched the envelope, but then he put it in his pocket.

"You can go right ahead and read it now," Beer said. "I have time."

"No, I'll read it later."

"Then I'll go back to the hospital now. I'll tell her definitely that I have seen you. Do you want to give me something to take along?" Beer took a fountain pen and writing paper out of his coat pocket. "I brought these for you."

"Thanks. Thanks a lot!" Kern hurriedly wrote a letter: He was all right, Ruth must get well quickly. If he were deported first he would wait for her in Geneva. Every day at twelve o'clock in front of the Post Office. Beer would give her all the details.

He put the twenty-franc note the judge had given him in the envelope and sealed it. "Here."

"Don't you want to read her letter first?" Beer asked.

"No, not yet. Not so quickly. I have nothing else to do all day."

Beer gave him a startled look. Then he put the letter in his pocket. "All right, I'll come to see you again in a couple of days."

"You'll be sure to?"

Beer laughed. "Why not?"

"Yes, you're right. Now everything is settled, at least in these circumstances. In the next twelve days nothing can happen. No surprises. That's really a comforting thought."

When Beer had gone Kern took Ruth's letter in his hands. So light, he thought, a scrap of paper and a few lines of writing — and yet what happiness!

He laid the letter on the edge of his bunk and took his exercises. He knocked Ammers down again and this time gave him a couple of foul blows to the kidneys. "We won't let it get us down," he said to the letter, and with a beautiful straight right to the beard sent Ammers crashing to the floor again. He rested for a moment and continued his conversation with the letter. Not until afternoon when the light was beginning to fail did he open it and read the first lines. Each hour he read a little further. By evening he had come to the signature. He saw Ruth's trembling apprehension, her love and bravery. He sprang up and went to work on Ammers again. This battle, to be honest, was a little lacking in sportsmanship. Ammers received cuffs on the ear, kicks, and finally his white beard was torn out by the roots.

*   *   *

Steiner had packed his things. He wanted to get to France. It had become dangerous in Austria and the *Anschluss* with Germany was only a matter of time. Besides, the Prater and Director Potzloch's enterprise were preparing for their long winter sleep.

Potzloch took Steiner by the hand. "We traveling people are used to partings. Somewhere or other we always meet again."

"Certainly."

"Well then!" Potzloch made a grab for his glasses. "Have a good winter. I hate farewell scenes."

"So do I," Steiner replied.

"Do you know," Potzloch blinked, "it's simply a matter of routine. After you've see as many people come and go as I have, it all ends by being a matter of routine. As if you were going from the rifle gallery to the carrousel."

"A fine simile! From the rifle gallery to carrousel — and from carrousel back again to rifle gallery. It's a magnificent simile."

Potzloch grinned at the flattery. "Between us, Steiner, do you know what the most terrible thing in the world is? In strict confidence it's this: in the end everything gets to be a matter of routine." He jammed his glasses back on his nose. "Even the so-called ecstasies."

"Even war," Steiner said.

"Even pain. Even death. I know a man who has had four wives die in the last ten years. Now he has a fifth and she's getting sick. I don't need to tell you he's looking around for a sixth. All a matter of routine."

"Only not your own death."

Potzloch dismissed the thought with a wave. "You never really believe in that, Steiner. Not even in time of war; otherwise there wouldn't be any wars. Each man thinks he'll be the one to get by. Am I right?"

He cocked his head on one side and looked at Steiner. Steiner nodded in amusement. Potzloch extended his hand again. "Well, so long. I've got to rush over to the rifle gallery and see whether they're packing the silver service properly."

"So long. For my part I'll go over to the carrousel again."

Potzloch grinned and bustled away.

Steiner went to the wagon. The dry leaves rustled under his feet. Night hung silent and indifferent over the forest. From the rifle gallery came the ringing sound of hammers. A few lanterns swung in the partially dismantled carrousel.

Steiner was about to say good-by to Lilo. She was going to stay in Vienna. Her identification papers and permit to work were only valid in Austria. She would not have gone with him even if it had been possible. She and Steiner were comrades of destiny, whom the winds of the times had blown together — and this they both knew.

She was in the gipsy wagon setting the table. As he entered she turned around. "A letter came for you," she said.

Steiner took the letter and looked at the postmark. "From Switzerland. I guess it's from our kid." He tore open the envelope and read the letter. "Ruth's in the hospital," he said.

"What's the matter with her?" Lilo asked.

"Inflammation of the lungs. But apparently not serious. They're in Murten. The kid makes fire signals to her every evening in front of the hospital. Perhaps I'll run into them if I go through Switzerland."

Steiner stuck the letter in his breast pocket. "I hope the kid knows how to arrange things so they can get together afterwards."

"He will know how to arrange it," Lilo said. "He has learned much."

"Yes, but just the same . . ."

Steiner wanted to explain to Lilo that it would be hard for Kern when Ruth was taken out of the hospital and escorted to the border. But then he reflected that they themselves were seeing each other for the last time that evening — and that it would be better not to talk about two people who hoped to stay together or at least see each other again.

He went to the window and looked out. In the light of carbide lamps workmen in the midway were packing the swans, horses and giraffes from the carrousel into gray sacks. The animals stood and lay around on the ground as though a bomb had suddenly shattered their happy communal life. In one of the detached gondolas two workmen were sitting and drinking beer out of bottles. They had thrown their jackets and caps over the antlers of a white stag that was leaning against a chest with its legs stretched wide apart as though transfixed in eternal flight.

"Come," Lilo said behind him, "supper is ready. I have made piroshki for you."

Steiner turned and put his arm around her shoulders.

"Supper," he said, "piroshki. For us roving devils simply eating together almost takes the place of home and country, doesn't it?"

"There is something else. But you don't know anything about it." She paused an instant. "You don't know anything about it because you cannot weep and you do not understand what it means to be sad together."

"You're right. That's something I don't know," Steiner said. "We weren't often sad, Lilo."

"No. Not you. You are savage or indifferent or you laugh or you are what you call brave. It isn't really brave."

"Then what is it, Lilo?"

"It's the fear of giving way to your feelings. Fear of tears, fear of not being a man. In Russia men could weep and still be men and still be brave. You have never opened your heart."

"No," Steiner said.

"For what are you waiting?"

"I don't know. I don't want to know, either."

Lilo watched him attentively. "Come and eat," she said presently. "I shall give you bread and salt to take with you as we do in Russia, and I shall bless you before you go, O restlessness that cannot flow. Perhaps you'll laugh at that."

"No."

She put the dish of piroshki on the table.

"Sit down with me, Lilo."

She shook her head. "Today you eat alone. I shall wait on you and hand you what you eat. It is your last meal."

She remained standing and handed him the piroshki, the bread, the meat and the pickles. She watched him as he ate and silently she prepared his tea. She moved lithely about the little wagon with long steps, like a panther that has grown accustomed to a too-narrow cage. Her slender bronze hands cut the meat for him, and her face had a composed and enigmatic expression; to Steiner she appeared suddenly like an Old Testament figure.

He had traded his knapsack for a bag since he had secured a passport. He opened the door of the wagon, went down the steps and left the bag outside. Then he came back.

Lilo was standing by the table leaning on one hand. Her eyes mirrored a blind emptiness as though they saw nothing and she were already alone. Steiner went up to her. "Lilo — "

She moved and looked at him. The expression in her eyes changed. "It's hard to go away," Steiner said.

She nodded and put her arm around his neck. "I shall be really alone without you."

"Where are you going to go?"

"I don't know yet."

"You'll be safe in Austria. Even if it becomes German."

"Yes."

She looked at him earnestly. Her eyes were very deep and brilliant.

"Too bad, Lilo," Steiner murmured.

"Yes."

"You know why?"

"I know, and you know about me too."

They went on looking at each other. "It's strange," Steiner said, "only a bit of time and a bit of life that stands between us. We have everything else."

"All time, Steiner," Lilo answered softly, "all time and our whole lives — "

Steiner nodded. Lilo framed his face with her hands and spoke a few words in Russian. Then she gave him a piece of bread and some salt. "Eat it when you are gone. It is to bring you bread without sorrow in foreign lands. Now go."

Steiner was going to kiss her. But when he looked at her he forbore to do it. "Go now," she said softly. "Go — "

He walked into the forest. After a while he turned around. The city of tents was swallowed in night, and there was nothing there but the immense whispering darkness and the bright rectangle of a distant open door and a tiny figure that did not wave.

Chapter Fifteen

AT the end of two weeks Kern was arraigned again in the District Court. The heavy man with the apple face looked at him unhappily. "I have bad news for you, Herr Kern — "

Kern braced himself. Four weeks, he thought. I hope it won't be more than four weeks. If it's necessary Beer will certainly be able to keep Ruth in the hospital that long.

"The appeal in your behalf to the higher court has been denied. You had been in Switzerland too long. Your action could no longer be considered as arising from a state of distress. Besides, there was the affair with the policeman. You have been sentenced to fourteen days imprisonment."

"Fourteen days more?"

"No. Fourteen days in all. Your detention for examination is counted in."

Kern took a deep breath. "And so I can be released today?"

"Yes. All you have to do is remember you spent the time in prison and not in detention. The only bad feature is that now you have a prison record."

"I'll be able to stand that."

The judge looked at him. "It would have been better if your name hadn't been put in the prison record. But there was no way to help it."

"Will I be deported today?" Kern asked.

"Yes. By way of Basle."

"By way of Basle? To Germany?" Kern gave a lightning glance around the room. He was prepared to leap out the window immediately and flee. He had heard once or twice of emigrees being deported to Germany. Most of them had been refugees who had come directly from Germany.

The window was open and the courtroom was on the ground floor. Outside the sun was shining. Outside the branches of the apple tree were swaying in the wind, and beyond was a hedge over which one could leap, and beyond it was freedom.

The judge shook his head. "You will be taken to France, not to Germany. Basle is on both our German and French borders."

"Can't I be put across the border at Geneva?"

"No, unfortunately that won't do. Basle is the nearest place. We have express orders about that. Geneva is much farther."

Kern was silent for a moment. "Is it certain that I shall be put into France?"

"Perfectly certain."

"Is no one who is arrested here without papers sent to Germany?"

"No one so far as I know. The only place that might happen would be in the border cities. But I have heard practically nothing about it even there."

"It's certain that a woman would not be sent back to Germany then?"

"Certainly not. At all events I wouldn't do it. Why do you ask?"

"For no special reason. It's just that I've occasionally run into women on the road who had no papers. Everything is even harder for them. That's why I asked."

The judge took a document from among his papers and showed it to Kern. "Here is the order for your deportation. Do you believe now that you'll be taken to France?"

"Yes."

The judge laid the paper back in his portfolio. "Your train leaves in two hours."

"And it's quite impossible to be taken to Geneva?"

"Quite. Refugees cost us a great deal in railroad tickets. There is a strict regulation that they must be sent to the nearest border. I really can't help you there."

"If I were to pay for the trip myself could I be taken to Geneva?"

"Yes. That would be possible. Do you want to do it?"

"No, I haven't enough money to do that. It was just a question."

"Don't ask too many questions," the judge said. "Actually you ought to pay your fare to Basle if you have money with you. I have refrained from inquiring." He stood up. "Good-by. I wish you the best of luck and I hope you will get along in France! And I hope, too, things will be different before long."

"Yes, perhaps. Otherwise we might just as well hang ourselves right now."

Kern had no further opportunity to communicate with Ruth. Beer had been there on the previous day and had told him she must stay in the hospital about a week longer. He decided to write him immediately from the French border. He was sure now of the most important thing — that in no case would Ruth be sent to Germany. And that if she had money for the trip she could be taken to Geneva.

Promptly at the end of two hours a detective in plain clothes came to get him. They walked to the station, Kern carrying his bag. Beer had got it for him the day before and brought it to him.

They passed an inn. The windows of the dining room, which was on the ground floor, stood wide open. A group of zither players were playing a slow country waltz and a male chorus was singing. Beside the window two singers in alpine costume were yodeling. Their arms were around each other's shoulders and they were swaying back and forth in time to the music. The detective stopped. One of the yodelers, the tenor, broke off. "Where've you been all this time, Max?" he asked. "Everyone's here waiting."

"On duty," the detective replied.

The yodeler eyed Kern with contempt. "What offal!" he growled in a suddenly deep voice. "Then our quartet's shot to hell for this evening?"

"Not a bit of it. I'll be back in twenty minutes."

"Are you sure?"

"Yes, sure."

"Good. We've got to get that double yodel right to-night, understand. Don't catch cold."

"I won't."

They walked on. "Then you're not going to ride to the border?" Kern asked after a time.

"No. We have a new patent device for you."

They arrived at the station. The detective found the conductor of the train. "Here he is," he announced and pointed to Kern. Then he gave the conductor the order of deportation. "Have a good trip, sir," he said, suddenly very polite, and stamped off.

"Come with me."

The conductor took Kern to the caboose on one of the freight cars. "Get in here."

The little cabin contained nothing but a wooden bench. Kern pushed his bag under it on the floor. The conductor closed the door and locked it from the outside. "There! They'll let you out in Basle."

He walked off along the dimly lighted platform. Kern looked through the window of the caboose. He tried cautiously to see whether he could squeeze his way through it. It wouldn't work; the window was too narrow. A few minutes later the train pulled out. The bright waiting rooms slid past with their empty tables and their blank senseless lights. The stationmaster, with his red cap, was left behind in the darkness. A few crooked streets glided by, a parking lot with waiting automobiles, a small café in which a few people were playing cards — then the city had disappeared.

Kern sat down on the wooden bench. He put his feet on his bag. He pressed them close together and looked out of the window. The night outside was dark and unknown and windy, and suddenly he felt very miserable.

In Basle he was fetched by a policeman and taken to the customs house. He was given supper. Then an officer took him by streetcar to Burgfelden. In the darkness they went by a Jewish cemetery. Then they passed a brickyard and turned off from the main road. After some time the officer stopped. "Go on from here — straight ahead." Kern went on. He knew just about where he was and he walked in the direction of St. Louis. He made no attempt to hide himself; it didn't matter if he were arrested immediately.

He had made a mistake in the direction. It was almost morning when he arrived in St. Louis. He reported immediately to the French police and explained that he had been put across the border from Basle the night before. He had to avoid being put in prison. And he could only do that by reporting each day to the police or to the customs officials. In that way he was not subject to any punishment and could only be sent back.

The police held him in detention during the day. In the evening they sent him to the border customs house.

There were two customs men there. One was sitting at a table writing. The other was sprawled on a bench beside the stove. He was smoking cigarettes of heavy Algerian tobacco, and he glanced at Kern from time to time.

"What have you got in your bag there?" he asked after a while.

"A few things that belong to me."

"Open it up!"

Kern raised the top. The customs man got up and strolled over indifferently. Then he bent over the bag with a show of interest. "Toilet water, soap, perfume! See here, did you bring these things with you from Switzerland?"

"Of course."

"You're not going to pretend you need all this yourself — for your own personal use?"

"No. I have been peddling it."

"Then you'll have to pay duty," the customs man announced. "Empty it out! Now this rubbish" — he pointed to the needles, shoelaces and other small things — "I'll let pass."

Kern thought he was dreaming. "Pay duty?" he asked. "You want me to pay duty?"

"Why naturally! You're no diplomatic courier, are you?

Or did you think I wanted to buy these bottles? You have brought dutiable goods into France. Come on, dump it out!"

The customs man reached for the list of tariffs and pulled up the scales.

"I have no money," Kern said.

"No money?" The customs man stuck his hands in his pockets and rocked back and forth from the knees. "All right, then, we'll just confiscate your things. Hand them over!"

Kern remained crouching on the floor and held onto his bag. "I did not enter France voluntarily," he said. "I reported when I got here in order to get back into Switzerland. I don't have to pay any duty."

"See here! Are you trying to teach me what's what?"

"Leave the youngster alone, François," said the customs man who was writing at the table.

"I wouldn't think of it! A *boche* who knows all about everything. Just like the rest of that crowd over there. Come on, out with those bottles!"

"I'm no *boche*," Kern said.

At that moment a third customs man came in. Kern saw he was of a higher rank than the other two. "What's going on here?" he asked curtly.

The customs man explained what was happening. The inspector examined Kern. "Did you report to the police at once?" he asked.

"Yes."

"And you want to go back to Switzerland?"

"Yes. That's why I'm here."

The inspector thought for a moment. "Then it's not his fault," he decided. "He's no smuggler. He was smuggled in himself. Send him back and make an end of it."

He left the room. "Look here, François," said the customs man at the table, "what's the idea of always getting so excited? It's bad for your blood pressure."

François made no reply. He stared angrily at Kern. Kern stared back. It occurred to him suddenly that he had spoken French and had understood French, and he silently blessed the Russian professor in the prison in Vienna.

Next morning he was in Basle again. Now he changed his tactics a little. He did not go to the police immediately. Not much could happen to him if he stayed in Basle for the day and did not report until evening, and for Basle he had Binder's list of addresses. It was, to be sure, more overrun with emigrees than any other place in Switzerland, but he determined nevertheless to try to make some money.

He began with the clergymen. It was fairly certain they would not denounce him. The first one immediately threw him out; the second gave him a sandwich; the third five francs. He went on working and luck was with him — by noon he had earned seventeen francs. He made an especial effort to get rid of the last of his perfume and toilet water in case he should meet François again. That was hard to do in the case of the clergy — but he had some luck at the other addresses. During the afternoon he earned twenty-eight francs. He went into a Catholic church. It stood open and it was the safest place to rest. He had gone two nights without sleep.

The church was dim and empty. It smelled of incense and candles. Kern sat down in one of the pews and wrote a letter to Dr. Beer. He enclosed a letter for Ruth and money for her. Then he sealed the envelope and put it in his pocket. He felt very tired. Slowly he slipped forward onto the prayer bench and rested his head on the rail. He only wanted to rest for a moment; but he fell asleep. When he woke up he had no idea where he was. He blinked his eyes in the feeble red glow of the eternal light, and gradually regained his bearings. At the sound of footsteps he was suddenly wide awake.

A priest in black robes was coming slowly down the middle aisle. He stopped beside Kern and looked at him. Kern prudently folded his hands.

"I had no wish to disturb you," said the priest.

"I was just about to go," Kern replied.

"I saw you from the sacristy. You have been here for two hours. Were you praying for something in particular?"

"Yes, indeed," Kern said, somewhat surprised but recovering himself quickly.

"You're not a resident of this place?" The priest looked at Kern's bag.

"No." Kern looked at him. The priest's appearance inspired confidence. "I'm a refugee. Tonight I must cross the border. In that bag I have the things I sell."

He had one bottle of toilet water left over from his afternoon's work, and he was suddenly possessed with the fantastic idea of selling it to the priest in the church. It was most improbable; but he was used to improbable occurrences. "Toilet water," he said, "very good, very cheap. I am just selling the last of it."

He started to open his bag.

The priest restrained him. "Let it be. I believe you. We won't imitate the money-changers in the temple. It pleases me that you have prayed here so long. Come with me into the sacristy. We have a little fund for the faithful who are in need."

Kern was given ten francs. He was a little ashamed but not for long. It meant fare for part of the way to Paris, for him and Ruth. My run of bad luck seems to have stopped, he thought. He went back into the church and actually did pray this time. He didn't know exactly to whom. He himself was a Protestant, his father was a Jew, and he was kneeling in a Catholic church — but he thought that in these times there would probably be a good deal of confusion in Heaven too, and he assumed that his prayer would find the right path.

That evening he took the train to Geneva. He suddenly had a feeling that Ruth might have been released from the hospital earlier than was expected. He arrived in the morning, checked his bag at the station and went to the police. He explained to an officer that he had just been deported from France. Since he had his order of deportation from Switzerland with him and since it was only a couple of days old, they believed him, kept him for the day, and that evening put him across the border in the direction of Coligny.

He at once reported to the French customs. "Go inside," said a sleepy official. "There's someone else there now. We'll send you back about four o'clock."

Kern went into the customs house. "Vogt!" he said in amazement. "What brings you here?"

Vogt shrugged his shoulders. "I'm still laying siege to the Swiss border."

"Since then? Since they took you to the station in Lucerne?"

"Since then." Vogt looked ill. He was thin and his skin

was like gray paper. "I've had a run of bad luck," he said. "I can't succeed in getting into jail. Besides, the nights are already getting so cold I can't go on much longer."

Kern sat down beside him. "I was in prison," he said, "and I'm happy to be out again. That's the way life is."

A policeman brought them bread and red wine. They ate and went to sleep immediately on a bench. At four o'clock in the morning they were awakened and taken to the border. It was still quite dark. The ripe fields gleamed palely at the edge of the road.

Vogt shivered from the cold. Kern took off his sweater. "Here, put this on. I'm not cold."

"Are you sure you're not?"

"Yes."

"You are young," Vogt said, "that's why." He pulled on the sweater. "Just for a couple of hours until the sun comes up."

A little way from Geneva they parted. Vogt was planning to get deeper into Switzerland, by way of Lausanne. As long as he was near the border they simply sent him back and he couldn't count on getting into jail.

"Keep the sweater," Kern said.

"That's out of the question. Something like this is a fortune."

"I have another one. A present from a priest in the Vienna jail. In the baggage room in Geneva."

"Is that true?"

"Of course. It's a blue sweater with a red band. Now do you believe me?"

Vogt smiled. He drew a small book out of his pocket. "Take this in exchange."

It was Hölderlin's poems. "That will be much harder for you to get along without," Kern said.

"Not at all. I know most of them by heart."

Kern went into Geneva. For two hours he slept in a church and at twelve o'clock he was standing in front of the Main Post Office. He knew Ruth couldn't possibly be there so soon, but nevertheless he waited until two. Then he consulted Binder's list of addresses. Once more his luck was good. By evening he had earned seventeen francs and thereupon he went to the police.

It was Saturday night and noisy. At eleven o'clock two drunks were brought in; they immediately vomited all over the place and then began to sing. Toward one o'clock there were five of them.

At two Vogt was brought in.

"It must be a jinx," he said in a melancholy voice. "But never mind, at least we're together."

An hour later they were taken out. The night was cold. The stars twinkled and looked very far off. The half-moon was as bright as molten metal.

The policeman stopped. "You turn to the right here, then — "

"I know," Kern interrupted him, "I know this road well."

"Good luck then!"

They walked on across the narrow strip of no man's land between border and border.

Contrary to their expectation, they were not sent back that night but taken to the prefecture. There a deposition was taken down and they were fed. The following night they were deported again.

It was windy and overcast. Vogt was very tired. He

scarcely spoke and seemed almost ready to give up. When they had gone a way beyond the border they rested in a haystack. Vogt slept until morning like a dead man.

He woke up as the sun was rising. He did not stir, he simply opened his eyes. There was something strangely moving for Kern about this slender, motionless figure under the thin overcoat, this bit of humanity with its great, calm, wide-open eyes.

They were lying on a gentle slope from which they could look out at the city and Lake Leman, bathed in the morning light. Smoke from the chimneys of the houses was rising into the clear air, awakening memories of warmth, security, beds and breakfast. The sun sparkled on the wrinkled surface of the Lake. Vogt quietly watched as the thin drifting mists were sucked up by the sun and vanished, and the white massif of Mont Blanc slowly emerged from behind tattered clouds, gleaming like the bright walls of a lofty heavenly Jerusalem.

Toward nine they started on. They came to Geneva and took the road along the Lake. After a while Vogt stopped. "Just look at that!" he said.

"What?"

Vogt pointed to a palatial building standing in a large park. The vast edifice shone in the sun like a stronghold of security and well-ordered life. The magnificent park was resplendent with the red and gold of autumn foliage. Automobiles were parked in long rows in the broad entrance court, and crowds of contented people were walking in and out.

"Marvelous!" Kern said. "Looks as if the Emperor of Switzerland lived here."

"Don't you know what that is?"

Kern shook his head.

"That's the Palace of the League of Nations," Vogt said in a voice tinged with sorrow and irony.

Kern looked at him in amazement.

Vogt nodded. "That's the place where our fate has been debated for years. Whether we are to be given identification papers and made human beings again or not."

An open Cadillac pulled out of the row of cars and glided toward the exit. A number of elegantly dressed young people were in it, among them a girl in a mink coat. She laughed and waved to a second car, making an engagement to lunch beside the Lake.

"Yes," Vogt said presently. "Do you understand now why it takes so long?"

"Yes," Kern replied.

"Hopeless, isn't it?"

Kern shrugged his shoulders. "I don't think those people are in any great hurry."

A doorman approached and suspiciously examined Kern and Vogt. "Are you looking for someone?"

Kern shook his head.

"Then what do you want?" the doorman asked.

Vogt looked at Kern. A weary spark of humor gleamed in his eyes. "Nothing," he said to the doorman. "We're just tourists. Simple pilgrims on God's earth."

"In that case it would be better for you to move on," said the doorman, thinking of crackpot anarchists.

"Yes," Vogt said. "Probably that would be better."

They went along the Rue de Mont Blanc looking in the shop windows. Vogt stopped in front of a jewelry store. "I'll say good-by here."

"Where are you going now?" Kern asked.

"Not far. I'm going into this store."

Kern did not understand; he looked through the plate glass at the display of diamonds, rubies, and emeralds arranged on gray velvet.

"I don't think you'll have any luck," he said. "It's well known that jewelers are hard-hearted. Perhaps because they constantly associate with stones. They never give anything."

"I don't expect them to. I'm just going to steal something."

"What?" Kern looked doubtfully at Vogt. "Are you serious? You won't get away with it in your condition."

"I don't expect to. That's why I'm doing it."

"I don't understand," Kern said.

"You'll understand in a minute. I've thought it over carefully. It's my one chance of getting through the winter. I'll get at least a couple of months for this. I have no choice. I'm in pretty bad shape. Another few weeks of the border would finish me. I must do it."

"But — " Kern began.

"I know everything that you're going to say." Vogt's face sagged suddenly as though the threads that had held it together had been torn. "I can't go on — " he murmured. "Good-by."

Kern saw it was useless to say anything more. He pressed Vogt's limp hand. "I hope you'll get well soon."

"Yes, I hope so. The prison here is all right."

Vogt waited until Kern had gone some distance and then entered the shop. Kern stopped at the corner and watched the entrance, pretending that he was waiting for a trolley. After a while he saw a young man dash out of the store and presently return with a policeman. I hope he gets some rest now, he thought as he went on.

*   *   *

A short distance outside Vienna, Steiner got a lift and was taken as far as the border. He did not want to take the chance of showing his passport to the Austrian customs officials and so he got out before they reached the border and went the rest of the way on foot. About ten o'clock in the evening he presented himself at the customs office and reported that he had just been sent out of Switzerland.

"All right," said an old customs man with a Franz Josef beard. "We're used to that. We'll send you back early tomorrow morning. Find a seat for yourself somewhere."

Steiner sat down outside in front of the customs house and smoked. It was peaceful. The customs man on duty was dozing. Only occasionally a car came by. About an hour later the man with the beard stepped out. "Tell me," he asked Steiner, "are you an Austrian?"

Steiner was immediately alarmed. He had sewed his passport into his hat. "What makes you think that?" he inquired casually. "If I were an Austrian I wouldn't be a refugee, would I?"

The customs man struck his forehead with the flat of his hand so that his silvery beard shook. "Of course! Of course! The things a fellow forgets! I only asked you because I thought if you were an Austrian you might be able to play tarots."

"I can play tarots. I learned it as a youngster during the war. For a time I was in an Austrian division."

"Splendid! Splendid!" The Emperor Franz Josef slapped Steiner on the shoulder. "Why you're almost a fellow countryman. How about it? Will you join us? We need just one extra."

"Of course."

They went inside. An hour later Steiner had won seven schillings. He didn't play in the manner of Fred the card-sharp — he played honestly. But he played so much better than the customs men that he always won whenever his hand was any good at all.

At eleven o'clock they ate together. The customs men said it was their breakfast; they were on duty until eight o'clock in the morning. The breakfast was abundant and good. Afterward they went on playing. Steiner got a good hand. The Austrian customs men played against him with the courage of desperation. By eight o'clock they were calling each other by their first names. By three o'clock they were saying "*du*." By four o'clock they knew each other so well that phrases such as "son of a bitch," "sprig of Satan," "horse's ass" no longer counted as insults but were spontaneous expressions of amazement, admiration and affection.

At five o'clock the customs man on duty came in. "Children, it's high time to get Josef across the border."

There was silence all around. All eyes were turned toward the money that lay in front of Steiner. The Emperor Franz Josef was the first to speak. "What's won is won," he said resignedly. "He's rooked us for fair. Now he goes off like an autumn swallow, the bastard!"

"I had good cards," Steiner replied. "Damned good cards."

"That's just it!" the Emperor Franz Josef said in a melancholy voice. "You had good cards. Tomorrow perhaps we will have good cards. But then you won't be here any more. There's injustice in it somewhere."

"That's right. But where will you find justice, brother?"

"Justice among card players lies in the fact that the winner must give a chance for revenge. Then if he wins again there's nothing you can do about it. But this way — " The Emperor Franz Josef raised his hands despairingly. "There's something unsatisfactory about this."

"But, children," Steiner said, "if that's all that's bothering you! You put me across the border, tomorrow evening the Swiss will put me back again — and I'll give you your chance."

The Emperor Franz Josef clapped his hands resoundingly.

"That's the very thing!" he shouted in relief. "We couldn't propose it to you ourselves, you know. Because we're officers of the State. It's all right for us to play cards with you. That's not forbidden. But we must not encourage you to recross the border. If you come of your own accord that's something else again."

"I'll come," Steiner said. "You can count on it."

He reported at the Swiss border station and said he wanted to go back to Austria that night. They did not send him to the police station but kept him there. It was Sunday. Right next to the customs building was a small inn. There was a lot going on that afternoon; but in the evening after eight o'clock it quieted down.

A few customs men who were having their vacation sat around in the main room. They had visited their friends and now they began to play jass. Before Steiner realized what was happening he was in the game.

The Swiss were wonderful players. They had iron nerve and enormous luck. By ten o'clock they had taken eight francs away from Steiner; around midnight he had made up five. But at two o'clock when the restaurant was closed he had lost thirteen francs.

The Swiss treated him to a couple of large glasses of brandy. He needed them, for the night was cold and he had to wade across the Rhine.

On the far side he caught sight of a dark shape against the sky. It was the Emperor Franz Josef. The moon was behind his head like a saint's halo.

Steiner dried himself. His teeth were chattering. He drank the remainder of the brandy the Swiss had given him and got dressed. Then he approached the lonesome figure.

"Where have you been?" Franz Josef greeted him. "I've been waiting for you since one o'clock. We thought you might lose your way and so I've been standing here."

Steiner laughed. "The Swiss held me up."

"Well, hurry up now! We've only got two-and-a-half hours left."

The battle began at once. At five o'clock it was still undecided; the Austrians happened to have held good cards. The Emperor Franz Josef threw his hand on the table. "What a break, now of all times!"

He put on his coat and fastened the buckle of his sword. "Come along, pal! There's nothing for it. Duty is duty. We'll have to put you across the border."

He and Steiner walked toward the border. Franz Josef was smoking a fragrant Nigeria cigarette. "Do you know," he said after a while, "I have a feeling the Swiss are especially on the lookout tonight. They're waiting for you to come across, don't you think?"

"Quite possibly," Steiner replied.

"Maybe it would be wiser to send you back tomorrow night. Then they'd think you'd got by us and would not be so much on the alert."

"That's reasonable."

Franz Josef stopped. "Look over there! Something gleamed. That was a flashlight. Now there on that side! Did you see it?"

"Very clearly." Steiner grinned. He hadn't seen anything, but he knew what the old customs man wanted.

Franz Josef scratched his silvery beard. Then he squinted slyly at Steiner. "You couldn't possibly get through. That's evident. Don't you think so too? We've got to go back, pal. I'm sorry, but the border is closely watched. We can't do a thing except wait till tomorrow. I'll make a report about it."

"All right."

They played until eight in the morning. Steiner lost seventeen schillings, but he was still twenty-two ahead of the game. Franz Josef wrote his report and turned Steiner over to the customs men who relieved him.

The daytime customs men were punctilious and formal. They locked Steiner up at the police station. He slept there the whole day. Promptly at eight o'clock the Emperor Franz Josef appeared to take him triumphantly to the customs house.

There was a short but hearty meal; then the battle began. At two-hour intervals one of the customs men was changed for the one who was coming off duty. Steiner stayed at the table until five in the morning. At twelve-fifteen Emperor Franz Josef burned off the top layer of his beard in the excitement. He had thought there was a cigarette in his mouth and had tried to light it. It was an hallucination due to the fact that for an hour he had had only spades and clubs. He saw black dots where there was nothing at all.

Steiner utterly routed the customs force. He wrought especial havoc between three o'clock and five. In his desperation Franz Josef fetched reinforcements. He telephoned to the tarots champion of Buchs, who came tearing up on his motorcycle. It did no good. Steiner took him too. For the first time since he had known Him, God was on the side of the needy. Steiner held such cards that he regretted only one thing — that he was not playing with millionaires.

At five o'clock the last hand was dealt. Then the cards were put aside. Steiner had won 106 schillings.

The champion of Buchs roared off on his motorcycle with no farewells. Steiner and the Emperor Franz Josef went to the border. Franz Josef showed him a different way from two nights before. "Go in this direction," he said. "Be sure to hide yourself tomorrow morning. In the afternoon you can go to the station. You've got money enough now. And don't let me see you here again, you highway robber," he added in a graveyard voice; "otherwise we'll have to apply for a raise in salary."

"All right. Sometime I'll give you a chance to get back."

"Not at tarots. I've had enough of that. At chess, if you like, or at Blind Cow."

Steiner crossed the border. He wondered whether he should go to the Swiss customs and demand a return engagement, but he knew he would lose. He decided to take a train to Murten and look for Kern. It was on the way to Paris and was no great detour.

*   *   *

Kern was walking slowly toward the general Post Office. He was tired. For the last three nights he had hardly been able to sleep. Ruth should have been there three days ago. During the whole time he had had no news of her. She had not written. He had resolutely told himself there was some trivial cause and had thought out a thousand explanations — but now he suddenly believed she would not come at all. He felt strangely numb. The noise of the streets penetrated as though from a great distance into his dull unformulated sorrow, and he walked like an automaton putting one foot in front of the other.

It took a moment for him to recognize the blue coat. He stopped. It's just any blue coat, he thought, one of the hundreds of blue coats that have been driving me crazy this week. He looked away, and then looked at it again. Messenger boys and a fat woman, laden with parcels, blocked his view. He held his breath and noticed he was trembling. The blue coat danced before his eyes between red faces, hats, bicycles, packages, and people who were constantly getting in the way. He walked on cautiously, as though on a tightrope and afraid he might fall off at any second. Even when Ruth turned around and he could see her face, he believed he was suffering from a diabolic trick of the imagination. It was not until her face lighted up that he rushed forward to greet her.

"Ruth! You're here! You're here! You've been waiting and I wasn't here!" He held her close in his arms and felt her clinging to him. They clung together as though they were standing on a narrow mountain ledge and a storm was tugging at them to pitch them into the abyss. They were standing in the middle of the doorway of the General Post Office in Geneva at the hour when the crowds were largest and people were pushing by, jostling them, turning around and laughing — they noticed none of it. They were alone. Only when a uniform appeared in Kern's field of vision did he regain his senses. He let go of Ruth.

"Come quick!" he whispered. "Come into the Post Office before something happens."

They hurriedly melted into the crowd. "Come this way!"

They took their places at the end of a line of people waiting in front of the stamp window. "When did you get here?" Kern asked. The Post Office had never seemed to him so bright before.

"This morning."

"Did they take you to Basle first or straight here?"

"No. In Murten they gave me a residential permit for three days. So I came right on here by train."

"Marvelous! Even a permit to stay! Then you needn't feel any fear at all. I had pictured you being alone on the border. You're pale and thin, Ruth."

"But I'm entirely well again. Do I look ugly?"

"No, much prettier. You're prettier every time I see you. Are you hungry?"

"Yes," Ruth said. "Hungry for everything — to see you, to walk along the streets, to breathe the air and to talk."

"Then we'll eat right away. I know a little restaurant where they have fresh fish from the Lake. Just like Lucerne." Kern beamed. "There are so many lakes in Switzerland. Where is your baggage?"

"At the station, of course! After all, I'm an old and experienced vagabond."

"Yes! I'm proud of you. Ruth, you've come to your first illegal border crossing. That's almost like a graduation. Are you afraid?"

"Not a bit."

"You needn't be, either. I know this border as well as my own pocketbook. I know everything about it. I've even got tickets. Bought them in France day before yesterday.

Everything is ready. I know the station thoroughly. We'll stay in a little tavern where it's safe up to the last minute and then go straight to the train."

"You've bought tickets? Where did you get the money for them? You sent me so much."

"In my desperation I plundered the Swiss clergy. I stormed through Basle and Geneva like a gangster. I won't dare let myself be seen here for six months at least."

Ruth laughed. "I have some money with me too. Dr. Beer got it for me from the Refugees' Aid."

They were standing close together, moving slowly forward with the line. Kern held Ruth's hand firmly in his. They were speaking softly in lowered voices and trying to appear as indifferent and unconcerned as possible.

"We seem to have uncanny luck," Kern said. "You not only turn up again with a permit, you actually bring money with you! Why in the world didn't you write to me? Wouldn't they let you?"

"I was afraid. I thought they might arrest you if you came to get a letter. Beer told me about the affair with Ammers. He thought too it was better not to write. I wrote a lot of letters to you, Ludwig; I wrote to you constantly — without paper or pencil. You know that, don't you?" She looked at him.

Kern squeezed her hand. "I'm sure of it. Have you rented a room yet?"

"No. I came straight here from the station."

She didn't tell him that she had been standing in front of the Post Office since nine o'clock that morning. "I thought I'd take a room in the same boardinghouse you're staying in. Isn't that the easiest way?"

"Yes, only — " Kern hesitated for a moment. "Look here, these last few days I've become a sort of nighthawk. I didn't want to take any chances. And so I've been making use of the state boardinghouses." He noticed Ruth's expression.

"No, no," he said. "Not prison. The customs houses. You can sleep there all night. They're warm and that's the important thing. All of the customs houses are beautifully heated when it's cold. But that's not the thing for you. You have a residential permit — We could make a fine gesture and take a room for you in the Grand Hotel Bellevue. That's where the representatives of the League of Nations stay. Ministers and similar useless people."

"We'll not do that. I'm going to stay with you. If you think it's dangerous, let's go away tonight."

"What?" the clerk behind the window asked impatiently. They had moved forward to the window without realizing it.

"A ten-centime stamp," Kern said, quickly recovering himself.

The clerk handed over the stamp. Kern paid and they went toward the exit. "What in the world are you going to do with that stamp?" Ruth asked.

"I don't know. I just bought it. I react automatically when I see a uniform." Kern looked at the stamp. The Devil's Falls in the Gotthard. "I could write an anonymous letter of abuse to Ammers," he remarked.

"Ammers —" Ruth said. "Do you know he's taking treatments from Beer?"

"What? Is that true?" Kern stared at her. "Now tell me they're treatments for liver trouble and I'll stand on my head with joy."

Ruth laughed. She laughed so that she swayed like a field in the wind. "Yes, that's right! That's why he went to Beer. Beer is the only specialist in Murten. Just think — that adds a problem of conscience to Ammers' difficulties — because he has to go to a Jewish doctor."

"Great God! This is the proudest moment of my life. Steiner told me once that the rarest thing in life was to have love and revenge at the same time. Here I am standing on the steps of the general Post Office in Geneva and I have them both. Perhaps right now Binding is sitting in jail or has broken his leg."

"Or someone has stolen his money."

"That's even better! You have fine ideas, Ruth!"

They walked down the steps. "It's safest where there are crowds," Kern said. "There nothing is likely to happen to you."

"Are we going to cross the border tonight?" Ruth asked.

"No. You must rest up first and get some sleep. It's a long way."

"And you? Don't you have to sleep too? After all, we could go to one of the boardinghouses on Binder's list. Is it really so dangerous?"

"I no longer know," Kern said. "I don't think so. As close to the border as this not much can happen. I've gone back and forth too often. The worst they can do is to take us to the customs authorities. And even if it were a little more dangerous, I still wouldn't go away alone tonight I think. At twelve o'clock noon, in the middle of a crowd, you can be very firm about the right thing to do — but at night when it gets dark everything's different. Besides, with every minute it's growing more and more improbable. You're here again — how could anyone go away of his own free will?"

"I wouldn't have stayed here alone either," Ruth said.

Chapter Sixteen

KERN and Ruth succeeded in crossing the border unobserved and took a train at Bellegarde. They arrived in Paris in the evening and stood in front of the station, not knowing where to go.

"Cheer up, Ruth," Kern said. "We'll stay at some small hotel. It's too late to try for anything else today. Tomorrow we'll have a look around."

Ruth nodded. She was tired from the night trip. "Any hotel will do."

In a side street they found a red electric sign: Hotel Habana. Kern went inside and asked the price of a room.

"For the whole night?" the porter asked.

"Yes, of course," Kern answered in surprise.

"Twenty-five francs."

"For two persons?" Kern asked.

"Yes, of course," the porter replied, amazed in his turn.

Kent went out and got Ruth. The porter glanced quickly at them and pushed a police form toward Kern. When he saw Kern hesitate, he smiled and said, "We don't take those too seriously."

In relief Kern put down his name as Ludwig Oppenheim. "That's all we need," said the porter. "Twenty-five francs."

Kern paid and a boy took them upstairs. The room was small, clean, and even had a certain elegance. It contained a large, comfortable bed, two washstands and a chair, but no wardrobe. "I guess we can get along without a wardrobe," Kern said, going to the window to look out. He turned around. "Now we're in Paris, Ruth."

"Yes," Ruth replied smiling at him, "and how fast it all happened."

"We don't have to worry much about police forms here. Did you hear the way I talked French? I understood everything the porter said."

"You were marvelous," Ruth replied. "I couldn't have opened my mouth."

"The funny thing is you speak French much better than I do. I'm just bolder than you, that's all. Come, now we're going to get something to eat. A city seems unfriendly until you have eaten and drunk in it."

They went to a little brightly lighted *bistro* near by. It was ablaze with mirrors and smelled of sawdust and anis. For four francs they received a complete meal and a carafe of red wine as well. It was cheap and good. They had had hardly anything to eat all day, and the wine rose to their heads and made them sleepy. They soon returned to the hotel.

In front of the porter's desk in the lobby a girl, wearing a fur coat, was standing with a rather drunken man. They were bargaining with the porter. The girl was pretty and well-groomed. She looked contemptuously at Ruth. The man was smoking a cigar; he did not move out of the way when Kern went to get his key.

As they climbed the stairs Kern said, "Pretty elegant here, isn't it? Did you notice that fur coat?"

"Yes," Ruth smiled, "it was an imitation. Just cat fur. Something like that doesn't cost much more than a good cloth coat."

"I would never have known that. I'd have thought it was mink."

Kern snapped on the light. Ruth let her pocketbook and coat slip to the floor, put her arms around his neck and pressed her face close to his. "I'm tired," she said. "Tired, and happy and a little afraid, but mostly tired. Help me get to bed."

"Yes."

They lay beside each other in the darkness. Ruth put her head on Kern's shoulder and with a deep sigh immediately fell asleep like a child. Kern lay awake for a while listening to her breathing. Then he too fell asleep.

Something woke him. He sat up with a start and listened to the noise outside. His heart began to pound; he thought it was the police. Quickly he leaped out of bed, ran to the door, opened it a hand's breadth and peered out. Someone was shouting downstairs and an angry, piercing woman's voice replied in shrill French. After a while the porter came up.

"What's wrong?" Kern asked in excitement through the crack in the door.

The porter looked at him in tired surprise. "Nothing, just a drunk who didn't want to pay."

"Nothing more?"

"What more should there be? Things like this happen occasionally. Haven't you anything better to do?"

He opened the door to the next room and admitted two people who had come up behind him, a man with a pitch-black mustache and a billowing blonde. Kern closed his door and felt his way back in the darkness. He bumped against the bed and as he steadied himself he suddenly felt Ruth's soft breast under his hand. Prague, he thought — and a wave of love swept through him. At the same moment Ruth's breast moved as she propped herself up on her elbows and an unfamiliar, frightened and constrained voice whispered: "What — what is it? For God's sake — " and became still and there was only a gasping sound in the darkness.

"It's me, Ruth," Kern said and got into bed. "It's me and I have frightened you."

"Oh, yes," she murmured and lay back.

Quickly she fell asleep again with her hot face on Kern's shoulder. That's what they've done to you, he thought bitterly. The other time in Prague you only asked, faintly disturbed: "Who's there?" But now you tremble and are afraid.

"Take everything off," said an oily male voice from the next room. "I'm crazy about a fat bottom."

The woman laughed. "I can supply that all right."

Kern listened. He knew now where he was. In a house of assignation. Cautiously he peered over at Ruth. She appeared not to have heard. "Ruth," he said almost inaudibly, "beloved tired little Ruth, go on sleeping and don't wake up. What's happening over there has nothing to do with us. I love you and you love me and we are alone — "

"Damn me!" The sound of a slap came through the thin wall. "That's what I call class. Damn me again! Hard as rock."

"Ough, you pig! You're a regular crazy pig," the woman cried happily.

"Sure. Did you think I was made of cardboard?"

"We're not here at all," Kern whispered. "Ruth, we're not here at all. We are lying in a field in the sunshine and around us camellias and red poppies are blooming. A cuckoo is calling and bright butterflies are hovering around your face — "

"The other way around! Leave that light on!" urged the oily voice from next door.

"What are you trying to do anyway? Ah — " The woman crowed with laughter.

"We're in a little peasant cottage," Kern whispered. "It's evening and we've just had buttermilk and fresh bread. Twilight touches our faces; everything is silent and we are waiting for the night. We are at peace and know that we love each other — "

A tumult came from next door with creakings and shouts.

"I'm resting my head on your knees and I feel your hands in my hair. You are no longer afraid; you have a passport and all the policemen nod genially to us. You go to the university every day and the professors are proud of you. And I — I — "

Footsteps came along the corridor. From the other side of the room where hitherto it had been quiet there was the rattling of a key. "Thanks," said the porter. "Thanks very much."

"What are you going to give me, dearie?" asked a bored voice.

"I haven't very much," a man answered. "How about fifty?"

"You're crazy. For less than a hundred I won't undo a single button."

"But my child — " the voice diminished to a throaty plaint.

"It's vacation and we're at the seashore," Kern said softly and insistently. "You have been in swimming and have fallen asleep on the hot sand. The ocean is blue and there's a white sail on the horizon. The wind is blowing and the sea gulls are screaming."

Something banged against the wall and Ruth trembled. "What's that?" she asked, drunk with sleep.

"Nothing, nothing. Go to sleep, Ruth."

"You're still here, aren't you?"

"I'll always be here and I love you."

"Yes, love me — "

She went to sleep again. "You are with me and I with you and no filth can touch us, none of the filth through which they drive us," Kern whispered amid the bawdy uproar of the short-time house. "We are alone and young and our sleep is clean, Ruth — beloved Ruth of the wide, flowery fields of love. . . ."

*   *   *

Kern came out of the office of the Refugees' Aid. He had not expected anything better than the news he had received. A permit to stay was out of the question. Donations only in extreme cases. Work, with or without a residential permit, was of course forbidden.

Kern was not especially depressed. It was the same in every country. And despite that, thousands of emigrees, who according to the laws should have starved to death long ago, were still alive. He stopped for a while in the anteroom of the office. It was full of people. Kern looked them over carefully one by one. Then he approached a man who was sitting a little to one side and who had a calm and collected appearance.

"I beg your pardon," he said, "there's a question I'd like to ask you. Could you tell me where one can live without being reported to the police? I've only been in Paris since yesterday."

"Have you any money?" the man asked without the slightest sign of surprise.

"A little."

"Can you pay six francs a day for a room?"

"Yes. For the time being."

"Then go to the Hotel Verdun in the Rue de Turenne. Tell the landlady I sent you. My name is Klassmann. Dr. Klassmann," he added in wry amusement.

"Is the Verdun safe from the police?"

"No place is safe. They get you to fill out an undated registration slip. But they do not send it to the police. If there should be a check-up their story is always that you came that day and the slip was going to be sent to the police next morning. The chief thing is you're not arrested right away. To escape that there is an excellent underground passage. You'll see when you get there. The Verdun is no hotel — it's something that God in his wise providence created for emigrees fifty years ago. Have you read your newspaper yet?"

"Yes."

"Then give it to me. We'll be quits."

"All right and many thanks."

Kern rejoined Ruth, who had been waiting for him in a café on the next corner. She had a map of the city and a French grammar in front of her. "Here," she said, "see what I bought in a bookstore while you were away. Cheap. Secondhand. I think they're the two weapons we need to conquer Paris."

"You're right. We'll make use of them immediately. Let's find out where the Rue de Turenne is."

The Hotel Verdun was an ancient dilapidated building from which the plaster had fallen in large pieces. It had a narrow entrance behind which there was a lodge and in the lodge sat the proprietress, a bony woman in a black dress.

In faltering French Kern explained his needs. The proprietress examined them from head to toe with gleaming, black, birdlike eyes. "With meals or without?" she asked curtly.

"What does it cost with meals?"

"Twenty francs per person. Three meals. Breakfast in your room, the other meals in the dining room."

"I think we'll take it for the first day with meals," Kern said to Ruth in German. "We can always change the arrangement. The main thing is to get in here."

Ruth nodded.

"All right then, with meals," Kern said. "Is there a difference in price if we take one room?"

The proprietress shook her head. "There are no double rooms free. You have one hundred forty-one and forty-two." She threw two keys on the counter. "Payment every day. In advance."

"All right," Kern said. Then he paid and took the keys. They were attached to huge wooden blocks on which the numbers had been burned. The two rooms were next to each other. They were narrow single bedrooms overlooking the court. The room in the Hotel Habana had been palatial by comparison.

Kern looked around. "These are regular emigrees' holes," he said. "Uncomfortable but familiar. They don't promise more than they can deliver. How do you like them?"

"I think they're fine," Ruth replied. "Each of us has a room and a bed. Just think how it was in Prague! Three and four in one room!"

"You're right. I'd forgotten all about that. I was thinking at the moment of the Neumanns' home in Zürich."

Ruth laughed. "And I of the haystack in which we got soaked in the rain."

"Your thoughts are better than mine. But you know why I think as I do?"

"Yes," Ruth said. "But it's wrong and it's insulting to me. We'll buy some tissue paper and make fine lampshades. We'll learn French right here at this table, and look out there over the roof at that piece of the sky. We'll sleep in these beds which will be the best in the world, and when we wake up and stand at the window this dirty courtyard will be full of romance, for it is a courtyard in Paris."

"Good," Kern said. "And right now we'll go to the dining room. The food there is French. And it too will be the best in the world."

The dining room of the Hotel Verdun was in the cellar. It was known to the guests as "the catacombs." To reach it you had to follow a long and twisting path up steps through passageways and strange rooms that had been moldering for decades and in which the air stood as still as water in a marshy pond. It was fairly large, for it also served the Hotel International which was situated next door and belonged to the sister of the proprietress.

This common dining room was the attraction of both ramshackle hotels. To the emigrees it was what the catacombs had been to the early Christians. If there was a check-up in the International everyone was whisked over through the dining room to the Verdun, and vice versa. The common cellar was the life line.

Kern and Ruth stood uncertainly in the doorway for a moment. It was midday, but since the dining room had no

windows it was lighted. The artificial light at this hour
had a strangely inappropriate and sickly look — as though
a slice of time from the evening before had been left over
and forgotten.

"Why, there's Marill!" Kern said.

"Where?"

"Over there beside the lamp. What luck! Right away
we see someone we know."

Marill saw them now. He gave an incredulous jerk at his
eyeglasses. Then he got up, came over and shook hands
with them.

"The babes in Paris! What do you think of that? How
did you discover the old Verdun?"

"Dr. Klassmann told us about it."

"Klassmann? Really? Well, you're in the right place. The
Verdun is first-rate. Are you taking your meals here?"

"Yes, but only for today."

"Good. Change that tomorrow. Pay only for the room
and buy the rest yourself. Much cheaper! Now and then
you can take a meal here to keep the proprietress in a good
humor. You were right to clear out of Vienna. It's getting
very hot down there now."

"How is it here?"

"Here? My boy, Austria, Czechoslovakia and Switzerland represent a war of movement for us exiles, but Paris
is a war of position. The front line of the trenches. Each
successive wave of exiles has rolled this far. Do you see the
man over there with the bushy black hair? An Italian. The
bearded one beside him? A Russian. Two places farther?
A Spaniard. Two beyond? A Pole and two Americans.
Next? Four Germans. Paris represents the last hope and
the final fate of all of them." He looked at the clock. "Come
on, children. It's almost two o'clock. If you want to get

anything to eat it's high time. The French are an exact people about meals. After two you can't get anything."

They sat down at Marill's table. "If you eat here let me recommend that fat waitress," he said. "Her name's Yvonne and she comes from Alsace. I don't know how she does it, but there's always more in her dishes than in the others."

Yvonne put the soup on the table and grinned. "Have you any money, children?" Marill asked.

"About enough for two weeks," Kern replied.

Marill nodded. "That's good. Have you given any thought yet to what you're going to do?"

"No. We only got here yesterday. How do the others here make a living?"

"That's a good question, Kern. Let's begin with me. I live by writing articles for some of the emigree papers. The editors buy them because I used to be a delegate to the Reichstag. All the Russians have Nansen passports and work permits. They were the first wave of immigration — twenty years ago. They are waiters, cooks, masseurs, doormen, shoemakers and what not. The Italians too for the most part have found places for themselves. They were the second wave. Some of the Germans still have valid passports. Very few of them have work permits. Some still have money which they are doling out with great care. But most of them haven't any left. They work illegally for food and a few francs. They sell whatever they still own. That lawyer over there does translating and typing work. The young man beside him takes wealthy Germans into night clubs and gets a percentage. The actress opposite him makes her living by palmistry and astrology. Some of them give language lessons. Some of them have become athletic instructors. A few go to the public markets and carry baskets. A number live on payments from the Refugees'

Aid. Some peddle; some beg — and some drop swiftly out of sight. Have you been to the Refugees' Aid yet?"

"I was there," Kern said, "this morning."

"Didn't get anything?"

"No."

"That doesn't matter. You must go again. Ruth must go to the Jewish one; you to the mixed; I belong to the Aryan." Marill laughed. "Misery has its own bureaucracy, as you see. Have you had your name put down?"

"No, not yet."

"Do it tomorrow. Klassmann can help you. He's an expert at it. In Ruth's case he can even try to get a residential permit. After all she has a passport."

"She has a passport," Kern said, "but it has expired and she had to cross the border illegally."

"That doesn't matter. A passport is a passport. Worth its weight in gold. Klassmann will tell you about it."

Yvonne put the potatoes on the table and a plate with three pieces of meat. Kern smiled at her. She gave him a broad grin.

"You see!" Marill said. "That's Yvonne. The regular portion is one piece of meat. She brings an extra one."

"Thank you very much, Yvonne," Ruth said.

Yvonne's grin broadened and she waddled out.

"Good heavens," Kern said, "a residential permit for Ruth. She seems to be lucky there. In Switzerland she got one too. To be sure it was only for three days."

"Have you given up chemistry, Ruth?" Marill asked.

"Yes. Yes and no. For the time being yes."

Marill nodded. "You're right." He pointed to a young man who was sitting beside the window with a book in front of him. "That youngster over there has been a dishwasher in a night club for two years. He was a German student. Two weeks ago he took his doctor's degree in

French. While he was studying for it he found out that he couldn't get an appointment here but that there was a chance in Capetown. Now he's learning English in order to take his doctor's degree in English and go to South Africa. That sort of thing goes on here too. Do you find it a comfort?"

"Yes."

"You too, Kern?"

"Everything's a comfort to me. How are the police here?"

"Fairly lax. You have to look out, of course, but they're not as sharp as in Switzerland."

"I find that a comfort," Kern said.

Next morning Kern went with Klassmann to the Refugees' Aid to have his name put on record. From there they went to the Prefecture. "There's no use at all in reporting," Klassmann said. "You'd just be deported. But it's a good thing for you to see, once at least, what's going on. It's not dangerous. Police offices, next to churches and museums, are the least dangerous places for emigrees."

"That checks with my experience," Kern replied. "To be sure I hadn't thought of museums until now."

The Prefecture was a great mass of buildings situated around a large courtyard. Klassmann led Kern through several archways and doors into a large room which looked just about like a station ticket room. Along the walls were a row of windows behind which clerks were seated. In the middle of the room there were a number of backless benches. Several hundred people stood or sat in long queues.

"This is the room of the elect," Klassmann said. "It is

pretty nearly paradise. Here you see the people who have residential permits and now only have to have them extended."

Kern felt the solemnity and crushing anxiety of the room. "You call this paradise?" he asked.

"Yes. Look there!"

Klassmann pointed to a woman who was leaving a window near by. She was staring with an expression of delirious joy at a permit which the girl behind the window had stamped and returned to her. She ran toward a group of those waiting. "Four weeks," she cried with suppressed delight. "Extended for four weeks."

Klassmann exchanged glances with Kern. "Four weeks; nowadays that's practically a lifetime, eh?"

Kern nodded.

An old man was now standing in front of the window. "But what am I to do?" he asked in bewilderment.

The clerk made some reply in rapid French which Kern could not understand. The old man listened to him. "Yes, but what shall I do?" he asked a second time.

The clerk repeated his explanation. "Next!" he said then and reached for the papers which the man behind was holding out over the old man.

The old man turned his head. "But I'm not through yet," he said. "I still don't know what I am to do. Where do you want me to go?" he asked the clerk.

The official made an inaudible reply and busied himself with the other man's papers. The old man gripped the ledge of the window as though it were a raft in the ocean. "What do you want me to do then, if you won't extend my permit?" he asked the clerk.

The official paid no attention to him and the old man turned to the people standing behind him. "But now what can I do?" He gazed at the stony wall of careworn, hunted faces. No one replied; but neither did anyone push him away. Over his head they handed their papers in at the window, taking special care not to jostle him.

He turned to the clerk again. "Really, someone must tell me what I'm to do," he said softly again and again. He was only whispering now, with frightened eyes and head bowed under the arms that curled over his head toward the window like waves. His old hands with their twisted and protruding veins were clamped to the window ledge. Finally his lips stopped moving and suddenly, as though his strength were exhausted, he let his arms fall and left the window. His big useless hands swung from his body as though attached by ropes and with no vital connection and his bowed head seemed no longer capable of sight.

But while the man still stood there completely lost, Kern saw the next face at the window grow rigid with horror. There followed hasty gestures and once more the dreadful inconsolable stare, the blind inward searching for some impossible rescue.

"So this is paradise?" Kern asked.

"Yes," Klassmann replied. "This is paradise, at least by comparison. Many are refused; but there are many too who get extensions."

They went along several corridors and came to a room that no longer looked like a ticket room but like a fourth-class waiting room. It was filled with a mixture of nationalities. There were not enough benches, and people were standing or sitting on the floor. Kern saw a heavy dark woman sitting on the floor in one corner like a broad-beamed nesting hen. She had impassive regular features. Her black hair was parted in the middle and done up in braids. Around her a number of children were at play. She had the smallest child at her bared breast. She sat there un-embarrassed amid the confusion with the striking nobility of a healthy animal and the rights of every mother, paying attention only to her brood who played around her knees and back as though around a statue.

Beside her stood a group of Jews, with quivering gray beards, wearing caftans and ear-locks. They stood waiting with an expression of imperturbable resignation as though they had already been waiting for centuries and knew they would have to wait for centuries more. On one bench sat a pregnant woman, beside her a man who kept up a con-stant rubbing of his hands. Beside him a man with white hair was softly comforting a weeping woman. On the other side a pimply young fellow was smoking cigarettes and furtively, like a thief, staring at a beautiful and elegant woman opposite him who was putting on and taking off her gloves. A hunchback was writing in a notebook. A number of Roumanians were hissing like steaming kettles. A man was looking at some photographs, putting them in his pocket, immediately getting them out again, to stare at them again and once more put them away. A fat woman was reading an Italian newspaper. A young girl sat there completely sunk in sorrow, taking no notice.

"These are all people who have applied for permits," Klassmann said, "or are about to apply for them."

"What sort of papers do you need to do that?"

"Most of them have valid passports, or passports that have expired and not been renewed — or in some way or other have got into the country legally, with a visa."

"Then this is not the worst department?"

"No," said Klassmann.

Kern saw that in addition to the male clerks there were some girls sitting behind the windows. They were pretty and smartly dressed; most of them wore bright blouses and half-length black-satin sleeve protectors. For an instant it seemed strange to him that behind the windows there should be human beings to whom it was a matter of consequence to protect the sleeves of their blouses from getting dirty, while in front there was a crowd of people whose whole lives were sunk in dirt.

"In the last few weeks it has been especially bad in the Prefecture," Klassmann said. "Whenever anything happens in Germany to make the neighboring countries nervous, the emigrees are the first to suffer. They are the scapegoats for one and all."

Kern saw a man with a thin, intelligent face, standing at one of the windows. His papers appeared to be in order; after a few questions the young girl behind the window took them and began to write. But Kern saw that the man had begun to sweat just standing there at the window waiting. The big room was cold and the man was wearing a thin summer suit, but the sweat streamed out of every pore. His face gleamed with moisture and bright drops ran over his forehead and cheeks. He stood motionless, with his arms resting on the window ledge, in a polite but not subservient attitude, prepared to answer questions — and his wish was being fulfilled; nevertheless he was nothing but a death sweat, as though he were being roasted on invisible fires of heartlessness. If he had screamed, lamented or begged it would not have struck Kern as so horrible. But that he should stand there in polite composure, courageously ready to accept his fate, and that only his sweat glands were traitors to his will — that was as if the man were drowning in himself. It was animal distress itself that was trickling through all the dams of conventional conduct.

The girl returned his paper with a friendly word. The

man thanked her smoothly in excellent French and moved quickly away. Not until he reached the door of the hall did he open the paper to see what was in it. There was a bluish stamp with a couple of dates, but all at once it seemed to the man as if it were the month of May and the nightingales of freedom were singing in the barren room.

"Shall we go?" Kern asked.

"Have you seen enough?"

"Yes."

They went toward the exit but they were stopped by a crowd of miserable Jews who circled round them like a flock of disheveled and hungry jackdaws.

"Pleece — help — " The eldest stepped forward with a sweeping gesture of obeisance. "We not speak French — pleece — help — man — man."

"Man — man — " the others joined in the chorus flapping their loose sleeves. "Man — man — "

It seemed to be the single word of German they knew, for they repeated it unceasingly, pointing with their worn yellowish hands to themselves, to their foreheads, their eyes, their hearts — over and over in a softly urgent, ingratiating singsong: "Man — man — " And only the eldest added "Fellow man . . ." He knew a few more words.

"Do you speak Yiddish?" Klassmann asked.

"No," Kern replied, "not a word."

"These are Jews who speak only Hebrew. They sit here day after day and cannot make themselves understood. They are looking for someone to translate for them."

"Yiddish, Yiddish," the eldest nodded eagerly.

"Man — man," buzzed the flapping chorus with excited and expressive faces.

"Help — help." The eldest pointed to the windows. "Not speak, only 'Man — man.' "

Klassmann made a regretful gesture, "No Yiddish."

The jackdaws surrounded Kern. "Yiddish — Yiddish — man."

Kern shook his head. The flapping died away. The eldest asked once more, in horrified attitude with bent head: "Not . . . ?"

Kern shook his head again. "Ah — " The old Jew raised his hands to his breast; his finger tips touched and his hands formed a little roof over his heart. Thus he stood, inclined a little forward as though he were listening for a voice from afar. Then he bowed and slowly let his hands sink.

Kern and Klassmann left the room. When they reached the outer corridor they heard martial music pouring from above, down the stone stairway. It was a rousing march with fanfare and peal of trumpets.

"What under the sun is that?" Kern asked.

"It's the radio. The police recreation rooms are up there. Midday concert."

The music surged down the stairs like a flashing stream — it gathered in the corridor and burst like a waterfall through the wide entry doors. It splashed over a small, lonely figure crouching on the lowest step, dark and colorless like an unmoving lump of black, a little hillock with mad, unresting eyes. It was the old man who had freed himself with such difficulty from the unrelenting window. He crouched in the corner, lost and done for, with bowed shoulders and knees drawn high, as though he would never rise again — and over him, and away in gay and flashing cascades, the music splashed and danced, strong, pitiless, unceasing as life itself.

"Come along," Klassmann said when they were outside, "we'll have a cup of coffee." They sat down at a wicker table in front of a small *bistro*. Kern felt better when he had drunk the bitter black coffee.

"What's the last stop?" he asked.

"The last stop for many is to sit alone somewhere and starve to death. Prisons. Subway stations at night. Under the bridges of the Seine."

Kern looked at the stream of people ceaselessly pushing past the tables of the *bistro*. A girl with a big hatbox on her arm smiled at him as she went by. She turned around again and threw him a quick glance over her shoulder.

"How old are you?" Klassmann asked.

"Twenty-one. Twenty-two soon."

"That's about what I thought." Klassmann stirred his coffee. "I have a son just your age."

"Is he here too?"

"No," Klassmann said. "He's in Germany."

Kern glanced up. "That's bad, I know."

"Not for him."

"So much the better."

"It would be worse for him if he were here," Klassmann said.

"Would it?" Kern glanced at him in surprise.

"Yes. I'd beat him until he was crippled."

"What?"

"He denounced me. It was because of him I had to leave."

"What the hell!" Kern said.

"I'm a Catholic, a good Catholic. But my youngster has belonged for years to one of the Party's youth organizations. They're called 'veterans' now. You can understand I wasn't too pleased, and there were words between us. The boy became more and more impudent. One day, just as if he were a non-com talking to a recruit, he told me to shut my mouth or something would happen to me. Threatened me, see? I gave him a good cuff on the ear. He rushed out in a rage and denounced me to the state police. Repeated word for word in a declaration the insulting things I had said about the Party. Luckily I had a friend there who warned me by telephone. I had to clear out right away. An hour later a squad came to get me — with my son in command."

"No joke," Kern said.

Klassmann nodded. "It'll be no joke for him when I get back again."

"Perhaps by then he'll have a son of his own who will denounce him. Perhaps by that time it will be the Communists to whom he denounces him."

Klassmann looked at him in dismay. "Do you think it will last that long?"

"I don't know. I can't picture myself ever getting back."

* * *

Steiner was fastening a badge of the National Socialist Party under the left lapel of his coat. "Magnificent, Beer," he said. "Where in the world did you get it?"

Dr. Beer grinned. "From a patient. Automobile accident just outside Murten. I set his arm. At first he was cautious and pretended he thought everything was wonderful over there; then we had a couple of cognacs together and he began to curse their whole economic set-up and gave me his Party badge as a souvenir. Unfortunately he had to go back to Germany."

"Blessings on the man!" Steiner picked up a blue portfolio from the table and opened it. There was a list with a swastika and a few propaganda releases in it. "I'm sure this will do. He'll fall for it ten times over."

He had received the list and the releases from Beer, to whom such things had been sent for years, for reasons that were not clear, from a Party organization in Stuttgart. Steiner had made a selection and was now going on the warpath against Ammers. Beer had told him what had happened to Kern.

"When are you moving on?" Beer asked.

"At eleven o'clock. Before that I'll bring back your badge."

"Fine. I'll be waiting for you with a bottle of brandy."

Steiner went off. He rang at Ammers' door. The maid opened it. "I'd like to speak to Herr Ammers," he said shortly. "My name is Huber." The maid disappeared and came back. "What did you want to see him about?"

Aha, Steiner thought, that's because Kern was here. He knew that Kern had not been asked. "A Party matter," he explained shortly.

This time Ammers himself appeared and stared at Steiner eagerly. Steiner raised his hand casually. "Party Member Ammers?"

"Yes."

Steiner turned over the lapel of his coat and showed the badge. "Huber," he explained. "I represent the Foreign Division and I want to ask a few questions."

Ammers stood in a stiff, bowed position. "Please come in, Herr — Herr — "

"Huber. Simply Huber. You know — the enemy have ears everywhere."

"I know! This is a great honor, Herr Huber."

Steiner had calculated correctly. It never occurred to Ammers to distrust him. Obedience and fear of the Gestapo

Flotsam

were much too deep in his bones. And even if he had been distrustful, he could have done nothing to Steiner in Switzerland. Steiner had an Austrian passport in the name of Huber. To what extent he was connected with the German organization no one could find out. Not even the German Embassy, which had long ago lost track of all the secret propaganda measures.

Ammers led Steiner into the living room. "Take a seat, Ammers," Steiner said, and himself sat down in Ammers' chair.

He leafed through the contents of the portfolio. "You know, Party Member Ammers, that we have one general principle in our foreign activities — silence."

Ammers nodded.

"We expected that in your case too. Silent activity. Now we hear you have made an unnecessary disturbance in the case of a young emigree!"

Ammers leaped from his chair. "That criminal! He made me absolutely sick, sick and ridiculous. The scoundrel — "

"Ridiculous?" Steiner interrupted him cuttingly. "Publicly ridiculous? Friend Ammers — "

"Not publicly, not publicly!" Ammers saw he had made a mistake. He almost fell over himself with excitement. "Only in my own eyes, I mean — "

Steiner looked at him piercingly. "Ammers!" he then said slowly. "A true member of the Party is never ridiculous, even in his own eyes! What's the matter with you, man? Have the Democratic moles been gnawing away at the roots of your principles? *Ridiculous* — there is no such word in our vocabulary! It's the others who are thoroughly ridiculous, do you understand?"

"Yes, of course, of course!" Ammers wiped his forehead. He already half saw himself in a concentration camp to freshen up his principles. "It was just this one case! Otherwise I'm strong as steel. My loyalty is unshakable —"

Steiner let him go on talking for a while. Then he cut him short. "All right, Party Member. I hope nothing of this sort will happen again. Pay no more attention to emigrees, understand? We're glad to be rid of them."

Ammers nodded eagerly. He stood up and brought a crystal decanter and two silver liqueur glasses with long stems and gold inlay from the sideboard. Steiner looked at his preparations with horror. "What's this?" he asked.

"Cognac. I thought perhaps you would like a little refreshment."

"You only serve cognac this way when it's very bad, Ammers," Steiner said with a touch of geniality, "or if you're giving it to a member of some order dedicated to chastity. Bring me a plain tumbler that's not too small."

"Very good!" Ammers was delighted that the ice seemed to be broken.

Steiner drank. The cognac was fairly good. But that was not thanks to Ammers. There was no bad cognac in Switzerland.

Steiner took the blue portfolio out of the leather brief case Beer had loaned him. "Here, by the way, is something else, friend. Strictly confidential. You know that our propaganda in Switzerland has not been going as well as it should?"

"Yes," Ammers agreed eagerly. "I've always said that myself."

"All right." Steiner genially dismissed the difficulty. "That's going to be changed. We're going to establish a secret fund." He glanced at his list. "We already have several large gifts. But smaller contributions are also welcome. This attractive house belongs to you, doesn't it?"

"Yes. To be sure there are two large mortgages on it. And so to all intents and purposes it really belongs to the bank," Ammers announced hurriedly.

"The mortgages are there so you'll have less taxes to pay. A Party member who owns a house is no four-flusher who doesn't have enough money in the bank. How much shall I put you down for?"

Ammers looked nonplused. "It's not at all a bad thing for you just now," Steiner said encouragingly. "We'll naturally send the list of names to Berlin. I think we can put you down for fifty francs."

Ammers appeared relieved. He had counted on a hundred at least. He knew how insatiable the Party was. "Why, of course," he agreed immediately. "Or perhaps sixty," he added.

"Good, we'll say sixty then." Steiner made a note. "Have you any given name beside Heinz?"

"Heinz, Karl, Goswin — Goswin with an S."

"Goswin is an unusual name."

"Yes, but thoroughly German! Old German. There was a king named Goswin during the Migration of Nations."

"I can well believe it!"

Ammers laid down on the table a note for fifty francs and one for ten. Steiner pocketed the money. "A receipt is out of the question," he said. "You understand why?"

"Of course! Secrecy! Here in Switzerland!" Ammers winked slyly.

"And no unnecessary rows in the future, Party Member! Keeping quiet is half the battle! Always remember that!"

"Certainly! I know how to behave! This was only an unfortunate accident."

Steiner walked through the winding streets back to Dr. Beer's. He grinned contentedly. Cancer of the liver! That Kern! How he'd look when he got the sixty francs from this expedition of revenge!

Chapter Seventeen

THERE was a knock. Ruth listened intently. She was alone. Since morning Kern had been out looking for work. For an instant she hesitated, then she got up quietly, went into Kern's room and shut the communicating door behind her. The two rooms were situated around the corner from each other. This was an advantage in case of raids. You could reach the corridor from either room without being seen by anyone standing in front of the other door.

Ruth noiselessly closed the outer door of Kern's room. Then she walked along the corridor and around the corner.

A man about forty years old was standing in front of her door. Ruth knew him by sight. His name was Brose and he lived in the hotel. For seven months his wife had been sick in bed. They lived on a small stipend from the Refugees' Aid and on a little money they had brought with them. This was no secret. In the Hotel Verdun each knew almost all there was to know about everyone else.

"Do you want to see me?" Ruth asked.

"Yes. I wanted to ask you a favor. You're Fräulein Holland, aren't you?"

"Yes."

"My name is Brose and I live on the floor below you," the man said in embarrassment. "My wife is sick and I have to go out to look for work. So I wanted to ask whether, perhaps, you had a little time — "

Brose had a narrow, tormented face. Ruth knew that almost everyone in the hotel ran from him at sight. He was always looking for company for his wife.

"She's alone a great deal — and you must know what that's like. It's easy for her to lose hope. There are days when she's especially sad. But if she has a little company she gets better at once. I thought perhaps you too would like some conversation. My wife is intelligent — "

Ruth was just learning to knit pullover sweaters out of light cashmere wool; she had been told there was a Russian firm in the Champs Elysées that would buy them in order to resell at three times the price. She wanted to go on working and probably would have refused to accompany Brose, but this pathetic word of praise, "My wife is intelligent," was decisive. In a strange way it made her feel ashamed. "Wait a minute," she said. "I'll get a few things and then I'll go with you."

She fetched her wool and the pattern and went downstairs with Brose. His wife was lying in bed in a little room that faced toward the street. Brose's face changed as he entered with Ruth. It radiated forced cheerfulness. "Lucy, here is Fräulein Holland," he said eagerly. "She wants to keep you company for a while."

Two dark eyes in a waxen pale face turned suspiciously toward Ruth. "Well, then, I'll go now," Brose said hurriedly. "I'll be back tonight. I'm sure I'll get something today. Good-by."

He waved to them, smiling, and closed the door behind him.

After a while the pale woman said, "He got you to come, didn't he?"

Ruth started to contradict her, but then she just nodded.

"That's what I thought. Thanks for coming; but I can

get along all right by myself. Don't let me disturb you in your work. I can get some sleep."

"I haven't any plans," Ruth said. "I'm just learning to knit and I can do that just as well here. I brought my wool and needles with me."

"There are pleasanter things than sitting with an invalid," the woman said wearily.

"Certainly. But it's better than sitting alone."

"Everyone says that just to comfort me," the woman murmured. "I know, people are always trying to comfort the sick. Why don't you admit you find it repulsive to sit with an unknown, bad-tempered invalid and that you're only doing it because my husband persuaded you to?"

"That's right," Ruth replied. "And I have no intention of comforting you. But I'm glad to have a chance to talk to someone."

"But you could go outdoors," the sick woman said.

"I don't care much for that."

Ruth glanced up when there was no answer. She saw a face from which all control had vanished. The sick woman had propped herself up and was staring at her, and suddenly tears streamed from her eyes. For an instant her face was inundated. "My God," she sobbed. "You can say that — and I — If I could only get out on the streets just once more — "

She fell back among the pillows. Ruth had risen. She saw the gray-white shoulders shake, she saw the miserable bedstead in the dusty afternoon light; and she saw beyond it the cold sunny street, the houses with their little iron balconies — and towering over the roofs a gigantic electric sign, the advertisement for Dubonnet *apéritif*, senselessly shining in broad afternoon; and for a moment it seemed to her as if all this were very far away, on some other planet.

The woman stopped crying. Slowly she straightened up. "You're still there?" she asked.

"Yes."

"I'm nervous and hysterical. Sometimes I have days like this. Please don't be angry with me."

"No. I was thoughtless, that's all."

Ruth sat down again beside the bed. She laid the sweater pattern she had brought with her in front of her and went on copying it. She did not look at the sick woman. She did not want to see that uncontrolled face again. Her own good health seemed in bad taste by contrast.

"You're not holding the needles right," the sick woman said presently. "And that's slowing you up. This is the way to do it."

She took the needles and showed Ruth. Then she took the part Ruth had knitted out of her hands and looked at it. "You've dropped a stitch here," she explained. "We'll have to unravel it. Look, this way!"

Ruth glanced up. The sick woman was smiling at her. Her face was now attentive and animated and entirely absorbed in her work. It showed no trace of the former outburst. Her pale hands were working easily and quickly. "There," she said eagerly. "Now you try it."

Ruth took the knitting. Strange, she thought in amazement; is it terrible that something like this can change so quickly or is it a tremendous comfort?

When Brose returned that evening the room was dark. Beyond the window was the apple-green evening sky and the huge flaming-red Dubonnet sign. "Lucy?" he said into the darkness.

The woman in the bed stirred and now Brose could see her face. It had a soft reddish glow from the reflection of the electric sign — as though a miracle had happened and she had suddenly become well.

"Were you asleep?" he asked.

"No, I've just been lying quietly."

"Has Fräulein Holland been gone long?"

"No, only for a few minutes."

"Lucy." He seated himself cautiously on the edge of the bed.

"My dear." She stroked his hand. "Did you find anything?"

"Not yet. But I will in time."

For a while the woman lay in silence. "I am such a burden to you, Otto," she said presently.

"How can you say such a thing, Lucy! What would I be without you?"

"You would be free. You could do what you liked. You could even go back to Germany and work."

"Could I?"

"Yes," she said. "Get a divorce from me. Back there they'll think very highly of you for doing it."

"The noble Aryan finally takes thought for the purity of his blood and divorces the Jewess, eh?" Brose asked.

"Very likely that's what they'll say. After all they haven't anything against you, Otto."

"No, but I have against them."

Brose rested his head against the bedpost. He remembered the time when his superior had come into the drafting room and had spent a long while talking about the times and about Brose's ability and what a shame it was that they would have to give him notice simply because he had a Jewish wife. He had taken his hat and left. A week later he had given a bloody nose to the janitor, who was also Party ward-heeler and spy, because he had called Brose's wife a dirty Jewess. That had been very nearly a disaster. Luckily his lawyer had been able to prove that the janitor had made drunken speeches against the Government; whereupon the janitor had disappeared. But his wife no longer felt safe on the street. She did not like being jostled by prep school boys in uniform. Brose could not find another position, and so they had left for Paris. On the way his wife had become ill.

The apple-green sky beyond the window lost its color. It became misty and dark. "Have you been in pain, Lucy?" Brose asked.

"Not much. I am just dreadfully tired. Way inside."

Brose stroked her hair. It gleamed in the copper reflection from the Dubonnet sign. "You'll soon be able to get up again."

The woman slowly moved her head under his hand. "What can it be, Otto? I've never had anything of this sort before and this has lasted for months!"

"It's just one of those things. Nothing serious. Women often get something like this."

"I don't think I'll ever be well again," his wife said in sudden despair.

"You are going to get well soon. You just have to keep up your courage."

Outside night crept over the roofs. Brose sat quietly, his head still resting against the bedpost. His face, which had been distressed and fearful during the day, became serene and peaceful in the last vague light.

"I love you, Lucy," Brose said softly, without changing his position.

"No one can love a sick woman."

"A sick woman is doubly to be loved, for she is a woman and a child at the same time."

"That's just it!" The woman's voice grew small and constrained. "I'm not even that. Not even your wife. You don't have even that. I am only a burden, nothing more."

"I have your hair," Brose said, "your beloved hair." He bent over and kissed her hair. "I have your eyes." He kissed her eyes. "Your hands." He kissed her hands. "I have you. Your love. Or don't you love me any more?"

His face was close above hers. "Don't you love me any more?" he asked.

"Otto — " she murmured weakly and pushed her hand between her breast and him.

"Don't you love me any more?" he asked softly. "Say it. I can understand you might no longer love a worthless fellow who isn't able to earn a living. Just say it once, Beloved, Only One!" he said threateningly to the wasted face.

Suddenly her eyes overflowed with happy tears and her voice was soft and young. "Do you really love me still?" she asked with a smile that tore his heart.

"Must I repeat it every evening? I love you so much I am jealous of the bed you lie on. You ought to lie in me, in my heart and in my blood!"

He smiled so that she would see it and once more bent over her. He loved her and she was all he had — but nevertheless he often had an inexplicable reluctance to kiss her. He hated himself for it. He knew the cause of her suffering and his healthy body was simply stronger than he was. But now in the tender warm reflection of the *apéritif* sign the evening was like an evening of years ago — beyond the dark power of the disease — a warm and comforting reflection like the red light from the roofs across the way.

"Lucy," he murmured.

She pressed her wet lips against his mouth. Thus she lay quietly, forgetting for a while her tortured body in which, in ghostlike silence, cancer cells ran riot and, under the spectral touch of death, uterus and ovaries were slowly falling like weary coals into gray amorphous ash.

*   *   *

Kern and Ruth were strolling along the Champs Elysées. It was evening. The shop windows blazed, the cafés were full of people, electric signs glittered; and dark, like an entrance to heaven, stood the Arc de Triomphe in the clear air of Paris which is silvery even at night.

"Just look there to the right," Kern said. "Waser and Rosenfeld."

In front of the huge show window of the General Motors Company stood two young men. They were shabbily dressed. Their suits were threadbare and neither of them wore an overcoat. They were arguing so heatedly that Kern and Ruth stood beside them for some time without being noticed. They were inmates of the Hotel Verdun. Waser was a technician and a Communist; Rosenfeld, the son of a banking family from Frankfort, who lived on the third floor. Both were car fanciers. Both lived on almost nothing.

"Rosenfeld!" Waser said imploringly. "Just try to be sensible for a minute. A Cadillac — not bad at all for old people! But what do you want with a sixteen-cylinder job? It drinks gasoline the way a cow drinks water and isn't a bit faster for all that."

Rosenfeld shook his head. He was staring in fascination at the brightly lighted show window, in which a tremendous black Cadillac was slowly turning on a revolving stand. "Suppose it does use up gas?" he exclaimed excitedly. "By the barrel, as far as I'm concerned! That's not the point. Just see how marvelously comfortable the body is, as safe and reassuring as an armor-plated turret!"

"Rosenfeld, those are arguments for a life insurance policy, but not for a car!" Waser pointed to the next window which belonged to the Lancia agency. "Just take a look at that. You have breeding and class there. Only four cylinders, but a low-slung nervous creature, like a panther ready to spring. In it you could run straight up the wall of a house if you wanted to."

"I don't want to run up the wall of a house. I want to drive to the Ritz for cocktails," Rosenfeld replied unmoved.

Waser disregarded this objection. "Take a look at its lines," he cried enthusiastically. "The way it seems to creep along close to the ground! An arrow, a bolt of lightning — by comparison even the eight-cylinder job strikes me as too heavy. A dream of speed!"

Rosenfeld broke into derisive laughter. "And how do you expect to get into that baby's coffin? Waser, Waser, that's a car for Lilliputians! Picture a woman in evening clothes with an expensive fur coat and perhaps a dress of gold brocade or sequins. You're coming out of Maxim's — it's December, say, with snow and slush on the street — and you in this radio cabinet on wheels. Can't you see you'd just be ridiculous?"

Waser got bright red in the face. "Those are the ideas of a capitalist. For pity's sake, Rosenfeld, you're dreaming of a locomotive, not an automobile. How can you get any satisfaction out of a mammoth like that? It's all right for captains of industry, but you're a young fellow. If you have to have something heavier, then for God's sake take a Delahaye. It has breeding and can always turn up one hundred sixty kilometers without trying."

"Delahaye," Rosenfeld snapped. "And fouled sparkplugs every few minutes. That's what you like, eh?"

"Not a chance, if you know how to drive! A jaguar, a projectile! You get drunk listening to the song of the motor. Or if you want something really marvelous, then take the new Supertalbot: it's good for one hundred eighty kilometers. You've really got something there."

Rosenfeld sputtered with indignation. "A Talbot! Yes, I've got something there! That's a car I wouldn't take as a gift. A machine with so much compression it boils in traffic. No, my friend. I'll stick to the Cadillac." He turned back to the General Motors window. "Just look at its quality; for five years at a time you don't even have to lift the hood. Luxury, dear Waser! Only the Americans really understand luxury. The motor is sleek and noiseless, you can't even hear it."

"But, man alive," Waser broke out, "I want to hear the motor. That's music when a nervous beast like that starts."

"Then buy yourself a tractor! That's even louder."

Waser glared at him wild-eyed. "Listen to me," he said, controlling himself with difficulty. "I propose a compromise: take a Mercedes Compressor! Heavy, but with breeding too. Agreed?"

Rosenfeld waved aside the suggestion. "Not for me, thanks. Don't waste your words. A Cadillac or nothing." He lost himself again in contemplating the black elegance of the huge car on the turntable.

Waser looked around and caught sight of Kern and Ruth. "Listen, Kern," he said in despair. "If you had a choice between a Cadillac and one of the new Talbots, which would you take? It would be the Talbot, wouldn't it?"

Rosenfeld swung around. "The Cadillac, of course. There's no doubt at all about that."

"I'd be satisfied with a little Citroën," Kern grinned.

"With a Citroën?" The car fanciers looked sadly at the black sheep.

"Or with a bicycle," Kern added.

The two experts exchanged a quick glance. "Aha," Rosenfeld commented in disgust, "so you don't know much about cars, eh?"

"Or about motor transport in general?" Waser asked coldly. "Well of course there are people who are interested in postage stamps."

"I'm one of them," Kern announced cheerfully. "Especially if the stamps are uncanceled."

"Well, then, we beg your pardon." Rosenfeld turned up the collar of his coat. "Come along, Waser, we'll step over there and take a quick look at the new models of the Alfa Romeo and the Hispano."

They went away together, reconciled through Kern's ignorance, two friends in shabby suits on their way to quarrel about the merits of racing cars. They had time enough, for they had no money to buy supper.

Kern looked after them in amusement. "Aren't human beings wonderful, Ruth?" he said.

Ruth laughed.

Kern could not find work. He tried everywhere, but could get no employment even at twenty francs a day. At the end of two weeks, their money was gone. Ruth received a small allowance from the Jewish committee and Kern from the Jewish-Christian one; altogether it amounted to about fifty francs a week. Kern had a talk with the landlady and arranged for them to keep the two rooms for this price and to get coffee and rolls in the morning as well. They were not especially unhappy about it. They were living in Paris and that was enough. They kept hoping for what the next day would bring and they felt safe. In this city, which had assimilated all the migrations of the century, a spirit of toleration prevailed; one could starve to death in it but one was harried only as much as was absolutely necessary — and this meant a great deal to them.

One Sunday afternoon when there was no admission charge Marill took them with him to the Louvre. "In winter," he said, "you need some way of passing your time. The emigrees' problems are hunger, a place to live, and time, which he doesn't know how to use because he can't work. Hunger and a place to live are the two mortal enemies he has to fight against — but unprofitable and unused time is the slinking enemy that destroys his energy, the waiting that exhausts him and the shadowy fear that takes away his strength. The others attack from the front and he has to fight them or succumb — but time creeps up from behind and poisons his blood. You are young; don't sit around cafés; don't complain, don't lose your zest. When things get tough, go to the great waiting room of Paris — the Louvre. It is well heated in winter. It's better to be sad in front of a Delacroix, a Rembrandt, or a van Gogh, than in front of a glass of brandy or a circle of angry, impotent and whining people. It is I who tell you this — I, Marill, who prefers to sit facing a glass of brandy."

Otherwise, of course, I wouldn't deliver these instructive lectures."

They wandered through the dim corridors of the Louvre — past the centuries, past the stone Pharaohs of Egypt, the gods of Greece, the Cæsars of Rome, past Babylonian altars, Persian rugs and Flemish tapestries, past the great works of human genius, Rembrandt, Goya, El Greco, Leonardo, Dürer — through endless galleries and corridors until they came to the rooms in which hung the paintings of the Impressionists. They sat down on one of the sofas that stood in the middle of the room. On the walls shone the landscapes of Cézanne, van Gogh and Monet, the dancers of Degas, Renoir's pastel portraits of women, and the bright scenes of Manet. It was quiet and no one else was there. Gradually it seemed to Kern and Ruth as though they were sitting in an enchanted tower and the pictures were windows opening on distant worlds: on gardens of placid joy, on generous feelings, on magnificent dreams — an eternal country of the soul beyond caprice, fear and injustice.

"Emigrees!" Marill said. "All of those men were emigrees too! Driven about, laughed to scorn, booted out, often without a place to stay, hungry, many of them abused and ignored by their contemporaries, living in misery and dying miserably — but just see what they have created! The culture of the world, that's what I wanted to show you."

He took off his glasses and polished them thoughtfully. "What is the strongest impression you get from these pictures?" he asked Ruth.

"Peace," she replied promptly.

"Peace? I thought you would say beauty, but it's true —

today peace is beauty. Especially for us. And yours, Kern?"

"I don't know," Kern said. "I would just like to own one of them so that I could sell it and get some money to live on."

"You're an idealist," Marill replied.

Kern looked at him suspiciously.

"I'm being serious," Marill said.

"I know it's stupid, but it's winter and I would like to buy a coat for Ruth."

Kern appeared dull in his own eyes; but actually he could think of nothing else and this idea had been in his mind the whole time. To his amazement he suddenly felt Ruth's hand in his. Her face was radiant and she pressed close against him.

Marill put his glasses on again, then he looked around. "Man is magnificent in his extremes — in art, in stupidity, in love, in hate, in egotism and even in sacrifice; but what the world lacks most is a certain average goodness."

Kern and Ruth had finished their supper. It consisted of cocoa and bread and for a week had been their single meal aside from the cup of coffee and the two *brioches* that Kern had arranged to have included in the price of the rooms.

"Today the bread tastes like beefsteak," Kern said. "Like good juicy beefsteak with fried onions."

"It seems to me it tastes like chicken," Ruth replied, "like a young broiler with fresh green salad on the side."

"Possibly it does on your end. Give me a slice of it. I could easily manage some chicken too."

Ruth cut a thick slice from the long loaf of white French bread. "Here," she said, "this is a second joint. Or would you rather have some of the breast?"

Kern laughed. "Ruth, if I didn't have you I'd be ready now to quarrel with God."

"And without you I'd lie down on the bed and howl."

There was a knock. "Brose," Kern said gloomily. "Of course, right in the middle of a tender love scene."

"Come in," Ruth called.

The door opened. "No," Kern said. "That's not possible! I'm dreaming!" He got up cautiously as if he were trying not to frighten away a phantom. "Steiner!" he stammered. The phantom grinned. "Steiner!" Kern cried. "God in heaven, it's Steiner!"

"A good memory is the basis of friendship and the ruin of love," Steiner replied. "Excuse me, Ruth, for marching in with a maxim — but I have just run into my old friend Marill downstairs. And so something like this was almost inevitable."

"Where did you come from?" Kern asked. "Straight from Vienna?"

"From Vienna. Round about by way of Murten."

"What?" Kern took a step backward. "By way of Murten?"

Ruth laughed. "Murten was the scene of our disgrace, Steiner. I got sick there — and this veteran of the borders was picked up by the police. That name has a cheerless sound for us — Murten."

Steiner grinned. "That's why I went there. I avenged you, children." He produced his wallet and took out of it sixty Swiss francs. "Here you are. This is fourteen dollars, or about three hundred and fifty French francs. A gift from Ammers."

Kern looked at him in bewilderment. "Ammers?" he said, "three hundred and fifty francs?"

"I'll explain it to you later, my boy. Put it in your pocket. And now let's have a look at you!" He scrutinized them. "Hollow cheeks, undernourished, cocoa and water for supper — and you haven't said a word to anyone, eh?"

"Not yet," Kern replied. "Every time we were on the point of it, Marill would invite us for a meal. As though he had some sixth sense."

"He has another beside that. For pictures. Did he drag you off to the museum after the meal? That's the usual penalty."

"Yes, to Cézanne, van Gogh, Manet, Renoir and Degas."

"Aha! To the Impressionists. Then you had your mid-day meal with him. After dinner he takes one to Rembrandt, Goya and El Greco. But come along now, children, put on your things! The restaurants of the city of Paris are blazing with lights and waiting for us!"

"We've just — "

"So I see!" Steiner interrupted grimly. "Put on your things at once! I'm dripping with money."

"We've got our things on already."

"Is that so! Sold your coats to a fellow believer who unquestionably swindled you — "

"No," Ruth said.

"My child, there are dishonest Jews too. Holy though your people appear to me at the moment as a race of martyrs! Well then, come along! We'll investigate the racial problems of roast chickens."

"Well, spill it. What's up?" Steiner said after the meal. "There's been a kind of jinx," Kern said. "Paris is not only the city of toilet water, soap and perfume, it is also the city of safety pins, shoelaces, buttons and apparently holy pictures as well. Peddling is almost impossible here. I've tried a lot of different jobs — I've washed dishes, carried market baskets, addressed envelopes, traded in toys — none of it was any real good. It was all in-and-out stuff. Ruth had a job for two weeks cleaning an office; then the company went bankrupt and she got nothing for her pains. For sweaters made of cashmere wool, she was offered exactly as much as the wool cost. As a result — "

He opened his jacket. "As a result I'm going around like a rich American. Marvelous when one hasn't a coat. Perhaps she'll knit this kind of sweater for you, too, Steiner — "

"I still have enough wool for one," Ruth said. "Black, to be sure. Do you like black?"

"And how! Black's the right color for us." Steiner lit a cigarette. "Well, that's clear enough! Did you sell your coats or pawn them?"

"Pawned them first, then sold them."

"Sure. The usual way. Have you ever been to the Café Maurice?"

"No. Only to the Alsace."

"Good. Then we'll just go to the Maurice. There's a man named Dickmann there. He knows everything. All about coats too. I want to ask him about a more important matter as well. About the International Exposition that's coming this year."

"The International Exposition?"

"Yes, Baby," Steiner said. "There's supposed to be work. And I hear they're not too fussy about papers."

"How long have you actually been in Paris, Steiner, to have found out all this?"

"Four days. Before that I was in Strassburg. There was something I had to look after there. I found you through

Klassmann. Ran into him at the Prefecture. I have a passport, children. In a couple of days I'm going to move into the Hotel International. I like the name."

The Café Maurice was like the Café Sperler in Vienna and the Café Greif in Zürich. It was a typical emigrees' exchange. Steiner ordered coffee for Kern and Ruth and then went across the room to speak to a middle-aged man. They conversed for a time, then the man glanced appraisingly at Kern and Ruth and went out.

"That was Dickmann," Steiner said. "He knows everything. I was right about the Exposition, Kern. The Foreign Pavilions are being built now. They are being paid for by the foreign governments. They bring some of their own workmen with them, but for day laborers' jobs, digging and that sort of thing, they hire their people here. And there's our big chance! Since the wages are paid by the foreign Committees, the French don't pay much attention to who works there. We'll have a try at it tomorrow morning early. There are a lot of emigrees working already. We're cheaper than the French — that's our advantage!"

Dickmann came back carrying two coats over his arm. "I think these will fit."

"Try on this coat," Steiner said to Kern. "You first. Then Ruth will try the other. Resistance is useless."

The coats fitted perfectly. Ruth's even had a shabby little fur collar. Dickmann smiled faintly. "I've a good eye," he said.

"Are these the best of your cast-off junk, Heinrich?" Steiner asked.

Dickmann looked offended. "The coats are all right. Not

new, as you can see. The one with the fur collar used to belong to a countess. In exile, of course," he added, catching Steiner's eye. "It's genuine raccoon, Josef. Not rabbit."

"All right. We'll take them. I'll be back tomorrow morning and fix things up with you."

"You needn't. You can just take them. I've got a lot more than that to pay you back for."

"Nonsense."

"Yes, I have. Take them and forget about it. I certainly was in a hell of a mess that time. Good God!"

"How are things otherwise?" Steiner asked.

Dickmann shrugged his shoulders. "I make enough for the children and me. But it's disgusting to live on rubbish."

Steiner laughed. "Don't get sentimental, Heinrich. I'm a forger, cardsharp, vagabond; I've been guilty of assault and battery and resisting the police and a lot more beside — and nevertheless my conscience is all right."

Dickmann nodded. "My youngest is sick. Grippe. Fever. But fever doesn't mean much with children, does it?"

He looked imploringly at Steiner. The latter shook his head: "Speeds up the healing process, that's all."

"I'll just go home a little earlier tonight."

Steiner ordered a cognac. "Baby," he said to Kern, "have one too?"

"Listen, Steiner — " Kern began.

Steiner silenced him. "Don't talk. These are Christmas presents that cost me nothing, as you just saw. A cognac, Ruth? You'll have one, won't you?"

"Yes."

"New coats! Work in sight!" Kern drank his cognac. "Existence is beginning to be interesting."

"Don't fool yourself." Steiner grinned. "Later on, when you have enough work, it will be the time when you didn't

have to work that will seem the interesting part of your
life. Wonderful stories for your grandchildren playing
about your knees. 'In those days in Paris — ' "

Dickmann went by. He bowed wearily to them and
walked toward the door.

Steiner looked after him. "He was once a Social Democratic burgomaster. Five children. Wife's dead. He's a
good beggar. Dignified. Knows everything. Does everything. Trades with everyone. His specialty is secondhand
clothes. His soul's a little too tender, as often happens with
Social Democrats. That's why they're such bad politicians."

The café began to fill up. Those who intended to sleep
came in and began to jockey for corner places for the night.
Steiner finished his cognac. "The proprietor is a splendid
fellow. Lets anyone sleep here who can find a place. Free.
Or for the price of a cup of coffee. If dives like this didn't
exist things would look bad for a lot of people."

He got up. "We'll be moving, children."

They went outside. It was windy and cold. Ruth turned
up the raccoon collar of her new coat and drew it close
around her. She smiled up at Steiner. He nodded. "Warmth,
little Ruth! Everything in the world is dependent on just
a little warmth."

He motioned to an old flower woman who was shuffling
by. She came trotting up. "Violets," she cackled. "Fresh
violets from the Riviera."

"What a city! Violets in the middle of the street in
December!" Steiner selected a bunch and gave them to
Ruth. "Violets for luck! Useless flowers! Useless things!
They're what give the greatest warmth." He winked at
Kern. "A lesson in living, Marill would say."

Chapter Eighteen

THEY were sitting in the canteen of the International Exposition. It had been pay day. Kern arranged the thin paper notes in a circle around his plate. "Two hundred and seventy francs!" he said. "Earned in a single week! And this is the third time it's happened! It's like a fairy tale."

Marill looked at him for a moment in amusement. Then he raised his glass to Steiner. "We'll shudder and drink a toast to paper, my dear Huber. It is astounding what power it has gained over people. Our ancient forefathers trembled in their caves for fear of thunder and lightning, tigers and earthquakes; our more recent forebears trembled at swords, robbers, epidemics and God; but we tremble at the printed word — be it on a banknote or a passport. Neanderthal man died by the club; the Roman by the sword; the man of the Middle Ages by the plague; and all it takes to extinguish us is a few scraps of printed paper."

"Or to bring us to life," Kern added and looked at the notes of the Bank of France lying around his plate.

Marill looked at him askance. "What do you make of this boy?" he asked Steiner. "Turning into something, isn't he?"

"You bet! He thrives on the raw winds of exile. Now he's even able to kill the point of a story."

"I knew him when he was a mere child," Marill explained. "Tender and trusting. A couple of months ago."

Steiner laughed. "He lives in a topsy-turvy century. A time when it's easy to be rubbed out — but also a time when you mature fast."

Marill took a sip of the light red wine. "A topsy-turvy century," he repeated; "the great unrest. Ludwig Kern, the young Vandal in the second Migration of Nations."

"That doesn't fit," Kern retorted. "I'm a young half-Jew in the second Exodus from Egypt."

Marill looked at Steiner reproachfully. "Your pupil, Huber," he said.

"No — he learned the trick of aphorisms from you, Marill. Besides, a steady weekly wage improves the wit of any young man. Long live the return of the prodigal son to the pay roll!" Steiner turned toward Kern. "Put the money in your pocket, Baby. Otherwise it will fly away. Money doesn't like the light."

"I'll give it to you," Kern said. "Then it'll be gone right away. You're due for a lot more than this from me."

"Just get this straight. I'm a long way from being rich enough to have money paid back to me."

Kern looked at him. Then he put the money in his pocket. "How long are the stores open tonight?" he asked.

"Why?"

"This is New Year's Eve."

"Till seven, Kern," Marill said. "Are you planning to buy something to drink for tonight? It's cheaper here in the canteen. Excellent Martinique rum."

"No, no drinks."

"Aha! Apparently you're getting ready to spend the last day of the year in the ways of bourgeois sentiment, eh?"

"That's about it." Kern got up. "I'm going to Salomon Levi's. Perhaps he's sentimental today, too, and has topsy-turvy prices."

"In topsy-turvy times the prices rise," Marill replied. "But go ahead, Kern! Habit is nothing — impulse all! And don't get so engrossed in your haggling as to forget dinner at eight for the old warriors of the emigration, at Mère Margot's."

Salomon Levi was a nimble, weaselly little man with a trembling, ragged, goat's beard. He lived in a dark, vaulted room amid clocks, musical instruments, worn rugs, oil paintings, kitchen utensils, plaster gnomes and porcelain animals. In the window were artificial pearls, cheap imitation jewelry, old silver ornaments, watches and old coins mixed helter-skelter together.

Levi recognized Kern immediately. His memory was a ledger that had stood him in good stead in many deals.

"What gives?" he asked, ready for battle at once since he assumed Kern had something more to sell. "You come at a bad time."

"How's that? Have you sold the ring already?"

"Sold, sold?" Levi wailed. "Sold, you said, if I didn't misunderstand you. Or have I made a mistake?"

"No."

"Young man," Levi went on fencing, "don't you read the newspaper? Do you live on the moon? Don't you know what is happening in the world? Sold! Old trash like that! Sold! How can you say such a thing, magnificently like a Rothschild? Do you know what it means to make a sale?" He paused for effect and then explained mournfully: "It means that a stranger comes and wants something and that then he draws his purse out of his pocket — " Levi took out his wallet. "Opens it." He opened it. "And gets out cold kosher money." He plucked out a fifty-franc note. "Puts it down." The note was smoothed out on the counter. "And then the most important thing of all!" Levi's voice rose to falsetto. "He permanently separates himself from it!"

Levi put the note away. "And for what? For some trinket, some gewgaw, cold kosher money. Am I to laugh? Only crazy people and *gojim* act like that. Or an unlucky fool with my passion for business. Well, what have you today? Much I cannot give. Four weeks ago — now, those were fine times."

"I don't want to sell anything, Herr Levi. I'd like to buy back the ring."

"What!" For an instant Levi's mouth fell open like a hungry yellowhammer in its nest. His beard was the nest. "*Ach*, already I know. You want to trade. Nix, young man. I know that trick. A week ago I was caught — a watch, sure it did not go, but a watch is a watch, after all. For that I got a bronze inkwell and a fountain pen with a gold nib. What shall I tell you? Tricked I was because I am a blind trusting fool; the fountain pen does not work. Sure, the watch does not go for more than a quarter of an hour, but is it the same thing when a watch does not go and when a fountain pen does not work? A watch is still always a watch, but a fountain pen that is empty, what is that? That is a contradiction; it is like it wasn't there at all. And what did you want to trade?"

"Nothing, Herr Levi. I said buy. Buy!"

"With money?"

"Yes, with real money."

"I know — some Hungarian money or Rumanian money or no-good Austrian money or inflation notes. Who can tell what they are worth? Not long ago came in a man with curled mustaches like Charlemagne — "

Kern brought out a hundred-franc note and placed his wallet on the counter. Levi stiffened and emitted a low whistle. "You are in money? The first time I have seen such a thing. Young man, look out for the police — "

"I earned it," Kern beamed, "earned it honestly. And now where is the ring?"

"This instant." Levi rushed out and came back with the ring that had belonged to Ruth's mother. He was polishing it with the sleeve of his coat, blowing on it and then polishing it again. Finally he laid it on a square of velvet as though it were a twenty-carat diamond. "A fine piece," he said reverently. "A true rarity."

"Herr Levi," Kern said, "you gave us a hundred and fifty francs for the ring. If I give you one hundred eighty you'll have a twenty per cent profit. That's a good bargain, isn't it?"

Levi didn't hear him. "A man could fall in love with a piece like this," he murmured in dreamy ecstasy. "No modern trash. Value! Real value! I planned to keep it myself. I have a little private collection for my own pleasure."

Kern counted out one hundred eighty francs on the counter.

"Money," Levi said scornfully. "What is money today? With devaluation. Goods, they are the only real value. A lovely little ring like this gives a man pleasure and also it goes up in value. A double joy! And just now gold is so high," he remarked thoughtfully. "Four hundred francs would be cheap for such a beautiful piece. A connoisseur's price you might get for it."

Kern recoiled. "Herr Levi!"

"I am human," Levi said nobly. "I shall part with it. I will give you this happiness with no profit to myself. Because this is New Year's Eve. Three hundred francs, done, even though it costs my heart's blood."

"That's twice what you paid," Kern said angrily.

"Twice! You say that casually without knowing what you mean. What is twice? Twice is half, as Rabbi Michael von Howorodka wisely says somewhere. Have you ever heard of overhead, young man? It costs and costs; taxes, rent, coal, assessments, losses. To you that is nothing, but for me it is staggering! Each day it amounts to as much as a little ring like this — "

"I'm a poor man, an emigree — "

Levi dismissed the point. "Who is not an emigree? He who wants to buy is always richer than he who has to sell. Well, and which of us two wants to buy?"

"Two hundred francs," Kern said, "that's my last word."

Levi picked up the ring, blew on it and carried it out. Kern put his money in his pocket and walked to the door. As he was opening it Levi screamed after him: "Two hundred and fifty, because you're young and I like to be a benefactor."

"Two hundred," Kern shouted back from the door.

"*Schalom alechem!*" Levi saluted him.

"Two hundred and twenty."

"Two hundred and twenty-five. On my word of honor because I have to pay the rent tomorrow."

Kern returned and with a sigh laid down the money. Levi packed the ring in a little pasteboard box. "This box you shall have for nothing and the fine blue cotton. Ruined I am because of you."

"Fifty per cent," Kern growled. "Usurer!"

Levi paid no attention to Kern's last remark. "Take my

word for it," he said, sincere for the moment. "At Cartier's, in the Rue de la Paix, a ring like this costs six hundred. It is worth three hundred and fifty. That's the truth."

Kern rode back to the hotel. "Ruth," he said in the doorway, "we're on our way up and going fast. Here! The last of the Mohicans is home again."

She opened the little box and looked inside. "Ludwig —" she said.

"Useless things, that's all!" Kern said quickly in embarrassment. "What is it Steiner says? They're supposed to give the greatest warmth. Just wanted to test it out. And now put it on! We're all going to eat today in a restaurant. Like real workmen with weekly wages!"

*　　*　　*

It was ten o'clock in the evening. Steiner, Marill, Ruth and Kern were sitting in the "Mère Margot." The waiters were beginning to push the chairs together and sweep the floors with tremendous brooms and water. The cat on the cashier's desk stretched and leaped down. The proprietress was asleep, tightly wrapped in a knitted jacket. But from time to time she opened a watchful eye.

"I believe they're trying to shove us out of here," Steiner said, motioning to the waiter. "High time, too. We've got to go to Edith Rosenfeld's. Father Moritz arrived today."

"Father Moritz?" Ruth asked. "Who's that?"

"Father Moritz is the dean of the emigrees," Steiner replied. "Seventy-five years old, little Ruth. Knows all borders, all cities, all hotels, all boardinghouses and private lodgings where one can live unreported, and the jails of five civilized countries. His name is Moritz Rosenthal and he comes from Godesberg-on-the-Rhine."

"Then I know him," Kern said. "I crossed with him once from Czechoslovakia into Austria."

"And I went with him from Switzerland into Italy," Marill said.

The waiter brought the check. "I've crossed a few borders with him myself," Steiner said. "Have you a bottle of cognac I can take with me?" he asked the waiter. "Courvoisier? At store prices of course."

"Just a moment. I'll ask the *patronne*."

The waiter went across to the sleeping woman in the knitted jacket. She opened one eye and nodded. The waiter came back, took a bottle from one of the shelves and gave it to Steiner, who put it in his overcoat pocket.

At this instant the street door opened and a shadowy figure entered. The *patronne* put her hand to her mouth, yawned and opened both eyes. The waiters made wry faces.

The man who had come in went, as silently as a sleep-walker, straight through the room to the big *rôtisserie* in which a few roasting chickens were turning on spits above the glowing wood coals.

The man examined the chickens with X-ray eyes. "How much is that one there?" he asked the waiter.

"Twenty-six francs."

"And that one?"

"Twenty-six francs."

"And that one?"

"Twenty-six francs."

"Do they all cost twenty-six francs?"

"Yes."

"Why didn't you tell me that at once?"

"Because you didn't ask me at once."

The man looked up. For a moment healthy rage showed through his somnambulism. Then he pointed to the biggest chicken. "Give me that one."

Kern nudged Steiner. Steiner was watching attentively. His mouth was twitching.

"With salad, roast potatoes, rice?" the waiter asked.

"With nothing. With a knife and fork. Hand it over."

"The Chicken," Kern whispered. "The old Chicken, as I live and breathe."

Steiner nodded. "That's who it is! The Chicken from the Vienna jail."

The man sat down at a table. He took out his wallet and paid out the money. Then he put it away and solemnly unfolded his napkin. In front of him rested the magnificent roast chicken. The man lifted his hands like a priest bestowing a blessing. A fierce and radiant air of satisfaction enveloped him. Then he lifted the bird and put it on his own plate.

"We'll not disturb him," Steiner whispered softly. "He's earned his roast chicken the hard way."

"Exactly. I propose we get out at once," Kern replied. "I've run into him twice before. Both times in prison. On each occasion he was arrested at the moment when he was about to eat a roast chicken. If he runs true to form, the police will be here any minute!"

Steiner laughed. "Then let's get going! I'd rather celebrate New Year's Eve with those disinherited by fate than in the guardroom of the Prefecture of Police!"

They got up. At the door they looked around again. The Chicken was just detaching a crisp brown leg from the body of the prize. He regarded it, like a pilgrim looking at the Holy Sepulchre, and bit into it reverently. But after that he went at it with determination and enormous appetite.

Edith Rosenfeld was a delicate, white-haired woman of sixty-six. She had come to Paris two years before with eight children. She had found places for seven of them. Her eldest son had gone to China as an army doctor; her eldest daughter, who had been a philologist at Bonn, had secured a position as a servant girl in Scotland through the Refugees' Aid; the second son had passed the French Government examinations in law; when he could not find a practice, he had become a waiter in the Hotel Carleton in Cannes; the third had enlisted in the Foreign Legion; the next had migrated to Bolivia; and the two other daughters were living on an orange plantation in Palestine. The only one left was her youngest son. The Refugees' Aid was trying to get him a job as a chauffeur in Mexico.

Edith Rosenfeld's apartment consisted of two rooms: a larger one for her, and a small one in which this last son, Max Rosenfeld the auto fancier, lived. When Steiner, Marill, Kern and Ruth came in, there were already about twenty persons assembled in the two rooms — all refugees from Germany, some with residential permits but most of them without. Those who could afford it had brought along something to drink. Almost all had chosen cheap, red French wine. Steiner and Marill sat among them like two pillars with their cognac. They poured it out generously, hoping to avoid unnecessary sentimentality.

Moritz Rosenthal arrived at eleven o'clock. Kern barely recognized him. He seemed to have aged ten years in less than one. His face was yellow and bloodless, and he walked with difficulty, leaning on an ebony cane with an old-fashioned ivory handle.

"Edith, my old love," he said, "here I am again. I couldn't come earlier. I was very tired."

He bent over to kiss her hand, but he could not reach it. Edith Rosenfeld stood up. She was as light as a bird. She held his hand and kissed him on the cheek.

"I almost believe I'm getting old," Moritz Rosenthal said. "I can no longer kiss your hand. But you brazenly kiss me on the cheek. Oh to be sixty once again!"

Edith Rosenfeld looked at him smiling. She did not want to show him how shocked she was at his altered appearance. And Moritz Rosenthal didn't show her that he knew how shocked she was. He was calm and cheerful and he had come to Paris to die.

He looked around. "Well-known faces," he said. "Those who belong nowhere meet each other everywhere. Strange stories! . . . Steiner, where were we the last time? In Vienna, right! And Marill? In Brissago, and later in Locarno in the police station, wasn't that it? Why, there's Klassmann too, the Sherlock Holmes of Zürich. Yes, my memory's still functioning fairly well. And Waser! Brose! And Kern from Czecho! Meyer, the friend of *carabinieri* in Palanza! God yes, children, the good old times! Now things are no longer the same. My legs don't want to go on."

He lowered himself cautiously. "Where do you come from now, Father Moritz?" Steiner asked.

"From Basle. Children, let me tell you one thing: avoid Alsace! Be cautious in Strassburg, and flee Colmar! Penitentiary atmosphere. Mathias Gruenwald and the Isenheim altar have had no influence. Three months in prison for illegal entry; there is no other court that gives more than fifteen days. Six months for a second offense, and the prisons are workhouses. So avoid Colmar and Alsace, children! Go by way of Geneva!"

"How's Italy now?" Klassmann asked.

Moritz Rosenthal took the glass of red wine that Edith Rosenfeld had placed beside him. His hands trembled badly as he lifted it. He was ashamed of this and put the glass down again. "Italy is full of German agents," he said. "There is nothing more for us there."

"And Austria?" Waser asked.

"Austria and Czechoslovakia are mousetraps. France is the single country in Europe we have left. Make sure you stay here."

"Have you heard anything of Mary Altmann, Moritz?" Edith Rosenfeld asked after a pause. "She used to be in Milan."

"Yes. She's in Amsterdam now as a chambermaid. Her children are in an emigrees' home in Switzerland. In Locarno, I believe. Her husband's in Brazil."

"Have you seen her to speak to?"

"Yes, just before her trip to Zürich. She was delighted they had all found places."

"Do you know anything of Josef Fessler?" Klassmann asked. "He was waiting in Zürich for a residential permit."

"Fessler shot himself and his wife," Moritz Rosenthal answered as calmly as if he were talking about breeding bees. He didn't look at Klassmann. His eyes were turned toward the door. Klassmann made no reply. Nor did any of the others. There was a moment's silence. Each one acted as if he had heard nothing.

"Have you run into Joseph Friedmann anywhere?" Brose asked.

"No. But I know he's in prison in Salzburg. His brother went back to Germany. He's said to be in a concentration camp now." Moritz Rosenthal took his glass in both hands, as cautiously as though it were a sacramental goblet, and drank slowly.

"What's Minister Althoff doing now?" Marill asked.

"He's in splendid luck. He's a taxi driver in Zürich. Residential permit and permit to work."

"Just as you'd expect!" said Waser the Communist.

"And Bernstein?"

"Bernstein is in Australia. His father's in East Africa. Max May has had especial good luck; he has become assistant to a dentist in Bombay. Black, of course. But he has to eat. Loewenstein took all his law examinations over again in English, and now he's an attorney in Palestine. The actor Hansdorff is at the State Theater in Zürich. Storm hanged himself. Did you know Councilor Binder in Berlin, Edith?"

"Yes."

"He got a divorce. On account of his career. He was married to an Oppenheimer. His wife poisoned herself and their two children."

Moritz Rosenthal reflected for a while. "That's about all I know," he said. "The others are wandering around as usual. Only there are even more of them now."

Marill poured himself a drink of cognac. He used a water glass that bore the inscription *Gare de Lyon*. It was a souvenir of his first arrest and he always carried it with him. He emptied the glass at one gulp. "An instructive chronicle," he commented then. "Long live the destruction of the individual! Among the ancient Greeks thought was a distinction. After that it became a pleasure. Later a weakness. Today it is a crime. The history of civilization is the story of the sufferings of those who have created it."

Steiner grinned at him. Marill grinned back. At that

instant the bells outside began to ring. Steiner looked at the faces around him — the many little destinies blown together here by the Wind of Destiny — and he lifted his glass. "Father Moritz!" he said. "King of the wanderers, last scion of Ahasuerus, eternal emigrant, accept our greetings! The devil knows what this year may bring. Long live the subterranean brigade! So long as we're here, nothing's lost."

Moritz Rosenthal nodded. He lifted his glass to Steiner and drank. In the background of the room someone laughed. Then there was silence. They all looked at one another with embarrassed faces as though they had been surprised doing something shameful.

From outside in the street came cries. Fireworks exploded. Taxis rushed by honking. On a balcony of a house opposite a little man in vest and shirt sleeves set off a pan of green fire. The whole façade was lighted up. The green light streamed blindingly into Edith Rosenfeld's room and made it unreal — as though it were no longer a room in a hotel in Paris, but a cabin in a sunken ship deep under water.

* * *

The actress Barbara Klein was sitting at a table in a corner of "the catacombs." It was late and there were only two electric light bulbs burning, one over each doorway. Her chair stood in front of an arrangement of palms, and whenever she leaned back the leaves touched her hair like stiff hands. She felt it each time and her head jerked; but she no longer had the strength to get up and find a seat elsewhere.

From the kitchen came the clatter of dishes and the

plaintive tones of an accordion over the radio. The Toulouse broadcasting station, thought Barbara Klein. A new year. I am tired. I don't want to go on living. What did any of them know about how tired a person could be?

I'm not drunk, she thought. My thoughts have just become slower. As slow as flies in wintertime. Flies in which death is growing. It's growing in me, too, like a tree. It's growing like a tree in my veins which are slowly freezing. Someone gave me a glass of cognac. The one called Marill or the other one that went away. He said it would warm me. But I'm not even cold. I just haven't any feeling at all any more.

She sat there and saw, as through a glass wall, someone coming toward her. He came nearer and she saw him more clearly now, but there was still glass between them. Now she recognized him; it was the man who had sat beside her in Edith Rosenfeld's room. He had had a diffident, indistinct face with large eyeglasses and a twisted mouth and restless hands and he limped — but now he limped right through the transparent wall and it closed behind him with soft iridescence like a curtain of liquid glass.

It was some time before she understood anything of what he was saying. She saw him go away with his halting gait as though he were swimming, and she saw him return and sit down beside her and she drank what he gave her and had no feeling of swallowing. In her ears was subdued roaring and amid it voices, words, useless senseless words from far away, from another shore; and then suddenly it was not a human being any more in front of her, hot, blotched and restless — it was only something pathetic, moving, something maltreated and beseeching. It was only hunted, imploring eyes, just an animal caught in this loneliness of glass and the Toulouse radio station and the alien night.

"Yes — " she said, "yes — "

She wanted him to go and leave her alone for only an instant, a few minutes, a little portion of the long eternity that stretched before her — but he was getting up now and standing in front of her and bending over and taking her arm and drawing her to her feet and speaking and taking her away, and she was wading through a mire of glass. And then came the stairway which was ductile and snapped at her legs with its steps, and doors and brightness and a room.

She sat on her bed and felt she could never get up again. Her joints seemed to fall apart. There was no pain. It was just a noiseless sundering as when overripe fruit in the stillness of autumn falls at night from a motionless tree. She bent forward, she looked at the worn carpet as though she expected to see herself lying there, and then she lifted her head. Someone was looking at her.

It was strange eyes under soft hair, it was a strange, thin face, bent forward, masklike, and then it was a chilling shudder and a convulsion and an awakening from far away, and she saw that it was her own face that was looking at her out of the mirror.

She did not move. And then she saw the man kneeling beside her bed in a curiously ridiculous posture, holding her hands.

She drew her hands away. "What do you want?" she asked sharply. "What do you want of me?"

The man stared at her. "But you said — you told me I could come with you — "

She had become weary again. "No — " she said. "No — "

The words came again. Words of unhappiness and pain

and loneliness and suffering, words, words that were much too big — but did small words exist for small beings that were ground down and abased? And that he had to go away tomorrow, and that he had never had a woman, and that it was only fear and his infirmity that paralyzed him and made him ridiculous, a smashed foot, only a foot, and the despair and the hope that just tonight — after all, she had looked at him all evening and he had thought . . .

Had she looked at him? She did not know. All she knew was that this was her room and that she would never leave it again, and that everything else was mist and less than mist.

"It would mean a new life for me!" whispered the man beside her knees. "Everything would be different for me — please understand that! No longer to feel myself an outcast — "

She understood none of it. She looked in the mirror again. That was Barbara Klein there, bending forward, twenty-eight years old, untouched her whole life long, treasured-up for a dream that had never come, and now without hope and at the end.

She got up cautiously, still watching the image in the mirror. She looked at it. She smiled at it, and for an instant a flicker of irony and macabre mockery answered her. "Yes," she said wearily, "yes — all right — "

The man stopped speaking. He stared at her almost incredulously. She paid no heed. Everything was suddenly too heavy. Her dress weighed on her like armor. She let it fall. She let herself fall, the heavy shoes, the thin, heavy body — and the bed grew and became huge and took her in its arms, a soft white grave.

She heard a switch snap and the rustling of clothes. With

an effort she opened her eyes. It was dark. "Light," she said into the pillow. "The light must stay on."

"One instant! Please, just one instant more!" The man's voice was embarrassed and hasty. "It's just that — please understand — "

"The light must stay on — " she repeated.

"Yes. Certainly — at once — only . . ."

"It will be dark for so long afterward," she murmured.

"Yes — yes, certainly — the nights in winter are long — "

She heard the switch click. The light was once more a soft red twilight on her closed eyelids. Then she felt the other body. For a second everything inside her tightened — then she relaxed. This would pass, like everything. . . .

Slowly she opened her eyes again. A person she did not know stood by her bed. She had had a memory of something restless, beseeching, miserable — but what she saw now was a warm, frank face alive with tenderness and happiness.

She looked at him for an instant. "You must go now," she said. "Please go — "

The man made a gesture. Then the words came again. Quick, trembling words. At first she did not understand. It was too sudden and she was too burned-out. All she wanted now was for him to go. Then she understood part of it — that he had been desperate and broken, and that this was no longer so. And that he had regained his courage. Now, at the very moment when he had been ordered out of France —

She nodded. He must stop speaking. "Please — " she said. He was silent.

"You must go now," she said.

"Yes — "

She lay beaten and exhausted under the blanket. Her eyes followed the man as he went to the door. He was the last human being she would see. She lay very quiet in a strange peace — nothing concerned her any more.

The man paused at the door. He hesitated and waited for a moment. "Tell me one thing more," he said. "Have you — Did you do that just — out of — more out of pity — or — "

She looked at him. The last human being. The last link with life. "No — " she said with tremendous effort.

"Not out of pity?"

"No."

The man at the door stiffened. He was breathless with anticipation. "Then what . . . ?" he asked as softly as though he feared he might fall into an abyss.

She was still looking at him. She was very calm. The last little bit of life. "Love — " she said.

The man at the door was silent. He looked like one who had expected a blow from a cudgel and had stumbled into an embrace. He did not move, but he seemed to grow. "My God!" he said.

Suddenly she was afraid he would come back. "You must go now," she said. "I am very tired — "

"Yes — "

She no longer heard what he was saying. Exhaustion seized her and closed her eyes. Then the door was there again, blank and empty, and she was alone and had forgotten him.

She remained for a time lying quiet. She saw her face in the mirror and smiled at it — very wearily and tenderly. Her head was quite clear now. Barbara Klein, she thought.

Actress. Precisely on New Year's Day. Actress. But wasn't one day like another? She looked at her clock on the bedside table. She had wound it that morning. The clock would go on ticking for a whole week. She looked at the letter beside it. The dreadful letter that contained death.

She took the little razor blade out of the drawer. She held it between her thumb and index finger and drew the covers over her. It didn't hurt much. The landlady would be furious in the morning. But she had nothing else. She had no veronal. She pressed her face into the pillow. It became darker — then it came again — far away. The Toulouse radio. Nearer and nearer. A faint rumbling. A funnel into which she was slipping. Faster and faster. And then the wind . . .

Chapter Nineteen

MARILL came into the canteen. "There's someone outside looking for you, Steiner."

"Under what name, Steiner or Huber?"

"Steiner."

"Did you ask him what he wanted?"

"Of course. As a precaution." Marill looked at him. "He has a letter for you. From Berlin."

Steiner pushed back his chair with a jerk. "Where is he?"

"Over in the Rumanian Pavilion."

"Not a spy or anything like that?"

"Doesn't look it."

They walked across together. Under the bare trees a man of about fifty was standing. "Are you Steiner?" he asked.

"No!" Steiner said. "Why?"

The man looked at him sharply for an instant. "I have a letter for you from your wife." He took a letter out of his portfolio and showed it to Steiner. "You probably recognize the handwriting."

Steiner knew that he was standing still but it took all his strength, for suddenly inside him everything was unsteady and quivering. He could not lift his hand; he believed if he tried to it would fly away.

"What made you think Steiner was in Paris?" Marill asked.

"The letter reached me from Vienna. Someone took it there from Berlin. When he tried to find you he was told you were in Paris." The man pointed to a second envelope. *Josef Steiner, Paris,* was written on it in Lilo's large handwriting. "He sent it to me along with other letters. I've been looking for you for several days. Finally at the Café Maurice they told me I would find you here. You needn't tell me whether you are Steiner. I know how careful one has to be. All you need do is take the letter. I want to get rid of it."

"It's for me," Steiner said.

"Good."

The man handed him the letter. Steiner had to force himself to take it. It was different and heavier than any other letter in the world. But once he felt the envelope between his fingers you would have had to cut his hand off to get it away from him.

"Thanks," he said to the man. "You've been to a lot of trouble."

"That's nothing. When people like us get mail it's important enough to do a little searching. I'm glad I found you."

He waved to them and left.

"Marill," Steiner said, completely beside himself. "From my wife. The first letter. What can it be? She ought not to write me, you know."

"Open it — "

"Yes. Stay here with me. Damn it, what can have gone wrong with her?" He tore open the envelope and began to read. He sat like a stone and read the letter to the end; but his face began to change, it became pale and drawn. The muscles in his cheeks tensed and the veins stood out.

He let the letter fall and sat for a time silently staring

at the floor. Then he glanced at the date. "Ten days — "
he said. "She's in the hospital. Ten days ago she was still
alive — "

Marill looked at him and waited.

"She says she can't be saved. That's why she wrote. She
doesn't tell me what's wrong. It doesn't matter now. She
writes — you understand — it's her last letter — "

"In what hospital is she?" Marill asked. "Did she tell you
that?"

"Yes."

"We'll call up at once. We'll call the hospital, under
some other name."

Steiner stood up unsteadily. "I must go there."

"Call first. Come, we'll go to the Verdun."

Steiner gave the number. In a half-hour the telephone
rang and he went into the booth as though into a dark
cavern. When he came out he was dripping with sweat.

"She's still alive," he said.

"Did you speak to her?" Marill asked.

"No. To the doctor."

"Did you tell him your name?"

"No. I said I was one of her relatives. There has been an
operation and there is no hope for her. Three or four days
at most, the doctor says. It was for that reason she wrote.
She didn't think I'd get the letter so quickly. Damn it!"
He still had the letter in his hand and he looked around as
though he had never before been in the dirty lobby of the
Verdun. "Marill, I'm taking the train tonight."

Marill stared at him. "Have you lost your mind?" he
asked softly.

"No. I'll get across the border. I have a passport, you know."

"The passport won't do you any good once you're over there. You know that perfectly well yourself."

"Yes."

"You also know what it means once you cross the border?"

"Yes."

"That you're probably done for."

"I'm done for if she dies."

"That's not true!" Marill was suddenly very angry. "It may sound tough, Steiner, but I advise you to write her, telegraph her — but stay here."

Steiner shook his head absent-mindedly. He had scarcely heard.

Marill seized him by the shoulder.

"You can't help her. Even if you get there."

"I can see her."

"She will be horrified if you go. If you were to ask her now, she would make every effort to have you stay here."

Steiner had been staring into the street without seeing anything. Now he turned around quickly. "Marill," he said, and his eyes wavered, "she is still all there is for me, she is alive, she breathes, her eyes are still there and her thoughts, I am still there behind those eyes — and in a few days she will be dead; there will be nothing left of her; she will lie there and be nothing but a strange, disintegrating body. But now, now she is still alive for a few days longer, the last days — And I am not to be with her? Try to understand that I must go. There is no other way. Damn it, the world is ending; if I don't see her I'll simply break. I'll die with her."

"You won't die with her. Come, telegraph her, take my

money, take Kern's money, telegraph her every hour, pages, letters, anything — but stay here."

"It's not dangerous for me to go. I have my passport. I'll get back with it."

"Don't talk nonsense to me. You know it's dangerous! They have a damned good organization over there."

"I'm going," Steiner said.

Marill tried to seize him by the arm and lead him away. "Come, we'll empty a couple of bottles of brandy. Get drunk! I promise you I'll telephone every couple of hours."

Steiner shook him off as though he were a child. "It won't do, Marill. That won't fix it. I know what you mean. I understand it, too. I'm not crazy. I know what the stakes are, but if they were a thousand times higher I'd still take that train and nothing could stop me. Can't you understand that?"

"Yes," Marill roared. "Of course I understand it! I'd take the train myself!"

Steiner packed his things. He was like a frozen river when the ice breaks up. He could hardly believe he had talked to someone under the same roof with Marie; it seemed almost inconceivable to him that his own voice had droned so close to her inside the hard black rubber of the telephone receiver; it all seemed unimaginable — that he was packing, that he would take a train and that tomorrow he would be where she was.

He threw the few things he needed into his bag and shut it. Then he went to find Ruth and Kern. They had already heard everything from Marill and were waiting for him, in sorrow and sympathy.

"Children," he said, "I'm going away now. It's taken a long time but I always knew at bottom this is how it would be. Not exactly this way," he added. "But then I don't believe that yet. I only know it."

He smiled a sad, twisted smile. "Good-by, Ruth."

Ruth gave him her hand. She was crying. "There's so much I'd like to say to you, Steiner. But now I've forgotten what it is — I'm just sad. Will you take this with you?" She handed him the black sweater. "I just finished it today."

Steiner smiled and for an instant was as he used to be. "That turned out just right," he said. Then he turned to Kern. "So long, Baby. Sometimes things go dreadfully slow, don't they? Sometimes damn fast."

"I don't think I'd be alive if it hadn't been for you, Steiner," Kern said.

"Sure you would. But it's nice of you to say that to me. It means the time wasn't entirely wasted."

"Come back to us," Ruth said. "That's all I can say. Come back. There's not much we can do for you, but everything we are is yours. Always."

"Fine. We'll see. So long, children. Keep your chins up."

"We'd like to go with you to the station," Kern said.

Steiner hesitated. "Marill is going along. Yes, you come too."

They walked down the steps. On the street Steiner turned around and looked back at the shabby gray front of the hotel. "Verdun — " he murmured.

"Let me carry your bag," Kern said.

"Why, Baby? I can do it all right myself."

"Give it to me," Kern begged with a shy smile. "I showed you just this afternoon how strong I've grown."

"Yes, so you did. This afternoon. How long ago that was!" Steiner gave him the bag knowing that Kern wanted to do something for him and that there was nothing else to do but this trifling service of carrying his bag.

They arrived just in time to see the train off. Steiner got in and lowered a window. The train had not begun to move; but it seemed to those on the platform that the window already separated Steiner irrevocably from them. With burning eyes Kern looked at the stern, lean face — trying to impress it on his mind for all time. This man had been his friend and teacher for many months; for whatever in himself had become tempered and resilient, he had Steiner to thank. And now he saw this face, composed and calm, going voluntarily to destruction; for none of them counted on the miracle of Steiner's coming back.

The train began to move. No one spoke. Steiner slowly lifted his hand. The three on the station platform looked after him until the cars disappeared behind a curve.

"Damnation!" Marill said presently, in a hoarse voice. "Come along. I need a drink. I've seen many a man die but I was never present at a suicide before."

They returned to the hotel. Kern and Ruth went to Ruth's room. "Ruth," Kern said after a while, "everything is suddenly empty and it makes you feel cold — as if the whole city had died."

That evening they went to visit Father Moritz, who was now bedridden. "Sit down, children," he said. "I know all about it and there's nothing to be done. Every human being has the right to decide his own fate."

Moritz Rosenthal knew he would never get up again. And therefore he had had his bed so placed that he could look out the window. There wasn't much he could see —

just a section of the row of houses opposite. But since he had nothing else, that was a great deal. He looked at the windows and they became the epitome of life. In the mornings he saw them opened, he saw faces appear, he knew the sullen servant girl who cleaned the panes, the weary young wife who sat in the afternoon almost motionless behind the open shutters, staring into the street, and the bald-headed man on the top floor who exercised in the evenings in front of the open window. In the afternoon he saw the lights behind drawn curtains, he saw shadows moving back and forth; in the evenings he saw some windows that were dark as abandoned caves and others where lights burned far into the night. That and the muffled noise from the streets represented the outer world, to which now only his thoughts belonged, not his body. The other world, the world of memory, he had on the walls of his room. With the last of his strength, aided by the chambermaid, he had put up with thumbtacks all the photographs he possessed.

On the wall above his bed hung faded pictures of his family: his parents; his wife, who had died forty years before; the portrait of a son who had lived to be fifty and who had died; the picture of a grandson who died at seventeen; the picture of a daughter-in-law who had lived to thirty-five — the dead, among whom Moritz Rosenthal, old and impassive, now himself awaited death.

The wall opposite was covered with landscapes. Photographs of the Rhine, towns, castles and vineyards, interspersed with colored clippings from newspapers, sunrises and thunderstorms over the Rhine, and at the end a series of pictures of the little town of Godesberg-on-the-Rhine.

"I can't help it," Father Moritz said in embarrassment. "I really ought to have pictures of Palestine hanging there, at least a few in the collection — but they don't mean a thing to me."

"How long did you live in Godesberg?" Ruth asked.

"Until I was seventeen. Then we left."

"And later on?"

"Later on I never went back."

"That was a long time ago, Father Moritz," Ruth said.

"Yes, it was long, long before you were in the world. Perhaps your mother was born about that time."

How strange, Ruth thought. When my mother was born these pictures were already memories in the brain behind that forehead — and she lived her difficult life and is gone, and these same memories live on like ghosts behind this ancient forehead as though they were stronger than many lives.

There was a knock and Edith Rosenfeld came in. "Edith," Father Moritz said, "my eternal love! Where have you been?"

"I've come from the station, Moritz, I've just seen Max off. He is on his way to London, and from there to Mexico."

"Then you're alone now, Edith — "

"Yes, Moritz. Now I've found places for them all and they can work."

"What's Max going to do in Mexico?"

"He's going as a day laborer. But he plans to try to get into the automobile business."

"You're a good mother, Edith," Moritz Rosenthal said after a pause.

"I'm like all of them, Moritz."

"What will you do now?"

"I'll rest a little. And then I've already found something else to do. There's a baby here in the hotel. Born two weeks ago. The mother will soon have to get back to work. Then I'll become its adoptive grandmother."

Moritz Rosenthal raised himself a little. "A baby? Two weeks old? Then he's already a Frenchman. That's more than I've been able to achieve at eighty." He smiled. "Can you sing it to sleep despite that, Edith?"

"Yes — "

"The songs you sang my son to sleep with! It was a long time ago, Edith. Suddenly everything is a very long time ago. Won't you sing one of them again for me? Sometimes I'm like a child that wants to go to sleep."

"Which one, Moritz?"

"The song about the poor Jewish child. It's forty years since I've heard you sing that. You were young then, and very beautiful. You are still beautiful, Edith."

Edith Rosenfeld smiled. Then she straightened herself a little and began, in her frail voice, to sing the old Yiddish lullaby. Her voice tinkled a little like the thin melody of an old music box. Moritz Rosenthal lay back and listened. He closed his eyes and drew his breath peacefully. In the barren room the old woman sang the nostalgic melody of homelessness and the sad words that accompanied it: —

> "With almonds and with raisins
> You'll earn your daily keep,
> You'll trade, Yiddele, haggle and trade
> Sleep, Yiddele, sleep."

Ruth and Kern sat listening in silence. Above their heads roared the wind of time — forty years, fifty years rushed by, in the conversation of the old woman and the old man. The ancient pair seemed to find it natural that those years had passed. But in their company crouched these two people of twenty, for whom a single year was endless and almost unimaginable, and they felt a kind of shadowy dread: that everything passes and must pass, and that presently time would reach out for them too. . . .

Edith Rosenfeld got up and bent over Moritz Rosenthal. He was asleep. She looked at the old man's large face for a while. "Come," she said then. "We'll let him sleep."

She turned out the light and they went out noiselessly into the dark corridor and found their way across to their own rooms.

* * *

Just as Kern was pushing a heavy wheelbarrow of dirt from the pavilion over to Marill, he was stopped by two men. "One moment, please." One of them turned to Marill. "You too."

Kern ceremoniously set down the wheelbarrow. He knew what this was. The tone was familiar; anywhere in the whole world he would have leaped up out of the deepest sleep at hearing these polite, low, inexorable accents beside his bed.

"Will you be so kind as to show us your papers of identification?"

"I haven't mine with me," Kern replied.

"Please identify yourselves first," Marill said.

"Certainly, with pleasure. Here, this will do, won't it? I am from the police. The gentleman here is an inspector from the Ministry of Labor. You understand, the large number of French unemployed forces us to make a check-up."

"I understand, sir. Unfortunately, I can only show you a residential permit; I have no permit to work; you could hardly have expected that — "

"You are quite right, sir," the inspector said politely. "We did not expect that, but what you have is sufficient. You may go on working. In this particular case — in the construction of the Exposition — the Government has no desire to be too strict in enforcing regulations. We beg your pardon for disturbing you."

"Not at all. It's your duty."

"May I see your papers?" the inspector asked Kern.

"I have none."

"No *récépissé?*"

"No."

"You entered the country illegally?"

"There was no other way."

"I am very sorry," said the man from the police, "but you must come with us to the Prefecture."

"That's what I expected," Kern replied and looked at Marill. "Tell Ruth I've been nabbed. I'll come back as soon as I can. Tell her not to worry."

He had spoken in German. "I have no objection if you want to talk to your friend for a moment more," the inspector said obligingly.

"I'll look out for Ruth until you get back," Marill said in German. "Tough luck, old fellow. Get them to deport you by way of Basle. Come back again by way of Burgfelden. Telephone from the Steiff Inn to Hotel Steiff in St. Louis for a taxi to Mühlhausen and from there to Belfort. That's the best way. If they take you to the Santé, write me as soon as you can. Klassmann will keep a lookout anyway. I'll telephone him immediately."

Kern nodded to Marill. "I'm ready," he said then.

The representative of the police turned him over to a man who had been waiting near by. The inspector looked at Marill and smiled. "A nice way to say good-by," he said in perfect German. "You seem to know our border well."

"Unfortunately," Marill replied.

* * *

Marill was sitting with Waser in a *bistro*. "Come on," he said, "let's have one more drink. Damn it, I hate to go into that hotel! This is the first time something like this has happened to me. What'll you have, a *fine* or a Pernod?"

"A *fine*," Waser said with dignity. "That anisette stuff is for women."

"Not in France." Marill summoned a waiter and ordered a cognac and a straight Pernod.

"I could tell her," Waser proposed. "In our circles that sort of thing is an everyday affair. Every few minutes someone is picked up and then you have to tell his wife or his girl. The best thing for you is to start off with the great, common cause that always demands sacrifices."

"What sort of common cause?"

"The Movement! The revolutionary enlightenment of the masses, of course!"

Marill regarded the Communist attentively for a while. "Waser," he said calmly, "I don't think we'd get far that way. That's good for a socialist manifesto, but for nothing else. I forgot you were mixed up in politics. Let's finish our drinks and start marching. Somehow or other I'll get it done."

They paid, and walked through the slushy snow to the Hotel Verdun. Waser disappeared into "the catacombs" and Marill climbed slowly up the stairs.

He knocked at Ruth's door. She opened it as quickly as if she had been waiting behind it. The smile on her face faded a little when she saw Marill. "Marill — " she said.

"Yes. I'm not the one you were expecting, am I?"

"I thought it was Ludwig. He'll be here any minute now."

"Yes."

Marill walked into the room. He saw a plate on the table, an alcohol stove over which water was boiling, bread and sliced meat and a few flowers in a vase. He saw all this, he saw Ruth standing expectantly in front of him, and irresolutely, just for something to do, he picked up the vase. "Flowers," he murmured. "Even flowers — "

"Flowers are cheap in Paris," Ruth said.

"Yes. That's not what I meant. Only — " Marill replaced the vase as cautiously as though it were not made of cheap thick glass but of eggshell porcelain. "It's just that it makes it so damnably hard, all this — "

"What?"

Marill made no reply.

"I know," Ruth said suddenly. "The police have picked up Ludwig."

Marill swung round to face her. "Yes, Ruth."

"Where is he?"

"At the Prefecture."

Ruth silently picked up her coat. She put it on, stuffed a few things into the pockets, and tried to go past Marill and out the door. He stopped her. "It's silly," he declared. "It won't help him or you at all. We have someone at the Prefecture who will keep us informed. You stay here!"

"How can I? I could see him again! Let them lock us both up. Then we could go across the border together."

Marill kept hold of her. She was like a compressed steel spring. Her face was pale and seemed to have grown smaller with anxiety. Then she suddenly gave up. "Marill," she said helplessly, "what shall I do?"

"Stay here. Klassmann is at the Prefecture. He'll tell us what happens. All they can do is deport him. Then in a couple of days he'll be back again. I promised him you would wait here. He knows you'll be reasonable."

"Yes, I will be." Her eyes were full of tears. She took off her coat and let it drop to the floor. "Marill," she said, "why do people do all this to us? After all, we've not harmed anybody."

Marill looked at her thoughtfully. "I believe it's for that very reason," he said. "Actually, I think that's it."

"Will they put him in jail?"

"I don't think so. We'll find out from Klassmann. We'll have to wait until tomorrow."

Ruth nodded and slowly picked up her coat from the floor. "Didn't Klassmann tell you anything more?"

"No, I only spoke to him for a moment. Then he went straight to the Prefecture."

"I was there with him this morning. They ordered me to come." She took a paper out of her coat pocket, smoothed it out and gave it to Marill. "For this."

It was a residential permit for Ruth, good for four weeks.

"The Refugees' Committee arranged it. I had an expired passport, you know. Klassmann brought me the news today. He's been working on it for months. I wanted to show it to Ludwig. That's why I got those flowers too."

"So that's the reason!" Marill held the permit in his hand. "It's marvelous luck and a damned shame at the same time," he said. "But mostly luck. This is a kind of miracle. It doesn't happen often. But Kern will come back. Do you believe that?"

"Yes," Ruth said. "The one's no good without the other. He must come back!"

"Fine. And now you're coming out with me. We'll have dinner somewhere. And we'll have something to drink — to the permit, and to Kern. He's an old soldier. We're all soldiers. You too. Am I right?"

"Yes."

"Kern would let himself be deported fifty times with howls of joy to get you what you have there in your hand. You know that, don't you?"

"Yes. But I would a hundred times rather not — "

"I know," Marill interrupted. "We'll talk about that when he's here again. That's one of the first rules of a soldier."

"Has he money to get back with?"

"I assume so. All of us old campaigners always have some with us for that emergency. If he hasn't enough, Klassmann will smuggle in the rest. He's our advance post and patrol. Now come along! Sometimes it's a damned good thing that there's drink in the world! Especially in these times!"

*　　*　　*

Steiner was awake and alert when the train stopped at the border. The French customs men went through it quickly and perfunctorily. They asked for his passport, stamped it and left the compartment. The train started and rolled slowly on. Steiner knew that at this moment his fate was sealed; now he could not go back.

After a time two German officials came in and bowed. "Your passport, please."

Steiner took out the booklet and gave it to the younger of the two.

"For what purpose are you going to Germany?" the other asked.

"I'm going to visit relatives."

"Do you live in Paris?"

"No, in Graz. I was visiting a relative in Paris."

"How long do you intend to stay in Germany?"

"About two weeks. Then I shall return to Graz."

"Have you funds with you?"

"Yes. Five hundred francs."

"We must make a note of that on your passport. Did you bring the money with you from Austria?"

"No. My cousin in Paris gave it to me."

The official scrutinized the passport, wrote something on it and stamped it. "Have you anything to declare?" the other man asked.

"No, nothing." Steiner took down his bag.

"Have you a trunk as well?"

"No, this is all."

The official hastily inspected the bag. "Have you newspapers, printed matter or books with you?"

"No, nothing."

"Thank you." The younger official gave the passport back to Steiner. Both bowed and went out. Steiner sighed with relief. He noticed suddenly that the palms of his hands were drenched with sweat.

The train began to run faster. Steiner leaned back in his seat and looked through the window. Outside it was night. Low clouds raced across the sky and between them the stars shone. Little, half-lighted stations flew past, red and green signal lights dashed by, and the rails gleamed. Steiner

lowered the window and put his head out. The damp wind
of passage tore at his face and hair. He took a deep breath;
it seemed a different air. It was a different wind, it was a
different horizon, it was a different light, the poplars along
the road swayed in a different and more familiar rhythm,
the roads themselves somehow led into his heart. Feverishly
he drew the air into his lungs; his blood pounded, the landscape rose and faced him, enigmatic but somehow no longer
strange — Damn it, he thought, what's this? I'm getting
sentimental.

He sat down again and tried to sleep — but he could not.
The dark landscape outside beckoned and enticed, it was
transformed into faces and memories, the heavy years of
the war rose up again as the train thundered across the
bridge over the Rhine; the flashing water, flowing by with
a sullen murmur, threw a hundred names at him, names
whose echoes had died in the past, dead names, almost forgotten names — names of regiments and comrades, of towns
and camps, names out of the night of the years. It was like
a physical impact and Steiner was suddenly caught in the
whirlwind of the past. He tried to defend himself and
could not.

He was alone in the compartment. He lighted one cigarette after another and walked up and down in the narrow
space. He would never have thought all this could have
such power over him. With a violent effort he forced himself to think of the next day, of how he would have to try
to enter the hospital without arousing suspicion, of his own
situation and which of his friends he could look up and
consult.

But for the moment all that appeared strangely misty
and unreal; it eluded him when he tried to lay hold of it.
Even the danger that surrounded him and toward which

he was rushing paled to an abstract idea with no power to calm his feverish blood or force him to reflect. On the contrary, it seemed to lash his blood into a whirlpool, in which his life revolved in a mysterious dance with mystic repetition. Then he gave up. He knew it was the last night; tomorrow all this would be over — shadowed by something else — it was the last night he would spend in pure uncertainty, in the whirlwind of his feelings, the last night without grim knowledge and the certainty of destruction. He stopped trying to think. He surrendered himself.

The immense night unfolded before the windows of the rushing train. It was without end; it arched over forty years of a man's life, a man for whom forty years was all the time there was. The villages, which slid by with their sparse lights and the occasional barking of dogs, were the villages of his childhood — he had played in all of them, over all of them had swept his summers and winters, and the bells ringing in their churches had rung everywhere for him. The black and sleeping forests that swept by were all the forests of his youth — their golden-green twilight had shadowed his first wanderings, their smooth ponds had mirrored his breathless face as he watched the speckled, red-bellied salamanders, and the wind that sighed in the beech trees and sang in the pines had been the age-old wind of adventure. The palely glimmering roads, spreading like a net across the night fields, had all been the roads of his restlessness — he had walked them all, had hesitated at their crossings, he knew their places of departure, their promise and return from horizon to horizon, he knew their milestones and the farms that lay along them. And the houses under whose low roofs the light was caught, redly gleaming through the windows like a promise of warmth and home — he had lived in each of their rooms, he knew the soft pressure of their door latches; and he knew who was waiting in the circle of lamplight with head a little bowed and the light striking sparks from her fiery golden hair — she whose face had waited for him everywhere, at the end of all roads and at all corners of the world, sometimes in shadow, often almost invisible, flooded by yearning and a desire for forgetfulness, the face of his life towards which he was traveling, the face that now covered the night sky, the eyes that gleamed behind the clouds, the mouth that whispered soundless words from the horizon, the arms that he could feel in the wind and the swaying of the trees, and the smile in which the landscape and his heart sank in a wild rush of emotion.

He felt his veins dissolve and open, he felt his blood stream out and become part of a luminous river that flowed outside him, that absorbed his blood and returned it, enriched, to him. It carried away his hands to meet other outstretched hands; its eddies broke him apart, piece by piece, and washed him away, as a torrent in spring breaks up an ice pack, putting an end to his isolation. In this one endless night it brought him the solitary joy of union with the universe. It brought him on its waters the sum of things — his life, the dead years, the splendor of love, and the profound knowledge of a recurrence beyond destruction.

Chapter Twenty

STEINER arrived at eleven o'clock in the morning. Leaving his bag in the station checkroom he went immediately to the hospital. He did not see the city; he was only aware of something flowing by on either side of him, a stream of houses, cars and people.

In front of the big white building he stopped and hesitated, staring at the wide entryway and the endless rows of windows, floor after floor. Somewhere there — but perhaps not there any longer. He clenched his teeth and walked in.

"I should like to inquire when visitors are admitted," he said at the reception desk.

"Which class?" the nurse asked.

"I don't know. This is the first time I've been here."

"Whom do you wish to see?"

"Frau Marie Steiner."

Steiner had a moment of astonishment as the nurse began calmly leafing through a thick book. He had almost expected the white walls to crash about his ears or the nurse to jump up and summon a watchman or the police when he pronounced his name.

The nurse was turning over the pages. "First-class patients may receive visitors at any time," she said continuing to search.

"It wouldn't be first class," Steiner answered, "perhaps third."

"Visitors' hours for the third class are from three to five."

The nurse went on searching. "What was the name again?" she asked.

"Steiner, Marie Steiner." Steiner's throat was suddenly dry. He stared at the pretty doll-like nurse as though she were about to pronounce his death sentence. He knew she was going to say: Dead.

"Marie Steiner," the nurse said, "second class. Room five hundred five, fifth floor. Visitors' hours from three to six."

"Five hundred five. Thank you very much, nurse."

"Not at all, sir."

Steiner still stood there. The nurse reached for the buzzing telephone. "Was there something else you wanted to ask, sir?"

"Is she still alive?" Steiner asked. The nurse laid down the telephone. In the receiver a low tinny voice went on squeaking as though the telephone were an animal.

"Certainly, sir," the nurse said and glanced in her book. "Otherwise there would be a note after her name. Demises are always reported immediately."

"Thank you."

Steiner forced himself not to ask whether he could go up at once. He was afraid they would ask why, and he had to avoid making himself conspicuous. And so he went out.

He wandered aimlessly through the streets, passing the hospital in wider and wider circles. She's alive, he thought. My God, she's alive! Suddenly he was overcome with fear that someone might recognize him and he took refuge in

an obscure bar where he could wait in safety. He ordered
something to eat but could not swallow it.

The waiter looked offended. "Don't you like it?"

"Yes, it's good. But bring me a kirsch first." He forced
himself to eat the meal and then ordered a newspaper and
cigarettes. He pretended to read the paper and really tried
to, but nothing registered in his mind. He sat in the half-
darkened room that smelled of food and stale beer, and
went through the most horrible hours of his life. In his
mind he saw Marie dying, now at this very hour, he heard
her desperately calling him, he saw her face drenched with
death sweat and he sat like a lump of lead on his chair with
the rustling newspaper in front of his eyes and clenched
his teeth in order not to groan and leap up and run out.
The crawling hand on his watch was the arm of fate that
dammed up his life and almost choked him by its slowness.

Finally he put down the paper and stood up. The waiter
was leaning on the bar picking his teeth. He approached
when he saw the guest getting up.

"Want to pay?" he asked.

"No," Steiner said. "Another kirsch."

"All right." The waiter poured it out.

"Have one with me."

"I don't mind if I do." The waiter poured out another
glass and raised it with two fingers.

"Here's to health!"

"Yes," Steiner said, "to health!"

They drank and put down their glasses. "Do you play
billiards?" Steiner asked.

The waiter looked at the shabby table that stood in the
middle of the room. "A little."

"Shall we play a game?"

"Why not? Do you play well?"

"I haven't played in a long time. We can play a trial game first if you like."

"Right."

They chalked their cues and played a few balls. Then they began a game, which Steiner won.

"You're better than I am," the waiter said. "You'll have to give me ten points."

"All right."

If I win this game, Steiner thought, everything will be all right. She will be alive, I shall see her, perhaps she will even get well —

He concentrated on the game and won. "Now I'll give you twenty points," he said. These twenty points represented life, health and escape together; and the clicking of the white balls was like the key of fate turning in the lock. The play was close. In a good run the waiter came within two points of the full score, and missed the last ball by a fraction of an inch. Steiner took his cue and began to play. There were flashes before his eyes and sometimes he had to pause, but he ran out the string without an error.

"Well played!" said the waiter admiringly.

Steiner nodded his thanks and looked at the time. It was after three. He quickly paid his check and went out.

He mounted the linoleum-covered steps, his whole being a strange, high-pitched and tormenting vibration. The long corridor writhed and undulated. And then a chalk-white door sprang up to meet and confront him: Five hundred five.

Steiner knocked. There was no answer. He knocked again. A dreadful fear that something might already have happened twisted his stomach as he opened the door.

The little room lay in the light of the afternoon sun like an island of peace in another world. It seemed as if the roaring onward rush of time had lost its power over the infinitely quiet figure that lay in the narrow bed and looked at Steiner. He swayed a little and his hat fell from his hand. He started to bend over and pick it up but in the act he felt as if he had been pushed from behind and, not knowing how he got there, he found himself kneeling by the bed and weeping silently with the tumultuous emotion of home-coming.

The woman looked at him for a time with an expression of peace in her eyes. Then gradually they became uneasy. Her forehead began to wrinkle and her lips moved. Something like panic flickered in her eyes, her hand, which had rested motionless on the cover, rose as though she wanted to reassure herself by touch of what her eyes had seen.

"It's me, Marie," Steiner said.

His wife tried to raise her head. Her eyes searched his face, which was close before her.

"Be calm, Marie. It's me," Steiner said. "I have come."

"Josef — " his wife whispered.

Steiner had to lower his head. His eyes were filled with tears. He bit his lips and swallowed. "It's me, Marie. I have come back to you."

"If they find you — " the woman whispered.

"They won't find me. They can't find me. I can stay here. I shall stay with you."

"Hold me, Josef. I want to feel that you are really here. I've so often seen you — "

He took her fragile, blue-veined hand in his and kissed it. Then he bent over her and pressed his lips on hers, those tired lips that seemed already part of another world. When he stood up, her eyes were full of tears. She gently shook her head and the drops fell like rain.

"I knew you could not come but I have waited for you always."

"Now I shall stay with you."

She tried to push him away. "You can't stay here. You must leave. You don't know what it has been like. You must go at once. Go, Josef — "

"No. It is not dangerous."

"I know better. It is dangerous. I have seen you; now go. I shall not last much longer. I can face it all right alone."

"I have made arrangements so I can stay here, Marie. There is going to be an amnesty and I fall under it."

She looked at him incredulously.

"It's true," he said, "I swear it to you, Marie. No one need know that I am here. But even if they find out it won't matter."

"I shall say nothing, Josef. I have never said anything."

"I know that, Marie." The blood rushed to his head. "You have not divorced me?" he asked softly.

"No. How could I? Please don't be angry."

"It was only for your sake, so that things would be easier for you."

"I haven't had a bad time. People have helped me. That's how I happen to have this room. It has been nicer to be alone; you were with me more."

Steiner looked at her. Her face was drawn, her cheekbones stood out and her skin had a waxy pallor with blue shadows. Her neck was thin and frail and her collarbone stood out prominently from the shrunken shoulders. Even her eyes were veiled and her mouth was colorless. Only her hair sparkled and glowed, it seemed to have become heavier and thicker as though all her former strength were concentrated there in triumph over her wasting body. Spread out in the afternoon sun it was like an aureole of red and gold, like a wild protest against the weariness of the childlike body, of which hardly enough remained to show beneath the sheets.

The door opened and a nurse came in. Steiner got up. The nurse was carrying a glass filled with a milky fluid which she placed on the table. "You're having company?" she said, examining Steiner with sharp blue eyes.

The sick woman nodded her head. "From Breslau," she whispered.

"From so far? Isn't that nice? Now you will have a little entertainment."

The blue eyes swiftly inspected Steiner once more as the nurse drew out a thermometer.

"Has she been having fever?" Steiner asked.

"No indeed," the nurse replied cheerfully. "She hasn't had any for days now." She put the thermometer in the patient's mouth and went out. Steiner drew a chair up to the bed and sat down close to Marie. He took her hands in his. "Are you glad I'm here?" he asked, conscious of how foolish the question was.

"It's everything," Marie said without smiling.

They looked at each other in silence. There was little to say, for being together meant so much. They looked at each other and there was nothing else that mattered. They were lost in each other and had come home to each other. Life no longer had a future or a past; it was all present. It was rest, quietness and peace.

The nurse came in again and made a note on the fever chart; they barely noticed her. They were looking at each other. The sun slowly advanced; it reluctantly abandoned the beautiful flaming hair and lay down like a soft kitten of light on the pillow beside it; then it moved over, still reluctantly, to the wall and slowly climbed it; they looked at each other. Blue-footed dusk stole into the room and filled it. They looked at each other and could not stop, till the shadows drifted from the corners of the room and with their wings covered the white face, the one face in the world.

The door opened and the doctor entered in a flood of light with the nurse behind him. "You must go now," the nurse said.

"Yes," Steiner said, getting up. He bent over the bed. "I'll come back tomorrow, Marie."

She lay like a play-weary child already half asleep, already half in the world of dreams. "Yes," she said, and he could not tell whether she spoke to him or to a figure in a dream. "Yes, come back."

Steiner waited outside for the doctor and asked him how long it would last. The doctor inspected him sharply. "Three or four days at most," he said. "It's a miracle she has lived this long."

"Thank you."

Steiner went slowly down the stairs. In front of the entrance he stopped. Suddenly the city lay spread before him. He had not really seen it on his way there; but now it stretched in front of him at once clear and inescapable. He saw the streets, he saw the houses and he saw danger, silent invisible danger, lying in wait for him at every corner, in every doorway, in every face. He knew there was not much he could do. The place where he could be caught like a wild beast at a drinking hole in the jungle was this white stone building behind him. But he knew, too, that

he must hide in order to be able to come back to it. Three
or four days. An instant and an eternity. For a moment
he debated whether he should try to find one of his friends,
but in the end he decided on some nondescript hotel. That
would be the least conspicuous place to go for the first day.

*   *   *

Kern was sitting in one of the cells in the Santé prison,
with the Austrian Leopold Bruck and the Westphalian
Moenke. They were pasting together paper bags.

"Boys," Leopold said after a while, "I've got gas on my
stomach — fit to burst. What I'd like to do is eat this paste —
if there wasn't a penalty!"

"Wait ten minutes," Kern replied; "then the evening
grub will be here."

"What good's that? Afterwards I really will have gas."
Leopold blew into a paper bag and smashed it with a bang.
"It's a misery in these rotten times that people have stom-
achs. When I think of boiled beef or roast pork I could
pull this whole joint to pieces."

Moenke lifted his head. "My thoughts run more to a
big rare beefsteak," he announced. "With onions and roast
potatoes. And an ice cold beer to go with it."

"Shut up," Leopold groaned. "Let's think of something
else. Flowers for instance."

"Why flowers in particular?"

"Anything that's beautiful, don't you understand? To
distract us."

"Flowers won't distract me."

"Once I saw a bed of roses." Leopold made a violent effort to concentrate. "Last summer. In front of the jail in

Pallanza. In the evening sunlight when we were released.
Red roses. As red as — as —"

"As a rare beefsteak," Moenke helped him out.

"Oh what the hell!"

There was the rattling of keys. "There comes our grub,"
Moenke said.

The door opened. It was not the turnkey with their food;
it was the warden. "Kern — " he said.

Kern got up.

"Come with me. Visitor!"

"A visitor?" Kern asked in amazement.

"Very likely the President of the Republic," Leopold
suggested.

"Perhaps it's Klassmann. He has papers. Maybe he's
brought along something to eat."

"Butter," Leopold said yearningly. "A big piece. Yellow
as a sunflower."

Moenke grinned. "Oh boy, Leopold the lyricist! Now
you're even thinking about sunflowers."

Kern stopped in the doorway as though he had been
struck by lightning. "Ruth!" he said breathlessly. "How did
you get here? Have they arrested you?"

"No, no, Ludwig!"

Kern threw a hasty glance at the warden who was dis-
interestedly leaning in the corner. Then he walked quickly
across to Ruth.

"For God's sake get out of here right away, Ruth," he
whispered in German. "You don't know what you're doing. You might be arrested at any moment and that means

four weeks in jail and six months for a second offense! So go quick — quick!"

"Four weeks," Ruth looked at him in horror. "Do you have to stay here four weeks?"

"That's nothing. That was just bad luck. But you — Let's not be silly. Anyone here might ask for your papers! At any instant."

"But I have papers!"

"What?"

"I have a residential permit, Ludwig!"

She got the slip of paper out of her pocket and gave it to Kern. He stared at it. "Christ," he said slowly after a pause, "it's a fact! Really and truly! Why that's as if a dead man had come to life. Then it really worked this time. Who was it? The Refugees' Aid?"

"Yes. The Refugees' Aid, and Klassmann."

"Warden," Kern said, "is a prisoner permitted to kiss a lady?"

The warden looked at him indifferently. "As long as you like, so far as I'm concerned," he replied. "The only thing is she must not use the opportunity to slip you a knife or a file."

"That wouldn't pay anyway for the couple of weeks that are left."

The warden rolled a cigarette and lit it.

"Ruth," Kern said, "have you heard anything from Steiner?"

"No, nothing. But Marill says that would be impossible anyway. He certainly won't write. He'll just come back again. Suddenly he'll be with us."

Kern looked at her. "Does Marill really believe that?"

"We all believe it, Ludwig. What else can we do?"

Kern nodded. "Yes, what else really is there for us to do? He's only been gone for a week after all. Perhaps he'll get through."

"He must get through. I can't conceive of anything else."

"Time," said the warden. "That's all for today."

Kern took Ruth in his arms. "Come back," she whispered, "come back quickly. Will you stay here in the Santé?"

"No. They'll transport us. To the border."

"I'll try to get another permit to visit you. Come back. I love you. Come quickly. I am afraid. I'd like to go with you."

"You can't do that. Your *récépissé* is only good for Paris. I'll come back."

"I have money here. It's stuck under my shoulder strap. Take it out when you kiss me."

"I don't need any. I have enough with me. You keep it. Marill will look after you. And perhaps Steiner will be back soon."

"Time," the warden admonished them. "Children, after all no one's going to the guillotine."

"Good-by." Ruth kissed Kern. "I love you. Come back, Ludwig."

She looked around and picked up a package from the bench. "Here's something to eat. They looked it over downstairs. It's all right," she said to the warden. "Good-by, Ludwig."

"I am happy, Ruth! Good God, I'm happy about your permit. That's Heaven here and now."

"Now off with you," the warden said. "Back to Heaven."

Kern took the package under his arm. It was heavy. He went back with the warden. "Do you know," the latter said thoughtfully, "my wife is sixty and is slightly hunch-backed. Sometimes that's brought home to me."

The turnkey with the bowls of food had just reached the cell door when Kern got back.

"Kern," Leopold said with a disconsolate expression, "potato soup again without potatoes."

"This is vegetable soup," the turnkey announced.

"You might even call it coffee," Leopold replied. "I believe everything you say."

"What's in that package?" the Westphalian Moenke asked Kern.

"Something to eat. I don't know what yet."

Leopold's face shone like a communion chalice. "Open it up! Quick!"

Kern untied the string. "Butter," Leopold said reverently.

"Like a sunflower," Moenke added.

"White bread! Sausages! Chocolate!" Leopold went on ecstatically. "And here — a whole cheese."

"Like a sunflower," Moenke repeated.

Leopold paid no attention. He drew himself up. "Guard," he said with authority, "take your miserable slop and — "

"Stop," Moenke interrupted. "Not so fast! These Austrians! They're the reason we lost the war in 1918. Hand over the bowls," he said to the guard.

He took them and put them on a bench. Then he arranged the other things beside them and looked at this still life. On the wall above the cheese was an inscription in

pencil by a former inmate of the cell: "*There's an end
to everything, even a life sentence.*"

Moenke grinned. "We'll use the vegetable soup as tea,"
he announced. "And now let's have dinner like civilized
people! What do you say, Kern?"

"Amen," the latter replied.

*   *   *

"I'll come again tomorrow, Marie."

Steiner bent over the still figure and then straightened
up. The nurse was standing by the door. Her sharp glance
swept over him, but she avoided his eyes. The tray in her
hand trembled and the glass on it clinked softly.

Steiner walked out into the corridor. "Stop!" a voice
commanded.

On each side of the door stood a man in uniform with
drawn revolver. Steiner stopped. He had no feeling of
panic.

"What's your name?"

"Johann Huber."

"Come over here to the window."

A third man approached and looked at him. "It's
Steiner," he said, "no doubt of it. I recognize him. You
probably recognize me too, eh Steiner?"

"I've never forgotten you, Steinbrenner," Steiner replied
quietly.

"You'll catch it this time!" the man snickered. "Welcome home! I'm really overjoyed to see you again. Very
likely you're planning to stay with us for a little while this
time, eh? We have a marvelous new camp with every
modern convenience."

"I can believe it."

"Handcuffs!" Steinbrenner commanded. "As a precaution, my sweet. It would simply break my heart if you were to desert us again."

There was a click of a door latch. Steiner looked over his shoulder. It was the door of his wife's room that had opened. The nurse looked out for an instant, then quickly drew back.

"So that's how it was," Steiner said.

"Oh, yes — Love," Steinbrenner snickered: "it brings the toughest birds back to their nest — for the good of the State and the joy of their friends."

Steiner looked at the blotched face with receding chin and blue circles under the eyes. He looked at it calmly; he knew what that face portended for him, but it was all very remote — like something that did not actually concern him at all. Steinbrenner blinked his eyes, licked his lips and took a step back.

"Still not a grain of conscience, Steinbrenner?" Steiner inquired.

The man grinned. "Only a good conscience, sweetheart. It gets better and better the more of you I have under my thumb. My sleep is first-rate. But in your case I'm going to make an exception. I'm going to visit you at night so that I can chat with you a little. All right, take him away!" he commanded suddenly in a sharp voice.

Steiner went down the stairs with his escort. The people who met them stopped and let them pass in silence. In the street too this silence prevailed as they went by.

Steiner was arraigned. A middle-aged official questioned him and the facts were put down in the records.

"For what purpose did you come back to Germany?" the official asked.

"I wanted to see my wife before she died."

"Which of your political friends have you met here?"

"No one."

"It will be better for you to tell me before you are sentenced."

"I have already told you: no one."

"On whose instructions did you come here?"

"I had no instructions."

"With what political organizations were you associated abroad?"

"None."

"Then how did you live?"

"From the money I earned. As you see, I have an Austrian passport."

"With what group were you to get in touch when you arrived here?"

"If that had been my intention I'd have hidden myself better. I knew what I was doing when I went to see my wife."

The official continued to question him for a while longer. Then he scrutinized Steiner's passport and his wife's letter, which had been taken from him. He looked at Steiner, then he read the letter once more. "You will be transferred this afternoon," he said finally, shrugging his shoulders.

"I want to make one request," Steiner said. "It's a small matter but to me it means everything. My wife is still alive. The doctor says that at most she can only live for one or two days more. She knows that I intended to come back tomorrow. If I do not come, she will know I am here. For myself I expect neither sympathy nor favors of any kind; but I should like my wife to die in peace. I beg you to keep me here for one or two days and allow me to visit my wife."

"Not a chance. I can't give you such an opportunity to escape."

"I won't escape. The room is on the fifth floor and has only one entrance. If someone takes me there and watches the door, there will be nothing I can do. I make this request not for myself but for a dying woman."

"Impossible," said the official. "I have no authority to grant it."

"You have the authority. You can order another hearing for me and you can make these visits possible. You could give as a reason that I may tell my wife something that is important for you to know. That could be the reason too for having my guard wait outside. You could arrange for that reliable nurse to stay in the room and listen to what was said."

"That's nonsense. Your wife won't tell you anything, nor will you tell her."

"Of course not. She doesn't know anything. But she would die in peace."

The official reflected and leafed through the documents.

"We examined you formerly on the subject of Group VII. You did not give us any names. In the meantime we have caught Müller, Boese and Welldorf. Will you tell us the names of the others?"

Steiner was silent.

"Will you tell us their names if I make it possible for you to visit your wife for two days?"

"Yes," Steiner said after a pause.

"Then tell them to me."

Steiner was silent.

"Will you give me two names tomorrow evening and the rest the day after tomorrow?"

"I will tell you the names day after tomorrow."

"Do you promise that?"

"Yes."

The official stared at him for a time. "I'll see what I can do. Now you will be taken back to your cell."

"Will you give me back my letter?" Steiner asked.

"Your letter? It has to stay with the rest of the evidence." The official looked at him, undecided. "There's nothing incriminating in it. All right, take it with you."

"Thanks," Steiner said.

The official rang and had Steiner taken away. Too bad, he thought, but what can a man do? You're in the fire yourself the minute you show any sign of being human. Suddenly he banged his fist down hard on the table.

* * *

Moritz Rosenthal was lying in bed. For the first time in days he had no pain. It was an early evening in February. The first lights were beginning to gleam through the silvery blue dusk of Paris. Without moving his head Moritz Rosenthal could see the windows grow bright in the houses opposite; it was like a gigantic ship in the twilight, an ocean liner ready to sail. The wall between the windows threw a long shadow toward the Hotel Verdun like a black gangplank lowered for those who were to go aboard.

Moritz Rosenthal did not move; but as he lay on his bed he saw the windows suddenly open wide and someone who looked like himself get up and stride out over the shadowy gangplank to the ship, which lay rolling gently in the long groundswell of life; now the anchor was raised and the ship glided slowly away. The room collapsed about him like a fragile pasteboard box and went swirling away in the eddies; streets rushed by, forests slid past under the bow, there was fog, the ship rose gently in the subdued roar of eternity, clouds and stars swam by in the deep blue and then like a comforting cradle-song the red and gold of a majestic coast rose before him, the dark gangplank was lowered noiselessly, Moritz Rosenthal walked down it, and when he looked around the ship was no longer there and he was alone on a foreign shore.

A long, smooth road stretched before him. The old wanderer did not hesitate for long; a road was meant to be followed — and his feet had known many roads.

But after a short time he saw, behind silver trees, an immense, shining gate and farther on flashing domes and towers. A massive figure radiant with light stood guarding the entrance, a shepherd's crook in his hand.

The customs! Moritz Rosenthal thought in dismay, and jumped behind a bush. He looked around. There was no going back; that way led into emptiness. There's no help for it, the old refugee thought resignedly, I'll have to stay hidden here till it's dark. Then perhaps I can steal around to one side and get by somehow. He peeked through the crotch of a limb made of garnet and onyx and saw the mighty guardian motioning with his staff. He glanced around again; there was no one else there. The guardian continued to wave. "Father Moritz!" called a soft sonorous voice. Call all you like, Father Moritz thought, I'm not going to show myself.

"Father Moritz," the voice called again. "Come forth from behind the bush of tribulation."

Moritz stood up. Nabbed, he thought. That giant can

certainly run faster than I can. There's no way out; I'll
have to go.

"Father Moritz!" the voice called once more.

"That he should know my name, too, what luck!" Moritz
murmured. "I must have been deported from this place before. According to the latest regulations that means not
less than three months in prison. I hope at least the food's
good and they don't give me *The Ladies' Magazine* for the
year 1902 to read, but something modern. Something by
Hemingway is what I'd like."

The gate became brighter and more radiant the nearer he
approached. What flood-lighting they have on the borders
now, Moritz reflected. You can't even recognize where
you are any more. Perhaps they've recently lighted the
whole frontier so it'll be easier to catch us. What extrava-
gance!

"Father Moritz," said the keeper of the gate, "why are
you hiding?"

What a question, Moritz thought, when he knows my
name and all about me.

"Enter," said the keeper of the gate.

"Look here," Moritz replied. "According to my opinion
I've done nothing illegal yet. I have not crossed your
border. Or does the section behind me count too?"

"It counts too," said the guardian.

Then I'm lost, Moritz thought. It seems to be an island.
Perhaps it's Cuba where so many people have been trying
to get to recently.

"Don't be afraid," the guardian said, "nothing will happen to you. Just go right in."

"Look," Moritz replied, "I'll tell you the truth at once.
I haven't a passport."

"You haven't a passport?"

Six months, Moritz thought, listening to the resonant voice. And he shook his head submissively.

The keeper of the gate lifted his staff. "Then you do not need to spend twenty million years standing in the back of the celestial theater. You will be given immediately an upholstered wing-chair."

"That's all well and good," Father Moritz replied, "but it won't do. I have no entrance visa and no residential permit. For the moment we'll say nothing about a permit to work."

"No residential permit? No visa? No permit to work?" The guardian lifted his head. "Then you will be given a box in the middle of the first row in full view of the Heavenly Hosts."

"That wouldn't be bad," Moritz said, "especially as I'm very fond of the theater. But now we come to something that spoils it all. As a matter of fact I'm surprised you haven't a sign posted out here saying we can't come in. You see, I'm a Jew. Deprived of German citizenship. Illegal for years."

The keeper of the gate raised both arms. "A Jew? Deprived of citizenship? Illegal for years? Then two angels will be assigned to your personal service and a trumpeter as well." He shouted through the gate: "The Angel of the Homeless!" And a towering figure clad in blue raiment with a face like all mothers of the world strode forth beside Father Moritz. "The Angel of Those Who Have Suffered Much!" called the guardian again, and a white-clad figure with an urn of tears on its shoulder moved to the other side of Father Moritz.

"Just a minute," the latter begged, and then asked the guardian: "Are you sure about what's in that thing?"

"Don't be alarmed. Our concentration camps are down below."

The two angels took hold of his arms, and Father Moritz, the old wanderer, the dean of exiles, walked confidently through the gate toward an immense light over which suddenly bright-colored shadows began to whirl faster and faster. . . .

"Moritz," Edith Rosenfeld called from the doorway. "Here's the baby. The little Frenchman. Do you want to look at him?"

There was no reply. She approached cautiously. Moritz Rosenthal of Godesberg-on-the-Rhine no longer breathed.

* * *

Marie regained consciousness. She had lain the whole morning in a twilight agony. Now she clearly recognized Steiner.

"You're still here?" she whispered in alarm.

"I can stay here as long as I like, Marie."

"What does that mean?"

"The Amnesty has been proclaimed. I am included. So you needn't be afraid any more. Now I shall stay here always."

She looked at him doubtfully. "You only tell me that to comfort me, Josef — "

"No, Marie. The Amnesty was announced yesterday." He turned to the nurse who was busying herself in the back of the room. "Isn't it true, nurse, that since yesterday there's no further danger of my being arrested?"

"That's true," the nurse answered indistinctly.

"Please come closer. My wife would like to hear you say it."

The nurse was still bending over. "I've already said it."

"Please, nurse," Marie whispered.

She remained silent. "Please, nurse," the sick woman whispered once more.

The nurse reluctantly approached the bed. Marie watched her anxiously. "Isn't it true," Steiner asked, "that since yesterday I can stay here permanently?"

"Yes," the nurse gulped.

"There is no further danger of my being arrested?"

"No."

"Thank you, nurse."

Steiner saw the dying woman's eyes become veiled. She no longer possessed the strength to weep. "Now everything is all right, Josef," she whispered. "And now, just when I could be useful to you, I must go —"

"You are not going, Marie —"

"I should like to be able to get up and go away with you."

"We will go away together."

She lay for a time watching him. Her face was gray and the bones seemed to be working through the skin. Overnight her hair had become dull and lifeless like a burned-out fire. Steiner looked at all this and did not see it; all he saw was that she still breathed, and as long as she was alive she was Marie, his wife, clothed in the glory of youth and their life together.

Evening crept into the room, and from beyond the door Steinbrenner could be heard from time to time, urgently and impatiently clearing his throat. Marie's breathing became shallow, then it came in gasps with pauses. Finally it was almost inaudible, and ceased, like a gentle breeze falling asleep. Steiner held her hands until they grew cold. He died with her. When he got up to go out he was an insentient stranger, an empty shell that had the motions of a man. He looked at the nurse with indifferent eyes.

Outside he was taken in charge by Steinbrenner and another man. "For more than three hours we've been waiting for you," Steinbrenner growled. "We'll have plenty of chances to talk about that later on, you may be sure."

"I am sure of it, Steinbrenner. I always count on you in such matters."

Steinbrenner moistened his lips. "You know perfectly well the way to address me is Herr Major, don't you? Go right on calling me Steinbrenner and being chummy, but for each time you do it you'll spend weeks weeping bloody tears, sweetheart. From now on I shall have plenty of time with you."

They went down the broad stairway, Steiner between his two guards. It was a warm evening and the long windows in the oval bay of the wall were open wide. There was a smell of gasoline and a hint of spring.

"I shall have such an eternity of time with you," Steinbrenner declared slowly and gloatingly. "Your whole life, sweetheart. And our names go so well together, Steiner and Steinbrenner. Sometime we'll have to see what we can make of that."

Steiner nodded thoughtfully. The open bay window grew larger, came nearer; very near — He thrust Steinbrenner toward it, leaped against him, over him, and pitched with him out into space.

*   *   *

"You don't need to have any scruples about taking the money," Marill said. He was sad and distracted. "He left it with me expressly for you two. I was to give it to you if he didn't come back."

Kern shook his head. He had just arrived and was grimy
and tattered from the trip. He had come from Dijon as a
helper on a moving van. Now he was sitting with Marill in
"the catacombs."

"He will come back," he said. "Steiner will come back."

"He won't," Marill replied emphatically. "Good God,
don't go on making things worse with your everlasting
'He will come back.' He won't come back. Here, read
this."

He drew a rumpled telegram from his pocket and threw
it on the table. Kern took it and smoothed it out. It was
from Berlin and was addressed to the owner of the Verdun.
"Cordial birthday greetings — Otto," he read.

He looked at Marill. "What does it mean?" he asked.

"It means he's been nabbed. That's what we'd agreed on.
One of his friends was to send the telegram. It was easy to
foresee. I told him what was going to happen. And now
shut up and take these filthy bills."

He pushed the notes toward Kern. "There's two thousand, two hundred and forty francs," he explained. "And
here's something more." He took out his wallet and ex-
tracted two tickets. "Here's passage for two, from Bor-
deaux to Mexico. On the *Tacoma*. A Portuguese freighter.
For you and Ruth. Sails on the eighteenth. We bought
them with Steiner's money. This is what's left over. The
visas have been attended to. The Refugees' Aid Committee
has them."

Kern stared at the tickets. "But — " he said uncompre-
hendingly.

"No buts," Marill interrupted him angrily. "Don't be
difficult, Kern. All this has cost some pains. The damnedest
piece of luck! There was an announcement three days ago.
The Refugees' Aid Committee had got permission from
the Mexican Government to send over one hundred and

fifty refugees. Provided they could pay for the trip. We booked passage for you and Ruth instantly. Before everything was taken. Money for the trip was available just at that moment. Well now — "

He was silent. "Yvonne, bring me a kirsch," he said presently to the fat waitress from Alsace. Yvonne nodded and paddled out to the kitchen with swaying hips.

"Bring two," Marill shouted after her.

Yvonne turned around. "I'd have done it anyway, Monsieur Marill," she announced.

"Fine. There's at least one understanding soul."

Marill turned back to Kern. "Made up your mind now?" he asked. "A bit surprising, all this, I admit. If you show your ticket and visa at the Prefecture you'll get a residential permit for France good up to the date when the ship sails. Even if you entered illegally. That's something the Refugees' Aid Committee arranged. Go there first thing tomorrow morning. It's the one chance for you to get out of this mess. You know what the penalty is now, if you're arrested again?"

"Yes. One month for a first offense — six months in jail the second time."

"That's right, six months. And sometime or other you'll be nabbed again as sure as fate!" Marill looked up. Yvonne was standing in front of him, about to place a tray with two glasses on the table. One was an ordinary glass; the second was a tumbler filled to the brim with brandy.

"That's for you," Yvonne announced, grinning and pointing with her thumb at the tumbler. "For the same price."

"Thanks. You're a bright child. It would be a damned shame for you to marry and turn into a Xantippe, as you undoubtedly would. Or into a noble martyr. *Prost!*"

Marill emptied half the glass at one gulp. "*Prost*, Kern!" he repeated. "Why aren't you drinking?" He put his glass on the table and looked Kern full in the face for the first time. "All we need now," he said, "is for you to begin howling! Man, is that your idea of the way to behave?"

"I'll not howl," Kern retorted. "And if I do howl, who cares? But, damn it, all the time I thought Steiner would be here when I got back, and now you hand me money and tickets and I'm saved because he's lost — that's a God-damned miserable thing, don't you understand?"

"No! I don't understand. You're talking sentimental rubbish. No sense in it anywhere. That's the way things always happen. And now empty your glass. The way — Well, the way he'd have emptied it. What the hell! Don't you think I feel it in the marrow of my bones too?"

"Yes — "

Kern emptied his glass. "I'm all right now," he said. "Have you a cigarette, Marill?"

"Of course. Here you are."

Kern drew the smoke deep into his lungs. In the dim light of "the catacombs" he suddenly saw Steiner's face — bending forward with a slightly ironic expression in the flickering candlelight, as it had looked an eternity ago in the Vienna jail. And it seemed to him that he heard the deep, unhurried voice: "Well, Baby?" Yes, he thought — Yes, Steiner!

"Does Ruth know?" he asked.

"Yes."

"Where is she?"

"I don't know. Probably at the Refugees' Aid. She didn't know you were coming."

"No. I didn't know myself just when I'd get here. . . . Can one work in Mexico?"

"Yes. I don't know at what. But you'll get a permit to stay and a permit to work. That's guaranteed."

"I don't know a word of Spanish," Kern said. "Or do they speak Portuguese there?"

"Spanish. You'll just have to learn it."

Kern nodded.

Marill leaned toward him. "Kern," he said in a suddenly altered tone. "I know it's not easy. But my advice to you is: Go. Don't stop to think. Go! Get away from Europe! The devil knows what's going to happen here. A chance like this isn't likely to come a second time. And you'll never get as much money together again. Take ship, children. Here — "

He finished his drink.

"Will you come with us?" Kern asked.

"No."

"Isn't there enough money for three? After all, we still have some left over."

"That's not the point. I'm going to stay here. I can't explain to you why. I'm going to stay. No matter what happens. You can't explain it. You just know, that's all."

"I understand," Kern said.

"There comes Ruth," Marill exclaimed. "And just as certainly as I am going to stay here, you are going to go. Do you understand that too?"

"Yes, Marill."

"Thank God!" Ruth paused for a moment in the doorway. Then she rushed into Kern's arms. "When did you get here?"

"Half an hour ago."

Ruth lifted her head from the embrace that had been endless and yet shorter than a heartbeat. "Do you know. . . ?"

"Yes. Marill has told me everything."

Kern looked around. Marill was no longer there.

"And do you know. . . ?" Ruth asked hesitantly.

"Yes, I know. We won't talk about it now. Come on, let's get out of here. We'll go out on the street. Somewhere outside. I want to get away from here. Let's go out on the street."

"Yes."

They walked along the Champs Elysées. It was evening and a pale half-moon hung in the apple-green sky. The air was silvery and clear and so mild that the sidewalk cafés were filled with people. They walked in silence for a long time. "Do you know exactly where Mexico is?" Kern asked finally.

Ruth shook her head. "Not precisely. But then I no longer know where Germany is."

Kern looked at her. Then he took her arm. "We'll have to buy a grammar and learn Spanish, Ruth."

"I bought one, day before yesterday. Secondhand."

"Secondhand, eh?" Kern smiled. "We'll make out, won't we, Ruth?"

She nodded.

"Anyhow we'll see a little of the world. That's something we wouldn't have had otherwise, back home."

She nodded again.

They walked on past the Rond Point. The first tender green leaves were showing on the trees. They gleamed in the early lamplight like the flickering of St. Elmo's fire rising from the earth and running along the branches and twigs of the chestnut trees. The soil of the gardens had been spaded and its strong scent mixed strangely with the smell of gasoline and oil that always hung over the broad avenue. In a few places the gardeners had planted flowering narcissi that shimmered in the darkness. It was the hour when the shops were closing, and the crowds were so thick it was hard to move.

Kern looked at Ruth. "How many people there are!" he said.

"Yes," she replied. "Frightfully many people."

THE END

About the Author

ERICH MARIA REMARQUE, who was born in Germany, was drafted into the German army during World War I. Through the hazardous years following the war he worked at many occupations—schoolteacher, small-town drama critic, racing driver, editor of a sports magazine. His first novel, *All Quiet on the Western Front*, was published in Germany in 1928. A brilliant success, selling over a million copies, it was the first of many literary triumphs. When the Nazis came to power, Remarque left Germany for Switzerland. He rejected all attempts to persuade him to return, and as a result he lost his German citizenship, his books were burned, and his films banned. He went to the United States in 1938 and became a citizen in 1947. He later lived in Switzerland with his second wife, the actress Paulette Goddard. He died in September 1970.